It awoke something wild and very sensual
deep within her . . .

She continued to stare into the thick foliage, straining to make out a shape, a shadow. Was it a large snake? A python perhaps—they grew to enormous sizes.

She felt a dark premonition of danger, of something dangerous hunting her. Stalking her. Watching her intently with a fixed, focused stare. Defensively she put a hand to her throat as if warding off the strangling bite of a leopard. Maggie took a cautious step backward, toward the safety of the house, her gaze never leaving the tree above her head . . .

—from Christine Feehan's *The Awakening*

FANTASY

CHRISTINE FEEHAN
SABRINA JEFFRIES
EMMA HOLLY
ELDA MINGER

JOVE BOOKS, NEW YORK

FANTASY

A Jove Book / published by arrangement with the authors

PRINTING HISTORY
Jove edition / April 2002

Visit our website at
www.penguinputnam.com

ISBN: 0-515-13276-4

A JOVE BOOK®
Jove Books are published by The Berkley Publishing Group, a division of Penguin Putnam Inc., 375 Hudson Street, New York, New York 10014.
JOVE and the "J" design are trademarks belonging to Penguin Putnam Inc.

PRINTED IN THE UNITED STATES OF AMERICA

10 9 8 7 6 5 4 3 2 1

CONTENTS

The Widow's Auction

Sabrina Jeffries

1

Isobel Lamberton, Lady Kingsley, could hardly believe her ears. The longer she listened to Justin Antony, the Marquess of Warbrooke, the more horrified she became. This was his "brilliant" new plan for the Lamberton Boys' School? This . . . this outrageous proposal?

Lord Warbrooke had taken leave of his senses. Yet the other members at the school's governing-board meeting seemed oblivious to his sudden bout of insanity. They drank in every word dropping from his handsome mouth. They approved of every slashing gesture of his broad, masculine hand, every compelling look from those magnetic eyes.

While all she could see were the tenpenny nails he drove into the coffin of her own plans for the school. She'd intended to present those plans today, until Lord Warbrooke had beaten her to it with his ghastly suggestion.

"What an inspired idea," one board member proclaimed, thumping the top of the meeting room's ancient table, a castoff from some lord's manor. "It'll be good for the lads and teach them responsibility."

"It'll make money for the school as well," added Mr. Dawson, Lamberton's headmaster. No surprise that *he* liked it. He thought that Lord Warbrooke not only walked on water, but ran on it as well.

The other five men on the board chimed in their admiration, each one more effusive than the last. Even the only other woman on the board—Mrs. Chambers—turned traitor to express her approval. Phoebe Chambers had shown great caring two years ago when Isobel had lost her husband. Since then, the older widow had come to be Isobel's closest friend. So if the staunchly supportive Phoebe agreed with his lordship, then Isobel would never convince the rest of them how wrongheaded this idea was. Not even Lord Bradford's apparent reluctance to voice an opinion helped, since everyone knew how much he resented Lord Warbrooke.

Which meant she was essentially alone in her outrage. And she dared not even explain why.

Suddenly everyone fell silent, and all eyes turned to her. "Lady Kingsley?" Lord Warbrooke asked in that husky voice that always scrambled her thoughts. "What do you think?"

She took a breath, gathering her energy to don the "fine lady" role she'd perfected through the years, the role she didn't truly deserve. The only role that they would accept or understand. Especially Lord Warbrooke.

"I think," she said slowly, "that the idea of establishing a factory on the school grounds is appalling." Yes, that sounded firm enough. She went on in a haughtier tone, "It's unwise and unfeasible and certainly immoral."

Though the others cringed at her blatant disapproval, the man she most needed to intimidate merely cocked an eyebrow. "I don't see why. Boys of that age require activity. It's the lack of it that sends them looking for trouble."

Legend had it that the Antony family was descended

from the Romans who'd ruled Britain long before William the Conqueror had swept in from Normandy. If she'd been skeptical of that legend before, she wasn't now—his lordship's Roman blood fairly screamed its presence this morning. Despite his immaculate cravat and well-tailored morning coat, Lord Warbrooke had the look of a victor about him—jet hair swept back from sharp, intent features . . . broad shoulders fixed for battle . . . unearthly blue eyes glittering a warning that he wouldn't be gainsaid.

Well, he wasn't the only one. "Our boys don't go looking for trouble, I assure you. They participate in sports or engage in further study to improve their minds. That's quite enough activity for any young man."

He looked skeptical. "Is it? As I came in, I saw several idle souls watching the clock in the library. A boy of fifteen can endure only so much study, Lady Kingsley. Nor can he play sports all day long. No, young men need additional sources of intellectual stimulation and challenge."

"His lordship has a good point," Mr. Dawson said gingerly. When she glared at the headmaster, he shrugged and dropped his gaze. "A good point, that's all I'm saying."

When she returned her attention to Lord Warbrooke, his unfazed expression sparked a panic in her chest. He knew he'd win this time—she could see it in his eyes. "My husband didn't intend this school to be a vehicle for moneygrubbing," she said. "Furthermore—"

"Furthermore, your husband is dead." Lord Warbrooke's bald statement rent the stale air.

At her shocked gasp, the other members shifted and squirmed awkwardly in their seats.

But Lord Warbrooke went on remorselessly. "Lord Kingsley gave precious little direction on how to handle the fortune he bequeathed to all his charities. You may be his widow, but he chose us—all of us—to decide such matters. So despite whatever edicts you hand down from Olympus, I intend to have my say in the running of this school."

"You aren't prime minister yet, Lord Warbrooke," she snapped. But some said he would be if he continued to attract political support as fast as a sweating stallion attracted flies. He regularly dined with prominent Whigs like current prime minister Lord Grenville and Foreign Secretary Charles Fox.

And this was the man she thought to thwart? Whose blue blood enabled him to command respect? Who would surely banish her from this board if he ever learned the truth about her own lineage?

God help her. "Henry did choose all of us to govern," she went on, "but he made *me* director of the board. And I take my responsibilities very seriously."

There came that conqueror's smile of his—satin over steel. "Oh, we're all quite aware of your seriousness, Lady Kingsley. You remind us of it often enough."

Because you give me no choice, she wanted to protest. *How else am I to convince you that women can be serious about more things than gowns and jewelry? Especially when you're so blasted sure of yourself and arrogant and . . .*

Male. So very, very male. And so unlike Henry.

Not that her husband hadn't been masculine. But Henry believed in gentle persuasion. He never raised his voice, never questioned her judgment or disagreed with her. Quite unlike the relentless Lord Warbrooke.

"This isn't the sort of factory you think," he persisted. "I'm speaking of a facility that would allow the boys to experiment with different skills and positions of authority. They would manage it themselves as much as possible."

"It's a progressive idea," Mr. Dawson ventured. "You must admit—"

"Progressive?" she cried. "To take them from their studies for the dubious opportunity of doing precisely what they'd do outside the institution—work from dusk until dawn so their betters can profit from their hard labor?"

"I agree with her ladyship," Lord Bradford interjected.

"Don't like all this talk of going into trade, old fellow. Supporting a charity is all well and good, but dabbling in factories and such . . . Seems a nasty business to me."

When Lord Warbrooke's lips twitched and his eyes danced, she sighed. Yes, Lord Bradford was an insufferable snob, but his father leased the land to Lamberton School. So Bradford's opinion counted for something, no matter how muddleheaded his reasons.

"Lord Bradford has a point, but I don't see it as going into trade a'tall," Mr. Dawson chimed in. "Since the purpose of this institution is to educate—"

"Yes, exactly—to educate, not exploit!" She seized the opportunity to show them a better possibility. "That's why I think we should establish four or five educational endowments for the boys so they can attend Oxford or Cambridge. We could even give competitions with the endowments as prizes. That would provide the boys with something to work toward."

"If you could fund four or five endowments, Lady Kingsley," Lord Warbrooke bit out, "We wouldn't be having this discussion."

Oh, why must the clever devil always be so blasted logical?

He went on without a care for her agitation. "At least my proposal is self-supporting. The income from the factory would fund it, while teaching them—"

"That they're only good as workhorses for their betters," she finished, feeling her control of the board slipping away from her despite all her protests. "Is that really what we want to teach them?"

"You'd prefer to prepare them as scholars? When you know very well most of them want only a way to care for themselves and their families?"

Despair clutched at her heart. He would never understand. How could he? "You don't know what they want. You come here only for these meetings. I'm the one Mr.

Dawson turns to whenever decisions must be made. I'm the one who speaks regularly with the boys."

"She does have a point—" Mr. Dawson began.

"Yes, we all have a point, don't we?" Lord Warbrooke snapped at Dawson. His mouth tightened into a grim line. "In any case, it's absurd to debate the matter without knowing the details. Have you brought along a written proposal for *your* idea, Lady Kingsley?"

"As a matter of fact, I have." She held up the stack of proposals that had taken Henry's man of affairs a day to copy out, then set them on the table.

"Good. So have I." He set his own thick pile of papers next to hers. "Why don't we all take some time to examine them both, and then vote on the best proposal at our meeting on Tuesday, four days from now?"

The other members of the board readily agreed. They sorted out the copies among them, and then she adjourned the meeting. One by one the board members left the room until only Isobel, Phoebe, and Lord Warbrooke remained.

He rose and turned for the door, then paused to glance back at her. "Lady Kingsley, when you read this, do attempt to keep an open mind."

"I will if you will," she retorted hotly.

To her surprise, he chuckled. "I daresay neither of us will. It's a pity, too, because if we could ever see our way clear to agreeing on a matter, we might accomplish a great deal of good in this world."

It infuriated her that he could pretend to care even one whit for these boys. "Now you've confused me. I'd assumed that your reason for serving on so many charitable boards was to further your political aims. Yet all the time you were merely hoping to accomplish some 'good in this world.' How very astonishing."

Just that quickly, his amusement vanished. "While I don't pretend to be as morally superior as you and your late husband, my intentions are good, no matter what you make of them. It may shock you to learn that those of us with character flaws sometimes do as much good as those of you without."

She had no answer for that. If he knew how fragile was her appearance of superiority and how many were her character flaws, he'd never say such a thing. But he didn't know, and she could only pray he never found out.

When she merely sat there mute, he added, "Good day, Lady Kingsley. I do hope you sleep well tonight on your pedestal." Then without waiting for her response, he left.

As soon as the door closed behind him, she shot to her feet. "My pedestal! Ohhh, how I wish I could wipe that knowing smile from his face! And he calls *me* superior! He's the one who's so smug and sure of himself!"

"And handsome as the very devil," Phoebe put in.

"That's exactly what he is—a devil! Him and his ideas for a factory . . . why, he might as well take those poor boys and put them to work in coal mines!"

"You're looking at his proposal all wrong, you know. You're not considering the possibilities."

"For what? Exploiting children? Those poor boys—"

"Those poor boys run our good Mr. Dawson ragged. Except for the few who thrive on their studies, most are restless and, as his lordship says, need stimulation."

"Hard labor? Is that what you call 'stimulation'?"

"It's better than the alternative. Would you prefer that they act like the boys at Harrow and Eton? Become a plague on every maid around? Or worse?"

A sudden helplessness overtook Isobel. "Oh, Phoebe, what am I to do? The very thought of establishing a factory on the grounds makes my blood curdle."

Phoebe reached over to pat her hand. "I know, Bella, I know. You're just too gentle a soul to consider it."

That wasn't it at all, but she could hardly explain. Even Phoebe didn't know the truth about her. That she was a fraud. That she might be called a lady, but only because of her husband's ineffable kindness and careful grooming of her.

She curled her fingers into fists. "Lord Warbrooke can say what he wishes, but I know Henry would never have approved of his measures."

"Or of the way his lordship looks at you either," Phoebe commented dryly.

Isobel glanced up, startled. "What do you mean?" She'd thought nobody else noticed. She'd thought she imagined those alarmingly heated looks Lord Warbrooke sometimes flashed her way.

Phoebe chuckled. "That man wants you badly. The two of you spark off of each other like flint and steel."

"We do not!" What an awful idea! Truly dreadful! She and Lord Warbrooke together? The very idea was absurd, impossible . . .

Entrancing.

No, she mustn't even think it. She mustn't dwell on how the rough timbre of Lord Warbrooke's voice occasionally spiked her pulse up a notch. Or how the accidental brush of his hand against hers sometimes—only sometimes, mind you—made her body quiver in odd places. He would never accept her as she was, nor give her his approval.

Not that she wanted him to. No, indeed. She didn't care what that . . . that arrogant lord thought of her.

"I certainly wouldn't protest if his lordship eyed *me* like that," Phoebe said. "Can you imagine how he'd be in bed? All lean muscle and stormy passion and—"

"Phoebe!" she protested weakly, the images far too vivid. A pox on her friend for evoking them. Isobel had learned long ago that such odd yearnings and desires came to nothing but disappointment. They could certainly never be satisfied by a man with aims and opinions so decidedly opposed to her own.

"There's nothing wrong with wanting a man, you know," Phoebe said. "It's not as if you're a virginal miss who must protect her virtue. As long as you're discreet, you can engage in a love affair or two." She eyed Isobel curiously. "Or even marry again. Have you never thought of doing so?"

"Of course." She stared down at the hands she always kept gloved. "But it's not that easy to find a suitable husband. He'd have to be the sort to put up with my charity work and not expect me to be always at home."

More important, he'd have to accept the truth about her past. She doubted such a man existed. Once any respectable man learned who she really was, he'd never want her.

He might even be unscrupulous enough to reveal her secret to others. If the truth became widely known, how would she ever convince anybody to contribute to the charities ever again? They listened to her because she was Henry's wife—a viscountess. They'd never listen to poor Isobel Smith, no matter how many deportment lessons Henry had purchased for her and how much French she knew.

"Some men would tolerate your involvement with Henry's charities. Lord Warbrooke, for example—"

"Don't even think such a thing! His lordship might have a passion for charitable causes, but I can guess the sort of wife he'd want—one better suited to a politician. He'd want me to stay at home and entertain while he did the real work."

"Well, I think you're wrong, but it needn't be him. Choose some other gentleman. You've pined after Henry long enough. He was thirty years your senior—he wouldn't expect you to mourn him all your life. And don't you miss the intimacies of marriage?" A faraway look crossed Phoebe's face. "God knows I do."

Isobel blushed. "I don't understand why. I suppose that the kissing can be nice, but the rest of it—" She gave an involuntary shudder. "It's embarrassing and uncomfortable and not the least pleasant."

Phoebe gaped at her. "Do you mean to say . . . that is . . . from the way you spoke of Henry, I'd thought— So you find it unpleasant, eh?" She settled back against her chair with narrowed eyes. "Tell me something, Bella. When Henry . . . er . . . came to your bed, how long did he take to do his business?"

"Phoebe!" She couldn't believe her friend was even talking about this!

"Just answer the question."

She hesitated, yet she found it curious that Phoebe would ask such a thing. Curious enough that she answered her. "I suppose . . . five minutes. Fortunately, Henry was a considerate husband, for I don't see how a woman could endure more than that."

Phoebe burst into laughter. "Oh, Bella, you have no idea! Trust me, when a man does it right, you want it to last forever."

Isobel gazed at her friend, truly perplexed. She couldn't imagine wanting the dreadful act to last forever. Still, hadn't she often wondered if there were more to it? She'd heard married women giggling over their lovers and seen many a country girl go astray. And for what? If lovemaking were as awful as it had been in her experience, why did they even do it when they didn't have to?

She wanted to ask Phoebe to explain, yet she was almost afraid to know more and be disappointed yet again. After all the sly remarks at her and Henry's wedding breakfast, she'd eagerly anticipated their time together, only to find it sad and awkward and painful. Perhaps it was simply *her*. Perhaps she was made wrong.

"Phoebe?" she heard herself say. "You said, 'when a man does it right,' but . . . well . . . how do you know if he's doing it right?"

"When it makes you feel as if the heavens have rained joy all over you."

She'd certainly never felt *that*. "Perhaps some women just don't—"

"If a woman doesn't, it's usually because her lover is inept. And while bumbling males do abound, you can find the competent ones if you look hard enough." Phoebe's voice filled with sympathy. "Have you truly never enjoyed . . . I mean . . . wasn't there anybody besides Henry?"

Isobel shook her head. "He's the only man I've even kissed."

"Then you don't know what you're missing, Bella. It can be so very lovely when it's with a man who knows what he's doing."

A lump of longing caught in Isobel's throat. She gazed down at the table. "Or perhaps I'm just . . . well, flawed somehow." Though the thought that she'd failed Henry in that respect struck her to the heart.

"I'd lay odds that you're not." Phoebe's face brightened. "And I know how you can find out for sure."

"What do you mean?"

"Come with me tonight to the Widows' Auction." Scooting her chair closer, Phoebe glanced furtively out the open door, then lowered her voice. "It's held at the Mayfair Bachelors' Club every year. Respectable widows offer themselves in an auction for one night of . . . well . . . passion. The bachelors bid and the widows receive three-quarters of the auction price. The other quarter goes to the club."

Isobel's shock knew no bounds. "You're not . . . You don't mean to—"

"Oh, I certainly do. I've done it before, you know. At last year's auction, I met the most marvelous—" She broke off with a smile. "Let's just say that once you've enjoyed the sweets, it's difficult to abstain. And Mr. Chambers has been dead quite a while."

"But, Phoebe, I know you've had men interested in marriage."

"Yes, but I don't want another husband, just a little . . . er . . . taste of pleasure from time to time. For all his faults, Mr. Chambers could lay out a feast for a famished woman, and I miss that."

Isobel gnawed on her lower lip. She didn't know what the feast was like. She hadn't even realized until this moment that there might be a feast at all. "What about your reputation and your future?"

"The auction is entirely anonymous. The women are masked, and no man may remove a woman's mask without her permission. Otherwise the widows would balk at participating every year. It allows the gentlemen to have their fun, and the women to supplement their income—"

"You mean, to sell themselves like whores."

Phoebe shrugged. "If you wish to see it that way. I don't. They don't make a profession out of it. Some of the women even give the money to charity. And it's not as if they have any virtue to lose." A pleading note entered her voice. "It's just one night for a lonely woman, Bella. One night of pleasure free from any dire consequences."

"Oh? What about the possibility of children?" she snapped.

Phoebe flashed her a smug smile. "There are ways to prevent that."

And she hadn't known? Oh, but why should she? Henry had wanted children. That had been his primary reason for marrying her. It had been one of her great regrets that she'd been as unable to give him a son as his previous two wives.

With a saucy tilt of her head, Phoebe surveyed Isobel critically. "You could do it, too, you know. For a night with you, a man would pay substantially. With that mass of blond hair and your rosy lips and fine form—"

"I am *not* putting myself up for auction to the highest bidder! I'm certainly not spending the evening in the bed of a perfect stranger."

Still, the idea of being desired by a gentleman just for her body and naught else had a strangely enticing appeal.

Oh, Lord, how could she even think it? It was the most wicked thing she'd ever heard of!

Phoebe tsked at her. "You can't go all your life moldering away in your lonely town house. You're barely twenty-seven. It would be a crime for a woman like you to never truly experience the pleasures of the flesh."

"There's no guarantee that the man who bids on me will be any better able to show me . . . um . . . the pleasure of the flesh than Henry was."

"True, but they're all experienced gentlemen or they wouldn't participate. It takes a jaded man to bid on a widow when he could simply pay a common whore. These are men who find excitement in pleasing a woman who's been long without." A glint of mischief entered her eyes. "Besides, you could use the proceeds to fund your educational endowments for the boys."

A pox on Phoebe for knowing exactly how to tempt her. The idea took hold, much as Isobel tried to banish it. Wouldn't it be grand to go into that meeting next week and throw that money in Lord Warbrooke's face? With all of Henry's estate tied up in his charities except for the modest living allowance given to her, she had no other way of raising the funds.

Much as she hated to admit it, she was even more intrigued by the possibility of finding out the truth about lovemaking. Throughout her marriage, she'd wondered why Henry's perfectly pleasant kisses always ended in such a miserable act. If Phoebe were right, and it had naught to do with *her* . . .

She sighed. "If only it didn't sound so . . . so . . ."

"Exciting? Thrilling?"

"Dangerous. If I'm found out, think what would happen!"

"You'd risk far more with any other method of tasting the fruits of the flesh."

Phoebe did have a point. To engage in a typical love affair would mean exposing herself to some man who might use the knowledge to ruin her if he liked. But Phoebe had done this before, and nothing had happened. Besides, she'd be masked.

"I–I don't know . . ." she began, even as she felt herself weakening.

"Come now, Bella, it will be fun, and we'd be doing it together. Don't you think it's high time you learn what you've been missing in the bedchamber?"

When Phoebe put it that way, the bleakness of Isobel's life stretched before her—a wasteland of duty and long, lonely days followed by even longer, lonelier nights. She wanted to marry, truly she did, if only for companionship. But first she needed to know if she was too flawed for the act of lovemaking.

"All right," she heard herself saying. "If you're sure no one will find out."

"It'll be our secret," her friend responded.

But the cat-in-the-cream smile Phoebe tendered made Isobel wonder if she wasn't making an enormous mistake.

2

That evening, Justin did something he wouldn't have considered under any other circumstances. He agreed to join the odious Lord Bradford for dinner at the Mayfair Bachelors' Club.

Justin had never had a desire to join or even visit Bradford's club. The organization was made up of young rascals, all of whom competed to see who could be the more debauched. But thanks to this morning's disastrous meeting of the governing board, he needed the young earl's vote. If Bradford voted with Lady Kingsley, others might be swayed to their side and that simply wouldn't do.

Lady Kingsley. He snorted. If not for that bloody woman voicing her unfounded opinions this morning, he'd be having a nice dinner at home instead of having to endure some undoubtedly inedible meal in Bradford's company. He still smarted over her parting jabs about his motives for serving on charitable boards. The lady had to be the most annoyingly superior creature in Christendom.

And it was a pity, too. Because beneath her lofty airs lay a pretty woman whose good taste, fine breeding, and intelligence would make her a very good wife for some man. That is, if any man could put up with her high-minded nonsense long enough to marry her.

Bradford met him at the door as he arrived, then quickly led him into a cavernous room packed with gentlemen. A stench of sweat and tobacco and brandy hung in the air, exacerbated by the summer heat. Justin surveyed the mob with distaste. "Is it always this crowded on a Friday evening?"

"Only tonight. It's the Widows' Auction."

That's when he noticed the dais erected at the front of the room for the occasion and the array of masked females lined up to one side of it. Good God, the infamous Widows' Auction. That explained the smell of lust permeating the room. He should've guessed Bradford would frequent a club notorious for such nonsense. "Perhaps we should go elsewhere—"

"No, indeed!" Bradford nudged him in the ribs and winked madly. "Where's your spirit, man? I never miss this. You'll like it. It's great fun. Who knows? You might even find a lady worth having for an evening."

Justin shot Bradford a skeptical look, but Bradford missed it in his eagerness to assess the "goods" being offered. Justin sighed. If he wanted Bradford's vote, he'd have to endure this. At least until the man bid on some hapless female and took her off.

"Very well," Justin said, though the whole thing disgusted him. He supposed it wasn't any different than taking a mistress or bedding a soiled dove, both of which he'd done often enough in his salad days. The act of love was a viable tender in all levels of English society. But an auction made it seem so much more blatant.

As they took seats at a back table, a servant scurried over to offer them wine and take their order for dinner. At the front of the room, an auctioneer barked attributes of women as if they were horses on the block at Tattersall's. Justin shivered involuntarily. What woman in her right mind submitted to such a bloodless description of her fine qualities? And then to go off with the highest bidder . . .

But a glance around the room told him no one else shared his distaste. The other men cried their bids with regularity, heedless of the lewd comments and jesting of their companions. Even the woman presently on the dais seemed to revel in the attention, for when some balding fellow won the bid and went to claim her, she smiled as sweetly as a schoolgirl.

Justin shook his head. There was no accounting for human behavior, was there? He turned back to Bradford, whose attention was fully engaged by the activity on the dais. "Now about this proposal of mine—"

"Give it a rest, won't you, old fellow?" Bradford interrupted. "We can talk about all that later. Don't know why you even care what happens with that damned school anyway. A man like you dabbling in all this reform nonsense . . . I tell you this—once I inherit the title and I'm not on Father's leash anymore, I'll flee that governing board at once. Boring stuff, all of it."

"Some of us see it as our Christian duty," Justin said tightly.

"Well, I'm not one of them." He flicked his hand toward the dais with a smug grin. *"That's* my Christian duty—looking after the widows and orphans. That's what the Bible says to do, y'know."

If Bradford had ever read one word of a Bible, Justin would be much surprised. "Somehow I don't think this is what the writers of the Bible had in mind."

"Don't be so sanctimonious. You're not exactly immune to lust yourself. I've seen how you eye Lady Kingsley in those meetings."

Justin started. "What the devil are you talking about?"

"Lofty Kingsley of the governing board. Personally, I think Mrs. Chambers would be a bit warmer in bed, but I wouldn't kick Lady Kingsley out if she showed up in mine, to be sure. And judging from how fiercely you two spar, I'll wager you wouldn't kick her out of yours either."

"That's absurd. I've never thought of Lady Kingsley in that way."

"Not even when she wears that dark blue gown that's a little too smug? The one that makes her bubbies stick out in front, and her bottom look plump enough to make a man want to sink his teeth—"

"Not even then," Justin snapped. "And you shouldn't talk so crudely of Lady Kingsley. She's not that kind of woman."

Devil take Bradford. Bad enough that Justin had indeed thought of her "in that way" from time to time. Hearing that Bradford did, too, annoyed him in the extreme.

It was ludicrous anyway. The woman would never countenance attentions from either of them. She filled out her gowns well, but so did cold marble. And her rigid morality was surpassed only by her worshipful adoration of her late husband.

Those two must have made quite the dull pair. Justin had barely known the viscount, but Lady Kinglsey spoke of him as if he were a saint. No doubt her background was equally colorless and respectable, or Saint Kingsley would never have married her. And she wouldn't be continuing his legacy with such single-minded determination.

Not that he didn't admire what she'd done with Kingsley's charities. But a young woman ought to have more of a life than a short marriage and a long widowhood, locked away from the world like some pharaoh's wife in a sarcophagus, waiting to join her lord and master in the afterlife.

He looked at the dais. Then again, some widows *ought* to be locked away. He'd never seen so many gaudily dressed, overpainted females in all his life, tittering and gabbling in their low-cut gowns and feather-trimmed masks. He wouldn't pay a farthing for the lot of them.

Except perhaps for the one being led onto the dais now.

"Deuce take it, would you look at that blonde," Bradford broke in. "What a fine wench. A damned beauty, I'll bet. It's a pity about the masks—stupid rule, if you ask me, though easily got round if the woman agrees. Most of 'em do . . . given a little persuasion." He winked at Justin, who shot him a baleful glance in return.

But Justin couldn't keep his gaze from the dais for long. He hated to agree with Bradford, but that was indeed a "fine wench." Her freely flowing blond hair stood out among the indeterminate brown and hennaed coiffures of her companions. Her simple white satin mask covered the upper part of her face, allowing only a glimpse of her eyes through the slits, though it did expose a generous, soft mouth and flushing cheeks. Like Bradford, he wished he could see the rest, but he had to admit that the mask heightened her allure. Beneath it lay the mysteries of a woman, mysteries any man would want to explore.

Especially when coupled with her gown, a classical Roman sort of thing, probably a leftover costume from some masquerade ball. The white satin draped her curves suggestively, skimmed her breasts and hips so snugly that it drew a man's eye inexorably to her attractions.

Which were ample and unmistakably female. He cursed when his loins grew heavy. But he wasn't made of stone, after all.

"What's your name, luv?" the auctioneer asked the woman.

"Now see here," she said in an oddly imperious voice, "I thought this was supposed to be anonymous."

Everybody laughed at her haughtiness, including Justin. Where had they found this impudent chit?

Strange, but her voice sounded familiar. He'd swear he'd heard it before, and recently, too.

"Not your real name, luv," the auctioneer said, smiling. "Your auction name. Don't want the gentleman wot buys

you calling you 'wench' all night, do you? Just choose a
pretty name. Like Lilith, perhaps, or Delilah."

"I certainly will not! If I must choose an immoral name,
at least it will be something original. And certainly nothing
as appallingly obvious as that!"

As laughter rolled from the audience, Justin's eyes narrowed. This morning a certain unyielding woman had
called his ideas "appalling" in just that superior tone of
voice.

No, it was impossible. Unthinkable. Lady Kingsley?
She would never do something like this.

Or would she? She was a widow, after all. And she had
the same blond hair and the same height and build as this
woman. Not to mention the superior manner. Despite how
he tried to banish the absurd thought, it continued to nig-
gle in his brain. He leaned forward, wishing he could move
closer still.

"Give us a name, luv," the auctioneer prodded.

The woman steadied herself. "You may call me Bella,"
she said primly.

His heart hammered in his chest. Lady Kingsley's given
name was Isobel, but he'd once heard Mrs. Chambers call
her Bella. That was too much of a coincidence, given the
other similarities.

Impossible it might be, and unthinkable it certainly was,
but the woman on that dais was Lady Kingsley all the
same. He'd stake his fortune on it.

The little morally superior hypocrite! She had no business looking down her nose at *him* when she was here offering her body in a highly scandalous auction.

It made no sense at all. Why would she do such a thing?
Could it be for the money? From what he understood, the
participating widows did receive a substantial portion of
the proceeds, but surely Kingsley had left her well enough
off that she didn't need to do *this*.

Not for herself, at any rate. But might she do it for the
sake of her precious scholarly endowments, her new pet

project? It would be just like her to go to such lengths to thwart him.

Whatever her reasons, the bloody woman was insane to do this. No doubt about it.

The auctioneer began his pitch, describing Lady Kingsley's assets with a boldness that made her duck her head. But not before he'd glimpsed the scarlet blush on the part of her face showing beneath the mask.

Good. She *ought* to be embarrassed, damn it. And what had she expected? This was a bachelors' club, for God's sake. They didn't mince words.

All the same, he grew inexplicably annoyed when her blushing drew laughter and sly comments from the men in the crowd.

"I say," Bradford spoke up beside him, "I think I know that little filly. Does she seem familiar to you?"

Justin froze. Bad enough that Justin had guessed her identity, but if Bradford did, he'd ruin the woman for certain. The thought didn't sit well. "Never seen the chit before in my life."

"I could swear—"

"Do you come to this auction every year?" Justin broke in.

"Wouldn't miss it."

"Then perhaps you saw her here before."

Bradford's frown cleared. "You must be right." He settled back against his chair with a smug smile. "Might even be the one I bid on last year. She was yellow-haired and saucy, too, though a bit plumper. Still, could be the same one. I hope it is, for that one gave me quite the night to remember. You know these widows, randy as hell without a man in their bed. Think I'll bid on this Bella."

Bloody hell. Justin had meant to squelch Bradford's interest, not fuel it. "Do as you please, but she looks pale and sickly to me. Hardly worth the money." And if Bradford believed that, then he didn't have eyes in his head.

Unfortunately, Bradford's eyes were securely in place

and in good working order, too. The second the auctioneer solicited bids, Bradford bid fifty pounds.

Justin didn't stop to think; he just reacted. "Seventy-five pounds!" he called out.

"What the devil are you doing?" Bradford hissed. "I told you I wanted her. You trying to show me up? Is that it?"

"I want the woman for myself, that's all," Justin said coolly. "You told me I might find a wench worth bidding on, and I have."

It would cost him Bradford's vote on the proposal, not to mention God knows how much money, but he couldn't help it. He wasn't about to let Bradford win her. Bradford would take advantage, blackmail her into sharing his bed. The very thought chilled Justin's blood. One thing he knew—no matter what maggoty reason she had for coming here, Lady Kingsley would *not* enjoy any liaison with Bradford.

Besides, Justin had reasons of his own for wanting to win her. He wanted to know precisely why she was doing this. He wanted to see how far she'd take it.

And yes, some ungentlemanly part of him wanted to give her a taste of her own medicine. Lecture *him* on morality, would she? After tonight, she wouldn't try *that* again, not if he had anything to say about it. Oh, yes, he'd make her eat her words, he would.

But first he'd give her enough rope to hang herself. Let her quake in her boots when she saw who won the bid. Let her think he truly meant to bed her. If that didn't mortify her into begging his mercy, he didn't know what would. The foolish woman *needed* to be mortified if she was going to embark on idiotic schemes like this.

No, what she needed was to have someone strike the fear of God into her. Which he fully intended to do. Judging by her blushes, this was her first time at the Widows' Auction. She couldn't possibly realize how foolish, how dangerous this game was for a woman with her sheltered upbringing.

Well, he'd make sure she realized it by the time this night was over. He'd win this bid if he had to go into debt to do it. Because there was no way in hell he was passing up this chance to best the superior Lady Kingsley.

3

Isobel frantically tried to pick out the two men who'd placed bids, but it was difficult in the cramped room. This sordid assembly of drunken men making indecent comments wasn't at all what she'd expected. If one of these unkempt fellows had been the one to bid, she'd simply die.

She should never have listened to Phoebe. She should have realized this would turn out to be awful. How could it not? Scanning the room again, she fought to ignore her spinning head and the close, stale air that pressed in on her until she feared she'd faint.

And the embarrassment. The absolute mortification of being up here on public display . . .

"A hundred pounds," the first voice called again, and this time she located it.

Her heart sank. Oh, dear, not Lord Bradford. She'd had enough trouble resigning herself to this course of action. But to have it be *him* who bid on her . . . Why, it was too much to bear! He would guess who she was the instant she

neared him! Even if by some chance he didn't, she
couldn't endure having that disgusting creature put his
hands on her.

Heavens, this was such a dreadful mistake! She should
have fled the moment she realized what this was like.

But she'd seen what had happened to some poor woman
who'd balked earlier. They'd teased and taunted her and
then unmasked her . . . Oh, no, she dared not risk *that*.

All she could hope was that someone would bid against
the earl. A futile hope. The highest bid so far that night had
been a hundred pounds for a lithe beauty who'd flaunted
her wares with the practice of a dockside tart. No one
would bid that much for a blushing miss who looked utterly out of place amid the flashy gowns and low décol-
letage of the other widows.

"Two hundred," a dry voice called out from right beside
Lord Bradford, and her heart leapt.

Until she saw who it was. Lord Warbrooke? Here? Oh,
dear Lord in heaven. Only by holding on to the auctioneer's arm did she keep from fainting. This was even more
horrible! Lord Warbrooke would surely use this to his advantage if he won. Oh, if only she could flee!

God Almighty had clearly handpicked the two men
she'd least want to see her here. It must be His idea of an
appropriate punishment for a woman engaging in such a
rash and immoral act.

She could think of no other reason than divine inter-
vention for Lord Warbrooke's presence. The very eligible
and self-assured marquess didn't need to purchase companionship; he could have all he wanted for free. And if he
did purchase it, he wouldn't do it at an auction where he
might actually lose.

"Five hundred," Lord Bradford said with an air of triumph.

Perspiration ran down her nose from beneath her satin
mask. No one in their right mind bid five hundred pounds
for one night with a woman. Certainly no one would bid

more than that, even Lord Warbrooke. And though being won by either man would be disastrous, she was sure Lord Bradford would be the worse of the two. Lord Warbrooke might send her temper soaring half a dozen times a week, but her instincts told her he'd never hurt a woman. Strip her of her pride perhaps and play havoc with her self-control, but not hurt her. Whereas Lord Bradford . . .

She shuddered.

The bidding had so rapidly escalated to a competition between the two men that the rest of the audience was speculating on the meaning of it in hushed whispers. Chairs creaked and glasses clinked as people drank, but eventually even those sounds died out as everyone held their breath for the outcome.

"Going once—" the auctioneer began.

"A thousand pounds," Lord Warbrooke called out.

A collective gasp and then wild applause shook the audience, but shock stunned her into silence. The man had lost his mind. A thousand pounds? For some woman he didn't even realize he knew? It was an obscene amount of money! Lord Warbrooke was rich, but a thousand pounds would tax any man's finances.

Apparently Lord Bradford thought the same, for with a curse he rose and slammed down his glass, then pushed his way out of the room. He wasn't going to bid again. Thank heavens.

The auctioneer said, "Going once. Going twice . . ."

Oh, Lord, but that meant Lord Warbrooke had won her for the night. What was she to do now? She'd been mad to try this. Mad!

"Sold!" the auctioneer said.

Though her heart threatened to thunder its way right out of her chest, she could do nothing to prevent this disaster. Keeping a firm hand on her elbow, the auctioneer ushered her off the dais, barely giving her time to don her pelisse and grab her large reticule before he led her into the crowd.

With a feeling of impending doom, she saw Lord Warbrooke rise from his seat and head toward them.

Dear heaven, she was trapped. His lordship wouldn't take kindly to any refusal to honor the bid. Even if she could think of a reasonable explanation for refusing, he'd demand reparation. Or worse—he'd demand that they unmask her.

"A thousand pounds—that's quite a bid," the auctioneer told her as he steered her across the room. "Largest one we've ever had. That means seven hundred fifty pounds for you, Bella."

At last the reality of how much Lord Warbrooke had paid for her sank in. *Seven hundred fifty pounds*. Why, she could easily fund *three* scholarships with that money! And it would be *Lord Warbrooke's* money, too. There was a perverse sort of justice in that. If she brought seven hundred fifty pounds to the meeting next week, that would sway them all to her side.

But not if Lord Warbrooke figured out who she really was. Oh, and he would certainly enjoy exposing her wicked nature before the governing board, wouldn't he? He'd make her sound like the worst wanton imaginable, while he, being a man, would receive no censure at all.

Then she'd never be able to face any of them again. She'd lose control of Henry's charities, for who'd want an immoral woman like her on their boards? And then what would become of the charities? Pushy men like Lord Warbrooke and Lord Bradford would always hold sway.

No, she couldn't let that happen. There was only one thing to do. Keep Lord Warbrooke from figuring out who she was. Surely she could do that for one night. How difficult could it be?

Especially considering how Lord Warbrooke regarded her—as a serious, highly proper lady. He would never expect Lady Kingsley to be participating in this sordid auction. He certainly wouldn't expect her to go through with it after she'd been won, so if she went along willingly, she might allay any suspicions. She was safely masked, and the auction rules said he couldn't remove the mask without her permission.

Of course, Lord Warbrooke had never been one for following rules . . .

She squared her shoulders. No, she wouldn't let him intimidate her. She must play her part so well—acting like a widow eager for his attentions—that he would never, *ever* dream it was her.

Yes, that's what she must do. Be bold, be daring. Be the wicked Bella.

Besides, she *had* wanted to find out if she was capable of being a true wife to a man. She just hadn't expected to perform her experiment on *him*, of all people.

A shiver of anticipation swept through her despite all her fear. She tried fruitlessly to squelch it. She did find him attractive, after all. And if any man could guide her through the "pleasures of the flesh," it would be *him*, with his Roman conqueror's blood and his heated looks.

Suddenly he was upon them, and she had no more time to decide. But she'd already made her decision. Bella—and only Bella—was spending the night with Lord Warbrooke.

"That's quite a bid you placed, sir," the auctioneer said genially as Lord Warbrooke met them. "I'm afraid I don't know you—"

"I'm the Marquess of Warbrooke." His lordship's eyes never left her masked face. "A guest of Lord Bradford's."

The auctioneer chuckled. "I daresay he wished he hadn't invited you."

"No doubt." Never one to waste time with pleasantries, he held out his arm to her. "Shall we go, madam?"

His gaze was so searching and curious she feared she'd already given herself away. Scrambling for a further way to disguise herself, she pitched her voice at a lower timbre. "Of course, my lord."

His eyes narrowed. "You sound different from before."

The hint of challenge in his tone raised her hackles. Lady Kingsley might have to endure his impudence, but Bella didn't. "My voice is higher when I'm nervous, that's all."

His gloved hand curved warmly over hers, making her breath catch in her throat. "Why were you nervous? Surely you've done this before."

"No, never."

"That makes two of us," he admitted as he led her toward the door, leaving the auctioneer behind.

A devilish mischief seized her. "I hardly believe that. You seemed to know precisely what you wanted and how to get it."

"I should hope any man above the age of seventeen would."

"Yes, but few men above the age of seventeen would pay a thousand pounds for it. I do hope I can make it worth your while."

His dark smile curled her toes. "You've already made it worth my while. Whatever follows will just be icing on the cake."

That drew her into a panic. Perhaps she'd underestimated the safety of her disguise. Oh, Lord, what if he'd already guessed who she was? What if he was toying with her, waiting to see how far she would sink into depravity before he exposed her? "Wh–what do you mean?"

His hand stiffened on hers. "I finally got to publicly humiliate a man I despise. That was easily worth a thousand pounds."

"Oh." Despite her relief that he hadn't guessed her identity, his explanation filled her with an unaccountable disappointment. "So this wasn't about me at all. Any woman would have served your purpose. It was merely a battle between you and Lord Bradford."

"Not quite." His heated gaze made a slow circuit of her body. "I bid on you because I wanted you. And I wanted no one else to have you."

His possessive tone and the glitter in his eyes ought to have sent her fleeing. Instead, it melted her into a puddle.

Swallowing hard, she glanced away. She shouldn't react so powerfully to his attentions. She should keep up her guard.

Yet some ancient feminine part of her exulted to hear how badly he wanted her. Even if only for one night. Even though he thought she was Bella, an anonymous widow of no consequence.

They were outside now and descending the stairs toward his waiting carriage. When he handed her in, a feeling of inevitability swamped her. She was going home for the night with a man. Not just any man, but one descended from the Romans who'd briefly ruled Britain, a man used to conquering and commanding and—

Oh, dear, what a ridiculous imagination she had. It was all the fault of this flimsy toga-like costume Phoebe had loaned her. It made her feel like the spoils of war—a vestal virgin being carted off over some soldier's shoulder.

How silly was that? She'd chosen to do this, after all. It wasn't as if she was acting against her will. So why did she feel like a statue being hauled away as so much plunder?

As she settled against the squabs, Lord Warbrooke instructed the coachman, then got in, too. Her heart pounded faster when he dropped onto the seat beside her instead of opposite her. Nor did her nervousness ease when he removed his gloves one finger at a time, exposing hands every bit as strong and finely shaped as she'd imagined. Hands that would soon be roaming over her body, stripping off her clothes, and doing God knows what other things.

The thought turned her knees to water. Oh, how she wished she'd asked Phoebe to be a bit more forthcoming on what to expect.

He reached for her hand and started to unbutton her glove.

"No!" she protested, jerking it back. "I'd rather leave it

on." She dropped her gaze to her hands, which she never let *anyone* see.

"Part of your disguise, is it?" he quipped.

"You might say that." She was being silly. What did it matter if he saw Bella's hands? Still, she'd rather keep her hands covered. They weren't at all pretty.

"It doesn't matter," he bent close to murmur. "As long as you're willing to remove the pertinent items of clothing when the time comes, I don't much care if you keep your gloves on."

His blatant innuendo made her jerk her head up, only to find him eyeing her with decided mischief. Why, the scoundrel was deliberately provoking her!

Well, two could play that game. "I'll remove the pertinent items of clothing *now*, if you prefer."

At first her frankness seemed to startle him, but then he smiled. "No need to rush, is there?" After ordering the coachman to drive on, he returned his probing gaze to her. "Are you hungry, Bella?"

She gazed at him warily. Did some other wicked meaning lie behind the question? Or was he merely asking if she wanted food? "To be honest, I'm famished." She added, for clarification, "I had no chance to eat, I'm afraid."

"Neither did I." He tossed his gloves on the opposite seat. "So I thought our first order of business should be dinner. We'll dine in private at the Clarendon."

She relaxed against the seat. "You mean you don't want to throw me down and ravish me right here?"

"Is that what you expected?"

"Actually, I did. You paid a lot of money for only the one night, after all."

"True." He shifted on the seat to see her better. "But I'm not foolish enough to guzzle an expensive wine the moment it's set before me. Especially when it's so very fine."

An unwarranted thrill coursed down to her toes. She ought to take insult at being compared to a bottle of wine.

But a *fine* bottle of wine . . . well, that was another matter entirely, wasn't it?

He leaned closer, his features shadowy in the faint gaslight trickling into the carriage. Lifting his hand, he traced the lower border of her mask with one finger, grazing her cheek, then the tip of her nose, then making a detour down to her lip. Idly he outlined her mouth. "Before I indulge in a superior bottle of wine, I prefer to take a moment to admire its beautiful color."

She tried to breathe and failed miserably. And had she imagined his emphasis on "superior"?

"Then," he rasped, bending in to nuzzle her hair, "I sniff its bouquet and savor its scent." He breathed in deeply, and she thought she'd shatter right then and there. He loomed so close, and this felt so intimate. She almost wished he *had* thrown her down and ravished her. She could have endured that easier than this inch-by-inch assault on her senses.

With the faintest touch of his finger, he tipped her face up to his. His eyes glittered at her like shards of silver. "Only after that do I allow myself the first sip . . ."

That was all the warning he gave before his mouth covered hers, warm and sensuous and soft. His kiss blotted out the black night and the carriage and all her silly fears. It sent her pulse racing and startled a quiver in her belly. If this was a sip, God help her when he got around to drinking.

As if he'd read her mind, he did the most astonishing thing. He slipped his tongue between her lips. Henry had never done *that*, to be sure. And Lord Warbrooke mustn't guess that she had no idea what he was doing.

So she mimicked his actions and slid her own tongue into *his* mouth. He halted, but only for a moment. Then with a groan he caught her to him and thrust his tongue inside with a boldness that took her off guard.

She was still reeling from the intimacy of it when he repeated the motion . . . again and again, his tongue caressing the inside of her mouth, tangling with her own tongue until she was dizzy from the dance. What an odd way to kiss . . . seductive and maddening all at once. It made her hot in strange places . . . in her breasts . . . her belly . . . in that wicked place between her legs that Henry had so rudely assaulted every time they'd coupled.

She tore her mouth free long enough to catch her breath. "Dear heaven, Lord Warbrooke. This is . . . all very . . . interesting."

Chuckling, he pressed an open-mouthed kiss to her cheek. "Do you like it?"

"Oh, yes," she breathed.

"Then call me Justin."

"Justin," she whispered, and slid her hands about his neck.

With a guttural sound of approval, he took her mouth again, hard and deep, invading her as surely as any Roman conqueror. Scents of brandy and musk drifted through her senses as he dug his fingers into her arms to keep her close.

Which was entirely unnecessary. She wasn't going anywhere, not when he was kissing her so deliciously. She couldn't think, couldn't breathe for fear that any movement might make it all end.

And she didn't want it to end yet. Not when she was beginning to realize how very little her late husband had known about kissing. Henry's kisses had tickled her curiosity, then failed to satisfy it. But Lord Warbrooke's kisses made naughty, exciting promises that he clearly intended to satisfy in spades. The very thought made her sway against him.

He tore his mouth from hers to murmur, "Ah, Bella, you're not what you seem . . ."

"No one is ever what they seem," she whispered back, arching her neck as he began to kiss his way along the pulse that beat so fast beneath his mouth.

Suddenly she felt him slide his hand over to stroke her breast. At first she hardly noticed, too fogged by all the other glorious sensations to register this new one. But as his hand progressed from tender caresses to a bolder kneading motion, she gasped and drew back to say shakily, "I take it you're done with sipping."

His eyes opened, heavy lidded and dazed. "What?"

She glanced down at his hand, still cupped over her breast. "The wine. You're done with the sipping and have decided to go on to drinking."

He jerked his hand back. When he caught her bewildered gaze on him, his face grew shuttered. "No . . . I only got carried away."

"So did I. But isn't that what we're supposed to do?"

Releasing his breath in a ragged sigh, he stroked her cheek. "Yes, but not yet. Not until after dinner. We have the entire night ahead of us, after all."

Then he shocked her by leaving her side to throw himself over onto the other seat. As he laid his head back against the squabs and raised a shaky hand to shove the hair from his eyes, the streetlamps cast a lambent glow over his face. Soft light swept his taut features and the lines of strain about his mouth.

From the way he sat, with legs splayed apart, she would guess that she'd aroused him. So why had he stopped when he had? Had she done something wrong? Was it indeed as she'd feared—that she was inept at this lovemaking business? "You prefer to drink your wine slowly, do you?" she ventured to ask.

His gaze swung to her, stormy with suppressed need. "Only when the wine's worth drinking."

"Or when you paid too much for it, perhaps?"

"Too much?" His laugh held an edge. "It's the fact that I paid so little that worries me. I suspect there will be another reckoning later that may exceed what I wish to pay."

She could gather only one meaning from his peculiar words. "If you're concerned about getting me with child, then you needn't be. I'm not even sure I can bear children. During my marriage I was never able to conceive."

He shifted his gaze to the window. "But you and your husband did try."

"Of course. Many times." Then she caught herself. She couldn't believe she was actually telling Lord Warbrooke how often she and her husband shared a bed. It was a wonder he wasn't appalled to hear a lady discuss—

No, not a lady. She was Bella, the masked widow. She could say exactly what she pleased, when she pleased.

The full reality staggered her. She really could, couldn't she? It didn't matter if he found her tart-tongued or bold or improper—he'd never see Bella again. She was truly free to say what she wished, to *do* what she wished.

Such heavenly freedom emboldened her. "And even if I could conceive, my friend showed me how to prevent it."

His head swung around so fast, she thought he'd lose it. "Your friend did *what*?"

"Told me about French letters and sponges and such." She waved her well-packed reticule. "She even gave me a sponge. I have it right in here."

He gazed at her as if she'd gone mad.

"You do know about them, don't you?" she went on nervously. "I–I was told that all the ladies use them. First they're soaked in vinegar and then they're put—"

"I know where they're put," he ground out. "I'm merely astonished that *you* do."

"Why? Surely you didn't think I'd attend the auction unprepared."

He looked exceedingly flustered, then mumbled, "Nice young widows aren't supposed to know about things like that."

"To be honest, I didn't until my friend told me. She felt honor-bound to instruct me in how to protect myself, since she was the one who convinced me to do the auction."

"Convinced you— Good God, what kind of friend is this? A whore?"

She gaped at him. "You're passing judgment on my

friend after *you* bid an ungodly amount to spend the night with a strange woman?"

"I . . . um . . . that is—"

"And why is it any worse for a woman to prevent conception than for a man to go about doing the conceiving willy-nilly?"

"Now see here—"

"You ought to be ashamed of yourself!" Her dander was fully up now. "Do you *want* a lot of your little bastards running about?"

He blinked at her, then burst into laughter. "No, indeed I don't. How good of you to consider that. It hadn't entered my thoughts in the least."

"Well, it should have," she scolded.

"You're quite right," he choked out, clearly trying to repress any further laughter.

His amusement annoyed her. "And if that didn't worry you, then what did you mean by all that nonsense about a reckoning? Did you think I'd steal from you tonight? Or blackmail you . . . or . . . or something degenerate like that?"

He cast her a glance of mock solemnity. "No, certainly nothing degenerate."

"Then what?"

Mischief glinted in his eyes. Leaning forward suddenly, he caught her hands in his. "The reckoning I fear is that one night with you won't be enough for me. That I'll want you time and again. And that you'll make me pay for that need very dearly in the long run."

4

Justin relished the expression of panic that crossed "Bella's" face. It was about bloody time she realized the possible ramifications of her actions.

Good God, he'd nearly taken her right here in the carriage! And that had *not* been his intention. He'd meant only to draw her out. By playing along, he'd hoped to coax her into revealing her reasons for doing this. Then he could unmask her, give her a stern lecture, and take her home. After which, her gratitude at his discretion would make her moderate her opposition to him on the governing board.

That had been the plan . . . until she'd looked up at him with that strange, yearning expression. Next thing he knew he was spouting all that nonsense about wine and bending to kiss her sweet, lush lips . . .

And enduring a lecture about preventing conception. From *her* of all people!

He groaned. She was tying him in knots, this enchanting creature who'd taken over Lady Kingsley—the one with the sense of humor and the tempting mouth. He was having trouble remembering who she really was, for God's sake.

The enchanting creature finally found her voice. "One night *must* be enough for you," she said fiercely. "It simply must. After this is over, it's over. We can't meet or see each other again."

"I don't see why not." If he pressed hard enough, she might admit the truth. "I'm not married. And unless you entered that auction under false pretenses, *you're* not married either. So if we take pleasure in each other's company and want to spend time together—"

"I'm not that kind of woman!"

"You mean the kind to share a stranger's bed without knowing his background or his character?"

She drew her hands from his. "I mean . . . the kind to be a man's mistress."

Ah, now he was getting somewhere. "Your actions speak otherwise. Clearly you're looking for a protector or you wouldn't be here."

"No! That's not why I did it at all!" Her pretty eyes flashed at him through the slits of the mask.

He found her ridiculous moral outrage highly comical. "I can't imagine what other reason you'd have."

Glancing away, she gnawed on her lower lip as if considering telling him more. Finally she sighed. "It's merely that . . . I'm testing the waters, that's all. I'm not quite ready to marry again, and I want to see if I can even bear to be with another man."

That possibility hadn't occurred to him. Understandably so, since it was insane. "A stranger? You want to test the waters with a perfect stranger?"

"Every man is a stranger to a woman the first time she shares his bed."

Clever wench. Settling back against the seat, he eyed her with new respect. "An interesting point and one I'd never considered."

"Why does that not surprise me, Lord Warbrooke?" she said dryly.

"I thought you were going to call me Justin."

"That was before you started acting as overbearing and pompous as—" She stopped herself with a look of chagrin.

"As who?" he prodded, though he'd swear she'd been going to say, "as usual."

She glanced away. "Another man I know, that's all."

"Ah. Your late husband, perhaps?"

"No, indeed!"

His curiosity about her deepened. "Your husband wasn't overbearing?" Kingsley had never been overbearing in public, but as she'd said, a man could be a very different person in the marriage bed.

"My husband was the most amiable man I ever knew," she said softly.

The pang of jealousy that struck him out of nowhere made him peevish. Why the devil did he care anyway? Of course she spoke well of her late husband. He'd think less of her if she didn't.

Instead of letting it pique him, he should be using it to bring her to her senses. "What would this 'amiable' husband of yours think of your going off with a strange man for the evening?"

"He'd be appalled," she said in a small voice.

"And that doesn't matter to you?"

"Certainly it matters." She eyed him through the mask with a steady gaze. "But as a friend of mine recently said, I have to stop pining after my late husband and learn how to be with someone else."

So Justin was the "someone else" she planned to "be with" to test the waters? Like hell he was! And who was this bloody friend advising her to do all this nonsense anyway?

He only had to think a moment to come up with the answer. Phoebe Chambers. No doubt she'd been somewhere on that dais, too. The two widows were as thick as thieves.

Although he'd never heard any scandal attached to Mrs. Chambers's name, she did seem the sort to know about sponges. "I suppose this is the same friend who urged you to participate in the auction."

"What if it is?" Her stubborn chin quivered. "She gave me good advice. I don't regret following it."

"Glad to hear it," he said wryly. "If you did regret it, it would mean I hadn't proved much of a companion so far." The carriage jolted to a halt, and lamplight flooded the carriage. In the next moment, the door was opened by a liveried footman. "Time for dinner," Justin added.

As they left the carriage, he slipped his arm about her waist to lead her inside, wanting to see how she might react. He'd expected her to flinch or draw away, but instead she leaned timidly into the curve of his arm and shoulder.

Desire bolted through him, sudden and unanticipated. Bloody hell, she made him want to wrap his arms around her and kiss her senseless again. And all just by cozying up to him!

This unaccountable lust was insane. Irrational. Infuriating.

And no less infuriating because she seemed determined to satisfy it. That was the most outrageous thing of all. Lady Kingsley ready to leap into his bed for a night of wanton pleasure? It was impossible. She'd never really do it.

Unfortunately, part of him was more than eager to test her willingness. Part of him thought that taking Bella to his bed was an enormously appealing idea. Which was why he must remember that she was *not* Bella but Lady Kingsley, no matter what she pretended.

A few moment's discussion with the hotel manager and a handful of gold coins was all it took to procure them a private room adequately furnished for a night of wild debauchery.

So Lady Kingsley wanted to see if she could "bear to be

with another man"? Very well, he'd humor her awhile longer. He seriously doubted that her resolve would stand firm when she was faced with the stark reality.

As they climbed the stairs behind the hotel manager, he told her, "Forgive me for not taking you to my town house, but my mother and sister are there, and I didn't think they'd appreciate my bringing a masked woman to dine. Or stay the night."

"I should hope not. But why didn't you take me to wherever you take your lights o' love and your mistress?"

He gaped at her. "Good God, woman, do you think I have a bloody harem?"

"Well, no, but a man like you—"

"Has better things to do than loll about with a variety of loose women all day." What kind of profligate did she think he was, for God's sake? "When I have a mistress, I keep her in a house of her own."

"And when you don't?"

He couldn't believe he was having this highly inappropriate discussion with Lady Kingsley. Then again, until today he'd never thought to have been kissing her passionately either. "When I don't, I abstain."

She eyed him askance.

"Men of sense don't engage in liaisons with whores." A wicked impulse made him add, "Only liaisons with merry widows like yourself."

She had nothing to say to that, though a pretty blush suffused her cheeks.

In the next moment, they reached their floor. The apartment they were shown into was as close to a private love nest as he could have wanted. It lacked any scandalous sculptures or lurid paintings—this was the Clarendon, after all—but the furnishings were lush, the bed prominent and inviting at one end of the room, and the fireplace stoked high enough to reveal a thick fur rug lying before it. A classic setting for seduction if ever there was one.

He watched her closely for her reaction. When she re-

mained silent for several long moments after the hotel
manager left, Justin felt compelled to speak. "Have you
any complaint with the room, madam?"

She started. "Not at all. It's wonderful. Almost exactly
as I imagined."

"As you imagined?" So much for shocking her.

"Oh, yes." She slanted a shy look his way that made his
blood pound. "Though I could never have imagined what
happened in the carriage."

"Nor could I," he mumbled under his breath.

"What?"

"Nothing." He tried to leer at her, though the concept of
leering was foreign to him. "I merely wondered if you'd
been imagining what's going to happen here." He nodded
toward the bed. "Or rather, over there."

"Of course." Slowly she faced him. Then with shaking
hands, she opened her pelisse and let it slide from her
shoulders onto the floor. "I only hope that I can be . . .
um . . . satisfactory."

When she approached him with a hesitant smile and a
swing to her hips that would have done any light o' love
proud, every muscle in his body sprang to attention.

Then a knock came at the door—the servants bringing
their dinner. He nearly tripped over a chair in his haste to
let them in. At this rate, he'd never last the night. He began
to wonder if Lady Kingsley had a twin. A wanton
temptress of a twin bent on driving him insane.

The servants laid out a vast spread of covered dishes
and left. She surveyed the crowded table, her unabashed
delight further inflaming his desire. "What's for dinner?"

Fornication. And for dessert, more fornication. "Take a
look," he choked out.

She circled the table, uncovering the first few dishes—
pea soup and turbot in lobster sauce and mutton cutlets and
boiled potatoes. Then she paused, her eyes twinkling up at
him through the mask. "Are you sure we have enough?
Perhaps we should add another six courses or so."

"I didn't know what you'd like, so I ordered everything that sounded appetizing."

She uncovered the remaining dishes, her smile widening as she revealed sausages and cauliflower and pigeon pie, a capon in caper sauce and roast tongue, pickles and asparagus and a cucumber salad redolent with vinegar. Not to mention the Portugal cakes and tansy pudding that provided the final touch.

"Apparently you find the entirety of Clarendon's kitchen appetizing," she teased. Then she added more earnestly, "It was truly lovely of you to do all this for me. You aren't . . . that is, I didn't expect *you*—I mean, the man who bought me—to be so generous."

"Thank God I've managed to defy your expectations. You've been defying mine all night."

"I do hate to be predictable." She leaned low to sniff the pigeon pie, and her costume fell forward enough to reveal the lush, pale breasts hanging free within the satin sheath and lacy chemise. No corset. Good God. He thought his breeches would burst right there.

Nor did it help when she straightened, eyes gleaming, to pick up a bottle and ask, "Would you like *wine*, my lord?"

When coupled with that low, husky voice she'd adopted as a disguise, her blatant innuendo made him reel. "Are you offering me the beverage? Or something else?"

"Both, I think."

Images of licking wine off every inch of her naked body flashed into his brain. Bloody hell, she was driving him mad. "Then I'll have the beverage." When she actually looked disappointed, he added, "For now."

Her tinkling laughter filled the room and made his loins tighten painfully. How much more of this teasing could he take?

She poured two glasses and handed him one with a knowing smile that made his blood thunder in his temples. Fighting to restrain his rampant urges, he held out her seat for her, then rounded the table to his own seat. Silence reigned for the next few moments as they filled their plates.

When she picked up her fork, he noted that she still refused to remove her gloves. The woman never ceased to surprise him. One moment she was offering him "wine," and the next she was behaving with extreme propriety. Fortunately, that tiny glimpse of the real Lady Kingsley helped him bank some of his lust.

"Tell me something, Lord Warbrooke," she said.

"Justin." He took a couple of bites of the turbot.

"Justin. Of course." She ate some pigeon pie as prettily as a duchess, then set down her fork. "You said earlier that you weren't married. Why not?"

He shrugged. "I never found the right woman, that's all."

"Out of the hundreds of eligible women who parade through London every year in search of husbands, you couldn't find a single one to suit you?"

He took her skeptical tone for a challenge. Settling back in his seat, he folded his hands over his belly. "I don't fancy marrying some grabbing young female whose only object in life is to spend my money and flaunt my title under the noses of her friends."

"My, my, you do think highly of your attractions. But surely not all women of good society are out to spend your money and flaunt your title."

Impudent minx. "If they aren't, they're certainly hiding it well. At any rate, I have no time to separate the wheat from the chaff. Unlike most of my peers, I actually *do* something with my money and my title. I'm on the board of several charities, and I take my duties in Parliament very seriously. My mother and my sister eternally complain that I spend too much time and money on those activities. I can only imagine what a wife would have to say about it."

He watched her out of the corner of his eye as he

swirled his wine. "Which is why I'd rather stick to keeping a mistress. Are you sure you won't fill the position?"

"Certainly not!"

At this hint of the real Lady Kingsley, he couldn't help laughing. "Such a disappointment. You'll force me to seek out one of those bits of muslin who cavort through the theaters."

She stared down at her plate. "You *could* look for a wife who might support your aims."

Like her. It was an intriguing thought, one he'd had before. But he'd always been stopped by two things—her overly fastidious moral sense and her adoration of her late husband. While the first was obviously in question, the second still rankled. He didn't fancy following an act like Henry Lamberton.

And even if he could, he could never get past her dislike of him. Even if at the moment that dislike seemed decidedly absent.

"I haven't had much luck finding a wife who'd 'support my aims,'" he replied. "In my experience, most women of good society would rather entertain callers and redecorate their town houses." All except Lady Kingsley, that is.

She cut her meat with precise little jabs. "Isn't that what you'd . . . um . . . want of your wife? Someone who'd tend the home fires while you're out *doing* something with your money and your title? Someone who'd stay behind the scenes to make you look good?"

"Good God, no . . . er . . . Bella." Bloody hell, he'd almost called her Lady Kingsley and given himself away. It was easy to think of her as the alluring Bella when she was melting in his arms, but not so easy when she started talking like the officious viscountess. "Such a soft-brained creature sounds deadly dull." He shot her a perplexed look. "Why would you assume I'd want that sort of wife?"

Swallowing, she concentrated on dicing her potato into bits. "Men with political aspirations usually prefer it."

He pounced on her slip. "And what makes you think I have political aspirations?"

Her head shot up, her face showing panic. "I–I . . . isn't that why you serve on all those boards and such? What other reason would a marquess have for doing so?"

Still smarting from her earlier allegations, he snapped, "Can't a man with political aspirations also have a social conscience? And be interested in politics precisely because of that conscience?" He leaned back and glared at her, daring her to repeat her unfair assertions from this morning.

But she mostly seemed surprised by his statement. "Well . . . I . . . yes, I suppose so."

He relaxed. "That's why I'd prefer a wife who'd participate in activities where she felt useful—either to me or to others. If that turned out to be working for reform at my side, I'd welcome it."

Suddenly it occurred to him that he might use this conversation to coax her into revealing her true identity. "Besides, there are times when a woman's fine instincts and knowledge of domestic life can be a real asset, especially on charitable boards."

"Oh?"

"Take, for example, a governing board I serve on for a boys' school." He drank some wine, gazing at her over the rim of the glass, but she wouldn't look at him. "With coal prices being what they are and our budget limited, we were having trouble heating the two large halls the boys slept in. It took a woman on the board to figure out that we were attacking the problem from the wrong angle. Instead of heating the rooms, she said, we needed to heat the beds."

Bella seemed to have developed an inordinate interest in her cucumber salad, given the way she dredged the slices back and forth through the dressing.

He went on. "Lady Kingsley suggested that during the day we store the boys' blankets in a closet adjacent to the chimneys that lead from the kitchens. She also said the lads should put hot bricks from the oven into their beds every evening before bedtime. Between the warmed blankets and the bricks, the boys are kept quite comfy, and we aren't forced to pay exorbitant prices for extra coal."

"What a good idea." She lifted a smug gaze to him. "This Lady Kingsley sounds very resourceful."

He stifled a grin. "Oh, yes, very resourceful indeed. But then it takes a woman to be resourceful in such matters. We men would have spent all our time trying to figure out how to lower the cost of coal in England so we could afford to purchase more for heating Lamberton School."

She laughed, and the warm sound settled in his chest. They are in a companionable silence for a few moments.

But he wasn't done with her yet. "Of course, those womanly instincts and emotions can sometimes also be a liability."

"How so?"

"I recently suggested that we build a factory on the grounds of the school. And this same astute lady—reacting as the gently bred creature that she is—opposed it without even listening to my proposal."

She drew her mouth up in a mutinous line. "Perhaps the idea of child labor revolted her."

"Ah, but these are older boys, eager to learn a skill and find ways to support their parents and siblings. Besides which, I don't mean to have them do anything taxing. The way I envision it, the factory's activities can be integrated with their studies. They'll learn about mathematics in class, then see it applied at the factory. They'll learn how to run a business through the factory, then be more motivated to read those books and essays that inspired the men of trade who went before them."

"I see. It does sound . . . rather intriguing when you put it like that." She toyed with a piece of asparagus, twirling it round and round on her plate with her fork. "And did the other members of your board approve of this idea?"

"Some of them. Not all." He broke off some bread and

buttered it. "In fact, that's why I was at that auction—I was trying to convince Lord Bradford to support my position."

Her gaze shot to his. "But you bid against him!"

"Yes. I bid against him." He added dryly, "I think it's safe to say that I've lost *his* support."

"Why would you do that? Enter into a foolish bidding competition when it went against your best interests to do so?"

Tossing the bread aside, he leaned forward to clasp her hands. "Because I couldn't bear to see a woman as lovely and refined as you in the clutches of a man like him."

The blood drained from her face. "So you were trying to . . . to protect me?"

He nodded. All right, so that wasn't all he'd wanted to do, but that had certainly been part of it.

"You weren't really wanting to spend the night with a widow at all?" she asked in a small voice.

"No. It's not my sort of entertainment. I only bid because Bradford did."

Drawing her hands free of his grasp, she murmured, "Then you don't really want to bed me."

Her plaintive tone confused him. "It's not that I don't *want* to bed you exactly . . . it's just that—"

"I should have known." Her head was bowed, and she kept twisting her hands together. "I was afraid of this—that I might lack the figure and the . . . the female attractions to tempt a man like you—"

"Good God, I only wish that were true," he broke in. She was making him feel awful. And were those tears glimmering in her eyes, for God's sake? "See here, Bella, there isn't a bloody thing wrong with your figure or your female attractions. If this were a different situation, I'd already have you naked in that bed."

Her startled gaze swung to him. "What do you mean— a different situation? Even if you started out by trying to protect me—and I do appreciate that—you did win me. And you can tell I'm willing to go through with my end of it. I *want* to be naked in that bed, so why not take advantage of it?"

"Because you only think you want it, that's why! You don't really want it."

She rose from the chair, her eyes bright. "You have *no* idea what I want!"

"Not a sordid night with a stranger, I'll wager." He rose from his chair, too, his blood running hot as he waited, hoping she'd admit that he wasn't a stranger to her. When she only glanced away, he snapped, "No matter what your foolish reasons for participating in that auction, you couldn't possibly have known what you were getting yourself into."

"I knew precisely what I was getting myself into: a night with a man. That's all I wanted!"

"Someone who might abuse you or hurt you?" He dropped his voice to a threatening murmur. "You don't know what men can be like."

Her head snapped around, her fierce eyes boring into him. "Then perhaps you should show me!"

Without warning, she began to unfasten the ties that held her flimsy satin costume together, and all the blood in his body rushed to one inexorable spot.

She freed the last tie, then shimmied defiantly out of her gown to reveal a chemise so sheer he could see the tips of her breasts straining against the silk. He couldn't help it—he gaped at them, his mouth going dry at the sight.

"Devil take you, Bella!" His muscles tightened, and the heaviness of his desire settled between his thighs. "You won't stop this madness until I give you a taste of what you think you want, will you?"

That seemed to provoke her even further. With a grim, determined smile, she thrust her breasts up for his perusal. That made it even worse, for the loving drape of the silk left nothing to the imagination. They were perfect—as plump and luscious as he'd imagined in his fevered fantasies of her.

She strode up to him, practically daring him to touch her. "If you want me naked in that bed, Justin, then do something about it. Because no matter what your reasons for bidding, you paid a lot of money for one night with me. So I think it's time you put your mouth where your money is."

When she began to unbutton her chemise, revealing her lovely bare skin inch by inch, all his control snapped. Taking the few steps to meet her, he caught her head in his large hands. Need surged through him as he stared down at the full, tempting lips and the eyes that gleamed mysteriously behind the white satin mask.

He wanted to shake her. He wanted to kiss her.

She'd made him desperate to bed her, but it was impossible. Because it wasn't only Bella he'd be bedding, but Lady Kingsley, too. And though Lady Kingsley seemed to think she wanted this, once she came to her senses, she'd hate him for taking advantage of her whim. She'd never be able to face him across the table at meetings, and their encounter would lie solidly between them until it became an ugly thing they couldn't get around.

He wished there could be more between them. But much as he'd teased her about taking her for his mistress, that would never work. Nor could he marry a woman still in love with the gentle Saint Henry. What Justin felt for her wasn't gentle, and he'd be damned if he'd compete with her late husband for her affections.

But he could at least make her see the idiocy of what she was doing. "Never say I didn't warn you," he growled, then brought his mouth down hard on hers.

He'd tried to be careful before, heedful of the sort of woman she was and sure that she'd stop him at any moment. But now anger rode him, anger and desire and a need to put her silly notions to rest once and for all. So he spared her nothing in that kiss, taking her mouth with all the passion he was capable of, making sure not to blunt the force of his desire in any way.

But she didn't seem to mind. Her mouth was eager beneath his, warm and open and yielding. She tugged at his coat until he shrugged out of it, and then she went to work on his waistcoat buttons.

A haze of need fogged his brain. He filled his hands with her breasts, reveling in the full weight of them, the nipples that pebbled beneath his touch even through the fabric. Oh, God, she was soft . . . and sweet and more woman than he'd ever imagined. He had to taste her or he'd go mad.

Trailing kisses down her neck, he shoved her chemise off her shoulders and down far enough to bare both breasts—both beautiful, bountiful breasts. They made his mouth water. He dropped to one knee so he could kiss them properly.

She smelled of lemons and woman—a scent designed to entice. And it was working, too. All he wanted was to lay her out and take her like a savage.

He settled for taking her breast in his mouth instead, laving it with his tongue, teasing the sweet little nipple with his teeth. When she uttered a groan and arched into him, that only maddened him further. He sucked and caressed her lush breast endlessly, fondling the other with his hand, until he was so aroused he thought he'd erupt right there.

Bloody hell, he must end this soon, before he did something he regretted, before he cried out her real name.

Which he now realized he could never do. They might not have lain together, but they'd done and said enough to mortify her for life. So it was best that she think he hadn't guessed her identity. Then she could return to her real life without embarrassment, repenting only in private the reckless encounter from which she'd escaped by the skin of her teeth.

But before he thrust her aside, he'd give her something reckless to repent, by God.

So he slowly slipped his hand under her chemise . . .

5

Isobel was already half in ecstasy from what Justin was doing to her breasts. Henry had never even touched her breasts, but Justin made up for it with his wicked lips and flicking tongue. Who would have dreamed it could feel this exciting to have a man's mouth there? The way he teased and sucked . . . it sent a luscious heat melting down through her belly, down . . . down . . .

To where his hand was sliding under her chemise. A thrill of awareness shot through her. He was going to touch her down *there*, in her secret place. She held her breath, half-afraid, half-eager. But when his finger burrowed through her tangled curls to stroke the flesh already aching for a caress, she thought she'd jump out of her skin.

The sensations were so intense that she dug her fingers into his shoulders. His mouth grew fierce and devouring on her breast, and his finger . . . oh, dear heaven, his finger! It was *inside* her, for pity's sake, delving inside her with a deft stroke that made her gasp. He delved again, more deeply, and she squirmed. It felt so good. Strange, but good.

Soon he had two fingers inside her and was using his thumb to fondle a sensitive spot that sent her right out of her mind. Ohhh, the things he was doing with those devilish fingers! A tension built between her legs, a tension that he fed with every stroke and caress.

She'd never imagined such a thing! It was better than kissing, better by far . . . better than anything . . . so very exciting . . . Oh, Lord, now the tension grew almost unbearable, making her strain against him to get more, feel more of those magical fingers.

Until suddenly the tension peaked, sending her soaring into a realm of pleasure she'd never, ever known.

A cry erupted from her mouth . . . his name, over and over. That seemed to encourage him further. He went on fondling her until she peaked again more fiercely, her hands tearing at his shirt, her throat hoarse from her cries.

Only when her knees buckled did he stop, drawing his hands from beneath her chemise to steady her. His mouth left her breast, and his eyes shone with need as he gazed up at her. She reveled in it. Who would have ever guessed that Lord Warbrooke was capable of such intensity? Or that he could show a woman such pleasures?

She cupped his face, fumbling for words to express how wonderful it had been and how eagerly she anticipated the rest, but he jerked away from her touch.

Her heart caught in her throat as he rose slowly to his feet. To her shock, he pulled the chemise back up to cover her breasts. Reaching for the ties, he began to fasten them again, and she caught his hand. "Stop that! What are you doing?"

He stepped back from her, his breath coming in unsteady gasps. "You've had your taste. That ought to be enough."

"But . . . but we're not finished!" She knew enough about lovemaking to know *that*, for pity's sake.

His eyes glittered in the stark hunger of his face. "Yes, we are. That's as much as you're getting from me tonight, Bella."

She blinked. It took a few seconds for his words to register, but when they did, her heart dropped into her stomach.

How could he make her want him, then turn around and refuse her so cruelly? She'd begun to believe he wasn't the man she'd thought, that he wasn't at all the calculating creature eager for power that she'd assumed.

But perhaps she'd been wrong to trust all his kind words and sweet attentions.

"Why?" she whispered. An awful possibility suddenly occurred to her. "Is it because I did something wrong? I failed to excite you?"

"God preserve me from stupid women!" He threaded his fingers through his hair in clear frustration. "I can hardly stay on my feet for the weight of my arousal, and you can ask such a bloody foolish thing?"

Her gaze shot to his trousers, which did seem to be rather . . . filled out. "Then why not satisfy your urges? And mine?"

Hot, wanton need flared in his face. "Good God, woman, don't you understand? Any satisfaction of your 'urges,' any pleasure you might feel if we make love, won't last beyond tonight. Not for a woman like you."

A chill went through her. A woman like her? Could he have guessed that she was Lady Kingsley? Could all of this be just his way of tormenting her?

No, how could that be? Surely if he'd guessed, he would have said something by now. Lord Warbrooke would never have kept silent on such a subject. And the way he'd kissed her and caressed her . . . well, she couldn't imagine Lord Warbrooke taking such liberties with a woman he'd always seemed to dislike.

Still, to be safe . . . "What kind of woman do you think I am? What could you possibly know about me, aside from the fact that I'm a masked widow who participated in a scandalous auction?"

He averted his gaze from her. "I don't have to know—I can easily guess it. You're a lady of breeding. It's in your speech, your bearing, your superior attitude." Striding over to a tray of brandy and glasses, he poured himself a generous portion. "I'll wager you spent your childhood at a country estate under your father's tender protection, then went straight to London for your coming out, where you met your 'amiable' man who never lifted a hand to you a day in his life."

He gulped down some brandy, then wiped his mouth with the back of his hand. "And after the man you loved died and left you alone, you couldn't bear the emptiness of your life without him, so you got some maggoty idea in your head about this bloody auction."

He whirled on her, eyes flashing. "But you aren't the kind to dally with men for sport. You're the kind to feel shame after it's done, to torture yourself for giving in to your 'wicked' impulses. And frankly, I don't want to be the one you hate for encouraging them." Knocking back another swig of brandy, he shifted his gaze to the fireplace. "I don't want to be the man to defile the memory of the husband you seem to have worshiped."

She wanted to laugh. Him and his noble impulses—he was worse than Henry. In fact, she began to think he might even be a better man than Henry, in more ways than one. But that made her yearn all the more to share his bed.

"Oh, Justin, your protectiveness is very sweet, but entirely unnecessary. Yes, I did worship my husband. Shall I tell you why?"

A muscle tightened in his jaw. "I'd rather you didn't."

"Too bad. I think you should hear. Especially when you persist in these strange notions about me."

She took a steadying breath. She'd never told a soul in good society these things, and it wasn't easy to relate them now. Especially to *him*. If not for the safety of her disguise, she could never say it. "I worshiped my late husband because I was grateful for what he'd done for me. You see, he's the one who saved me from a life of drudgery in a cotton mill."

His gaze swung back to her, confused, incredulous. "What?"

"This ladylike façade you see before you is precisely that. A façade." Bitterness crept into her voice . . . and regret that she could never be a real lady, no matter how much she tried. She would always be an impostor. "This image was built through years of education and countless lessons in etiquette and deportment. It took tutors and dance instructors and—"

"I don't believe you."

She let herself fall into an accent long in disuse, a manner of speaking as foreign to her now as her "proper lady" role sometimes felt. "Well, sir, it ain't my problem if you believe it or no."

Jerking off her gloves, she approached him and thrust her hands up to his face. "See the scars? They ain't from workin' needlepoint. Them scars come from startin' work in the mill at the wee age o' six. After twelve 'ours of work, a child starts to nod off an' can't keep up with the machines. So 'er 'ands catch the rough end an' take a slice 'ere an' there. I know a girl wot lost 'er thumb. An' there was a boy—"

"Enough," he whispered. Catching her hands in his, he fingered her scars. Revulsion mingled with pity in his face.

She could hardly bear to see it. It was difficult enough exposing her true nature to him, but to have him pity her for it . . .

Tugging her hands free, she turned her back to him and reverted to her usual manner of speaking. "Not quite the childhood at a country estate under a father's tender protection that you envisioned, is it?"

A ragged oath erupted from him. "But how—"

"I was an orphan. And not the secret child of noble parents that you see in children's tales either, in case that's what you're thinking. Just a plain, ordinary orphan who lived with a poor aunt. I worked at the cotton mill in Lancashire until I was twelve."

Though these were painful secrets, she felt an odd relief in being able to tell someone—*anyone*—who she really was. After all, she'd hidden it for so very long. Apparently anonymity did have its uses, one of which was allowing her to unburden herself without fear of the consequences.

She went on more easily. "That was the year a reformer came unannounced to inspect the mill." She smiled, remembering that day. "He caught the overlooker dunking a child's head in the cistern to wake her up. He acted on impulse: he punched the overlooker out and then bought the mill. And the first thing he did was ban children under the age of fourteen from working there."

Lost in the bittersweet memories, she balled her gloves up in her hands. "But by then my aunt had died, and I had nowhere to go. I'd been taking care of myself in her cottage, but without the work at the mill . . ."

She shrugged. "I threw myself on his tender mercies. I asked to be a servant in his house, a kitchen maid, anything." A lump filled her throat. "I still don't know what he saw in me, but he took pity on me and brought me back to his estate. He had me educated as a gentlewoman. He told me if I worked hard to improve myself, I could have a shop or even be a governess. I think it pleased him to watch my progress."

"You lived alone with him?" he asked in an uneasy voice.

"It's not how it sounds. His second wife had only recently died, but his sister lived with him. It was all very proper, believe me."

A long, awkward silence filled the room. He was the one who broke it. "So how did you come to marry him?"

"As I grew older, I began helping him with his work. I suppose we sort of . . . fell into marriage. I don't think he would have bothered to marry again at all except that he hadn't yet fathered an heir. He was a man of property, a gentleman, and he needed a son. And it occurred to him . . ." She trailed off, loath to reveal these intimate secrets about Henry.

"*What* occurred to him, Bella?"

It wasn't as if Justin would know whom she spoke of, was it? Justin had barely known Henry, and few people talked of Henry's previous wives. "Well, his first two wives had been the refined sort. He always said the aristocracy was overbred, and that it was killing them. He thought perhaps an infusion of the stronger blood of peasant stock, as he put it, might help him produce a son."

"And you didn't mind providing him with the 'peasant stock'?" he choked out.

"How could I? He'd done so much for me—the least I could do was marry him and try to give him an heir." Her gaze dropped to the gloves she kept twisting in her hands. "But I failed in that respect. Doesn't say much for the power of my stronger blood, does it?"

"You can't blame yourself for that." The thrum of his low voice washed over her like a caress. "These things happen. It might have been his fault, after all. Either way, no one is truly to blame except God, and He isn't apologizing. So I don't see why you should."

She faced him with a wan smile. "An interesting point and one I'd never considered."

He didn't smile at her echo of his earlier statement. Indeed, the look on his face was so full of sympathy and concern that it brought tears to her eyes. How had she ever thought this man incapable of true feeling?

Ruthlessly she blinked her tears back, grateful for the mask that helped to hide them. "In any case, I'm not the well-bred lady you thought I was. That's all I was trying to illustrate. So your balking at making love to me is entirely unnecessary, you see."

"Oh, no, you're wrong," he said fiercely. "If anything, your tale has made it even more necessary. I'm sorry, Bella, but I won't make love to you. Not now, not ever."

6

Though Justin knew he'd made the right decision, it cost him a great deal to hold to it. Especially when she stood there looking so lost.

But what she'd told him explained so much. It was no wonder she'd reacted violently to his proposal at the governing board. If he'd been in her place, he'd have done the same.

Unfortunately, it also explained why she worshiped Henry Lamberton. She would never accept another man in Lamberton's place. And who could blame her? What man could replace a real saint?

That must be why she'd participated in the auction instead of just looking for a husband—she didn't *want* a man to replace Lamberton. Except for one night. And Justin couldn't be only that to her, not now that he'd seen how truly rare a woman she was.

"I should take you home," he said.

He regretted the words when he saw tears leak out from

beneath her mask. Bloody hell, he hadn't wanted to make her cry! Not after all she'd endured.

"I—I see," she stammered. "Now that you realize how very far beneath you I am—"

"Don't be absurd." It hurt that she could even think that of him. "Your origins have nothing to do with it. If anything, they make me respect you more. Indeed, I respect you too much to take advantage of you when you still have only room for your husband in your heart."

She blinked at him. "What? You think . . ." She laughed harshly. "Dear heaven, so that's what this reluctance is all about." She stepped nearer, her face full of supplication. "Oh, Justin, didn't you understand what I was saying? My marriage wasn't like that at all."

"Like what?"

"A love match. Yes, I was grateful to my husband for what he did, but—" With a sigh, she glanced away. "Have you ever heard the myth of Galatea and Pygmalion?"

He sifted through the years of his Eton education. "Pygmalion was the one who created a statue of a woman so perfect that he fell in love with it, right?"

She nodded. "He suffered for his love, but Venus took pity on him and turned Galatea into a real woman. Then Pygmalion and Galatea married."

His eyes narrowed. "You're saying that your husband was Pygmalion, and you were Galatea."

A bitter smile touched her lips. "Exactly. Except that my Pygmalion hardly ventured beyond adoration of his statue. He had no idea how to be Galatea's husband. All those lovely things you just did . . . the way you touched me and kissed me? Hen—my husband would never have done any of them."

He couldn't fathom such madness. "Why not?"

She strode up to him, her eyes glittering beneath the mask. "My husband considered that sort of behavior too wicked for his precious creation. Despite all his talk about peasant blood, once he made me into the image of a perfect wife, he didn't want to defile that image in any way."

Justin stared at her, wanting but hardly daring to believe what she was saying.

She went on relentlessly. "He couldn't avoid committing the actual act of love—not if he wanted to sire a son—but he made it . . ." She halted, no doubt reluctant to speak of the intimacies of her marriage. Then she went on. "He made it as short and perfunctory as possible. There was no enjoyment, no pleasure, none of those heavenly feelings you gave me. Just a few painful thrusts while he apologized for inconveniencing me."

"Bloody hell," he whispered, the truth slamming into him. There were men with such proper ideas, but he'd never guessed Lamberton would be that sort. How could the man have wasted his hours with her in such a stupid fashion?

Though Justin hadn't been much better. When he could have been showing her how wonderful lovemaking between two people could be, he'd been acting like a pompous idiot, ignoring her protests, sure that he knew better.

What a fool he was. "I'm sorry, Bella, I didn't realize—"

"And I thought that was all there was," she went on as if she hadn't heard him. "I thought that was all I could expect of a husband. Until my friend told me it didn't have to be like that. I was sure she was wrong—that perhaps I was flawed—"

"You're not flawed." He grabbed her by the shoulders, needing to reassure her, to touch her, now that he knew he could. "You're not flawed in any way."

"It might be better if I was! Then perhaps you men would stop putting me on a pedestal where I don't belong! I don't *want* to be Galatea anymore, blast it!"

She twisted out of his grip, but he caught her about the waist and tugged her back against his body. When she froze, he pressed his mouth to her ear. "You can't stop being Galatea. It's who you are, whom he made you into. You couldn't return to being that orphan millworker even if you wished to."

A strangled sob erupted from her, and he went on hastily before she could misunderstand. "But it might not be so bad on that pedestal if you have the right man there with you."

"Th-the right man?" she echoed.

"Yes." It was time he showed her what Lamberton had not. She might only want him for tonight, but he'd give her that, no matter what it cost him. It was the least she deserved after risking so much for one wanton night. He lowered his voice to whisper. "If you ask *my* opinion, what Galatea needs is a lover."

She turned her head to gaze up at him, and the look of hope in her face nearly shattered him. "Where do you suggest I find this lover?"

"Right here." He cupped her cheek in his hand. "I'd be honored to fill the position."

"But what if I really am flawed—"

"The only flaw you possess, my darling Bella," he murmured as he turned her fully to face him, "is a deplorable inability to appreciate how wonderful you truly are."

A sudden smile broke over her face. "Oh, Justin, you say the sweetest things. Tell me, have you a method for ridding me of my 'deplorable' flaw?"

"Indeed I do." Feeling his hunger well up inside him, fierce, undeniable, he pushed the sleeves of her chemise off her shoulders. "What you need is to see yourself through the eyes of a man who *does* appreciate how wonderful you are. Like me, for example."

She sucked in a shaky breath as he dragged her chemise lower.

"First, there are your breasts." His voice thickened with need as he exposed them fully. "So beautiful and soft to the touch. I love having them in my mouth."

Dropping to his knees, he kissed them in turn. "I love

tasting them and teasing them and . . ." He trailed off as he seized one in his mouth, giving free rein to the urges that had plagued him endlessly all night.

But only for a moment. There was more of her he wanted to "appreciate." Sliding the chemise down farther, he smiled to see her slender waist. Lamberton must have been blind to ignore this angel's delights, to treat her body as something shameful when he should have been worshiping it.

Well, Lamberton's loss was his gain, and he'd make up for the man's stupidity if it took him all night. "Then there's your smooth belly," he rasped through a throat gone raw with desire. "One day, if you'll give me the chance, I intend to spread this belly with jam and spend an afternoon licking it all off."

Her skin quivered at his words, but her hands reached to caress his hair, and that was all the encouragement he needed. He kissed her navel, then pressed open-mouthed kisses in widening circles around it, inching lower and closer with every one.

Only after she swayed into him with a moan did he draw back to tug her chemise free of her hips. It dropped to the floor, baring her completely to his gaze.

With a little embarrassed cry, she covered the thatch of hair with her hand.

"Don't," he commanded. He looked up at her. "I want to see you, darling Bella."

Though her face grew pink, she nodded and pulled her hand away. "My husband never saw me without clothing," she said softly. "He told me that nakedness was indecent and . . . and shameful for a lady."

He felt a surge of anger toward Lamberton, anger mingled with pity. "What about when you made love?"

"He came into the bedchamber in his nightshirt, gave me a kiss, then got into bed. Only after he was under the sheets did he lift my nightshirt and . . . and . . . well . . . you know . . ."

Without sucking those pretty breasts? Or touching her lovely belly or— "Your husband was insane," he growled. He unfastened both her garters, then slid her hose down her legs. "Not to take advantage of his right to see these perfect thighs of yours? Bloody insane."

Stroking up the insides of her legs, he said hoarsely, "You don't know what they do to me—your elegant thighs. I can't help imagining them wrapped about my waist as I drive into your sweetness."

Her face flamed, especially when he sat back on his haunches and parted her curls with his fingers to expose the pink flesh beneath. "And as for *this* sweetness here . . ." he began.

"Justin, you shouldn't—"

He ignored her protest. "*This* is the holy altar at which I long to worship. It's so tender and dainty and eager for me."

Then he leaned forward and planted a kiss right on it. She jerked back with a little gasp of surprise, but he caught her hips to hold her still. "Oh, no, Galatea," he said, smiling up at her, "how can I be your lover if I can't worship every part of you?"

She looked uncertain, but he could already feel her relaxing in his hands. "Justin, are you sure—"

"Shhh," he murmured, then kissed her there again. But this time he used his tongue and his lips to caress her sweet petals, delighting in how the swollen flesh grew warm and fluid beneath his mouth.

Good God, her scent inflamed him—ripe with musk and hinting at lemon oil. It made him devour her, thrusting his tongue deep inside in his urgency to know more of her.

She shivered and shook, yet made no move to prevent him or chide him for his scandalous behavior. Her hands left his hair to knead his shoulders, and the mewling sounds she made in her throat turned his cock to iron. His mouth was ravenous on her now, and he could feel the heat build in her body, between her legs, beneath his hungry lips.

When at last she convulsed and cried out his name, he thought he'd come off in his breeches right there.

He needed to be inside her. He couldn't wait another moment. So while her knees were still buckling, he rose to sweep her up in his arms and head for the bed.

Isobel reveled in Justin's fierce, eager hunger. Like her very own Roman conqueror, he carried her off, his eyes dark with the intent to plunder and vanquish and mold her to his will.

She was quite eager to be molded after the way he'd sent her soaring just now. Why, her tender parts still thrummed from the excitement, and he hadn't even put himself inside her yet.

As he set her down on the bed, she stretched out to her full length, feeling languid and soft and all woman. He stepped back, and she propped herself up on one elbow to watch him drag his shirt off.

How odd that it didn't bother her in the least to recline here entirely naked. But he'd banished any shame in her body that Henry had tried to drum into her. He'd certainly banished any reluctance to see him scandalously bare his chest.

Such a fine chest it was, too! She hadn't seen a shirtless male since her girlhood in the mill, where the proprieties were rarely observed. Back then she'd been too young and tired to care what the boys looked like, but she did remember that their bony and grimy chests bore no resemblance to this wide expanse of male muscle, all sculpted and lean.

"Are you sure about this, Bella?" he asked, his hands pausing on his breeches buttons.

Her gaze flicked down to his bulging breeches, and curiosity overcame any lingering apprehension. "Oh, Lord, yes," she whispered.

A faint smile graced the firm mouth that had just sent her into ecstasies. "Like what you see, do you?"

She blushed, and turned her head. "I–I'm sorry. I didn't mean to—"

"There's nothing to apologize for." Catching her by the chin, he turned her back around. "I like having you look at me." Her gaze met his to find it smoldering with heat. He added in a ragged whisper, "I'd like it even better if you'd touch me, too."

Her heart knocked madly against her ribs. Sitting up, she ran her hands over his chest, over the muscles flexing beneath rough, hairy skin, over the taut belly that trembled beneath her questing fingers.

"My husband never let me touch him," she murmured. "I was supposed to lie still. He said if I touched him, he might do something awful."

"Like make love to you as you deserve?" he bit out. "Forget your husband. Forget every stupid thing he ever told you." He shoved his breeches off to bare drawers that strained with the fullness of his arousal. "Granted, there are men with such absurd notions about lovemaking, but I'm not one of them."

Opening his drawers, he slid quickly out of them, and her heart stopped. His shaft sprang free, long and rigid and arrogant—a conqueror's lance, to be sure. And she'd wager it was larger than Henry's had been, though she couldn't be sure since she'd only felt Henry's. She didn't know whether to be frightened or intrigued by Justin's size. If Phoebe were right, then her discomfort during lovemaking hadn't been related to the size of the blasted thing.

But if Phoebe were wrong . . .

"If you belonged to me, darling Bella," Justin rasped, "I'd take every opportunity to have your hands on my bare flesh."

"Like now?" she whispered a little nervously.

"God, yes, *now*. I'd like nothing better."

Reaching out, she stroked his silky thickness tentatively with her fingers. "Y—you'll have to show me how to give you pleasure. I don't know anything."

"You know plenty, almost too much for a man's sanity. But I'd love it if you'd grip it in your hand." Closing her fingers around him, he said, "Here, like this."

With a patience that she knew required great effort, he showed her how to caress him. It excited her to see him so rapt, to watch him throw his head back and utter heartfelt groans of pleasure. She'd never guessed it would be so wonderful to prompt this reaction in a man.

But she'd scarcely adapted to the new, delightful experience when he brushed her hand away, whispering, "I need to be inside you, Bella, I can't wait any longer." Pushing her down onto the bed, he knelt between her knees. "We have all night for playing, but for now, let me inside you . . ."

Her answer was to widen her legs and lift her hands to draw him down on top of her. Still, she couldn't prevent the trembling in her limbs or the subtle fear that made her fingers tighten on his shoulders. This was it. And what if she truly were flawed? What if this proved to be only more disappointment?

"Don't worry," he said, gentling her with one hand stroking up her thigh. "I'll make it good, I swear. Relax, just relax."

Surprisingly, she did. And even more so when his finger delved inside her as before. She knew this, knew what it felt like. So she hardly flinched when he replaced the finger with something larger. She even shifted to give him greater access when he began easing up inside her.

But it was nothing like having Henry force himself there. She didn't feel violated or hurt or embarrassed. She felt . . . filled. Yes, that was it, filled to the brim with Justin, surrounded by his scent, engulfed in his strength.

So *this* was why they called it "joining." No other word could adequately describe this intimacy, this intensity.

"Ohhh," she said, as any lingering anxiety drained from her. "I *like* this."

He choked out a laugh. "Good."

"Do . . . do you like it, too?"

"Can't you tell? Oh . . . darling . . . you feel wonderful. So tight . . . so warm. I wish I could stay like this forever."

"Why can't you?" she teased.

That Roman blood of his shone in every devouring glance he settled over her lips and breasts and belly. "Because it's even better when I do this."

That's when he moved. He drew himself out, then thrust so deeply into her that she gasped. Again and again, he drove into her, his blue gaze piercing her, his mouth whispering how he loved being with her, what he wanted to do to her, how often he wanted to do it.

Like a thread caught on a spindle, she felt as if he wound her tighter and tighter around him, joining them so they could never break apart, twisting their destinies together irrevocably.

Oh, dear heaven, what a feeling! The same glittering excitement that she'd felt earlier built again, only this time it was different because it seemed to come from him, too, to seize them both together until they were straining against each other, pressing together, fighting to be as much a part of each other as possible.

This time when the explosion came, like a white-hot searing of her soul, her cry of release mingled with his hoarser one. And joy rained down from the heavens all over her.

"Bella, Bella . . . my sweet Bella," he chanted as he spilled himself inside her.

His possessive tone gave her pause. Because this was a man she could easily lose herself to.

As he collapsed atop her, she clutched him close, her heart constricting in her chest. Oh, Lord, she'd fallen in love with him. With Warbrooke, who would never marry her. Lady Kingsley might fit some of his needs for a wife, but the orphan millworker Isobel would never do. He was headed for prime minister, for heaven's sake, the sort of man who required a matchless wife. Not one with her low past.

Yet perhaps she could be content with an illicit liaison. Plenty of widows engaged in them. If they were discreet . . .

No, she couldn't. He'd marry some politically appropriate wife one day, and it would destroy her.

With a growl of contentment, he rolled off her, then dragged her into the lee of his large body. Hooking one arm under her head to cradle it, he draped the other across her waist. "Well, Bella, what do you think—are you flawed or no?"

A sudden shyness seized her. "What do *you* think?"

He tipped her chin up until she was gazing into his face. "I think Bradford was a fool to stop at a mere thousand pounds."

Every uncertainty she'd ever had about her feminine qualities evaporated. She laughed, her heart flipping over in her chest. "You really are a dear, do you know that?" She stretched up to kiss his cheek. "That's for bidding so much for me." She kissed his other cheek. "That's for saving me from Bradford." Then she planted a hot kiss firmly on his mouth. "And that's for showing me how wonderful lovemaking can be."

His eyes darkened. "I have a better way you can show your thanks."

Her belly tightened in anticipation . . . until he lifted his hand to the ties at the back of her mask.

"Do we really need this anymore?" he murmured. "Let me see your face."

"No!" She gripped his wrist to prevent his tugging the ties loose. "No . . . I–I can't."

Rebellion showed in the clenching of his Roman jaw, and for a moment she feared he'd unmask her anyway.

Then he sighed and dropped his hand from the back of her head. "As you wish."

Relief made her weak. And grateful. "Thank you." She pressed a kiss to his neck, then another, lingering to taste the salty skin with the tip of her tongue.

He shuddered, his skin drawing taut under her kisses. "Bella, if you keep that up, I won't be responsible for my actions."

"Good." She lifted her head to grin at him. "I'd say we've a great deal of wine left to drink, and I'm still thirsty."

He froze, his eyes a stark, brilliant blue. Then with a growl, he caught her mouth in a blatantly plundering kiss.

Her heart filled as she gave herself up to him. She might have to swear off this particular bottle of wine in the morning, but for tonight she intended to drink her fill.

7

The prim and proper Lady Kingsley was going to kill him.

In the wee hours of the morning, Justin fell back against the pillows after their last lovemaking session, so completely drained that he couldn't even move to drag the cover up over their naked bodies.

It had been a long, tempestuous night. They'd made love on the table where he'd licked wine off her luscious little belly. They'd made love on the floor before the fireplace, writhing on the fur rug like cats in heat.

And just now they'd made love in the bath they'd called for shortly after midnight. What a tricky business that had been. But he must have managed it well, since "Bella" had climaxed three times.

He turned over to tease her about her insatiable "peasant blood," only to find that she'd finally reached her limit. She lay on her side asleep, her mask slightly askew, her hands folded like an innocent's under her cheek.

Even though they both desperately needed the rest, he

felt a twinge of regret. Their private night was over. There would be other nights, but never another like this.

In the morning, everything would change. He'd been willing to humor her about this mask nonsense for a while, because he hadn't wanted to ruin her enjoyment. But tomorrow was another matter entirely. They'd have to make plans and discuss marriage.

Because he knew beyond any doubt that he wanted no other woman in his bed and his life. No other woman could make him happy. And now that he'd learned he wouldn't be competing with Lamberton in the bedchamber, he felt certain he could beat out Lamberton for possession of her heart.

Which he fully intended to do. Somewhere between yesterday and the wee hours of today, he'd discovered that he very much wanted the clever, exasperating, and thoroughly bewitching Lady Kingsley to belong to him, and him alone. He didn't intend to share her with anyone, even her late husband.

In the morning, he would demand that she remove that bloody mask. If she didn't, he'd snatch it off her. But either way, they would be married as soon as he could obtain a special license.

Not that he expected her to refuse to marry him. No matter what she said about not having the sensibilities of a "real" lady, she would never have made love to him so eagerly without caring for him. Once he removed her mask, she'd have no choice but to admit it. Then marriage would be the next logical step.

Dragging her into the curve of his arms, he kissed the mask that had grown bedraggled in the course of their nighttime revels.

"Good-bye, Bella," he whispered. "And hello, Lady Warbrooke."

He was still holding her when he drifted off to sleep.

Just after dawn, he awoke to find his arms empty. He shot up out of the bed, realizing in an instant that something was wrong. The table was precisely as they'd left it—with plates heaped up to one side to make room for the second time they'd made love. The tub still sat in a puddle, and the empty wine bottle listed to one side atop a pile of the towels they'd dampened trying to clean up their bathwater.

But she was gone. Panic seizing him, he leapt from the bed and dragged on his drawers, then searched the room. Her costume had disappeared, along with her pelisse and her shoes. He did find assorted other pieces of clothing—a garter, both stockings, and one of her gloves—but that only showed she'd left in a hurry and probably dressed by firelight. She'd certainly fled, however, as evidenced by the absence of that bloody huge reticule she'd carried. With the sponges in it that they'd forgotten to use.

Thoughts of those sponges roused his temper. She'd left him, damn it! And after letting him make love to her four times without a thought for the consequences! The woman needed a keeper, that was for certain.

Striding to the door, he bellowed for a servant. One appeared in minutes.

"What time did the lady leave?" he demanded as he gathered up his stockings and breeches.

"Over an hour ago, my lord," the servant stammered. "She said to give you this." The young man held out a folded sheet of foolscap.

Justin paused in pulling on his breeches to take it. When he opened it to find the page covered with writing, he nodded toward the door. "Thank you, that will be all for now."

As soon as the servant fled, he scanned the missive.

Dear Justin,

Please forgive me for my cowardice, but I couldn't bear to stay for good-byes. You'd attempt again to remove my mask, and I couldn't allow it. Much as I am tempted to accept your offer to be my protector, I must respectfully decline. But thank you for a wonderful evening. I shall never forget your kindness, and I do hope I made it worth the price of your exorbitant bid.

Yours affectionately,
Bella

Feeling as if he'd been struck by a sledgehammer, he stared down at the words in disbelief. What "offer to be my protector" was she blathering about? He hadn't offered that. He hadn't had the chance to offer her anything! She hadn't stayed around long enough to let him!

Yes, he'd teased her early on about becoming his mistress, but that had been only to provoke her, to force her into telling him who she was, damn it.

His blood suddenly ran cold. How could she have known he was only provoking her? He'd never bothered to set her straight. He'd been so sure of himself, so sure of *her*, that he hadn't explained himself.

Then he would bloody well do it now, damn it. Tucking the letter under his arm, he buttoned up his breeches and went looking for his shirt. Enough of this nonsense. He'd head straight to the Kingsley town house and tell her everything, then demand that she marry him.

That's what he should have done last night. He should have ignored all her nonsense about holding on to that mask. A woman like her was meant to be married. Wasn't that why she'd participated in this auction in the first place?

He strained to remember what she'd said about it, then groaned as it came back to him: *I'm testing the waters, that's all. I'm not quite ready to marry again, and I want to see if I can even bear to be with another man.*

A sick despair settled in his gut, making him halt where he was. For the first time it occurred to him that she might not *want* to marry him. Or even to marry at all. What if she'd insisted on the mask for that reason alone? It didn't bode well for her feelings that she'd steadfastly refused to remove her mask even after they'd made love. What if she truly had wanted only an evening of pleasure, to "test the waters"?

Worse yet, what if she'd tested the waters and discovered she couldn't bear to be with another man after all? Then her fleeing would make perfect sense.

He sank onto the bed, feeling as if his heart were shredding apart inside his chest. After they'd made love, he'd simply assumed she would fall in with his plans like a good little girl, like the same starry-eyed young woman who'd married Henry Lamberton out of gratitude for the man's generosity.

But she wasn't that same young woman. Galatea had become flesh and blood, with a mind of her own. He'd been too full of himself to see it. He'd been so intent on playing his little games with her that he hadn't even considered what she might want. She was right—he was indeed overbearing and pompous.

Jerking out the letter again, he reread it, trying to decipher what she might have meant, but its brevity hampered him. All she said was that she "must respectfully decline" his offer. Which he hadn't actually made.

That meant she might also "respectfully decline" his offer of marriage.

With an oath, he crumpled the note in his hand. Going to her house and unmasking her wasn't an option. Much as he'd like to storm in and order her to marry him, he doubted such a method would impress Lady Kingsley. What if he confronted her only to discover that she had no interest in marrying him? Or that she was willing to marry him out of gratitude for what he'd taught her in bed? He didn't want her like that, to be sure.

A sudden chilling thought hit him. What if she agreed to marry him because she feared what he'd do with the knowledge he'd gained about her past last night? If he trapped her, she might very well respond that way.

He groaned. Damn, but he'd made a mess of things. He hadn't even considered that aspect until just now. She'd chosen not to take her mask off for a reason. Until he knew what it was, he couldn't act without forcing her into a corner.

So he must find a way to let her know how he felt about her without making her feel obligated to him. If he wanted to win her, he'd have to set it up so that she felt entirely free to choose. Or to keep her anonymity if she so wished.

He glanced down to see her glove still peeping from under the bed where they'd apparently kicked it last night. Picking it up, he mused over it a moment. An idea began to take shape in his mind . . .

Isobel hurried up the steps to the main building of the Lamberton School, fretting over the skirts that hampered her from moving faster. Oh, Lord, she was late. And for this meeting, of all meetings! Devil take her maid for not waking her.

Though she couldn't really blame the maid too much. Isobel hadn't slept well in three days—not since her night with Justin.

No, she must stop thinking of him like that. He was Lord Warbrooke. She'd best remember it, before she blundered in front of everyone.

That was the least of her worries, however. Far more important was how she would survive an entire meeting of the governing board without wanting to touch him or smile at him or say something flirtatious.

Which would not do at all. Despite having left a number of personal items at the Clarendon, she'd miraculously escaped detection. She'd be a fool to blunder now.

Never mind that she spent her nights reliving every sweet word and caress and taste they'd shared. That she spent her days trying to wear herself out for those awful, endless nights. She'd made her decision. Perhaps she'd been a bit hasty by not waiting around to see what he'd say, but she couldn't have borne it if he'd asked her to be his mistress again. If he'd cheapened what she felt for him.

In any case, she would make up for it today. After what he'd said during their night together, she had read his proposal for the boys' school very carefully. And when she'd examined it through eyes unclouded by suspicion of his motives, she'd discovered it had far more merit than she'd given him credit for. The least she could do was support it now, though she'd have to present her change of heart in a way that wouldn't rouse his suspicions.

When she reached the top of the stairs, Phoebe was waiting for her. "What is going on?" her friend demanded. "I've been trying to see you for three days. I can't believe you weren't at home to *me*."

"I–I was busy, that's all."

A knowing look spread over Phoebe's face. "Aha! But busy with *whom*? That's the question."

"Lower your voice, for pity's sake," Isobel hissed as she veered around her friend and headed purposefully down the hall. "Do you want to ruin me?"

"I saw Lord Warbrooke win you at the Widows' Auction," Phoebe said as she hurried after her. "I only want to know if it was everything you expected. And what did he think when he found out it was you?"

Isobel halted in her tracks. "I didn't tell him. Do you think I'm insane?"

"That bad, was it?"

"No!" At Phoebe's raised eyebrow, she colored. "No, it was as wonderful as you said it would be. But it could never work between me and Just—... Lord Warbrooke. He's not interested in marriage, and I'm not interested in anything else."

"He told you that?"

"Yes. Well, sort of." She continued down the hall.

"Ah, but he didn't know who you are. That might make a difference."

"It wouldn't," she said feebly.

"So you've become a Gypsy fortune-teller, have you? Bella, if you don't tell a man that you want him, how is he supposed to know? Especially when you take away his chance to decide by keeping your identity secret."

Isobel paused outside the closed door to the meeting room. "You don't understand—"

"Oh, but I do. You're a coward, Isobel Lamberton. You've finally found a man who suits you, but you're afraid to risk your heart. It's easier to go on with your plodding, lonely life than to take a chance on happiness. Well, you're a fool if you choose being safe over being loved."

Then with a sniff, Phoebe opened the door to the meeting room and marched in to take her place at the table.

Isobel stood in the doorway, Phoebe's words resonating in her brain. Phoebe was right. She *was* a coward. But she couldn't help it. She loved him so much she was afraid to be anything else. It would shatter her to have him admit he wanted only some sordid connection with her.

Mustering her strength for the long meeting ahead, she donned her old regal façade and walked into the room. "Good day, gentlemen. I'm sorry for being late, but I had some pressing matters to attend to."

As she skirted the table, she could feel Justin's eyes following her to her seat. Though that was nothing unusual, today it was different, at least for her. Because for the first time she wanted to meet his gaze boldly, to tell him who she was and how she felt.

But she couldn't take that chance.

She reached her usual chair and pulled it out, then froze. Directly in the center was a glove. *Her* glove, the one she'd lost. And attached to it was a note that read only, "Is this yours, Lady Kingsley?" It was signed, "Lord Warbrooke." Just that, and no other explanation.

Her pulse beat madly as she stood there, unable to do

anything but gape at it. God help her, he knew who she was! Did he mean to unmask her right now before the entire board? To reveal her immorality and ruin her? Would he do that?

She forced herself to look up, to meet his gaze. Around him, the others were chattering about this and that, oblivious to the drama playing itself out right there before them. But he sat quietly, patiently, his expression showing nothing. No cruelty, no hint of revenge.

But nothing else either. As if he waited for her to do or say something before he acted.

She glanced down again as something dawned on her. A glove was such an impersonal item. If he'd wanted to shame her, he could have brought something more damning, like the garter or stockings she'd left behind. But he hadn't.

So what did it mean? What did he expect her to do?

Then it hit her. He was offering her a choice—acknowledge the glove as hers and in so doing acknowledge their connection . . . or deny that it was hers and end their connection forever.

Oh, Lord, what a choice. If she took the glove, she'd be trusting him not to use it against her. And what if her trust were misplaced? What if their wonderful night had merely been leading up to this—to Lord Warbrooke's final public triumph over her?

No, she couldn't believe that. Not without believing that every word he'd spoken was a lie, every caress was feigned . . . every dark, hungry look had been only the basest form of lust. And she simply couldn't.

But what if she accepted, and he offered her only a place in his bed and not in his heart? Could she endure that?

She sighed. Whether she could or no, she owed it to him to tell him that to his face. Continuing as a coward was not fair to him.

Even if he *was* making it easy for her to refuse him. All

she need do was tell him that the glove wasn't hers and hand it back. She sensed that he'd accept such a gesture as her desire to keep her identity secret, not only from the rest of them but from him as well.

He probably wouldn't challenge it. But she'd lose him. If she'd ever had him at all.

She swallowed. Her other choice was to acknowledge their connection by accepting the glove. No one else would know what it meant. But he would. And after that, everything would change between them, regardless of what his intentions were. Did she dare to risk that?

"Lady Kingsley, are you all right?" Mr. Dawson queried.

That jolted her back to her surroundings. "I–I'm fine. I was merely remembering something I left behind."

She glanced to Justin, stunned to see him look suddenly vulnerable, even afraid. He didn't want her to deny him. And God help her, but she didn't want to deny him either, no matter what pain it might mean for her in the future.

She didn't want to be a coward anymore.

Taking a deep, steadying breath as she held his gaze, she bent and picked up the glove, then slid it into her apron pocket.

Relief flared in Justin's face, relief and something else. Could it possibly be love?

Hope sprouted within her as she sat down and wielded her gavel a bit unsteadily. "I call this meeting to order," she began. "At our last meeting—"

"Before we go on, Lady Kingsley," Justin broke in. "I'd like to make a suggestion."

"Yes?" she whispered, her heart in her throat.

"I've taken some time to read your proposal, and I find it a very worthy project. So I'd like to withdraw my own proposal and move that we adopt yours instead. I have some funds at present that I could funnel into your endowments, and I'm sure if others contributed—"

"I have a better idea, Lord Warbrooke," she interrupted

as hope took even firmer root in her heart. "What if we do both? I, too, spent some hours examining your suggestions, and I think we should embark on your factory idea at once."

A murmur of surprise ran round the table, and even Justin looked stunned.

She went on hastily. "But your proposal and mine aren't mutually exclusive, you know. I happen to have come into some funds recently that I'd be more than happy to contribute to the endowments. That would leave you to use your funds for the factory."

A slow, hopeful smile spread over his Roman conqueror's face. "What a brilliant idea, Lady Kingsley. It seems we've finally found something we can agree on."

"It does seem that way, doesn't it?" She allowed herself a smile in return.

The others could only sit and gape at them.

"I say," Mr. Dawson finally ventured, "whatever happened to you two since the last meeting? Have you both been neglecting to wear your hats in the sun?"

"It was wine, Mr. Dawson," she couldn't resist saying. "I had some wine that went straight to my head."

"How odd," Justin retorted. "So did I. Tell me, Lady Kingsley, was it as delicious as mine? Because the one I had—"

"We don't care about the damned wine, old fellow," Lord Bradford cut in. "Let's just put the proposal—whatever it is now—to a vote, so we can all go home."

Isobel exchanged a happy glance with Phoebe, who was grinning broadly enough to split her face open. "Certainly, let's vote at once. All those in favor of embarking on both projects, raise your hand."

Everyone raised their hand. Even the irascible Lord Bradford.

"Good," Isobel said. "Then that's settled. And I see no point to further discussion on the matter today. Why don't we all go home and examine both proposals in depth, then meet next week to talk about implementing them?"

She could tell her fellow board members were bewildered by her sudden amiable eagerness to adjourn a meeting, but she didn't waste too much time worrying about it. She merely tapped her gavel on the table and watched as Phoebe shooed the others out of the meeting room.

All except Lord Warbrooke. He was already rounding the table and coming toward her. She rose and tried not to read too much into that possessive glance of his, but it grew harder by the second. Glancing behind him to where Phoebe had paused in the door, she shot her friend a look of panic. But Phoebe merely smiled and blew her a kiss before walking out and closing the door behind her.

Isobel and Justin were alone at last.

He stood so close that she could touch him, but she didn't. Instead she stared down at the glove she'd just drawn out of her pocket. "How long have you known who I was?"

"From the moment you said your name was Bella on that dais," he said softly.

Her gaze shot to him. "As long as all that?"

He nodded.

"But why did you keep quiet? Why didn't you just unmask me right then and there?"

"In front of Bradford? I wouldn't be so cruel." He edged nearer, surrounding her with his heat, his scent. "At first I thought to shake you up a bit, bedevil you the way you'd been bedeviling me with your pronouncements about my character. I intended to give you enough rope to hang yourself before I unveiled you and gave you the lecture of your life about hypocrisy and morality and . . ."

He paused, lifting his hand to stroke her hair.

She flinched. He'd manipulated her from the moment he'd won the auction. He'd tricked her into telling him everything about her past, and then . . .

Then he'd made love to her with the most unbearable

sweetness. "And what?" she prodded. "What else did you intend to lecture me about?"

"The foolishness of participating in a widows' auction. I meant what I said about protecting you. I always intended to keep our little battle between the two of us. I would never have told anyone else about your appearance at that auction. So although I admit that I began by wanting to torment you a little, it was never meant to be more than that."

Hooking his finger beneath her chin, he forced her to look at him. "Then everything changed. The longer it went on, the more I was swept into it, and the more fascinated with you I became. It didn't take long before I realized I didn't *want* to unmask you unless you wanted it. All thoughts of lecturing or embarrassing you went right out the window." His voice grew husky. "Along with my self-control. Because by then I desired you more than I've ever desired anyone in my life. By then I could see the real woman beneath the lofty façade. And I wanted that woman for my own."

A thrill shot through her at his blatantly possessive words.

"Now I need *you* to explain something to *me*," he said, that vulnerability flaring in his face again. "Why did you leave before we could discuss any of this?"

She swallowed. "Because I was afraid you'd want me only as a mistress." With a sinking heart, she realized he hadn't yet said he wanted her for anything else. "Not that I blame you, of course. A man with your future doesn't need a wife with my past as a liability. But I just couldn't—"

"Oh, Bella, I'm so sorry I didn't make myself clearer. All that talk about having you for my mistress was meant only to provoke you into revealing yourself. Once I made love to you, there was only one role I wanted you to play in my life, and that was as my wife. I wouldn't settle for anything less."

Her fear began to ease. "But what about your future in politics?"

"I have no future in politics without you, darling. Because if I can't have you at my side, none of it is even worth pursuing." He flashed her a rakish grin. "If you refuse to marry me, I'll have to give it all up. Otherwise I'll make myself a laughingstock. They'll be gossiping all over town about poor Warbrooke and the widow who broke his heart."

A smile crept over her face. "You're exaggerating, you silly man, but I don't mind. That part about my breaking your heart is very sweet, even if we both know it's nonsense."

"It's not nonsense," he protested. "Are you blind? Can't you see I've fallen in love with you? Good God, woman, do you think I propose marriage every day?"

That Roman conqueror's look was in his eye now. She stilled, hardly daring to hope. "If you have indeed fallen in love, it's with Bella."

"No," he said firmly. "I fell in love with all of you—with Bella, the fetching temptress . . . with Lady Kingsley, the highly moral reformer . . . and even with Isobel, the orphan millworker."

She shook her head. "The only one of those who really is me is Isobel. Henry created Lady Kingsley, and as for Bella—"

"She's you, too. Just as Lady Kingsley is you. Yes, your husband set out the road for Isobel to follow, but it was Isobel who took it, Isobel who did the work, Isobel who transformed herself into Lady Kingsley. There would be no Lady Kingsley without Isobel working behind the scenes. And even Bella, that naughty minx, is Isobel when she's at home and relaxed . . . or in the throes of lovemaking. They are all you, my darling, and I'm in love with every single one of them."

"Oh, Justin," she said, hardly able to speak for the joy

filling her throat, "that is quite possibly the most wonderful thing any man has ever said to me."

"So that means you'll marry me? Even if you don't love me, perhaps in time—"

"*Now* who's blind?" she said, stretching up to silence his ridiculous uncertainties with a kiss. "Of course I love you." She mimicked his authoritarian voice. "Good God, man, do you think I accept a proposal of marriage every day?"

He raised an eyebrow. "This had better be the last. Because I don't intend to share you with anyone. I plan to be Galatea's only husband from now until eternity."

Then he swept her into his arms and gave her the most delicious kiss yet. Or perhaps it was the most delicious because they were in love. And being in love seemed to make everything more wonderful—the air, the room, the kiss . . . She couldn't wait to try this out in every room of her town house. And his. And *theirs*.

When he drew back, he wore a decidedly mischievous look. "Now that you've agreed to marry me, my lovely Isobel, I'll have to establish some rules."

She eyed him warily. "Oh? And what might those be?"

"Rule number one—no more masks."

With a laugh, she relaxed in his arms. "I think I can agree to that."

But he wasn't finished. "Rule number two—no more sponges."

"*More?* We didn't even use them the first time," she pointed out.

"Good. And we won't use them in the future either. At least not until we've had a few children."

She swallowed. "And if I can't have children?"

"Then we won't need them anyway, will we?" When she continued to stare at him uncertainly, he added, "Children or no children, I want you, Bella. But I should like to attempt to have some."

"So would I," she admitted shyly.

"And finally, rule number three—no more widows' auctions. I'll soon have pockets to let if I spend a thousand pounds every time I need to get your attention."

She laughed and tightened her arms about his neck. "Don't worry, my love. I've had enough of auctions to last me a lifetime. Unless you'd be interested in a *private* auction. I know this widow named Bella who for a certain price would be willing to commit the most naughty, outrageous acts imaginable."

As desire flared in his face, he growled. "Oh? And what precisely would that cost me?"

"Your heart," she whispered back. "Nothing but your heart."

He grinned as he lowered his head to hers. "Then thank God that's a price I'm more than willing to pay."

Look for Sabrina Jeffries's new historical romance,

After the Abduction

coming in June!

Luisa's Desire

Emma Holly

For Robert and Lana.
May your worlds always meet in love.

1

Tibet, 1600

The sun filled the air with diamond knives, its merciless
brilliance shooting spires of brightness off the ice-locked
Himalayan peaks. Beneath, on the precipitous path that
circled the tallest mountain, Luisa del Fiore huddled
deeper into her mink-lined hood. Black sheathed her from
head to toe: her kidskin gloves, her yakhide boots, even the
veil that draped her face was black as ink. Despite these
precautions, the effect of the sun was barely muffled. This
was Tibet, the roof of the world, and far closer to heaven
than a child of midnight ought to go.

The sun was a drug to her kind, a pleasure beyond com-
pare. Like all drugs, however, too large a dose could kill.
Indeed, she would not have risked this journey had her
need not been so great.

Unaware of her predicament, Dorje, her cheerful native
guide, beckoned her forward on the trail. The mere thought

of the drop to his right was enough to make her dizzy. The fall might not kill her, but even an *upyr* could break her bones.

"Come," he urged. "Only little way more."

He spoke the pidgin Chinese they used to communicate, the language of the traders to whom he sold yak butter and from whom he bought bricks of tea. A nomadic herdsman, Dorje was one of six whose pilgrimage to this lamasery she had joined. She knew she was lucky to have fallen in with them even though, had she been alone, she could have traveled in the sunless safety of the night.

Getting lost was not safe, of course, no more than freezing to death, a hazard to which she had not known she was vulnerable. Her first night in the mountains had taught her that hard truth. Thankfully, on the second night, she'd stumbled into Dorje's camp. He and his companions had offered her the foulest tea she'd ever pretended to drink and welcomed her to their fire. When she divulged her destination, they volunteered to guide her. Never mind she was a stranger, and a foreigner, and very outlandishly garbed. Never mind she posed a danger they could not begin to understand. They had heard that the *gompa*—the lamasery—at Shisharovar was holy. Anyone who helped her would gain merit from the trip.

At the moment, Luisa cared more for her next step than she cared for merit. Her exhaustion seemed a living thing, like one of the demons Dorje told tales of around the fire. She had no words for her hunger. She had not fed since she'd left the ship. She had not dared. It was not discovery she feared, nor others' violence against herself. Instead she feared she would feed until she slew these people who had saved her.

This was the crux of her dilemma, that she might kill when she had no wish to. Lately the urge had been getting stronger. She genuinely loved her life. The challenge of doing business among the humans kept her engaged. But with her years came an emptiness only blood seemed to fill, and only for a little while. When she had begun to drink from criminals—just in case she lost control—she knew she could not trust herself anymore.

She was not the hand of justice. Better to starve than to act as if she were.

As much as she believed in her choice, she could have wept for the intensity of her hunger. To drink . . . to be strong again . . .

But strength was the object of her journey: true strength, not the strength that came from theft.

Ahead of her, Dorje's crude felt boots punched holes in the snow she strove to follow. Like his fellows, he seemed to notice neither the cold nor the thinness of the air. Luisa felt both, her feet leaden, her blood-starved veins like overstretched wires of brass. She had not thought a mortal could be so strong. Forging steadily before her, Dorje seemed as tough as the grumbling yaks they had left in the spring green valley far below.

When she lagged, he laughed and urged her onward like a father exhorting a child to walk. She felt a child, so sun-addled she could scarcely stand. All around her the light was slow, sure poison, a wine of gold and blue, a scent as sweet and fragile as mountain flowers. It had been days now, weeks mayhap, that this deadly radiance had been seeping through her clothes. Drunk with it, she clung to reason by a thread.

Sleep, the sunshine whispered. *Pull off your cloak and bask in my golden rays. Be one with the beauty of the waking world.*

Luisa cursed and grit her teeth. She knew she must not listen.

The waking world was not her rightful sphere.

They came to a turning. Dorje pointed higher and ahead.

"See," he said. "Lamas here!"

As she rounded the scarp, the path widened into a table of land as flat as if it had been carved. Beyond this small plateau the mountain rose again, craggy and sharp, a final heavenward thrust of stone. Shisharovar nestled at its base. The lamasery was bigger than she had expected, many floors of white-limed walls and narrow, defensive windows. Lines of prayer flags fluttered against the sky. *The jewel is in the lotus,* she deciphered, the sum of what Tibetan she could read. A flash of silver drew her eye to men standing on the roof, tall brown men in flowing russet robes. She squinted. They held what appeared to be long trumpets. The low bleating the instruments made a moment later confirmed the guess.

"Oé!" Dorje exclaimed. With a sigh of resignation, he and his companions dropped their packs. "Lamas pray now. We wait."

He gestured for her to sit but she could not. Within those walls lay darkness and warmth and quite possibly an end to her travails. She was walking before she even knew she meant to, crossing the trampled snow like a woman in a trance.

"Wait!" Dorje cried. "No can go. Lama here very holy. Very big power. Luisa make *naljorpa* angry. Luisa be sorry."

He had her arm and was trying to drag her back. Anger rising, she spun around. Dorje's jaw dropped. Her hood had fallen with the movement and the light shone clearly through her veil. She caught a glimpse of how she looked through his eyes: pale, porcelain skin and hair as gold as new-minted florins. Her expression was startled, even innocent. But she was too perfect, her eyes too vividly green, her mouth too carnally red.

Beauty like hers was dangerous.

His interest shimmered in the air between them. A sound filled her head: his heart pumping harder with desire, forcing the life-giving fluid through it, forcing his sex to rise. For a moment she felt faint. Blood, she thought, seeing it, tasting it. She closed her eyes at the power of her hunger—not just for food but to destroy.

She didn't realize she had moved. When her eyes snapped open, her hand was wrapped behind his neck, already pulling him into biting range. Her gums were stinging where her teeth had broken through. She shook herself, then shook him.

He seemed not to notice the unfeminine force with which she did it.

"You go," she said, sternly, huskily. "You no stop me."

He stared at her, still under the spell of her foreign beauty. He licked his lips and she knew she'd done the same. Her mouth was watering, her eyeteeth razor sharp.

"You go," she repeated. "Me no want hurt you."

He grinned at that, as if he did not believe she could. "Haha," he laughed with a Tibetan's unpredictable humor. "No wonder you wear veil. You show face, you get too many husband!"

Her own laugh was weak but it allowed her to uncurl her fingers from his neck. His countrymen, she had learned, were polyandrists.

"Yes," she agreed. "Me no want too many husband."

She backed away, gesturing him to stay. He looked worried but this time he did not try to stop her. Perhaps he judged her a match for the terrible *naljorpa,* whatever in Creation that was. Steps led to the lamasery entrance, stone beneath the snow. She climbed them—one dozen, two . . . her eyes holding Dorje in his place.

At last she reached the top. Two large rings hung from the iron that bound the double door. Wincing at the bite of the frozen metal, she set her heels on the step and pulled. The hinges groaned. The door was too heavy for human hands, but impatience prevented her from pretending she could not move it. She was going in. Nothing, not prayers, not fears, not even her failing strength, was going to stop her now.

With a last grunt of effort, she heaved it open and slipped inside.

The shadows folded around her like a blessing, smoky

and sweet and warm. Butter lamps, the ubiquitous Tibetan illumination, flickered on various altars along the walls. She had entered a towering hall, its roof supported by heavy columns, its walls hung with banners of colored silk. Through clouds of incense she made out the hazy forms of many Buddhas praying, teaching, and looking much like those she had encountered in Calcutta.

A group of monks, young and old, were crossing the passage as she came in—presumably headed to their worship. As one, they turned to gape. Luisa did not care. She was too elated to be inside. Her head was pounding, sun drunk still, but at least it did not ache. Giddy with relief, she threw back her veil and grinned.

It was a mistake she would not have made had her mind been clear.

Two of the monks cried out and the larger of them rushed her. She barely had time to brace before his weight crashed her over into the floor.

"Towo!" he cried as she struggled to free herself. *"Tsem shes tsem!"*

Luisa realized she must have bared her fangs. He had taken her for a demon.

"I pilgrim," she protested in her limited Tibetan. "I come pray."

Unimpressed, the monk took her head in both hands and smashed it against the floor. He must have been very strong. Like the crackle of early winter ice, she felt a tiny fracture in her skull. The break healed almost as soon as it formed but, however ineffective, the injury snapped her control. Instinct took over, the remorseless drive for survival that marked her kind.

Taking his head in the same splay-fingered grip, she stunned the monk by coshing his brow against her own. Then, before he could recover, before she herself could think better of it, she rolled him beneath her and drove her teeth through the wind-roughened skin of his neck.

His blood filled her mouth, hot, rich, a feast for her

starving veins. Her head cleared at the first swallow. The second was just for greed. But she had to stop. She could not kill within arm's reach of her goal. When he moaned, she shoved off him and got up.

She might not be sated but she was sane.

"I am not a demon," she said, even as she drew her fine Spanish glove across her mouth. "Not *towo*."

The monk who had attacked her was on his knees, too shaken to rise. "No," he agreed, his eyes wide and locked to hers. "You are not a demon."

He sounded almost normal, almost, but she knew her bite had thralled him. He was hers to command, for an hour or a day, though she could not see what good that would do. The rest of the monks had closed around her, many of them as big as the one she'd bitten. She knew she could not overpower them all.

"I have come to learn your ways," she said, switching to her more fluent Mandarin. Pray God, someone here would speak it. "I beg the favor of studying with your abbot." Silence met her plea as she turned from one implacable visage to the next. "Look." Careful to move slowly, she reached into the folds of her fur-lined cloak. "I bring a gift for him, for Geshe Rinpoche, the holy lama of Shisharovar."

She held out her offering, wrapped as Dorje had advised in a white silk scarf. A rustle moved through the crowd, which suddenly parted to reveal another monk.

Everything seemed to hush as he approached—breath, heart, thought—as if the world itself had stopped turning on its axis. Even the terrible emptiness inside her stilled. Sun-drunk nonsense, she scoffed, but the sensation did not fade.

Here was a man to weaken knees.

Though young, the monk carried himself like a leader: upright, assured, with the grace of a creature whose body is completely in his control. He must be the lama she had come to see. His head had been shaved but not recently and new growth bristled out in a glossy brush. He looked healthy, smelled healthy. Helpless to quell the reaction, her pulse beat faster in her throat.

Swallowing, she tried not to stare at the way his stride moved the drapery of his deep red robe. Lifting her gaze did not help. The long, toga-like wrap bared one beautifully molded arm. As she watched, his hand settled on the shoulder of the kneeling monk. Without looking away from her, the lama gave the monk an order. Luisa could not suppress a shiver. His voice was as deep as the rumbling trumpets on the roof.

Whatever the lama's authority, Luisa knew her victim could not obey until she released her mental hold. She stepped forward to do so. Unfortunately, watching a woman wipe blood from her mouth did not elicit trust. The lama barked a word and extended his second hand.

As soon as he did, something pushed her belly, something she could not see. It felt like a wall not precisely of wind, but not unlike. Under its influence, she slid backward, slowly at first, then gathering speed, her heels dragging on the stone, her arms wheeling for balance until she hit the plastered wall. The force of the collision drove the air from her lungs. Beside her, on a lighted altar, a heap of barley spilled from an offering bowl.

Luisa could barely contain a gasp. In all her years she'd never seen anyone perform such magic, neither *upyr* nor human. This, it seemed, was the power of a terrible *naljorpa*. She should have been frightened but her skin was tingling strongly with excitement. She could learn from this man. She could finally achieve her goal.

Pinned to the wall by the lama's mysterious force, she watched him help the other monk to his feet. Her victim left the hall with no more than a reluctant glance in her direction. Amazing, she thought. No one but she should have been able to direct him in any way.

The lama continued his approach. Her body tensed, half with wariness and half with anticipation. Oh, she could happily have tied this one to her bed. He was staring directly at her, into her. The effect was eerie but oddly sensual, as if his gaze were touching places she had not known she had. His eyes themselves were lovely, the fold beneath slightly broader than the delicate one above. They did not slant so much as narrow at the ends.

When he stopped a foot away from her, she received another shock. In the light from the butter lamps' floating wicks she saw that his eyes were gentian blue. The back of her neck prickled. This man, this Tibetan sorcerer, had European blood.

His gaze dropped to the package she clutched before her breast.

"You should kneel when you offer that," he said.

She blinked at him. "You speak English."

His expression did not change. "As do you."

He must have assumed from her appearance that she would, a natural assumption and one that should not have unnerved her after all she'd seen him do. Nonetheless, she was unnerved. Though she was more gifted at putting thoughts *into* people's heads than taking them out, she was not accustomed to finding anyone such a blank.

If the lama was unnerved, he did not show it. He was close to her, the tiny spikes of his lashes shadowing his angled cheeks. Luisa was tall but he was taller, tall for any race, even hers. A warm soft scent rose from his robes, incense and yak butter and something sweeter: the scent that was his essence. She wanted to drag it into her lungs but knew she could not afford to, not now and maybe never. Already her attraction to him was stronger than she liked.

"You drank that man's blood," he said, "and you clouded his mind. If you are not a demon, what manner of creature are you?"

"I could ask you the same."

His lips twitched with what might have been a smile. Then, as if this lapse were somehow shameful, he sobered and stepped back. Luisa sensed she was losing ground.

"Forgive me," she said, doing her best to hide her consternation. "I did not mean to hurt that man. His attack surprised me. And I am not familiar with your customs." Dropping to her knees, she bowed her head and held her guest gift up before her. "Please, holy lama, accept this humble token of my esteem."

Someone giggled, a boy from the sound of it, quickly hushed.

"I am not Geshe Rinpoche," said the man with an edge of stiffness, "nor a holy lama. I am, however, honored to be the precious one's student. I will bring him to you when the service ends. If your request is sincere, I am sure he will honor it."

She was not certain, but his final statement seemed to hold a hint of drollness. The possibility did not reassure her. Nor was she happy when he led her down a corridor to a little room. A set of iron chains hung from the raw stone wall. Luisa took one look and wanted to run away. Instead, she let her escort guide her to them. What sort of monastery kept such devices so close to hand? The room wasn't even a dungeon! It had an ornate tea table and an extra cushion for a guest.

"You do not need to do this," she said, fighting panic as he closed the manacles around her sleeves. "I am not a threat."

The glance he shot her was sardonic. She had to admit he had cause to doubt her. But did he know iron was the only metal she could not break? Or had she simply imagined he had seen straight to her core? Either way, she could not fight. She needed these people's help. She could not afford to hurt them.

But then he bent and chained her ankles like her wrists. His soft bristled hair brushed the front of her thigh, an inadvertent intimacy she was sure. Despite the sensual distraction, her panic rose.

"I do not like being restrained," she said. She meant it

to be a warning, but her voice shook, betraying her sincerity more clearly than she wished.

He seemed to hear it. He straightened and stared at her with his extraordinary eyes. His pupils gleamed like ink, large in the dimness, or perhaps he also was aroused. Her beauty was not, after all, of the common run. Given his show of control, she was surprised when he cupped her cheek. His palm was warm, his fingers calloused. The comfort they brought made her want to clench her jaw. Too easily she could imagine those careful fingers between her legs. She frowned to herself. His pull was as dangerous as her instinct to fight the chains.

As if he, too, mistrusted the contact, his touch fell away. A second later, so did his gaze.

"It is not a long service," he said without his previous irony. "As soon as it is over, I will bring my teacher here."

His *teacher*, she thought, rolling the back of her head against the stone. If a mere student could do what he did, what did she need to fear from the man who'd taught him?

2

"So," *said the* abbot, his Mandarin even more elegant than hers, "Martin says you are interested in our ways."

Geshe Rinpoche was older than his pupil and, at first glance, less imposing. He was shorter, for one thing, with a peasant's solidity and bright black eyes that seemed an inch away from a smile. His robe was humble and the only badge of office he wore was the yellow stole around his neck. Martin stood guard at his side, stern and protective. His teacher, by contrast, did not behave as if she posed a threat.

And perhaps she didn't. Perhaps the magic Geshe Rinpoche commanded turned her own into the useless huffing of the wind. It was a strange possibility, one she had not faced since her first encounters with her kind. True, the smattering of *upyr* at Queen Elizabeth's court were more experienced than Luisa, but none of those backstabbers could take her without a fight—and certainly not by force of mind!

Knowing she must tread carefully, she bowed her head before she spoke. "I have heard much of Shisharovar, your holiness, and of your awe-inspiring power."

"Indeed," said the abbot. "How flattering."

"Perhaps you would allow me to introduce myself?" When she ventured to look up, a grin had creased the old lama's face, the lines fanning merrily outward from his eyes. He spread his hands in permission. Luisa composed herself. "Thank you, your holiness. My name is Luisa del Fiore and I am a prosperous Florentine merchant. My business takes me all over the world and also brings the world to me."

"You travel all over the world? A woman alone?"

"Usually I have companions but sometimes I go alone, sometimes in disguise as a man. It depends on the prejudices of those with whom I deal, and on which appearance will tend to my best advantage."

"Your skill at subterfuge must be great," said the abbot with a wry enjoyment that warned her not to underestimate his wit. "But surely you are not here to trade."

"No, your holiness. I am here because of a trader I met, one who traveled these regions long ago. His name was John Moore and he was rescued by your lamas when a snowstorm caught him in the pass. He remained some months and witnessed many wonders, one of which was a monk who had himself walled in a cave where he survived for three whole weeks on water and meditation. When he emerged, he was as strong as the day he'd left. That monk was, I believe, yourself."

For some reason, the abbot glanced at his student, then at her. "You come here to learn to fast? All this way, to learn a trick any hermit can perform?"

"Self-denial is one of the paths to enlightenment, is it not? I believe in learning from the best."

He furrowed his brow at her. The intensity of his concentration caught her unprepared. His gaze was even keener than his student's. It lapped at her skin like water, crawling over and under until the hairs on her arms stood up in waves. She gasped, abruptly unable to catch her breath. Then, with no more warning than he'd given when he began, the abbot released her.

"You have a strange energy," he said in a musing tone. "I see from the disposition of your subtle bodies that your thoughts and desires are very much concerned with your physical being. Our medical lamas claim such attachment leads to illness and yet your material self is very strong. I have never met a demon of your description, much less one who would enter a holy place. I confess, though, I cannot imagine what you are."

He waited then, a picture of Oriental patience. More than anything he seemed curious. No one who suspected she was not human had ever reacted in this way. Then again, in this country, demons and ghosts were treated as little more than inconvenient neighbors. Tibetans bought an amulet or a spell and continued on their way. Luisa sensed that even if she admitted to being a monster, this holy man would not condemn her.

Of course, a failure to condemn was not the same as giving aid.

At a loss, she looked to Martin. He was watching her just as calmly. She wondered if his composure were a pretense or if, like his teacher, he was prepared to accept her as she was.

"We can see this request is important to you," Martin said. "We would be interested to know why."

Luisa hesitated. Could she tell them? Should she? Would they help her if she did not? She fisted her hands within the iron shackles. The slow, draining chill pulled at her through her clothes. The metal would not kill her unless someone thrust it through her heart. Eventually, though, it would weaken her enough to be killed. By sunlight. Or fire. Or the severing of her spine. She supposed she could take her choice.

As if sensing her fears, the abbot lifted a key from a ring on the belt that tied his robe.

"No," she said before he could use it. "Let me answer before you decide to free me." Uncurling her fingers, she forced herself to relax. "I was born as human as you. One hundred twenty years ago, on the fortieth anniversary of my birth, my master changed me to the creature I am today. He was the descendant of an ancient race who came from a distant star. They lived in peace here once, until a few took to killing humans. We . . . feed off them, you see. It is the only sustenance we can take." She straightened her shoulders. "I am what the people of Russia call *upyr,* a blood-drinker, an immortal."

"An immortal." The abbot's head was cocked birdlike to the side. He seemed not so much shocked as fascinated. "An immortal who is neither ghost nor god. An immortal in human form." Suddenly he laughed. "You know, we of Tibet aspire to leave the world of illusion behind. To us, this earth is a kind of hell—a schoolroom, if you will— where we are repeatedly reborn in order to perfect our true, nonmaterial being. You, Luisa del Fiore, seem to have en- rolled for a very long term!"

His humor discomposed her. "I do not wish to give up my life," she said, wanting to be clear. "I simply wish to live more ethically. I wish to live without drinking blood."

"Ah," said the abbot, "now I begin to see. You must re- alize that may not be possible."

"Yes, your holiness, but surely if anyone can teach me it is you."

"Perhaps." His dark eyes narrowed in consideration. "I will have to meditate carefully before I act. It will not be easy to instruct you, who have not been raised in our sys- tem, and it may not be wise to try. We shall see." He turned to Martin, his expression warming with a father's fond- ness. "I leave it to you to make our visitor comfortable. Perhaps she would like a quiet room in the old east wing."

Martin looked as if he longed to forgo this duty, but he

bowed instead, his steepled hands moving smoothly from brow to throat to heart. "As you wish, rinpoche."

From his tone, Luisa gathered "rinpoche" was as much a term of honor as a name.

To her relief, Martin unshackled her and led her in a new direction down the stony, torchlit hall. Apart from instructing her to follow and shooting her the occasional measuring glance, he did not speak. Luisa was no stranger to solitude, but for some reason his taciturnity frayed her nerves. They climbed a set of ancient stairs.

"Have you taken a vow of silence?" she asked.

"No," was his short, basso response.

"Might I ask then why your abbot keeps a set of chains in his reception chamber?"

"They are for interrogating criminals. The neighboring villages sometimes bring their accused here. My teacher reads their auras to see if they speak true."

"Their auras."

"The aura is a second body. It is a match for the physical body, inhabiting the same space and extending slightly beyond it, but composed of life force instead of matter. The life force of the earth is what a hermit survives on while he fasts."

Luisa considered this as they turned down another corridor, apparently uninhabited and lit by narrow windows. The slits were open to the icy air. A dusting of snow swirled in eddies along the floor. She pulled her cloak closer but Martin, like Dorje, did not seem to mind the cold.

She thought longingly of her palazzo, so marvelously snug after living out her mortal life with wind whistling through unglazed windows, a wind that had too often blown her nothing better than the stink of her husband's fish. Resistance to the cold, she sometimes thought, was worth the price of turning *upyr* by itself.

Not that her homeland had ever seen cold like this. This

was beyond even the winter she'd spent at sea with Sir Francis Drake.

Ahead of her, Martin pushed open a heavy door and held it for her to enter. Irked by his seeming indifference, she paused on the threshold, not touching him but close enough to mark the subtle pulsing of his heat. To her gratification, a trace of color crept up his neck. So. Monk or not, he was not immune to her appeal. The discovery restored a portion of her confidence.

"I felt you touch my aura before," she said. "You were trying to look inside me like your teacher."

"Yes," he admitted. She thought he would say no more, but then his mouth quirked slightly to the left. "Studying someone's aura is not like a boy peeking under a woman's skirts, if that is what you were thinking."

Whatever riposte she might have made was lost when his gaze settled onto hers. Her spine tingled strongly. Again she had that sense of time held in suspension. She must have imagined the hint of teasing. He seemed the most serious man in the world.

How beautiful he is, she thought. How utterly male and comely. The admiration itself was pleasurable, though she knew it would not satisfy her long. Luisa was a creature who reveled in possession: a painting, a book, a perfect length of brocaded silk. Like her countrymen, she knew an object gained value by being owned: real value. In Italy, as in the rest of Renaissance Europe, a man was judged by what he had. Appearance was power. Illusion became reality. Luisa had survived and thrived by knowing that.

"You are big for a woman," commented the object of her lust.

She choked on a startled laugh. "Not much for flattery, are you?"

He did her the grace of flushing. "I meant you are tall. And you are stronger than our females. You fought that monk as if you were a man."

She was not sure how to respond. It didn't seem wise to

confess her strength had been at its lowest ebb. But Martin did not expect an answer. Without asking permission, he pushed her hood back to her shoulders. As if pulled by an unknown force, his hand slid into her golden waves. He seemed as bewitched as she.

"I have never seen a woman with hair like yours. It does not even tangle." His fingers spread gently behind her ear, his thumb stroking the shadowed contours of her cheek. "Your skin is as smooth as satin. Are all *upyr* like you?"

His touch sent a heated shiver to her sex. She had to clear her throat before she could speak. "In some ways. When we are changed, we become what we would have been had we achieved our full potential. Our perfect age. Our perfect height and weight. As a mortal, I was plain and dull."

And bruised, often as not—first by her husband and then, more sadly, by her sons. She shook off the memory with a frown. That life was over. In any case, she had darker sins on her conscience than any that stained those of the foolish brutes who, for better or worse, had been her mortal family.

They were dead now, those strapping boys. Sometimes she regretted her failure to save them from their father's sway. Sometimes she was grateful they were gone. She could pray for them if she wished, and forgive the blows they had no more power to strike.

Martin was watching her face as if he could follow the passage of her thoughts. When he spoke, though, he did not ask about her former life. "Why do your kind 'change' humans? Can they not have children of their own?"

She shook her head. "My master believed the sun kills *upyr* seed. But we have compensations. We are strong, as you said, and can influence human thought. I have heard some *upyr* are able to take the form of beasts, though I have not seen it done."

"How many of you are there?"

"That is difficult to say. Many of the old ones died by

human vengeance. Some simply grew tired. It is not easy
to make new *upyr*. And we are wary of one another. Territorial. I knew of a dozen in London and heard there were
similar circles in Paris and Seville. At least one more *upyr*
lived in Florence, but we rarely did more than nod in passing. He was different, that one, dangerous. I suspect he was
an elder."

"An elder?"

"One of the old ones who knows how to perform the
change. My master claimed there were only two—himself
and his student, Nim Wei—but I think he may have been
wrong."

His thumb smoothed the orbit around her eye. "And
you do not age once you are made?"

She shook her head. "Not physically."

He leaned so close she thought he meant to examine her
cell by cell. Knowing her passivity would increase his
trust, she allowed him the inquisition. Remaining still was
not easy. His scent curled around her while his breath
brushed her mouth like velvet. An inch would have
brought them to a kiss.

She made a sound she had not intended, soft and hungry in her throat.

At once he pulled away. "Forgive me," he said, reluctantly drawing his hand out of her hair. He rubbed it across
his chest as if it itched. "I have been rude."

"Some would say a creature like me deserves no better."

"Some lie. All living beings deserve respect."

She could see he meant it. Dazed for more reasons than
she could name, she obeyed his gesture to step inside. The
room was small: a stone floor, a low, beamed ceiling. One
arrow-slit window overlooked a snowy courtyard. The
only furniture was an unlit altar and a pile of squared-off
dusty cushions. Luisa assumed these were what she'd
sleep on.

"I will bring blankets," Martin said, "and a brazier."

She smiled at him. "That would be kind. I think I must have been changed to suit the climate of my birth. I can stand more cold than most, but we do not have these extremes at home." A burst of childish laughter drew her to the window. A group of boys were engaged in a kicking game with a ball. The shadows were long now, the sun sinking swiftly behind the peaks. After all she had been through, the lingering light did not affect her much.

"I hope the *chelas* will not bother you," Martin said. "They like to play there between their lessons."

"*Chelas?*"

"That is what we call young boys. Older students are *trapas*."

"And you?" She turned to find him a step behind her.

His gaze remained on the scene outside. "I am also *trapa*. I have not been here very long. A year only. There were . . . reasons I could not join the lamasery as a boy. But someday I hope to be *gelong*." If she had not been watching closely, she would have missed his tiny scowl. "*Gelong* is a special ordination. My teacher will tell me when I am ready."

"You seem quite advanced to me. Your powers—"

He waved her words away with his hand. "Having power is not the same as being holy."

"Certainly not in my case," she said with a coaxing smile.

Martin did not return it. "I have been a monk before," he said. "That is why my progress has been swift."

"Before?"

"In previous lives." He glanced at her, weighing her response to this exotic claim. "My memories drew me back to this place, to my teacher. He has never failed to guide me, even at my most stubborn. Always he took me in."

Devotion rang in his voice. As if he heard it himself, and judged it unsuitable for display, he pulled himself straighter and stepped away. "Unless you have further need of me, I will take my leave."

She inclined her head. "I await your teacher's convenience."

He paused beneath the lintel of the door. "If I bolt this, will it keep you in?"

She could not restrain a laugh. No one else would have expected her to be honest. "Probably not, but I pose no immediate danger to your colleagues."

"I can bring food," he offered. "Tea."

"And I could pretend to drink it, but it would not sustain me."

She watched him take this in, his thoughtfulness an echo of his teacher.

"Will you become ill if you do not eat?" he asked.

"There is time before that happens."

"But you will not be comfortable."

"No," she agreed, "I will not be comfortable."

He nodded at this. She sensed he also heard what she had not said: that she was more likely to take what she needed by force than to allow herself to grow much weaker. At any rate, she would try. From what she had seen of him, the outcome of a confrontation between them would not be sure.

Only when he pulled the door shut behind him did she remember where she'd first seen eyes his shade of blue.

"Clearly," said *Geshe* Rinpoche, "the trader she met was your father. You must admit the coincidence is striking, as if Fate were taking a hand in bringing you together."

Martin grimaced. That John Moore had drawn the woman here was hardly a point in her favor. A curse, more like, if she proved as unworthy of trust as he. Martin touched the pale jade horse that stood on the table by his teacher's window. The carving was a gift from the Mongol khan, a thanks for an herbal healing. Nestled on a scarf beside it, the woman's offering curled like a snake. It was a *mala,* a Tibetan rosary, a string of one hundred eight shining emerald beads.

Apparently she had not lied about being a prosperous merchant.

"I saw no sign she lied at all," said his teacher, "though there was much she hid."

His comment did not surprise Martin. He and his guide were so attuned Geshe Rinpoche could often read his mind. He, of course, would not presume to read his teacher's.

"Haha," laughed Geshe Rinpoche, "now I am presumptuous!"

Martin turned, face hot, but his embarrassment faded in the waves of warmth he felt from his friend.

"Yes, *friend,*" Geshe agreed, "for, as I have told you, you and I have shared many lives—lives in which *I* was not always the teacher." He beamed up at Martin from the floor, still seated in the attitude of meditation, his legs crossed, his hands curled easily around his knees. After a moment, his smile softened into a look of deep compassion. "I know you are troubled. I would be surprised if you were not. After all, this woman is a living reminder that half of you belongs in another world."

"None of me belongs anywhere but here," Martin declared. "This is the country of my heart!"

Shamed by the passionate outburst, he hung his head.

"The wise man feels neither attachment nor aversion," reminded his master with the patience for which he was renowned.

"I'm sorry, rinpoche. You know I am trying to follow the Path."

His teacher released a quiet sigh. "Yes, I know you are trying. Too hard maybe. There are things I have seen in your future . . . But that is a talk for another day. You will choose your own way, as everyone does. For now you need only know that I have decided to help this woman. Tomorrow we will consult the medical lama. If our pilgrim is as earnest as she claims, I think we may accomplish much."

" 'We,' rinpoche?"

His teacher's eyes held more than a hint of mirth. "Yes, 'we.' My meditation has told me you must help!"

3

The medical lama was a tall storklike man, as gauntly ascetic as Martin and the abbot were robust. He reminded Luisa of scientists she had known, truth seekers who burned for nothing but uncovering hidden things. She did not fear her nature would disgust him, only that at some point he would want to cut her open and look inside.

They had gathered—she, Martin, the medical lama, and the abbot—in Geshe Rinpoche's surprisingly comfortable quarters. They'd come soon after midnight, not for Luisa's sake but because midnight was when the lamasery's day began. Every so often the chant of the morning service drifted up from the floors below. Distant as it was, the sound could not compete with the rapid-fire barrage of the medical lama's questions.

Once he had taken her pulse at various places on her body, he interrogated her about her diet, her sleep habits, her strengths and weaknesses alike. Naturally, Luisa was reluctant to discuss the latter. She understood, though, that she must enter into this process wholly. As Geshe Rinpoche said: a doctor could not diagnose half a patient. All must be known or the treatment would not suit.

After an hour of this, the medical lama was so excited he was pacing back and forth across the colorful woven rug. "And you say you can consume food, but not digest it?"

"Yes."

"But wine you can imbibe, as well as filtered juice and tea."

"I cannot drink Tibetan tea," she clarified with an automatic wrinkling of her nose. "The yak butter and soda disagree with me."

The medical lama stopped to press his hands before his mouth. "Yes. Those additions are too coarse, too material. Blood is food a human has transformed for you and wine is sunlight on which the fruit has done the work. Are you certain you do not remember how you were changed into what you are?"

"Quite certain," she said. "The procedure is wiped from our memory as soon as it is done. Only the elders possess the secret and I'm afraid it is a power they do not choose to share. I do not even know how many of them exist. Two, according to my master, but I often thought he told me less than he knew. However great or small their number, they are shadow figures who rarely walk among their broods."

"Pity," said the lama as if their presence would present no more than a chance for intriguing study. Luisa was beginning to see that nothing in this world or any other could cow these Tibetan monks. The medical lama pondered the ceiling, then turned to the holy abbot. "I must study her *tsakhor.* Please instruct her to undress."

"Scusi?" said Luisa with a mixture of amusement and affront. She might not be a fount of modesty, but once upon a time she had been. Even now she drew the line at standing naked before three men—at least, three men she

did not intend to bed. That Martin's presence inspired the most discomfort, she chose not to examine.

To her relief, the abbot intervened. "*Tsakhor* are wheels of force within your subtle body. Examining them will tell Lama Songpan how your inner *mandala* channels energy. Your clothing would interfere with the emanations."

"If I understood more than two words of that," Luisa said, "I might be convinced."

Martin frowned at her as the medical lama threw up his hands. Calm as ever, the abbot smiled. "You must forgive us," he said. "We do not think of nudity as you do. To us the body is simply the vehicle of the soul. But perhaps you have something simple beneath those clothes? An undergarment that would preserve your privacy?"

"I am wearing a smock," Luisa conceded, suddenly feeling foolish. These were men of science, not a science she understood but that did not make them satyrs in search of thrills. Nor, given her history, was she in any position to throw stones. With a shrug at her own illogic, she doffed her fur-lined cloak. Her Turkish-style tunic and trousers spurred no comment, since they were more familiar to her watchers than the ruff and farthingale she would have worn at home.

Hiding her discomposure under her briskest manner, she stepped from the embroidered trousers and undid the tunic's pearl-studded buttons. The sleeveless shift she wore beneath fell past her hips, a cobweb silk woven by her own *bottega,* the best cloth-working shop in all of Florence. The silk was fine enough to pull through a woman's ring, as soft and shimmering as smoke. For all the shield it provided, she might as well have removed it. She kept it, though, perversely determined to maintain at least a pretense of maidenly reserve—not that Martin was likely to be fooled.

She stopped disrobing once she'd peeled off her long black gloves. Feeling the cold now, she handed them to

Lama Songpan, who exclaimed in wonderment as he turned them back and forth.

"Not a crease," he marveled. "Not a single sign of wear. Her garments are as fresh as if she never had put them on."

The abbot hummed and rubbed his chin. Only Martin seemed to view her barely clothed body as more than a scientific object. He had crossed his arms as she undressed and, while his face remained impassive, his knuckles were nearly white. Knowing his gaze was on her abruptly heightened her awareness of her flesh.

Yes, she thought, you know I am a woman. A draft stirred her hair behind her back and a shiver swept her breasts. She felt a tightening at their tips as if they had been pinched by gentle fingers. Martin's eyes met hers, hot now, and not the least bit monkish. She remembered carvings she had seen in India's northern temples: gods with thick, rearing phalluses, their consorts small of waist and round of breast. Phantom hands seemed to grip her around the ribs, lifting her, impaling her even as she hung splay-legged in the air.

It was not a position with which she was familiar. Then she knew. These memories were not hers. Martin wanted her. He was imagining how she'd feel. Tiny beads of sweat dotted his brow.

Perhaps he did not, after all, prefer a woman to be a maid.

She smiled at him and he immediately turned away— not, however, before she had seen the flush that tinged his ears.

"I will light the brazier," he said. "She is cold."

Lama Songpan, of course, had missed this little drama. "Hm," he said, circling her slowly on the rug. "In the average person, the earth's energy is continually being tapped for the replenishment of the aura. The process is as automatic as the beating of the heart. But her aura's barriers to penetration are very strong. I suspect this must serve some protective function, for she is virtually cut off from these natural forces. Her heart *tsakhor* in particular is quite guarded."

"You say she is virtually cut off," repeated the abbot, "but not completely?"

The medical lama crouched and laid the tips of three bony fingers on her feet. "I sense a small draw. Very small. Under normal circumstances not enough to sustain a child."

"She must be taught to increase it," said the abbot.

Lama Songpan rose creakily erect. "Perhaps. I do not know if she can." He shrugged. "I would recommend a cautious attempt. Otherwise, I do not know what to suggest."

"Very well," said the abbot. "Thank you for your advice."

His subordinate bowed and retreated, leaving the three of them alone.

The sound of Martin stoking the brazier seemed very loud.

Geshe Rinpoche turned to watch his student. From the look on his face, Luisa could only assume the abbot didn't expect *her* to be watching *him*. For once, his expression was not that of an indulgent teacher. It was considering, rather, almost cool, as if Martin were a racehorse he meant to bet on.

An instant later she thought she must have imagined it because he smiled at Martin just as fondly as before. "Come away from there," he said, a hint of laughter in the words. "If you keep that up, our guest will think we mean to roast her."

Martin straightened so quickly he nearly dropped the poker. "I'm sorry, rinpoche. I—"

"Sh." His teacher patted the air with open hands. "It is all right. Everything is well."

To Luisa's surprise, she caught a hint of her own gift in the lama's voice. He was putting calm into Martin's head, calm that was not really there. Given the expression she had caught a glimpse of, she couldn't help wondering what his motives were.

But maybe she'd grown too cynical. The love the abbot felt for his student lit more than his eyes. Luisa was not easily deceived. She doubted she could have misread that.

"Come," said Geshe Rinpoche, waving Martin closer. "I want you to show our guest how to pull up energy from the earth."

"Me?" Martin's reluctance was emblazoned on his face.

The abbot chuckled. "It is only a request, Martin. You may refuse. But she is drawn to you," he said, proving he had seen their exchange, "as you are to her. This sympathy will make teaching her easier. I will stay, though, if you feel yourself in need of a chaperone."

The implication that he intended to leave startled Martin and Luisa both. Did the abbot's trust run so deep? Or was this meant as a test of his student's self-command? Either way, Luisa was not certain she approved. She drew herself straighter, only to find that Martin had done the same.

"It shall be as you wish," he said, his chin raised up with pride.

This pricked her temper in a different way. Martin himself wished to be alone with her. He simply did not want to admit it.

Martin tightened his jaw against further lapses of control. He might have succeeded had he not recalled those long black gloves peeling down her shapely arms. They were foreign, those gloves, Western, a symbol of everything he'd turned his back on.

Just as his father had turned his back on him.

The gloves' removal should not have inflamed him, should not have dried his mouth or thickened the restless organ between his legs. They should not have aroused him even more than the sight of her skin shining through her filmy shift. As to that, he should not have cared if she did resemble a goddess in a temple, her breasts impossibly buoyant, her belly a creamy curve. The body was simply a vehicle for experiencing earthly life. It was nothing to worship, nothing to lust over until one ached in every part.

But her beauty shattered his efforts to stay aloof. She was a lake at sunset, a mountain touched with gold. Her skin glowed in the lamplight and her hair . . . her hair made him clench his hands and break into a sweat. She smelled of violets and he wondered if all her kind shared this not-quite-human scent. But all her kind did not matter. Only she did. He wanted to burrow against her and breathe her in. She made him forget what he meant his life to be. For that alone he would have kept his distance.

That is, he would have if Geshe Rinpoche had not left them by themselves.

"Well," purred his tempter, "why don't you show me how it's done?"

You know how it is done, he thought, far better than I.

"You seem to know what goes where," she said with a satiny smile and a pointed glance at his loins.

The insinuation hardened him even further, his shock at odds with his arousal. She must have seen the pictures in his mind, the union of god and goddess in the flesh.

It seemed a travesty that this woman could read him as easily as his guide.

"You were thinking very hard," she explained, her amusement gentler than it might have been. "Perhaps you were too distracted to shield your mind. I will stop listening if you prefer."

"No." He squared his shoulders. "Shielding my thoughts will not erase them. And you will learn better if you put no walls between us."

"As you wish," she said.

Her lashes fell in acknowledgment, then rose. Despite his reluctance, he could not look away. Her eyes were a rich, pure green, the color of innocence and nature, of drives both simple and complex. He forced himself to meet their unspoken promise. Whatever her experience in the sexual arena, he was her equal in many others. More to the point, he had faced lust down before. He was a man, after all, not a rock.

"Here." He took her hand, slipping it under his upper robe. "Keep your palm pressed lightly above my heart."

Her pupils dilated at the contact and the softest of flushes stained her cheeks. She licked her lips. The tip of her tongue was small and sharp. In spite of his resolve, he was not prepared for the strength of his reaction. His penis jerked upward, just once but hard, as if her tongue had wet its tip. Without warning, he became aware of the steady throb of an artery in his neck.

Her fingernails pricked his skin like a kitten's claws.

"Your chest is very hard," she said huskily, then shook her head with impatience.

The gesture reminded him she was hungry; that to her a man was more than a partner for her bed. What would it be like, he wondered, to gratify all those needs at once?

"Focus on your hand," he instructed, striving to keep both their attention where it belonged. "You must concentrate on the energy swirling above my skin. It will feel like the currents of a lake in which you are submersed while very still, or perhaps like a sort of tingle. I am going to meditate, to draw on the life force of the earth. You should feel the flow change. If you are able, I want you to follow the current down."

He closed his eyes and began to breathe, to slow his heart and calm the heated rushing of his blood. The touch of her hand was oddly pleasant, light now and quiet, with none of the twitches untrained people tended to betray. Without being told, she matched her breathing to his own. In and hold. Out and rest. He slipped quickly into the state he sought, enjoying for a moment the familiar sensation of weightless peace. He was more than Martin now, and less. He was, at least in part, the simple spirit Martin hid.

Before his sense of self could dissolve completely, he drew up a skein of force, slowly, letting Luisa see how it was done, letting her feel the gradual brightening of the spinning *tsakhor* above his heart.

There, he said, sensing he did not need to speak aloud, *now I shall send the energy through the channels of my subtle body.*

She shivered as he began. "Oh," she whispered, "I feel it."

She stepped instinctively closer, her thighs and belly brushing the woven folds of his robe. It seemed natural to wrap her lightly in his arms, to slide his hand into the small of her silk-draped back. Her temple nestled easily beside his jaw. Though he had witnessed the act of love, he had never held a woman. She was soft, a yielding pleasure to the touch. His arousal returned as calmly as a dream. The energy he had drawn from the earth fed its intensity, though its progress seemed honey slow. Hungry for more, he nuzzled her shell-like ear.

"Follow," he murmured, "follow where I go."

Her body pressed his, her free hand raking languorously up his skull. Sparks seemed to rustle through the shortness of his hair. She had been cool but now she warmed, reminding him this was no ordinary woman. No doubt her flesh followed strange rules of its own. When she rose onto her toes, the tips of her breasts matched his. The change in position made a place for his erection between her thighs. His skin tightened, his organ struggling against its own pounding weight. He longed to press her more closely, longed to slip his ache inside her hidden warmth. Even through their clothes he could feel her softness.

But this was not where his mind was supposed to go. He forced it back to the demonstration. "Do you see?" he said. "Do you feel the current flow?"

She shuddered as if she, too, had to pull herself from the brink.

"I see," she said, "but I don't see how."

He tried to explain, in word and deed, but could not make her comprehend. Control she had in overflowing measure. She could regulate her breathing and her pulse as well as the most masterful yogin. What she could not do was change her state of mind. Nor could he feed energy into her himself. When he tried, it flowed around her aura like a stream of water around an egg. She seemed, as far as he could tell, utterly impermeable.

"I'm sorry," she said. "I simply do not understand."

He drew breath to try again, then let his hold fall away. Luisa stepped back as he did. They stared at each other. At once, he missed her body's warmth. As if she felt the same, she hugged her upper arms. Her breasts swelled into the neckline of her shift, beautiful in a different way now that his trance had begun to fade. His too-worldly organ pounded in complaint.

"I am sorry," he said. "Perhaps my concentration was not complete."

Her laugh was low and sweet. "If your concentration had been complete, I would have been insulted."

He could not resist smiling back, at least for a moment. "I will consult my guide. He may have another idea."

"We could try this again."

Her eyes sparkled with teasing like a glacier in the sun. He knew better than to meet their temptation long. Touching her, and having her touch him—for however laudable a purpose—had strengthened her carnal tug. He knew how it felt to hold her, and he wanted that feeling again.

"I should escort you to your room," he said. "Dawn is near. I know you will want to sleep."

"Yes." Her gaze dropped to the floor.

"Is something wrong?"

She looked up, her smile wry but gentle. "No. I was debating whether to invite you to join me. I have heard that some of your monks . . ." Her voice trailed off at the stiffening of his shoulders. "But not you, I take it. Please forgive me for being forward."

"It is nothing," he said, wanting to sound casual but knowing he did not. "The vow I wish to take would preclude me from experiencing sexual pleasures."

"And in return you would gain what?" Her gaze was curious. His fell to the carmine fullness of her mouth, then slid away.

"A deeper spirituality. A chance to reach nirvana." He caught the question in her eyes. "Nirvana means enlightenment, a knowledge of oneness with the universe, a freedom from the cycle of rebirth."

"Like our concept of heaven?"

"Something like," he said, though from what he knew of Christianity the differences were great. No harps played in a Buddhist's heaven. No one lazed about or sang in heavenly choirs. And no sinner went to hell. Hell was here. Hell was earth. If one learned one's lessons well, one could advance to a higher plane and continue one's progress there.

To his surprise, a very human grin flashed across her face. "You don't want to tell me what you are thinking," she said. "You're afraid you will offend me." With a spontaneity that made his throat tighten, she squeezed his upper arm. "You must not worry. I may not be pious but my faith is firm. A matter of faith, I suppose you'd say, since—despite some people's claim that I am a creature of the devil—I have never met him, no more than I've met God. My beliefs require no proof, nor do I fear to hear others speak of theirs, even at the risk they will change my mind."

Martin blinked at her. His teacher would have approved of her attitude. "In that case, I shall tell you what you wish."

"Good," she said, and strode jauntily toward her folded clothes.

Watching her bottom jiggle was a pleasure he could not bring himself to forgo.

Martin and his guide stood shoulder to shoulder on the lamasery roof, gazing out toward the soft green haze of the nearest valley. Soon spring would bring herds of *gowa* to graze on the growing grass; herds of pilgrims, too, though not so many as trekked to the holier shrine at Kangrin-poche. He found himself glad they were not here yet. They would have been a distraction from Luisa.

She interests me, he thought, facing the truth as he had been trained. She pulls not just at my body but at my mind.

What would it be like to see history unfold in a single incarnation? To love the material world so deeply one never wished to leave? Martin shook his head. Luisa claimed faith in a higher power, but she did not experience its reality even as much as the youngest *chela.* She could not touch the truth behind the illusion. All things were one and yet Luisa seemed alone: separate from both her God and her fellow beings. She should have been miserable. He could not understand why she was not.

No doubt he would have pondered the matter longer if his teacher had not spoken.

"Do you remember," he said, "when your family first came to Shisharovar?"

"I shall never forget it. I ran straight up the stairs and tried to kick two monks out of 'my' room."

The abbot's eyes crinkled at the corners. "You were quite adamant for an eight-year-old."

"But it was all so clear to me. This was where I belonged."

"Yes," said his guide, "it must have seemed so. I admit, I felt the tug of it myself: to keep my old friend by my side. It is comforting to find again what you have lost, almost as comforting as finding what you have forgotten you ever had."

Martin wondered what the abbot was getting at, but his placid profile gave no clue. He felt his forehead pleat together. "I know sixteen years was a long time to stay away, but I could not have remained here then, not when it meant abandoning my mother. My father leaving before my birth was bad enough. I could not betray her, too."

The abbot patted his rumpled sleeve. "I did not mean to imply your choice was wrong. You had a lifetime in this monastery, more than one. To mindlessly repeat what one has done before can hardly be considered progress."

"But I belong here now," Martin said. To his dismay, his voice made the words a question.

The abbot smiled. "I do not doubt we are all where we're meant to be. Speaking of which"—his teacher shot him a sidelong glance—"what do you think of your new student?"

Martin's hands were clasped on the stony ledge. He stared at them, amazed they did not bear the silky imprint of her curves. "I regret I could not help her."

"We have only begun. No one could expect the first attempt to succeed. And I am certain you did your best."

Had he, Martin wondered, or had he allowed the clamoring of his body to drown out a better, quieter guidance? "I am not certain—" he began.

The abbot broke in. "She is settled in her room?"

"Yes," he said, though he was perturbed by the interruption. "I brought her blankets as the sun was rising. When she took them, she stumbled and nearly fell. I think she is weaker than she is used to. I sat with her for a while, to ensure she was well, but I do not think she knew I was there. She slept strangely, like a fakir on a bed of nails. Her body was stiff and cold to touch. I did not see her breathe more than twice in a quarter hour."

He did not add that her appearance had unsettled him, more statue than corpse but disturbing all the same. For a moment, he had feared she died in truth. But then her chest had risen with a shallow inhalation. The relief he'd felt had not been logical, no more than his gentle stroking of her hair. That contact could have comforted only him.

"She seemed . . . vulnerable," he said, the confession as troubling as the memory.

"Indeed," mused his guide, "if one wished to destroy such creatures, clearly their rest would be the time to try."

"Sir!" Martin was shocked beyond holding his tongue. Among Buddhists, the taking of life, any life, was a powerful prohibition.

His teacher raised his brows. "I am not proposing we murder our guest, only that we prepare for any eventuality."

His tone was eminently reasonable. Martin schooled his pulse to a steadier rate. "Forgive me. I know you will do everything possible to prevent such a necessity from arising."

He did not understand the small, satisfied smile with which the abbot turned back to the view. He seemed almost smug as he spoke again. "I have thought of something else," he said, "a meditation that might bring down her walls. We can drug some wine to induce the proper mental state. It will be dangerous, of course. Inexperienced as she is, she might get lost in the visions the herbs produce."

"Most likely she *will* get lost," Martin said, aghast. "Even trained monks sometimes mistake a vision for reality. Such a thing could break her mind!"

"Not if she has a guide."

Martin caught his breath. He sensed his teacher was not proposing to fill that role himself. "No," he said, before he could think better of it. "Rinpoche, please do not ask that of me. That kind of journey is too intimate. I would— She is already—"

The abbot cocked his head at him. "I know your response to her is strong, perhaps as strong as your first response to Shisharovar?"

"My reaction to her has nothing in common with that. Nothing! I have no memories of her. None!"

"One does not need a memory for there to be a karmic link. Dread can be as much a sign of connection as love. In any case, I know you have not forgotten the importance of facing fears."

Martin's head could scarcely hang any lower. "No, rinpoche."

"Good. Because I am asking you to help our guest face hers. Fear is invariably the barrier to achievement. Once she overcomes it, I suspect we will progress."

Martin had no doubt of that, but to what they would progress he dared not imagine.

4

Despite the abbot's sponsorship, Luisa's presence unsettled the other inhabitants of the lamasery. Because of this, her tiny, isolated cell was transformed into a chamber for meditation. She was given a robe to wear, a simple wrap of woven cloth. Pots of incense were carried in and a *thangka,* or banner of painted silk, was hung across one wall. The image was grim to say the least: a fire-enshrouded demon with a necklace of severed heads.

"That is Hayagriva," Martin said, "the deity of awakened energy. Those figures he is trampling represent the concepts of self and personality, both illusions of the earthly world. Illusion, of course, is the source of all human suffering."

Luisa hummed in response and tried to blank her face. When Martin explained the purpose of this exercise, she had acknowledged the importance of facing one's deepest fears. She could not, however, imagine wanting to lose one's sense of self. She had spent her human life as little

more than a beast of burden: unseen and unheard, almost
too beaten down to think. Even after she was changed, her
master had to bully her into learning. *You need a strong
mind,* he'd said, *to face the dangers of the world. You, my
little peasant, will bow to no one else's child.*

However dubious that claim, she relished being someone now, someone who could read and reflect and affect
not just her own future but that of others. If her identity
was an illusion, she was not sure she wished to know.

Behind her, Martin chuckled. "I'm sorry," he said when
she turned around. "If you could see your expression . . .
The self we seek to lose is only the self that is not true. Yes,
we believe all beings are part of a greater whole, but within
each is an essence that is unique."

Luisa suspected their concept of uniqueness differed.
Rather than debate him, she walked her fingertips up his
arm. "You know," she said silkily, "you have a beautiful
smile. You would cut quite a swath if I brought you back
with me to Florence."

Martin's eyes widened. Clearly his experience with flir-
tation was very small. She looked forward to seeing him
blush, but a quiet dignity fell over his face instead. He
bowed from the waist. "I thank you for your words," he
said. "I am sure you meant to honor me."

To her amazement, heat prickled over her cheeks. His
politeness shamed her. They both knew her intent had been
not to honor but to tease.

"I do honor you," she said, meaning it sincerely. "I have
to remind myself how earnest you are, and that there is no
show in you. You are different from other churchmen I
have known."

"As you are different from other Europeans I have
known—and not just because of what you are." His smile
returned, bringing a gleam of admiration to his eyes. The
admiration seemed for her both as a person and a woman.

Uncomfortable with the pleasure this inspired, she
turned her eyes to the wine into which he was mixing

herbs. The cup that held the brew was skillfully worked silver studded with turquoise and coral stones. The merchant in her wondered if the monks had similar creations she might buy. But better, mayhap, not to ask about that now.

"I am not certain this will work," she warned. "*Upyr* tend to resist the effect of drugs."

"These are not ordinary drugs. My teacher prepared these herbs himself."

Well, she thought, her humor recovering: if his *teacher* had prepared them, naturally they would not fail!

With a little bow, he handed her the cup and watched her drink it down. The taste was peculiar, heavy, with an oily bitterness overlaid. Whatever Geshe Rinpoche had concocted, it was strong. Still, she felt nothing as Martin led her to the cushion-bed and helped her to lie down.

"You should relax," he said, lowering himself to the floor beside her. She turned her head to watch his descent, awed again by his grace. His legs seemed to fold naturally beneath him and his spine bore a straightness an emperor would envy. His face was unearthly in its calm. That one so young should have such self-possession, she could only marvel.

He touched her cheek with the back of one curled finger. "It may be a while before the medicine takes effect. Why don't you breathe with me, as you did before?"

As she took his advice, a hush settled around her, and a dangerously seductive comfort. In they drew the incense-laden air; out they blew the breath of life. To soothe her, Martin trailed the tips of three fingers along the naked inside of her arm. She doubted he would have done this if he'd known the pleasure *upyr* took in touch—and no touch more than that of humans. Her kind loved the stroke of mortal hands almost as much as loving it made them wary. To crave a thing was to give it power. But perhaps God meant the need to humble them. Perhaps she was foolish to try to pull her own fate free.

Just as she might have been foolish to trust these lamas and their herbs.

"I'm afraid I do not feel anything," she confessed, "apart from apprehension. I wish you would talk to me while we wait."

"What would you like to talk about?"

"Would you tell me how you came to be a monk?"

His smile was as gentle as his touch. "You could say it was karma. I was conceived here, as you may have guessed."

She nodded. "Your father was the English trader who was stranded in the pass. I do not suppose you knew him well."

Martin's only sign of emotion was a subtle tightening of his lips. "He did not remain here long enough to meet his son, though he knew he was going to have one."

"When I spoke with him in London," she said carefully, not certain he wished to hear, "he seemed the sort of man no one can hold. A restless soul. A foreign fever had spoilt his health and his sight was not what it had been. I think he resented getting older because he could only talk about his adventures. I cannot be sure—his was not an easy mind to read—but I think, underneath, he regretted the human ties he left behind."

"I assume he did not regret them enough to mention me and my mother."

"No," she admitted, "though when he spoke of Tibet, his eyes were warm." Martin pulled a face and she left the sensitive topic behind. "Tell me about your mother. She must have been special."

At once his expression softened. Luisa did not need her powers to know he loved her.

"She was a woman of Kham," he said, "a member of a traveling performance troupe. The Khampa have a reputation for being beautiful and fierce, and my mother was no exception. She once broke a man's nose because he kicked a dog. One punch and he was down. But her voice was like birds warbling in the spring. With her brothers and cousins she would sing and dance and do acrobatic feats on horseback. I remember going from place to place, riding in front of her in the saddle and feeling luckier than any prince. My mother was completely fearless. She always kept me safe."

Which suggested there had been something to keep him safe from. "It cannot have been easy growing up between two cultures," she said, thinking of children she had known, of how cruel they could be to anyone who was different.

The curve of her thoughts caught a piece of memory: Martin as a boy backed into an alley by half a dozen ill-fed youths. Clods of dirt bounced off his lifted arms while tears of fury rolled down his cheeks. How dare they say such things about his mother! She loved him better than all their mothers put together, *was* better than them all.

The violence of his anger shamed the boy he was. He would have hurt those children if he could, even knowing he was much luckier than they.

She broke the link, not wanting to betray what she had seen.

"I was loved," he said, "and I always knew that someday I would live here. From my first glimpse of Shisharovar on the peak, it was my beacon, the place where I knew I would find a home. When my mother died in a fall a year ago, I returned."

The memory seemed to leave no mark on his face but Luisa saw beneath the calm recital. He claimed his mother kept him safe and yet it was he who felt compelled to remain with her, delaying his dream until she could not need him anymore. How great an outcast had she been because of her choice of lovers? She had given Martin an English name. That suggested there had been more between her and his father than an affair. When John Moore went back to England, he must have cut a painful wound.

"You are very loyal," she said.

His robe rustled softly with his shrug. "It is not hard to

be loyal to those you love, nor to return to a cherished home."

Luisa's breath escaped in a snort. "I have known people who could barely be loyal to themselves."

"That is their loss," he said as if what he'd done were a common thing. He seemed not to know how rare his integrity was.

Feeling oddly off balance, she covered his stroking hand. "Do you really believe you lived before?"

"I have dreamed of events from other incarnations and later had them confirmed. I have recognized possessions I used to own and people whose paths crossed mine. Of course"—his gaze met hers with banked amusement—"I do not expect you to take this on my word. As you said: faith is a matter of faith. There can be no proof for those who wish to doubt. But tell me of you. I am curious to hear of the man who made you, the *upyr* elder."

"You mean Auriclus." Luisa laughed quietly in remembrance. "My master was tall and dark. Sinfully handsome. The perfect lure for a fisherman's work-worn wife. He had a face like a tragedian, as weary and sad as if he had taken the weight of the world upon his shoulders, as if compassion for every suffering creature suffused his breast. Our kind are good at illusion. Even now I don't know if his face spoke true."

"Did he seek you out?"

"In a way. But I noticed him before he noticed me. It was just past sunset in Florence. The sky was the color of lemons, the clouds like shreds of cotton dipped in blood. He was leaning on the quay, wrapped in his somber cloak, watching the scattered traffic on the Arno. I remember wondering what a fine man like him must think of those rivermen, with their talk and their swagger and their garish clothes. Looking back, he was probably judging which one would make the better meal. That day, though, I felt lower than I ever had. I was less than the boatmen, less than their whores, less than the pink-eyed goat who gave us milk.

"Auriclus must have heard my thoughts because he turned to me, not smiling, just staring as if I were a puzzle he wanted to work out. His attention shamed me so badly I scurried away as quickly as I could, but I saw him the next day at the well, and again the following evening as I left the *mercato*. I had a pomegranate in my basket, a treat I would have to hide when I got home. He blocked my way, then took the fruit to draw it to his nose. His expression when he inhaled was like a man in the throes of climax. When he spoke his voice was as husky as if he'd had one. It made me shiver to hear it, as much as did his words. He told me I smelled better than the fruit, as sweet and clean as summer grass. It was the first compliment anyone had ever paid me. He had me for the price of it, so cheaply was I willing to sell my soul.

"Only later did I learn he was not supposed to choose me. He had a rival, a student to whom he had ceded the world's great cities to avert a war. I was an experiment to him, an attempt to create a child who would be a bridge between their broods."

"Did it work?"

"I do not know. Oddly enough, I have never met another child he made. I suspect he would say he failed. I may have begun as a peasant but in the end I succumbed to civilization's lure."

"Did he change you that first day?"

She rolled her head in negation against the cushion. "No. But I dreamed of him after our meeting, erotic dreams that made me long for sleep. I was scrubbing the wash and imagining his kiss when I tore my husband's best shirt, the only one that had no mend. I hardly minded when Giulio came into the courtyard to beat me. I had a secret, you see, a hopeless fantasy that made me strong.

"And then it was not hopeless because Auriclus appeared, my dark avenging angel. One sweep of his arm tossed my husband against the wall. He plucked me up and away before I could think to resist. He said he wanted to fan the spark in my eyes to life. Said I deserved to be showered with jewels and draped in silk. I knew he must be a madman but I let him do as he wished because his words were food to me and because, by that point, I did not care what it might cost. My children were grown. I had nothing left to lose."

"Your husband had beaten you before."

"Yes," she said calmly. "To his mind, I was no different from a dog who had misbehaved."

To her surprise, this—rather than her confession of adultery—roused Martin's ire. "He should not have done that. That is not the proper way between man and wife."

Luisa spread her hands. "My husband suffered for his abuse, though he knew it not. I could have been more to him than I was. But that was long ago. Another life, as you would say." Her mouth curved in a grin. "Now I do not even wish him to roast in hell."

"You are wise to let your resentment go," Martin said. "Strong emotion can bind people together for many incarnations. Perhaps you will not have to meet him on earth again."

Luisa began to laugh, the idea striking her as funny. What would her husband say if he saw her now? Probably fall to his knees and pray. *Get thee behind me, spawn of Satan . . . but please seduce me before you go!*

The room rocked sideways with her laughter. Her head was so light she thought it might float away.

Martin smiled at her hilarity. "Yes," he said, "the herbs have begun their work. Just remember, you must focus your mind on what you fear."

But her mind was beyond her control, cut loose from its moorings like an oarless boat swept down a river. A landscape of images rolled by on the bank. The day her father sold her to her husband to clear a debt. The dirty clay of the hovel floor. One of her sons a wriggling bundle at her breast. So sweet they'd been, a tiny ray of love in her loveless life . . . until they'd grown into smaller versions of their father.

She'd tried to prevent it—how she'd tried!—but their world, or perhaps their natures, stopped their ears to the pleadings of a woman. Kindness was weakness to them; respect the reward for brutish force. She watched her youngest steal a toy from a neighbor's child. When she paddled his bottom, her husband beat her. *Let him learn,* he had roared, *how to live in a heartless world.* Her cheek stung from the blow, a tooth spit bloody into her hand. Suddenly, with the muddled logic of a dream, Auriclus held her close with his face in her golden hair, her only beauty that remained.

Come to me, he'd crooned. *Let me bring you to life again.*

His bite had all the tenderness of death, lancing the stored-up bitterness from her soul. She was nothing then, only pleasure, clinging to his shoulders until the rising, throbbing silence swept her under, into oblivion and forgetting. When she woke she was alive as she never had been before. Strong, healthy, beautiful. So beautiful. Without merit or justice, the power of attraction was simply hers.

For that alone she would have adored him, but her master had not let her. *Little Luisa,* he'd teased, *adore what you can be, not what you think I am.* Sometimes she thought he was sorry he'd made her. He would watch her at her books or her correspondence as if he could not fathom who she was. *Clever little monkey,* he'd call her then, though he might as well have said *clever monster.*

Fourteen years later he was gone, driven out of Florence—so he claimed—by the rise of one infamous book-burning monk. Savonarola had seduced the masses, taught them to hate their bodies and their minds. *I will kill him,* her sire explained. *If I do not leave, I will spray his maddened blood across the square.*

Auriclus did not care that his abandonment broke her

heart, that she had a growing business she could not leave. But at least he taught her not to kill. *Charm the humans,* he always said. *Charm them and set them free.*

But it was not the humans who tested her adherence to his rule. That honor went to the *upyr* she met on a trip to London. Until she surprised them hunting for sailors by the docks, she had not known her kind were there. She guessed at once that Auriclus had not made them. They had a sleeker look than he, a darker, more urbane smell.

Mindful of his warnings about Nim Wei's brood, she had approached them with all the diplomacy she possessed. Staying away had not been an option. She longed too fiercely for the company of her kind. Perhaps they could teach her what she sensed her master had neglected. Sadly, far from teaching her, the English circle met her overtures with hostility, calling her *spy* and forcing her into situations where, had she been less strong and quick, she easily might have died.

Only when they discovered her skill at commerce did they begin to warm. Money they respected, money and ambition.

Ironically, finding them made her lonelier than ever: feeling so separate from those she should have been most like. Auriclus cared for humans. These *upyr* saw them only as animals to exploit.

In defiance, she gathered a mortal harem, three youths flush with manhood who vied for the privilege of fulfilling her every need. That was the beginning of her love affair with humans. She chose them for what they could teach her, about life or business or the mysteries of the spirit. Minstrels succumbed to her, adventurers and dukes. To her delight, her business grew by leaps and bounds. She never thralled the humans with whom she dealt; that did not seem fair play. Even so, her conquests at the court of Suleiman were productive, winning her trading rights few could boast. If cleverness failed, she did not scruple to use her immortal body as her coin. Sometimes it bought her influence, other times merely pleasure.

She remembered the pleasure now: hands, kisses, the passion-tensed curves of sweat-streaked skin. Men driven to madness by desire. Gasping. Trembling. Nearly bursting with their lust. *Take me,* they'd plead as she slid her tongue along their veins. *Take anything you want.*

Someone gripped her jaw and turned her face to his. Martin. Beautiful, noble Martin.

"Luisa," he said, his voice commanding, "this is not the way to face your fears."

His eyes burned like the center of a flame. She reached for him, her hand falling limply against his chest. "I want you more," she whispered, the truth freed by the drug. "More than any man I have known."

His gaze went black. She saw him swallow, his Adam's apple moving strongly in his throat. Never mind his oath. Part of him wanted to bed her now.

"Luisa," he said, "remember why you are here."

She sighed like the melancholy finish of a tale. Then she did as he advised.

The drug was meant to let him into her mind, but what he found there shocked him. The things she had done with those men, those many men, were beyond what he imagined. He knew, naturally, what the procreative act entailed. Growing up as he had, in communal tents and inns, the basic facts had been his from an early age. The more esoteric were part of his education since coming to Shisharovar. After all, the union of male and female essences had spiritual meaning, too.

What he hadn't known was the sheer physical joy one could take in sensual exploration. He had been there with her, had felt her body vibrate with longing and her teeth itch teasingly in their sheaths. He'd wanted to be those men, touching her, tasting her, forging thickly into her sex.

One pair of hands was not enough. He wanted to be them all.

And the places she had traveled! Stormy seas. Opulent palaces. Even England, so wet and dreary compared to the sunny sparkle of Tibet, possessed an appeal he could not deny. What, he wondered, were those curious platelike collars women wore around their necks? For what reason did they hang those fancy curtains on their beds? Velvets he'd seen, and lustrous embroidered silks, the exotic, nested backdrop to her play.

She was almost childlike in her love of her possessions, though he could not deny a discriminating mind lay behind her greed. Here in Tibet, a painting was an act of worship; no artist would sign his name. In her homeland, Luisa had gleefully added luster to the name of scores. Da Vinci, Michelangelo, Ghirlandaio, and Titian: her patronage had helped them all.

In truth, her life was a foreign jewel. The more he turned it, the more the facets shone. He reminded himself these were temporal pleasures that would soon pass away. The key to Luisa's freedom lay far from such glittering bits of stone.

When she told him she wanted him, though, more than she had wanted any man, the admission struck a resounding triumph in his soul, momentarily drowning out truths he knew.

She lured him because of what she was, not in spite of it.

He needed all his strength to pull them back to the path. "Luisa," he said, "remember why you are here."

His words took swift effect. A flash cut across his vision like the blade of a Mongol butcher's knife. He saw her dream self. She held a baby to her breast—her son—warm and plump. Dread closed around him. Her lips brushed the infant's milky neck. Sweet neck. Soft neck. She tipped the wobbling head back in her palm. Her gaze locked to the tiny pulse. Her baby. Her sweet, warm, sleepy baby.

Her hunger rose like a mournful wail, like a sin she could not name.

This was her fear, the monster lurking in her shadows.

"No," she whispered in his mind and in the room.

She set the child on the floor where it gurgled at her wide-eyed, waving its dimpled arms. She had not touched it. She would not touch it, not even in a dream.

"Luisa," he said, knowing this darkness had to be faced.

She shook her head and backed away. *No,* she said, no sound to it. Then she turned on her heel and ran.

He called after her, warning her she'd get lost. She was not familiar with the geography of dreams: how fantasy and fear could parade as truth. To his dismay, she did not heed him. She ran up a narrow and odorous city street, carts in her way, horses, men in tight-fitting hose. She shoved past them, shouting, "Make way! Make way!" They bowed down to her beauty with sweeps of feathered hats. Ignoring them, she flung open a wooden door.

Her harem waited inside the richly appointed room, the same three youths he had seen before. They were old now, walking skeletons with skin, their hands reaching ghoulishly from lace and velvet sleeves. "Don't let us die," they beseeched. "Make us what you are."

She covered her eyes and moaned. She did not know how to change them. She was powerless to help.

The emptiness inside her yawned like a pit.

And then she grabbed them, one by one, drinking them dry. When their bodies fell to the Turkish carpet they were young again, not so young as when they'd graced her bed but strong men still. She had made a terrible mistake. She had killed them in their prime. She had been too hungry, too rash, too loathe to see them age and die. She stumbled to her knees.

This had to be a nightmare. It made no sense for her to have done this. She thought she heard Martin say *Yes, these are only phantoms* but there was blood on her hands.

Sins enough to make an angel weep. Her hands were red. Her mouth.

She gripped the gate that rose before her and pulled herself to her feet. The bars were strong. Immovable even to her. They glowed with opalescence as if they'd been carved of pearl. Martin felt her relax, her head dropping back in tired surrender.

Yes, she thought, I am dead now and they must let me in.

But the gate did not open. The wind blew through it and the sun shone on it but no one came to see.

"Speak to me," she demanded, clenching the pearly bars. "Tell me if I am damned."

The air stirred behind her. Luisa spun. A man stood on the path in a dusty robe. He was tall and bearded, gaunt but strong. His eyes looked out from soulful hollows, their expression too beautiful to bear. Martin sensed Luisa knew who he was.

"Answer me," she said in a choking voice. "If I'm damned, I want to know."

The man said nothing, only stared at her sadly. Despite his humble garb, a golden shimmer bathed his skin. He reminded Martin of a bodhisattva, a wise old soul come to earth again.

"I want the ability to choose how I live," she said. "I want my free will freed."

You chose, said the man. *You chose when you let your master make you what you are.*

With that, the man disappeared, and the gate, leaving nothing but grass and sun as far as the eye could see.

"I *am* damned then," she said.

She waited in the silence, empty of everything but despair. Tiny, starlike daisies waved in the gentle breeze. They did not care. No one cared but her. She thrust back her shoulders and firmed her jaw. If she was damned, so be it. She still had herself to answer to. She would live what life she had as she saw fit. If it ended, she would pay the price without demur. Her God had rejected her. Perhaps He had a right to. But from now on, her heart and mind were the only judges she would heed.

Something changed with her decision. Martin felt it. The silence was ringing, the air brightening as if the sun were rising yet again. Each blade of grass glowed like a gem. Luisa's edges were dissolving. The barrier that had guarded her heart for seeming ages had been destroyed. Energy burst from the earth in a golden flood. The sweetness as it rushed inside her was indescribable, a heady mix of light and love and—

And then the link between Luisa and Martin snapped.

Thrust from her vision, Martin gasped. Here, in the material world, Luisa's body began convulsing. Martin could scarcely hold her shoulders down. She had succeeded in tapping the auric resources of the earth. Now energy poured into her unchecked, energy she obviously was not meant to have. To Martin's finely honed senses the flow seemed an angry, caustic river. With every second, the violence of her struggles heightened. Tendons stood out on her neck. Her hands curled into claws.

"Luisa!" he cried, pulling her to his breast.

He could not connect their minds. The energy was a torrent that swept his attempts aside.

The door crashed open. Geshe Rinpoche had been alerted by his distress. "Speak to her," he panted, robe askew. "You must reach into her vision with your voice."

"But how can she hear?"

"Those in trances still hear those they love," said his teacher. "You must have faith."

Martin could not refuse to try. "Luisa," he said, rocking her gently in his arms, "what you are doing is not safe. I know it feels lovely in your dream. I know it feels as if your angels had at last welcomed you home. But if you do not come back, your physical self will die. You said you did not want that. You said you loved your life."

His throat choked up but he forced himself to speak. "I

do not wish to lose you, Luisa. I wish . . . I wish to get to know you on this plane, in this life. Please do not make me wait. Please come back to me now."

With an abruptness that shocked him, her convulsions stopped. Her body relaxed, then went completely still.

He could not help but fear she died.

"Lay her down," instructed his teacher.

Reluctantly Martin did so. She was gaunt, her beauty burned thin, her skin as white and chill as snow. She looked even less human than when she slept.

The abbot knelt by her other side. "Luisa," he said commandingly, and laid both hands atop her heart. Martin knew he was trying to use his healing powers.

For one long, dark moment, nothing happened. She is gone, he thought, even as his mind groaned in denial. Then, like a person saved from drowning, she drew a ragged breath. Martin nearly collapsed in relief. Her eyelids fluttered. She licked her lips. "What— What happened?"

Though she looked at Martin, the abbot answered. "I misjudged, I'm afraid. That energy was poison to you. You must not try to take it again."

"Poison . . ." A slow, shining tear rolled down her cheek.

Martin knew what she was thinking: that all that love was not for her. She did not understand her vision had been a creation of her mind. No holy messenger had rejected her. No gates of heaven had been closed.

Throat tight, he brushed her tear away. "Luisa, the things you saw were just a dream. Your god, if he exists and if he is the source of what we call the energy of the earth, gives this bounty equally to saint and sinner. I do not know why you could not drink, but it is no judgment against your soul, merely an experiment that went awry— as if I were to eat a horse's hay."

She smiled but the attempt was weak. "Tired," she murmured, her eyes drifting shut. "Need to sleep."

Martin and his teacher watched her draw a score of breaths. Then, their thoughts in accord, they stepped quietly away.

The abbot rubbed his chin. "This troubles me," he said. "We have left her weaker than before. Even if I found another method to attempt, I am not sure she could withstand it. I am not even sure she would survive a journey home. She must feed, Martin, in the manner of her kind."

"We cannot ask any of the monks to let her drink."

"No," the abbot agreed, "we cannot"

Martin's heart thumped in his chest. He knew what the abbot was asking and he knew he could refuse. If he did not offer up his blood, Martin had no doubt his guide would volunteer. Even if it killed him, Geshe Rinpoche would do it. That was the kind of man his teacher was.

"She will put me in her thrall," Martin said, the rasp of words not quite a protest.

His teacher's gaze was steady. "I believe you are strong enough to resist her."

If I *want* to resist her, Martin thought, far from certain that he did. He remembered Luisa's harem, the slide of her slim, pale hands along straining skin. How easy it would be, how tempting, to make her *upyr* magic his excuse for giving in.

Then a flash of intuition struck. "This is a test," he said. "You want to know if I am worthy to take my vow."

His teacher neither confirmed nor denied the guess. He put his hand on Martin's arm. "You must decide soon," he said. "I do not think our visitor has much time."

5

Martin's strong arms lifted her from the cushions and eased her onto his lap. Even that small motion made the room spin around her head. She moaned against the musty sweetness of his robes, smelling incense and skin and an acrid touch of fear.

She thought the fear must be for her.

"Shh," he soothed. One hand stroked the pale gold curtain of her hair while the other cradled her back. He pressed her mouth to his neck. "Drink."

The word made her jerk with longing. She drew back from temptation and stared.

His gaze evaded hers. "I know you've been trying not to, but you are weak."

"Martin . . ."

"I know you will not hurt me." The words were fierce. "Just . . ."

"Just?"

"Please do not make me do things I would not wish."

Then she understood. Smiling softly, she flattened her palm against his smoothly shaven cheek. His skin was so warm it seemed to burn, its color rich against the whiteness of her hand. His eyes glittered in the dimness, wavering between trust and doubt. "Martin, when blood is offered freely an *upyr* does not, cannot, suborn her victim's will."

"She cannot?"

She combed his bristled hair around his ear. "No."

"Will you take very much?"

Luisa shuddered, aroused—or frightened—by a lingering fragment of her dream. "Enough to make you weak. But only for a while. When you recover you will be stronger than before, more resistant to harm or illness. The effect does not last forever: a week, possibly longer."

"No wonder those men—" He closed his mouth and flushed. "Forgive me. I did not mean to suggest you had no other charms."

"Were you thinking I took my harem against their will?"

"Well, I am sure you did not have to force them into your bed."

She laughed beneath her breath. "Thank you for that, though my scruples have not always been so fine. In this instance, I assure you their thrall was no more than any healthy young male might feel when an attractive woman offers him a sexual adventure. I may have added a few compulsions, of course, to ensure they did not speak of me where they should not."

"I imagine they were easier to control because they were young."

She saw he meant this as an observation and not an insult, but she squirmed beneath it nonetheless. "How uncomfortably perceptive you are! Yes, older men—or for that matter, younger men with strength of mind—are difficult to influence without the added coercion of a bite. As the years passed, I found I did not like to use that means."

"Friendship can be lonely when it is forced, or when it is not with an equal."

Tears sprang to her eyes at his understanding. Since her brush with death, Luisa had felt strangely vulnerable, not in body but in spirit—as if her heart had in truth been opened by her dream. His simple statement reached into the raw place, putting into words the yearning of many years.

"I have been lonely," she admitted. "That is why your . . . consideration for me means the world."

He smiled, an unexpectedly boyish grin. Seeing it, she was happy despite the danger to them both—not to mention to the achievement of her desire. Assurances aside, stopping before she hurt him would not be easy. Too much time had passed since she last fed and there were too many ways she found him appealing. With one nail she traced the strong blue thread that marked his neck. Her throat tightened. "Maybe I should not do this."

"My master says you must feed." Though Martin's expression was stubborn, worry lay beneath: worry and an intriguing glimmer of guilt. A muscle bunched in his jaw. "I want you to," he said, his innate honesty forcing the gruff admission. "I am curious to know how it feels."

She could not control the quickening of her pulse. So. He was curious. She skated her fingers down his vein and wet her lips. "It hurts for a moment, for the penetration." She lifted her eyes to his. "After that, it is erotic. Taking blood is the most intimate act a child of midnight can perform."

"More intimate than sex?"

His voice was husky. A quick, sharp sting told her her teeth had sharpened to feeding length. "More intimate than sex," she agreed, "though drawing what we need from another's veins awakens that desire as well."

"You will refrain from indulging it, though, won't you?"

"You may not want me to. Humans find the act exciting, too."

"I have faced attraction before. I am not afraid."

But he should have been. Martin could not guess how strong the urge to join could be, a frenzy of lust that sometimes hours of bed play could not sate.

"My resolve is strong," he said, sensing her hesitance. "I do not fear to put it to the test."

Her smile, gentle as it was, must have been too knowing. His eyes narrowed and he yanked the wrap of his robe halfway down his front. Her smile froze as her body heated. His muscles were tight and flat, their edges chiseled, their development perfectly balanced from sternum to shoulder cap. His chest hair was sparser than a European's, sheer dark swirls that clung to his flawless olive skin. His nipples were flushed and delicately erect. Yearning to pinch them, she curled her nails into her palms.

"Drink," he ordered in a tone that brooked no denial.

She had not the willpower to resist. With a moan she pressed her mouth to his neck, open, breathing heat and soul-deep need. His grip tightened on her shoulders but he did not push away. She licked him, dragging her tongue up the beating vein until a shiver swept his frame. He was hers now. She set her teeth against him and bit down.

Blood flowed, filling her mouth with power and life and will as strong as sugared ginger to her tongue. Here was vigor. Here was hot male strength. Enthralled by his taste, she drew on him, wrapping her arms with grateful fervor around his back. Oh, it was good to be close, better than good. Martin seemed to agree. Gasping her name, he slid his hand down her arching spine. She knew he was losing control but she could not hold back. She pushed even tighter to his chest. Her breasts flattened beneath her robe, her nipples as hard as his. When she writhed against him, he murmured what sounded like a prayer.

It was almost all she wanted, this evidence of his desire. Strength rushed into her with each swallow. She wanted to take him inside her, every throbbing, rigid inch. Desperate to touch his skin, she pushed her hand under his robe. The small of his back was smooth and dewed with sweat. She gripped his narrow buttock. His moan was even sweeter than his blood. Greed swamped her: to have him, to drink him down. Her heart pounded violently in alarm. With a groan of reluctance, she tore her mouth away.

"No," he said, a hiss that drew her eyes to his. His pupils were shining jet within rings of azure flame. She could tell he was dazed but not as deeply as most humans would have been. His protest was not the effect of any thrall. She had not taken anything he did not freely give. As if to assure her of this, he cupped her blood-flushed cheek.

"Let me make you strong. You haven't taken half of what I can offer. Here." He pressed her palm to his breast, his voice sinking to a growl. "Bite me here. Slowly. I want you to make it last."

A rush of moisture squeezed from the tender hollow between her legs. "Slowly," she repeated, the word shaking on her lips.

He nodded, shyness in it, but pride as well. His chin lifted in silent challenge. He did not care how others did this. He was asking for what he wished, drawing the veil from secrets most lovers hid. She thought she had never been so moved by someone's trust. She knew she could not refuse. "Just a little more," she agreed, then flashed a grin. "By sips."

She bit him slowly this time, letting him savor the dull cold sting of breaking skin. From what she had seen of his country, not to mention the discipline of the monks, she was not surprised he would welcome a little pain. It was a test to him, a hurdle to rise above. True to her expectations, he shuddered with enjoyment as her tongue swept his tightened nipple. Knowing he liked this, she suckled him as she drank. His breath came more harshly and his muscles tensed. His aura pricked like fire where it touched hers.

But she wanted to offer him more than this. She moved her second hand to the bend between his torso and his thigh. He flinched but did not withdraw. Slowly, giving him time to stop her, she shifted her caress to the rigid swelling where his erection pushed out his robe. Its crown bumped against his belly, its long thick ridge an invitation to measure how much he'd fill. A plenitude, she decided, her body softening deep inside. He was already too hard to get any harder. She could tell from the way his shaft resisted her gentle squeeze. He sighed at the pressure as if he'd been waiting an eternity to feel it. Taking this as permission, she slipped her hand beneath the cloth and held him bare.

The shock of Luisa's touch was not one for which he could have prepared. Her warmth, her strength, her devastating knowledge of male desire combined to set his nerves ablaze. His body tightened in every muscle, then melted with delight. He knew he ought to stop her; no man could resist this temptation long. Instead he closed his eyes and let his head drop on his neck. She was rubbing his aching length, her fingers tightening and releasing in a rhythm that made him wonder just how long such pleasure could be borne.

In all his life he had barely touched himself. Now those years of denied sensations seemed to squeeze together into the present, into those burning inches of stiffened flesh. Waves of rapture rolled through him, surging then ebbing, only to gather higher than before. He knew if she did not stop he would unravel like the sexual novice that he was.

But she had no mercy for his fears. Shifting in his lap, she began to draw on his organ with both hands. The strength of her hold pulled him outward from his body, his testicles drawn up, his tip seeming to burn and prickle each time her fingers tugged its rim. He was going to explode. He was going to burst like a Chinese rocket. Sweat ran into his eyes as he fought the desperate urge. The sounds he made were hardly human.

He had thought he knew desire; had believed he felt it when the young girls and the widows tried to lure him into their tents. They had smiled for him and tossed their braided hair. They had wagged their hips and let him see them with other men. To them, he was a challenge or a game: the handsome half Khampa who wanted to be a monk. Once or twice he had been tempted but never like this, never with more than his body.

This was a lust to sear the soul.

He cried out as she left his breast, and again as she found his mouth. Oh, the taste of her, the feel! She had to lead the kiss, his astonished, enchanting first. It was a mating, he realized, of lips and teeth and tongue. Sensation multiplied as they parried, wetly, sweetly. He tasted a hint of copper, then only her. Her incisors were sharp but they did not cut him.

So lost was he in pleasure that his body jerked at an unexpected touch. She had curled her thumb over the swollen crest of his erection, pressing the tiny slit as if to block his impending end. The move made him excruciatingly aware of the pressure that was building in his scrotum. An uncontrollable tremor seized his limbs.

"Touch me," she gasped against his cheek. "Put your hand between my legs."

Heart thumping wildly, he fumbled through sleek warm folds and tangled curls. This was a woman's *yoni*. This was a lover's prize. Her liquid welcome was a wonder as deep as any he had found through meditation. He had called forth her arousal. *He* had. He slid two fingers through the constriction at her gate and moaned at her forceful clasp. She was soft inside, as soft as the lotus flower most venerated by the sutras. To his gratified relief, her *madana-chatra* did indeed project like a plantain root from the upper petals of her sex.

Burnishing the tiny organ with his thumb, he drew his fingers in and out. The sound of her wetness made him swell even fuller with excitement. Her hand gentled on his shaft, but it did not help. His skin was as sensitive as if its nerves had been multiplied by ten. He was not sure he could bear this painful pleasure a second more.

"Your *kama-salila* is very generous," he said through gritted teeth, struggling to distract himself with words.

She laughed, a beguiling, throaty sound, and pushed her sheath up his hand. "I hope that is a good thing."

"It is recommended that the woman be wet in order for the man's organ to slide easily in the narrow—"

She cut him off with a kiss. He could not think at all then, except to wish most heartily that his penis and not his fingers were clasped inside her fragrant depths. As if she knew, her hand tightened on the sensitive ring beneath his crest.

"Move with me," she said. "Pretend that we are joined."

He did as she directed, tightening his hindquarters to push himself through her hold. Without even trying they began to breathe together, gasping in tandem, tensing in tandem, as the end he craved and wished would last forever rumbled like an avalanche into view.

It was a panic in him, to make it last, to engrave the moment in his mind. He showered her face with kisses, a gesture he could not withhold.

"Sweet Luisa," he said, her name a cry for things he'd lost so long ago their only trace was a tangled hurt. He nuzzled her swollen nipple, drawing it with her robe between his teeth.

"Take it," she said, tearing the wool away with her other hand. "Take what you want." She arched up to him and gave him what he longed for. The tip of her breast was softer than silk against his tongue. She moaned as he sucked and the sound was flames licking through his skin.

The final rise was more intense than he had dreamed a man could feel. He hung on a cutting wire, its promise of imminent fall sublime. To plummet, to give in . . . But wrong as the physical pleasure was, it was not enough. His body demanded more. Union. Penetration. He had no mind then; he only had desire.

With a curse of resignation, he wrenched his mouth away.

"I cannot pretend," he said harshly, drawing his fingers from her sweetly clinging sex. "I belong inside you."

"No. Don't relinquish your vow for me." Her hand pressed his fingers back to her softness and her mouth opened on his neck. He was dizzy, confused. Her tongue trembled briefly on his skin. "Now. Come with me now."

She did not even have to bite him. Energy rushed up through his feet, a flood of unstoppable golden-white. He felt the barrier around her aura give, swirling and blending into his. She caught her breath, but not in pain. He had a second to wonder at her reaction and then his climax burst like a never-ending fountain. One instant his shaft was pure, burning steel, the next a convulsing instrument of bliss. His groan echoed through the little chamber, as strange to his ears as this ecstasy was to his body. Again the tight, squeezing shock lanced through him, again, again, a release so deep it seemed to rake his soul.

He did not realize she had joined him until the last flickering pull of her sheath tugged at his hand.

She wriggled as it faded and relaxed against him, her mouth curled, her cheeks rosy, her eyes glowing like emeralds fringed with gold. He could not contain a flush of pride at her satisfaction. His head was light but strangely clear. Already his weakness was fading. Then he looked down at the much diminished organ she still held in her hand. She was petting it as if she relished its sticky softness. So much for pride, he thought.

It seemed important to acknowledge what she had done. "I must thank you," he said. "I would have taken you if you had not stopped me."

She batted her lashes and dragged one sticky finger across her tongue. The gesture nearly put him in a trance.

"Maybe I did save you," she said playfully. "And maybe you would have found your strength."

He shook his head to clear it. "You should not give me more credit than I deserve."

Her eyes hooded as if she were embarrassed to have been caught doing him a kindness. "I know you are not used to facing urges of that strength. It seemed unfair to let you do something you would regret. Especially when I still need your help."

Martin did not believe her explanation, though he chose to pretend he did. "I do not know what else I can try. Unless . . ." He pushed up from her, recalling the way her aura had momentarily seemed to welcome his. He knew orgasm called up a special energy from the earth, an energy transmuted by the nature of the connection between the partners.

All of which had been academic up till now. But if Luisa could utilize that special force, without ill effect, it could prove an alternate source of sustenance. Lost in thought, he rubbed the sides of his mouth, remembering too late that her scent clung to his fingers. To his embarrassment, his organ twitched and began to lengthen.

"Unless what?" she prompted.

He shook his head and rose, shaking his robe down as he did. The *chuba*'s fall was not as straight as it should have been. Frowning, he shoved his arms back in the sleeves. Apparently one encounter would not sate this new appetite. "It is only a thought," he said. "I do not wish to raise false hopes."

"Or anything else," she said, with a pointed glance toward the tenting wool.

Responding with dignity was a challenge but he managed as best he could. "The sun will rise soon," he said. "I am sure you want to rest."

He left her lolling on the cushions, more beautiful than a goddess, more nettlesome than a fly. He did not tell her he went to consult his guide; indeed, he hardly wished to admit to himself what he planned to do. Fairness, however, demanded he speak to the abbot immediately.

If Martin's theory had the slightest chance of being true, Geshe Rinpoche would know.

He found his teacher in the storeroom with the steward. They had pulled two dusty cushions together and sat, hunched and cross-legged, before a fat horizontal book. The single window cast a dawn gray light over their heads. Accounting, said their serious faces, is not a business for the faint of heart. Certainly it was not a small business. The consumption of barley, tea, butter, and other staples by nearly two hundred souls had to be closely tracked. Moreover, Shisharovar did not live by pilgrims' gifts alone. The lamasery was famed for its expertly fashioned religious objects—prayer wheels, butter lamps, *malas*—both in silver and in brass. Like most of the brothers, Martin had taken part in the various stages of production, though his gift was not that of a craftsman.

No, he thought sourly, his gift was the one he had so recently put at risk. His mind was strong; it could focus like a sunbeam through a lens of glass. Such a mind was meant to serve his country and his faith. If he let his carnal urges steal the upper hand, he would waste the very talent that gave him worth.

Or so he might have said before. Chewing his lip, he stared at his felt-topped boots. Luisa also had a right to expect his aid. If he failed to put his gift at her service, when he might be her only chance, would not the omission taint any good he might do later on? She had given much to come here, to learn to live a better life, and she had done so with no one to set her a good example. From what he had seen, the one who made her barely deserved the name of teacher. Certainly he was no beloved guide like Geshe Rinpoche. Martin admired her for forging her own morals, strange as he might find them, in a less than moral world. She deserved a chance to achieve her dream.

Just as he was about to clear his throat, the abbot looked up from the accounts.

"Ah, Martin," he said, with the smile that never failed to warm his pupil's heart, "we are finished here. Please come in."

"You are *not* finished," Martin said, reading the steward's startled look.

The abbot laughed. "Well, we are surely in need of tea. Do have a break, Myingmar. I will send the *chela* for you when Martin and I are done."

The steward bowed and left, his obvious eagerness at the prospect of nourishment drawing another smile from Martin's guide. The boy who had been sleeping in the corner scurried off to get them a pot and then Martin and his teacher were alone.

The abbot cocked one wispy brow in his direction. "I must say, you look none the worse for wear. I trust your sacrifice was not too onerous."

"I am well," Martin admitted. He took the cushion the steward had just left. As Luisa promised, his body hummed with vigor. He felt both relaxed and refreshed, his spine loose, his concentration crystal clear. Which did not mean what he had done deserved reward.

"You have a confession," guessed the abbot.

Only a day ago, Martin would have hung his head in shame. An impulse he did not understand kept it upright now. "Of a sort," he said. "Mostly I am here because I require advice."

He explained his theory that the power lovers drew from sex might be changed enough for Luisa to imbibe. Direct sunlight would burn but, as the ripening of a grape transformed its rays to healthful wine, so might lovemaking transform the forces of the earth—if Luisa had a partner who knew how to channel them.

"I felt her aura give," he said, "just as it did during her vision. I admit, the amount of energy that entered was small, but it did not seem to harm her. If what I suspect is true, this could serve as an alternate form of sustenance, perhaps even a replacement for drinking blood. Once she experiences the process in its entirety, she should be able to repeat it."

"An intriguing notion." The abbot tapped his ink-stained quill against the low, scratched surface of the desk. "But I do not think we can ask another man to try this. Even assuming she would accept a substitute, she might enspell him. Do you know, we had to barricade Brother Dhondrup in his cell? He kept begging us to let him serve her. Said he lived to be her slave." Brother Dhondrup was the monk Luisa had bitten on her arrival. Martin thought he had saved him from the brunt of her influence, but apparently her pull was stronger than he had known.

"He has not yet recovered?" he asked as he tried to tamp down his unease.

"He is beginning to, though I suspect her beauty dazzled him as much as her *upyr* power. She is not a woman a man could easily forget."

"No," Martin conceded, aware of the abbot's watchful gaze. Geshe Rinpoche was searching him, though for what he did not know. With an emotion akin to dismay, he realized Luisa's beauty was not what called to him most strongly now. She had become a person to him, her outer appearance not nearly as alluring as her inner fire. He thought of jewels again, of all those facets shining in the night.

When he looked outward, the abbot's attention was still on him. "If your theory is to be tested," he said, "you are the only one who can try."

Martin felt as if his guide had kicked him in the belly. Did Geshe Rinpoche place so low a value on his student's continued progress on the Path? Never mind his *gelong* vow, didn't he care that Luisa had the potential to tempt Martin far away? If her only attraction were carnal pleasure, Martin thought he might have fought. But she also offered adventure and mystery and, most persuasive of all, the chance to share an affection whose appeal he had just begun to savor.

Amazing as it seemed, Luisa *liked* him.

Didn't his guide understand how powerful that was to one who had rarely felt accepted? Or did some other motivation lay behind his actions, some agenda Martin was too slow to comprehend?

"Come," the abbot chided gently, "you cannot mean to say you expected, or even wanted, me to assign another lama to this task."

Martin knew his teacher spoke the truth. The thought of anyone else touching Luisa, knowing Luisa's innermost essence, was intensely repellent. "Of course not," he said, then huffed out a harried breath. "But I thought you might at least try to discourage me."

"When have I stood between you and an important choice?"

Martin had to admit he never had and yet his guide seemed oddly eager for him to risk his calling. That was what he could not understand, what seemed a betrayal of their bond.

Before he could find the words to explain, the abbot clasped Martin's upper arms. The growing light picked out the wind-worn lines around his eyes, eyes that shone as black as water in a cave. Martin knew his teacher's face better than he knew his own, but in that moment he might as well have been a stranger.

"Are you so certain," said the abbot, "that this course will lead you from the road you were meant to take? Maybe if you taste what you are proposing to give up, your sacrifice will have more meaning. Or maybe you will decide you don't want to be celibate after all. You know our sect does not require it, just as you know many yogins have taken lovers. Your spiritual progress need not be hampered unless you let it."

But I fear I will let it, Martin wanted to cry. I fear I will trade everything for her.

This, however, was not the abbot's problem.

"You must meditate," he said. "The answer will come."

The suggestion was clearly a dismissal. Martin rose, and bowed, and withdrew toward the door on less than steady legs. He would do as his guide advised. He would meditate. He only wished an answer existed that would be wholly good.

His teacher halted him at the threshold. "Your heart," he said, "is not your weakest organ. You should trust it, old friend. Through many lives it has not misled you."

Martin's throat was too thick to speak but he nodded in acknowledgment.

The abbot, it seemed, already knew what he wanted his choice to be.

6

Luisa rose from her bed shortly after sunset. Though the butter lamps had burned out, the light of the stars was enough for her *upyr* eyes. Catlike, she stretched her arms and spine. She had enjoyed her first sound sleep since arriving in Tibet. Her first meal, as well, not to mention her first good—

But her mind stopped short of calling what she had shared with Martin her first good tupping. Their encounter had been more rewarding than she expected, if also less than she desired.

Frowning, she straightened her robe and ran her fingers through her waist-length hair. No more than this was required to keep her tidy. What Martin called her aura kept her person and her clothes in immaculate condition—though she had never lost her fondness for a lengthy soak. She would treat herself to one, she vowed, the minute she got home.

But thoughts of Firenze made her restless. Swinging her

cloak around her shoulders, she headed for the door. Apparently the nervous monk who stood outside was there for her protection: he let her pass without a word.

Not wishing to disturb anyone else, she turned her steps down the abandoned corridor. The stiff yakhide soles of her boots made shushing sweeps through the eddies of frosted snow. Beneath its powdering the stones were cracked. Had this wing been new when Martin first lived in Shisharovar? Had he wandered down this hall as she did? Had his mind been filled with different dreams?

She smiled at the ease with which she had accepted his beliefs. But how could she not? Since turning *upyr* she had seen more marvels than she could count.

A narrow stairway led her upward, so dark even she had to feel her way by touch. The sound of air whistling drew her higher. Finally, after shouldering a heavy door aside, she reached the roof. Her breath caught at the vista that stretched before her: range upon range of rugged snow-capped mountains, their peaks milky and effulgent, their shadows streaks of sapphire ink. In every direction the towering crags marched over the horizon, as if their bulk filled all the world. The sky above them was the purest black she'd ever seen. Against its backdrop the stars seemed not like diamonds but pinprick holes through which the light of some higher sphere was breaking through.

God is here, they seemed to say, a greater god than humans can conceive.

Luisa felt simultaneously dwarfed and exhilarated. How can I exist? she thought. How can any creature? Why would God need more than the beauty of this night?

She stepped through the shallow drifted snow, past gilded, onion-peaked structures that rose from blocks of stone. From pedestal to peak the things were twice her height and strung one to another with lines of wind-torn prayer flags. They exuded an eerie vibration as she passed. Were these the reliquaries her native guide had called *chortens*: containers for the possessions, and occasionally the remains, of holy abbots? Dorje had claimed the bodies were boiled in yak butter and salted to preserve them. The practice seemed bizarre, but who was she to judge? Whatever lay inside them, the structures must be some sort of shrine. They reminded her of churches she had known. The lamas' beliefs had not quite let their contents die.

Reaching the wall at the perimeter of the roof, she crossed her arms atop the ledge. As she did, images of her sire came to her mind. What, she wondered, would Auriclus make of her present quest? For that matter, who would she be if he had not left her? If he had taught her more of his secrets, would her powers now be so great these lamas would be in awe of her? Would she even care about a thing like not living off stolen blood?

Martin would care, she thought, then shook her head at how easily the monk filled her awareness. Her own father she barely recalled, so completely had her master's shadow subsumed his. But even Auriclus could not obscure the shadow Martin threw.

Ever since he had withdrawn from her cell the night before, she had sensed him teetering on the cusp of a decision, one that would affect not just her mission but whatever chance they had of being more than a petitioner and her guide.

Troubled, she joined her hands in an attitude of prayer. I want that too much, she thought. I want everything from him too much. She closed her eyes, then opened them to the sky. The truth was as undeniable as the stars. She loved him. For the second time in her long *upyr* life, and perhaps for the first time that was real, Luisa del Fiore was in love.

She had not anticipated this development. How could she? Martin was no father figure like Auriclus. Nor was he a hedonist, despite having shown himself ready enough for pleasure the night before. He had a better heart than she did, and probably a stronger mind. God knew his soul was purer and yet, when she was with him, when she looked into his incomparable gentian eyes, she felt not diminished but complete.

He had never judged her. In truth, she could tell that he admired her.

Which was all the more reason she must not cause his fall.

Let him go, she thought, tightening her jaw against the blooming pain. Stop tempting him and you'll have earned your freedom from the blood. She could make it a bargain with the angels. Surely one good deed was not too much to ask.

And if the good deed gained her nothing, what then?

Luisa forced her muscles to relax. She stared at the mountains, their ceaseless winds blowing the hem of her mink-lined cloak against her thighs. As if in sympathy, her robe twisted around her ankles. Fur and wool, luxury and necessity—and her mind unable to say at the moment which was which. Blithely she had spoken of wishing to live more ethically, a half-truth at best, designed to impress the people whose help she begged. Much more important had been her desire to depend entirely on herself. To need a human for its blood, even a human she could suborn, was to be vulnerable. But now she needed much more than blood.

With a skin-chilling shock, she saw her quest had come to mean less to her than one man's good opinion.

Then she laughed, sharp and bitter, her breath clouding thickly in the air. Even now she hedged the truth. She wanted more than Martin's good opinion. She wanted his well-being.

From his interview with the abbot Martin had gone straight to his private chamber, where he turned at once to light his altar's lamps. Now a cone of his finest Indian incense smoldered sweetly in a dish. He had bathed and stretched and said his customary prayers. He had prostrated himself and fixed his inner vision on a point. Or he had tried to.

His body wanted nothing to do with prayer. His body wanted only to wallow in the memory of Luisa's touch. His phallus throbbed with readiness, hard and heavy and full, demanding union, demanding her.

His guide had claimed his heart was not his weakest organ. What, Martin wondered, would he have said of his cock?

His desires were at war with each other. He wanted to be the man of his own ambitions: a steadfast servant of his faith. Being recognized for his spiritual achievements was admittedly attractive, but more than that he wished to be true at heart.

Of course, he also wished to be the person who saved Luisa.

How else could he ensure that she remembered him? Not in bed. Too many men more skilled than he had gone before him. But this only he could do. A hundred years from now his image would brand her heart.

Sighing, he unfolded his body from the floor.

He had no business with her heart. Their likely paths in life could not have been more divergent. Except—

He brought both fists to his mouth and pressed them hard against his teeth.

Except his heart had business with her.

In spite of everything, he and Luisa were kindred spirits. Both were strong of mind, both concerned with a longer stretch of time than most lives could hold. Certainly both were trying to balance the promptings of the body against those of the soul.

Nor were those the only parallels. Luisa had twice been betrayed by the men who sired her: the first marrying her to a brute, the second simply leaving. To Martin's mind, neither abandonment was deserved. Whatever her flaws, his life was immeasurably richer for having met her. Auriclus had missed out. And so had Martin's father. Luisa had taught him that by proving how easy to love one imperfect soul could be.

His eyes went hot with the sting of truth. He did not simply admire Luisa's beauty or her spirit or her decadent Western mind. He loved her as any man loved a woman. He loved her as he loved the peace of meditation and the mountains in the spring. He loved her as the boyhood friends he'd never had. He loved her as he loved his cherished guide.

He also loved her as herself, in a manner unlike any other. He, who had never thought to love at all, loved her with all his being.

The discovery floored him. It was a miracle, a raw, exciting terror. He tottered under it like a two-year-old, neither knowing nor caring if the abbot had been right about there being a karmic bond between them. Whether they had shared a thousand lives or none could not have mattered less.

He loved her.

Stumbling to the door, he leaned his brow against its time-worn wood. He could not ignore this emotion. He had to sum it into his accounts.

Not here, though, not in his solitary monkish cell. He needed . . .

He did not know what he needed but he strode into the hall to find it, letting his instincts be his guide. The decision was there before him. He had only to clear his mind.

Martin was waiting in her cell when she returned. The sight of him made her heart sink to her belly. He sat tailor-fashion on the floor, in the position his people called the lotus, so still he might have been a statue. His string of wooden prayer beads was wrapped around one hand, their surface smooth as stone from many tellings. Gone was his agitation of the night before: his arousal, his embarrassment, anything that marked him a man of flesh. His absolute, effortless peace filled the room the way a stream of water fills a cup. Luisa inhaled without thinking, as if she could draw his serenity into herself. All she did was underscore the differences between them. Self-denial and contemplation were the essence of his world. She did not see how it would ever mesh with hers.

As if he'd known the moment she entered, his eyelids slowly rose. "I am glad you are here," he said, in his deep, heartbreaking voice. "I have something to show you."

He set down his beads and extended his hand to her, though she knew he needed no help to rise. His hold was warm, its illusion of camaraderie intense. He did not drop her hand even after he reached his feet. With a gentle smile, he led her to the cell beside her own.

She had assumed the space was empty, and maybe it had been. Now, however, it glowed with warmth. Butter lamps ringed the room and someone had softened the floor with a rich Pashmina carpet. The walls resembled a sultan's tent, draped in hangings of painted silk. Far happier than the banner of Hayagriva, these *thangkas* depicted various Buddhas and their consorts, each gracefully straddling the lap of her protector. The colors were bright and pure, the execution of the figures marvelously adept. Decorative as they were, she did not notice at first how explicitly they were joined.

But none of this was as suggestive as the pile of cushions on the floor. No dust marred them, no fading or frays of age. All red, all shining silk damask, they could not be the prop for anything but a seduction.

"No," she said, turning to her companion. "Martin, I don't think we should do this."

If anything, his manner grew calmer. "It is my wish," he said, his beautiful eyes like stars, "and possibly your need. Last night, at the moment we gave each other pleasure, I felt your barrier begin to fall. You opened your aura to mine and the flow of power did not harm you. Because of this, I believe you may be able to live off the energy lovers share. But there is only one way to find out."

"No," she said again. "Your vow . . ."

"I have not yet taken it."

"In your heart, you have." The scope of what he offered stunned her. She ran her fingers through her hair, distressed to the point where she knew she'd become disheveled. "Martin, I am honored. Truly, I am. But this is not a sacrifice I can accept. Perhaps I could make this experiment with someone else."

He frowned at her, his expression abruptly cool. "You are welcome to try, but I doubt you will see the same results, especially since—despite your many lovers—you never saw them before. Those men did not have my mental training. Nor, I think, did your soul view them as equals. Once you have experienced the process of exchanging energy in full, then perhaps your body will know the trick of repeating it with another."

"You are jealous," she said with a flattered laugh.

Martin drew himself up. "If I am jealous, it is no one's business but my own. I do not wish you to be a killer, not even against your will. If I were able to help and did not, any death you caused would be on my hands."

"I am responsible for myself! The minute I took what Auriclus offered that was true. Even if no one but you could aid me, I could not let you do this. You were born to be a monk."

"Was I?" he said. "I have lived as a monk before, taken my vows, followed a path no woman shared. Perhaps it is time to walk another way. Perhaps my spirit shall not progress until I do."

Luisa tossed her hair in exasperation. "How could someone like me help you progress? No. I am not going to let you risk everything just to keep me from drinking blood!"

He covered his face and shook his head, the gesture at odds with his usual self-control. When he dropped his hands, his eyes swam with emotion, part rueful laughter, part something deeper than she could read. "You underestimate the strength of your character—and overestimate mine. I am afraid more lies behind my offer than concern for you and your future meals."

"More?" she said warily.

"Much more," he admitted, his seriousness belied by a spark of humor in his eye. "There is my shamefully eager body, which remembers too well the pleasure of your touch. There is my teacher, who seems to think I should taste what I'm giving up. And let us not forget my curiosity. To know the full fruits of passion is an enticement no holy man should discount."

Luisa fiddled with the edge of her heavy cloak. Though she had no right to ask, she could not hold her next question inside. "Are those *all* the reasons you want to help?"

"No," he said, a laugh in it, but his amusement soon fell away. He looked sad then, as if his years truly were as great as hers. "No. There is one more reason. I am not sure you will want to hear it but, in truth, it is the only one that counts." He took her hand from the button it had been twisting and pressed it to his steadily thudding heart. Her own was fluttering with dread, with hope, with so many feelings she could not sort them out. "Luisa." He laughed again, an ironic puff of air. "How many times you must have heard this! I wonder if you will even understand what it means. I love you, Luisa. I love you and wish to give you the one gift no one but I can offer. I wish to free you. I wish to give you your heart's desire."

"You love me?" She knew she must sound astounded. She was astounded. Her heart felt as if it had been taken out and put in backward. "I—I—" She swallowed and willed her throat to work. "I love you, too."

He blinked, twice, and then his smile spread like honey across his face, slow and broad and, at the last, completely blinding. "Well," he said, "of all the answers I prepared for, I did not think of this."

"I have not— That is, I do not believe I have ever—"

"You are stammering," he said, and this also seemed to charm him. His arms found their way around her waist.

"I am trying to say I have never felt this way before. Not in a hundred sixty years."

He laughed. "I have not felt this way in a hundred sixty lifetimes."

"Martin." She struck his shoulder in gentle scold. "You cannot possibly remember so far back."

"Perhaps not," he conceded, his gaze falling heatedly to her mouth, "but it feels true."

She waited for him to kiss her, poised between expectation and impatience. He caught his lip in his teeth, and licked it, and finally lowered his mouth to hers. Their softness melded together like two parts of a whole. This time he needed no instruction. Deeper and wetter his kisses sank while he cradled her head and cupped her bottom in his hand. Yes, she thought, meeting the sweet intrusion of his tongue. Oh, yes, this was what she needed. His arousal pressed her hip, thickly eager and sun warm. If her bones hadn't been melting, she would have climbed him. Happily, one of his thighs found a home between her own. She rolled herself up it and clutched his muscled shoulders, moaning as his teeth lightly scored her neck.

"Luisa," he murmured, the sound a soft caress, "let us share what lovers know."

Her answer was a groan he had no trouble understanding. With endearingly awkward ardor, he divested her of her clothes. Her cloak fell with a thump, then her robe. He nearly tripped over both trying to wrestle his arms out of his sleeves.

The stumble was forgotten in an instant. His naked body was spectacular: long, lean, as graceful as any artist's masterwork. More graceful, really, because it was alive. His erection jerked and throbbed, its blood-dark thickness luring her to her knees.

"No," he gasped as her mouth engulfed the silky crest,

as his hips cocked forward in spite of his denial. He tasted of salt and lust, his pulse so quick she could not count it. "Luisa, stop." He was laughing but he meant it. With one final purse-lipped pull she set him free.

"Up," he urged, and pulled her to her feet.

Her hands went immediately to his chest, stroking, exploring. His skin was smooth, his hair a rasping warmth. She followed the line of it to his navel and twirled the tip of one finger just inside. His eyes went dark. With her touch still on him, he turned to toss her fur-lined cloak across the bed. Incense wafted as the garment settled neatly, mink side up.

She was behind him now, behind his beautiful tapering back. She pressed her breasts against it and kissed his nape. The dip of his shoulder invited her cheek to rest and she could not restrain a sigh. The comfort of holding him was stronger than shade at noon. He was so solid, so marvelously aroused. His body hummed silently with excitement. To her, his control was as alluring as his need. Wound tight with anticipation, she looked beyond him to the waiting cloak-draped cushions.

"You," she said, "want to see me on that fur."

He shuddered as her hands smoothed downward toward his groin. "Yes."

"Legs spread . . . sex wet . . ."

"I will spread your legs," he offered, then hesitated. "If you would allow it."

Her nails drew another shudder as they ruffled his pubic curls. "Yes," she said, "I believe I would."

She pulled away and circled him, hands trailing, gaze locked hungrily on his face. A muscle in his side twitched as she strafed it. He could not quite keep his attention on her eyes. Her naked body was clearly a distraction: her breasts, her belly, her pale and rounded thighs.

Look your fill, she thought with a secret smile as she lowered herself to the bed. Never had she been so grateful for her beauty. It was a gift she gave him, a gift that—pray

God—would please them both. Especially him, though. She felt young again beneath his reverent gaze, every nerve and sinew born anew. Her back settled to the cushions. With knees bent and pressed together, she reached up for his hands.

"Come," she said, "make a place for yourself where you belong."

His face darkened at her invitation, the blood rising up his chest and neck. He did not speak but knelt as if in supplication at her feet. His palms settled on her knees, their dampness just as erotic as their warmth. Gently, slowly, he pushed her legs apart until her golden triangle was bared to view.

He exhaled then, long and hushed, and slid his fingers up her thighs.

"You are a flower," he breathed, spreading her folds with such delicacy she had to strain to feel the touch. "I would paint you, if I could, and gaze at you every day."

His words and his gleaming, avid eyes robbed her of speech. Called forth by his admiration, a trickle of fluid slipped from her sex. As his thumb traced its downward course, his mouth fell open, then closed when he swallowed hard.

She wanted to laugh but she did not, no more than she told him what to do. These discoveries were his to make, his to learn on his own. With a mixture of confidence and shyness, he shifted between her legs. He was intent now, his breathing shallow, his pulse racing visibly in his throat.

Hush, love, she thought, her hands stroking down his back. Your body knows what to do. Indeed, his instinct led him better than he knew. His hips settled into the cradle of hers as if a lodestone drew them down. With heart-stopping accuracy, the tip of him probed her then pressed inside. His breath caught, held. He was testing the feel of her, taking in that first luscious clasp. She knew her softness pulled him, knew he wanted more. He pressed deeper, surer, his vision glazed, his senses tuned to that miraculous inner glide. He hilted with a sigh.

"Ah," he said, a sound of enchanted wonder. "Ah, Luisa, that is so *good*."

She laughed and hugged him with all her limbs. His hips ground back at her but it wasn't long before he complained.

"You must not hold me so tightly," he said. "I am certain I should move more vigorously in and out."

She let him do as he wished, loving his fits and starts and gasps.

"No," he said, after a rather amusing failure to find a working rhythm. "I need—"

With a strength that impressed her, he secured her against him, then tipped back and crossed his legs. The movement brought her over his lap, her thighs to either side of him, her sex pressed snugly onto his. His erection thumped inside her as if it approved the change. She could not help noting that their position echoed the sacred pictures on the walls.

"There," he said, happily flexing deeper with his hips, "now you are my consort."

"May your consort move?"

His eyes twinkled. "I should be grateful, for my hands would be free to touch you as you deserve."

He must have thought she deserved a lot. He caressed her as she rose and fell: her back, her haunches, her belly and hard-tipped breasts. His touch was like a drug. Her skin began to hum at the sweeping strokes. She would have purred if she'd had the means. His mouth glided up her neck and found her ear. The rush of his breath made her sheath tighten on his shaft. His fullness was exquisite, his living, vital pulse. His hands fell to her waist. He gripped her, half guiding, half greedy, then rested his forehead against hers.

"Let down your walls," he whispered. "I want to touch your soul."

Letting him in was as easy as drawing breath. Between one thrust and the next, her barriers simply fell. He was inside her then, as if her heart had always been his home. She could see with his eyes, feel with his body. His love was a sea that buoyed her in boundless warmth, deep, unstinting, as amazing as it was sure. No emptiness could survive it. This was her salvation, no matter what came to her in the end. She was loved and she could love, a blessing greater than any for which she'd dared to pray.

Their auras flickered together, shimmers of green and blue, ribbons of red and gold. Martin groaned and thrust so hard he lifted her from his lap. She could feel his swelling rise to climax, or maybe she felt her own. Sensation blurred, doubled, as if he were joining with her in truth, as if their bodies had lost their separate forms.

A hallucination, she thought. Real or not, the intermingling was delicious. Her body became her sex, yielding, giving, being taken in every cell.

And then she remembered.

This was how she had changed. This was how Auriclus had made her an *upyr.*

Exultation rose like new spring wine. She could make Martin what she was. She did not have to lose him, did not have to watch him age and die.

But— said the last sane corner of her mind.

But— said the first selfless corner of her heart.

If she made him what she was, she shared not just her gifts but also her burdens. He might have chosen to love her but he had not chosen that.

Her awareness expanded, then stilled. Colors pulsed in the hush like veils spun out of gems. She felt his attention, and his question, as if it were her own.

"We must stop," she said, or maybe only thought. "I cannot steal your future."

"And if my future lies with you?"

She wanted to believe so badly, the ache of it rang through her bones.

"Luisa," he said, his thought-voice as rich as velvet spice. "In all my lives, I have lost and found more treasures than I can count. But none of them, none, ever meant as much to me as you. There is no nirvana without you. There is only an empty night."

She searched him for the truth, though she knew he could not lie. What if he came to be sorry? What if she dragged him down?

"We will drag each other up," he promised. "Together we will be twice as strong."

"This is your choice? Truly?"

"I did not know how much I wanted this until I looked into my heart. I will not be sorry, Luisa. And I am not afraid."

All that he was infused the declaration: his pride, his courage, his curious, questing mind. It seemed impossible to fathom and yet she saw that loving her had made him stronger. Gone was his bitterness at his father, gone his fear that he never would belong. Because she loved him, all of him, he knew he belonged and always had. He did not need to renounce either West or East. Instead, all the world could be his home.

"Change me," he said, "and I will share the world with you."

A *shower of* stars burst within him, diamond cool and bright. His body disappeared, no boundaries, no limits, just sparks spread far and wide. I am the world, he thought, but a heartbeat later he slammed back in.

He was all body then, all tautly focused nerve and flesh. His phallus tightened. His throat burned with a swallowed scream. Luisa tugged at him, outside, inside. She was so wet, so warm. Sweat sprang from his pores, the pleasure like a cramp. When it swelled his cry broke free. He could not stop it, could not stop any of it. He came so strongly he almost turned inside out.

When Luisa arched, he came again.

And then a peace like none he'd ever known spread outward from his sex. It was purely a peace of the body but its power coursed sweet and deep. For the first time in his life, he knew what it was to be flawlessly in balance, every bone and muscle, every particle of being. Sighing at the liquid, golden feel, he toppled with her in his arms onto the bed. Apparently her strength had not abandoned her. She leaned over him, smiling, her hair hanging around them like new-washed silk. She seemed an angel to him, a *dakini* of the highest grade.

Angel or not, she traced the shape of his face with the tip of her longest finger. "You hardly look different," she mused, then laughed deep in her throat. "You must have been nearly perfect as you were."

The compliment pleased him, though it seemed vain to admit.

"I am sleepy," he confessed, watching her through pleasantly drowsy eyes. "If I let myself go under, will I forget what you have done?"

She smoothed his brow beneath her thumb. "I am not sure but I do not think so. Auriclus never taught me to blank a mind. Not that it matters. I would not alter your memory. I trust you with my secrets more than I trust myself."

This compliment he accepted without shame. "I shall strive," he said huskily, "to be worthy of your esteem."

He woke to a subtle twang inside his body. *Sunset.* It was almost a taste, like water from a spring: sweet, pure, the darkling dawn of his new day. At some point, he and Luisa had rolled out of bed onto the carpet. Despite the fading light, his vision was crystal clear. Different. Changed. I am *upyr* now, he thought. I am a foreign being. The recognition inspired exhilaration instead of fear. Maybe tomorrow would bring regret. For tonight he was simply glad.

He shifted, oddly at home in his altered form. The nerves in his back were alive to every strand of Kashmir wool. Luisa, bless her, lay sleeping across his chest. She was warm even now, or possibly he'd grown cooler. Her skin still felt like burnished silk. Desire overwhelmed him, sharper and harder than before. If this was what *upyr* felt, he did not know how she had held off. Too impatient to wake her, he rolled her under his body and thrust inside.

"Mm," she said, and cocked her calf around his hip. "I like an early riser."

The act was easier now, more natural. The rhythm came without duress. His arms were tireless, his thighs like tempered steel. And the pleasure . . . that was a roaring flood. When he threw back his head in climax her nails left approving half-moon pricks against his skin. Sadly, they had healed by the time she climbed atop and began to ride. He would have liked to bear her mark, just as the sages promised in the sutras. That one small disappointment, however, could not allay his joy.

As if she sensed this, she smiled through her flaxen hair. "You are not hungry," she said, wonder growing in her eyes.

Martin gripped her waist. "Only for you," he said, and thrust as deeply as he could. "From now on only for you."

"Shall I come with you?" she asked. She stood before him, her head lowered, her hands resting lightly on his breast. She was the picture of the wife he had not known he wanted.

"No," he said, "I have delayed this long enough."

She smiled at that, a secretive curling of her mouth. Since sunset they had put everything off but love. On the floor. Against the wall. Standing. Sitting. Twice they had even done it head to toe.

He had liked that. He thought it was a thing a god would do.

"I do not care what you say," he grumbled even as his body stirred again. "This incessant desire for coupling cannot be normal."

Her hands flowed seductively across his shoulders. "I did not say it was normal, I said it was natural. You were a healthy young man. Now you are a healthy *upyr*. Given your history, how could you not have numerous unmet urges to fulfill?"

"But I am turning into a fiend!"

She looked at him, her eyes round with concern. "Is that what you think? That I made you a fiend?"

"No, my love, no." He kissed her alabaster forehead. "I am merely feeling guilty for enjoying this so much. Or, rather, I am feeling guilty for not feeling guilty enough."

Her face lit up, as sunny as daybreak. "You called me your love."

He laughed. "You are my love. And now I must go, before you convince me I cannot."

She nuzzled the hollow beneath his throat. "Are you certain you don't want me to talk to the abbot with you?"

"I am," he said. "This task is mine alone to perform."

He was sorry to leave her despite his words. Her warmth had kept his anxiety at bay. Yes, his teacher had expected him to share the act of coition with their guest. He could not, however, have expected Martin to turn *upyr*.

Hands fisted determinedly at his sides, he strode through the lower hall. He stopped when two monks shrank in horror from his path. Only then did he realize how swiftly he had been moving, huge inhuman bounds that ate the distance.

"I am practicing a new power," he growled at the wide-eyed monks.

The men exchanged a wary look. Obviously this feat was more than they expected even from Shisharovar's best *naljorpa*.

I shall have to go, he thought. I do not fit in here now.

The knowledge hurt but not as much as he feared. Even

if Luisa had lived close, he would have been ready to leave. The wider world was calling. Perhaps it had been all along.

He closed his eyes and let the new awareness find a home. When he opened them, his teacher stood before him. The glow that lit his aura told Martin he had come from the midnight prayer.

"Rinpoche," he said, bringing his hands together for his bow.

"Martin," responded the abbot, "I see you have achieved all that I hoped."

Martin gaped at him. The abbot's eyes crinkled in amusement.

"Come." He took Martin's arm. "I think this calls for a cup of tea."

He led him to a small reception chamber, the same room in which Luisa had been chained. A pot waited on a table with two brown cushions pulled to its side. When his teacher poured a cup of pure gold Indian brew, Martin knew he had seen the truth. Luisa could not drink Tibetan tea, and neither now could he.

"How could you know?" he demanded. "And why are you not upset?"

"You have your gifts," said the abbot, "and I have mine."

"But—"

"I saw it," he said, "in a vision the day she came. You were gleaming in the moonlight white as stone. 'She is mine,' you said. 'She is the one for whom I have blindly waited all these years.' Oh, I knew my vision of the future was a chance and not a surety, and that it would be wrong to push, but I hoped . . ."

"You hoped!" Twice now his teacher had used that word. Martin was so flustered he had to put down his cup. "Rinpoche, I know I have come to view what happened as a blessing, but how could you hope? This change can only take me far away."

"That," said the abbot, blowing firmly across his tea, "is precisely what I hoped." To Martin's astonishment, his teacher's eyes welled up with tears. "Old friend, if you had seen the shadow I have seen hanging over our little country, you would know we will need every friend that we can make. You are no longer my charge, and I cannot give you orders, but I am not too proud to plead. Be our emissary, Martin, not to preach but to share our ways, to teach the world that Tibet is a treasure that must be saved." With heartfelt strength, he gripped Martin's icy hands. "It is a work of many years, but I know you will have them now."

A tremor swept Martin's newly sensitive *upyr* nerves. What sort of shadow could cause his guide to plead?

"Do not ask," said the abbot, one hand raised as if to fend off a blow. "We may yet find a way to turn this tragedy aside. Still"—he ventured a brilliant smile—"what country does not need friends?"

"It would be my honor," Martin said through his thickened throat, "to make them on your behalf."

He rose then before emotion could shame them both. An errant thought stopped him at the door. "What would you have done if I had not let her change me?"

The abbot's grin was impish. "I could lie," he said, "and say I would have asked your Luisa to change me. Alas, even if she would have, I fear you would see through my deceit. I have always aspired to win free of this earthly plane. You are the brave one, Martin. With all my heart, I bid you joy in your life to come."

"Thank you," Martin said, and hid his smile as he turned away. For all the abbot's wisdom, Martin knew he could not conceive how much happiness one life could hold.

With her hunger taken care of—and so enjoyably—the voyage back to Florence was far more comfortable than the voyage out. Just the same, Luisa was not sorry to be home, especially since she had come home with him. Home, home, home, to her stately fortress on the Arno, with her view of the Duomo and her courtyard and her private cellar of fine French wine—each pleasure doubled by being shared. Even sunset, she discovered, possessed a deeper charm. A glimmer of scarlet still blooded her windows' mullioned diamond panes. She had had her blessed soak and was now being dressed for her first dinner since their return.

Martin lounged against the bedpost to watch the maids prepare her. Outwardly amused, the gleam in his eye bespoke arousal. To him, her Western clothes were like a whiff of she-cat to a tom. His nostrils flared as her whalebone stays encased her smock, followed by the hip-widening cage of the farthingale. As her skirts were eased down the frame, he had to shift one ankle over the other. The way her breasts over-swelled the bodice made his gaze shoot aqua fire. When the maids began pinning jewels onto her slashed and embroidered sleeves, however, he could not restrain a laugh.

"Behold the glittering idol," he said, spreading his arms in a gesture he had been practicing for a week. The pose was convincingly Florentine. "Tell me, milady, is there an inch of that gown that does not bristle with lace and bows and a sultan's ransom in precious stones?"

"Pray God there is not!" she huffed, surprising the younger maid into a laugh. Both girls curtsied when she dismissed them, leaving her alone with her new spouse.

Unaccountably nervous, she adjusted her open ruff. With a small, quirked smile and a careful foot, Martin stepped into the circle of her skirts. In waves of emerald silk they spread around the giltwood stool on which she sat. As if to make certain she was real, he touched her powdered cheek. The cosmetic pinked her skin, a requirement for one so fair when mixing with mortal guests.

"My attire is part of doing business," she explained. "People do not believe you are successful unless you put on a show, and unless they believe you are successful, they will not help you to be more so."

"Is that what you want, to be more successful?"

Heart overflowing, she kissed his hand. "How I love you. When you ask a question, you never act as if you will judge the answer. I enjoy my success, yes. I worked hard for it. It is also a kind of safety. The Inquisition cast a shadow, you know, not as long in Florence as elsewhere, but such dark days I shall not soon forget. Besides"—she flashed a smile—"someone must fund the ventures of men whose stockings are full of holes."

"Is that what you do?"

"Among other things. I am not one lone woman anymore, I am a net of enterprise. My success supports that of others and that, too, warms my pride."

"And these partners do not know what you are?"

"No. Only my lawyer and his venerable father know. The Vasari are a proud Florentine family, back from when the great *casate* built towers to defend against being assassinated by their rivals. Old and young Piero understand loyalty—and discretion. I shall have to start silvering my hair, though, soon enough." She touched the youthful coils that supported her velvet cap. "After a time, I shall go into seclusion, perhaps even leave the country. Then, once I pass quietly away, I can return as some far-flung niece and heir."

Martin rubbed his nose. "It seems complicated."

"It is inconvenient," she admitted, "but necessary, and considerate in its way. If people do not know for certain why you are odd, they are content to have you be so."

"As long as you are successful."

Luisa smiled at his quickness. "Precisely."

"I have much to learn," he said, and plopped down on their bed. The feather bolster fluffed around his hips but could not detract from his dignity, no more than could his foreign clothes.

Much as Martin enjoyed her dress, he had been shocked by the fashions for men: their expense, their colors, their—to him—immodesty. But "I do not mind," he had assured her. "I cannot make friends for Tibet unless people see me as one of them. It is only, well, to wear this garb in public . . ."

Since he was determined to try, she had steered his disappointed tailor to the less flamboyant products of his trade. Now a pair of snug black venetians, sans padding, hugged Martin's well-formed thighs. The ice blue doublet displayed his shoulders to perfection and the blazing white neck ruff, small though it was, enhanced the still-warm color of his skin.

Despite his discomfort, his regal bearing and natural talent for mimicry carried off the style. With his hair growing out, his wonderful Asian face almost seemed Italian.

"You have learned so much already," she said. "I hope you do not think—"

He shook his head, hearing the words before she spoke. "I do not think you expect it of me. In truth, I find I must work hard to discover what you desire."

"As if you could not guess!"

His blue eyes darkened with amusement. "Yes, there are many things I can guess, but since most would require being shut up in this bedchamber . . ." His grin turned wolfish, but his gaze as always was sincere. "I am learning because I want to, my love. I wish to move smoothly in your world. Once I can, I will decide what I want to do." He laughed, the sound both deep and happy. "I cannot imagine what I shall be. A builder of ships? A lawyer?"

"Oh, not a lawyer, love."

He leaned in to nip her ear. "Then perhaps a famous sculptor. Shall you sponsor me, *donna,* if I model my creations on your form?"

"Our guests . . ." she murmured as his palm slipped down her pearl-decked bodice to her waist.

"Let them wait," he growled, beginning to gather her undergown. "Then they will savor you as I do."

His mouth breathed heat across her bosom, stirring the longing that never ebbed very far. Her teeth sharpened, then the peaks of her breasts. How lovely it was to feel this hunger without fear, to know it would be matched and met. Her hands seemed to drift of their own volition up his thighs. She found the extravagant swelling at their apex, the hardness of his desire.

With a moan of impatience, he pierced her neck.

"Oh, my," she sighed at the throbbing pleasure of his bite. "By all means, let them wait!"

Mr. Speedy

Elda Minger

1

"I can't believe he isn't letting me do this!"

Miranda Ward leaned back in the booth's comfortable seat and stared across the table at her friend Jim Barker. They'd left work twenty minutes early and headed for their favorite hangout, a sports bar, as soon as she'd found out she'd been turned down for this latest writing assignment. It was one she had really wanted, so this time it had really hurt.

"I mean, I was the one who brought the whole thing to his attention!"

"I know." Jim signaled the waitress, who started over toward their booth. "Miranda, I think this calls for fries. I know we're both trying to avoid fried food, but sometimes—"

"Fries would be good."

He ordered a large serving covered in chili and cheese, plus additional beers for both of them.

"Onions?" he said.

"Let's not go over the top."

Miranda studied her friend. Jim, at about five feet nine

inches, was a roly-poly sort of man, a real teddy bear with a full head of gingery brown hair and a ruddy complexion. In the six years they'd worked together at *Street Talk* magazine, she hadn't felt a shred of attraction toward him, though there were times when she wished she could. They were best friends. He could've been her brother.

And since she stood five ten in her bare feet, she kind of liked it when the men she dated were a little taller than she was. Call her shallow, but it was the one requirement she usually didn't deviate from.

She liked looking up to a man. Feeling a little feminine. And wearing heels on a date.

"Do you think it's fair?" she said, returning to the subject she just couldn't seem to relinquish.

"Fair isn't the issue. Ron doesn't think you could do the article justice—"

"Because I'm a woman!"

"Well, in this case, I have to agree with you."

Miranda took a sip of her beer and set it down. She'd come to Ron Hutchinson, their editor, with the idea on Wednesday morning. She'd found out about a popular seminar sweeping Los Angeles called The Swiftest Seduction. The seminar leader promised men that if they attended this weekend seminar and then followed to the letter the specific directions they learned, they could have a woman in bed and have glorious sex with her—*within twenty-four hours after meeting her!*

At first Miranda had been incredulous, but after doing the necessary legwork, she'd found out that not only was this seminar legit but business was booming.

As if women dating in Los Angeles don't have enough problems.

And to add insult to injury, Ron had informed her late this Thursday afternoon that she couldn't possibly do the assignment because Anton Levine, the man in charge, never let women into his educational seminars. He considered them "the enemy."

"Anton Levine?" Jim had said when she'd told him the outcome of her meeting with their boss. "Wasn't he the Satanist?"

"La*Vey*. The name was La*Vey*," Miranda had said. "Though I'd put this guy in the same league, with the stuff he's preaching."

So Ron had assigned the article to Bertie Hunt, one of the more uninspired writers on their staff, and a total lech.

Miranda was still furious. "I know Bertie won't take the angle I will, he'll probably attend the damn seminar and get some creepy ideas about how to treat female staff members—"

Their waitress set the plate of fries on their table and Jim reached for one, the cheddar cheese gooey, the spicy chili fragrant.

"Too bad you couldn't dress up as a guy and go do the seminar anyway—" He stopped, the messy fry halfway to his mouth. "Oh, Miranda, no. Don't go there. I don't like that look in your eye. Please tell me that I didn't—"

But she was already fumbling in her purse for her cell phone and notebook.

"I can't believe—" Jim began.

"Remind me," Miranda whispered as she found the phone number in her notebook and swiftly depressed the buttons on her cell phone, "to kiss you and thank you for the most brilliant idea after I finish this call— Hello?" she said, her voice lowering to a more masculine range. "The Swiftest Seduction? Yes, I'd like to sign up for your seminar, if you still have spaces available. You do? *Great!*"

Jim set down the French fry, wiped his hand carefully with a paper napkin, then put his head in his hands. Miranda almost laughed out loud.

"What? Oh no, I'll be using my—sister's credit card. . . . What do you mean, I sound like I'm already whipped?"

Jim started to laugh, his eyes still covered.

"Hey, then all the more reason for me to get in there this

weekend and find out how to *really* treat women!" Miranda smiled sweetly at Jim, who was now staring at her from between spread fingers. "Great. I understand. I'll go ahead and call the hotel and make reservations."

"Hotel?" Jim said as she ended the call.

"They have some rules and regulations, probably to keep people there once they find out how horrible the seminar is. You have to commit to staying at the hotel the seminar is held at, but it's just Friday and Saturday night. And you have to partner up with someone at the seminar so the two of you can go over homework." She rolled her eyes. "I can imagine what the assignments will be!"

"Do you have to room with this person?"

She frowned. "I'm not sure. I wouldn't think so." She leaned forward and touched Jim's arm. "I can't thank you enough for giving me this idea! When Ron sees my finished article, he's going to flip! And you can't tell anyone what I'm up to. I want the whole thing to be a complete surprise."

"What about Bertie? What if he recognizes you?"

"Bertie's an idiot. He won't have a clue."

Jim sighed. "Miranda, I hope you know what you're doing."

"I do. Hey, can I raid your wardrobe for a few pieces?"

The mournful expression he directed toward her almost made her laugh. "Sure, why not? In for a penny, in for a pound. But I want you to be careful."

"Oh, Jim, what could happen? And anyway, it's only a weekend. How bad can it be?"

Jake Blackhall stared out over the Los Angeles skyline from the cement patio surrounding his pool. He heard the sound of his secretary's heels tapping as she came up behind him.

"The Swiftest Seduction people called back," she said quietly. "You're all signed up for this weekend."

"Thank you, Helen."

He didn't know how he would've functioned without her. Helen Kendall, in her fifties and the best executive secretary he'd ever had, was his right arm. She kept his house running, made sure he ate on a regular basis, assisted his housekeeper in throwing food out of his refrigerator when it started to resemble a science experiment, and just generally made sure he had quiet, uninterrupted time to write.

And she was deadly when it came to research, fast and accurate. Anything he couldn't find, he assigned to Helen. She was worth every cent of the more than generous salary he paid her.

"And your sister is on the other line," Helen said. "Shall I have her call you back?"

He smiled at the mention of his twin sister, Jennifer. She lived with her husband and two sons three thousand miles away in Connecticut, but they managed to talk at least twice a week.

"I'll take it," he said, and started inside.

Once in his cool, shaded den, he sat down in the black leather chair behind his desk, reached for the phone, and put his feet up.

"Jen," he said.

"Oh, I can't believe you're actually going to do this! This man is an insult to all women everywhere!"

"Hey, relax. I'm going to write an article about the guy that will expose him for the scared little boy he is."

"How about woman hater? He sounds like Tom Cruise in *Magnolia*."

Jake sighed. "I have a feeling you're not that far off from the truth."

"I couldn't believe what I read! That article you faxed me was so—I can't even begin to describe—if George had approached me that way—"

"Jen, listen. I want to do this piece because I have a feeling that the story behind the story is even more interesting. I mean, how did this guy get this way? What made him want to even start these seminars? That's the part that interests me. That, and why any sane man would take a seminar like this one and actually believe it would work."

She laughed, then said, "I wonder if anyone will recognize you this weekend."

He sighed and stretched the kinks out of his shoulders. "Nah. I don't think men follow the gossip columns as closely."

"Hmmm. Who's being sexist now?"

He laughed, amazed that he could finally laugh about a time in his life that had been incredibly painful. A woman he'd thought he was deeply in love with, a marriage that had lasted barely three years, and a vicious divorce with a lawyer battling on his wife's behalf who had taken him to the cleaners—it had brought him to his knees and almost forced him to declare bankruptcy.

The tabloids had loved it. Because he was a public figure, they'd followed his every move, headlines screaming with different bogus information at every turn.

It had been a living nightmare. Pure hell. And in the process, Jake knew he'd developed a very thick skin. Nothing like having your every move scrutinized and analyzed to death to make a man wary.

And all he'd done to deserve it was to live his life. If he was good at making money by writing bestselling nonfiction exposés and investing that money to make even more, and if he liked to spend time with beautiful women, where was the crime in that? But the minute his personal life had gone down the toilet, the vultures had come out in the form of photographers and tabloid reporters.

Ah, he knew the rules. Whatever sold, whatever moved those papers out of the store, was fair game. Money was always the bottom line.

But it had been hard.

"Jake?" His sister's voice was soft. "Don't go back there. She's not worth it."

"Yeah." He hesitated. "I've got to go."

"Okay. Call me during the weekend if you want to talk. Any time."

"You bet. Give my best to George and hug those two little monsters for me."

"Always," his sister said.

He hung up the phone, then sat in his dark office, remembering.

"I draw the line at ugly underwear," Miranda said. "I'll wear my own."

Jim merely smiled.

"What?"

"You'd have to be a man to understand. The visual image—"

She had to laugh. "Hey, I have four older brothers. I think I understand male visual imagery quite well!" She threw a shirt at him.

"What, not the green one? I thought it would go so well with your eyes—"

"You are *such* a pain in the butt!"

Late that same Thursday night, she'd gone over to Jim's condo and assembled her wardrobe with choice pieces from his closet and a few more androgynous pieces of her own. Now all she had to do was call in sick on Friday and head down to the hotel in Santa Monica where the seminar was to be held.

Oh, and there was the small matter of getting a haircut.

"I'll cover for you," Jim said. "And listen, if you need to call and talk this weekend, any time's okay, got it?"

"You," she said, giving him a swift hug, "are the best friend a girl could have."

Jake threw some clothing in a weekend duffel bag without any real enthusiasm.

When had relationships become so hard? His own parents had been married for more than forty years and were still going strong. Not that they hadn't had their ups and downs, but somehow they'd managed to weather them. Every single year at the holidays, all he had to do was fly back to Pennsylvania, walk into the house he'd grown up in, and he could immediately feel the deep love that surrounded them.

He admired his parents. His father had always been his hero, his mother his confidant. And he'd hated calling them with the news of his divorce. They'd emotionally supported him through those dark days, assured him that he'd done nothing wrong, but Jake had still felt that he'd let them down. Jen had gotten it right. George was a terrific guy, and their two boys, Matt and Jake, had only added to their happiness.

He stalked into the bathroom and gathered up some toiletries, then tossed them into the duffel, and wondered if he was doing the right thing.

The writing had always gone well. He'd published his first book with not a whole lot of struggle and never looked back. It had been his personal life that had always been a problem.

At the age of forty-one, he'd come to the conclusion that the possibility of a real relationship, for him, was a total fantasy, something that probably wasn't going to happen in this lifetime. But something that, in a very quiet corner of his heart, he wanted badly.

He didn't often dwell on the subject. And he wondered why he was doing so now.

The various women he met in Los Angeles knew all about him. Who didn't? He'd been accused of breaking up marriages when he hadn't even met either the husband or wife. If a photographer managed to get a picture of him standing next to a total stranger, a woman outside the dry cleaners or the market, he was suddenly dating yet another woman.

Once they'd even taken a picture of him with Jen in

Malibu and claimed she was "the new mystery woman" in his life. Though he and George and his sister had had a good laugh over that one, it had still annoyed Jake. He understood that his life made him fair game for the press, but he drew the line when they pursued his family.

It would be difficult for him to even find the necessary privacy to get to know a woman. Though his every move wasn't as publicly scrutinized as it had been during those awful days after his divorce, the paparazzi knew he still sold tabloids, so they took every advantage.

Jake sighed, took one last look at his duffel bag, then zipped it shut. He was checking into the hotel in Santa Monica at noon tomorrow, which would give him time for a quick nap before the seminar got under way at six that evening.

He wasn't sleeping all that well at night these days.

The haircut was harder than Miranda had imagined.

Talk about giving everything for your art.

"You don't have to do this," Jim had reminded her just before the first cut. He'd come with her. She'd found at the last minute that she needed the extra support.

"Yeah," she had said, staring into the stylist's mirror. "I do."

Now the reflection that stared back at her looked like it belonged to a young boy. Her dark coppery hair had been shaped into a man's cut, and with her new short hair mussed up with styling wax, she looked about twelve. A clean-cut twelve.

Okay, on a good day, maybe fourteen. And Amish.

Pretty awful, considering she was thirty-three.

Jim must have read her mind. "So you're a late bloomer if anyone asks, right? Right?"

Her hazel eyes filled and she reached for his hand.

"Oh, Miranda—"

"I'm okay." She blinked, halting the tears. Her hair had

been short and shaped to her head, but this cut was definitely shorter. "I'm okay. It's going to be fine."

The lobby of the hotel was jam-packed with men of all shapes and sizes as Miranda maneuvered her way to the seminar registration desk. Her disguise seemed to be working so far, as no one looked at her in horror, made the sign of the cross with their fingers, and demanded she be strung up or thrown out.

"Randy Ward?" the uninterested man in charge of registration said, once she was at the area for R through Z.

"Yep, that's me."

After he found her name on the master list and she showed him her ID, he handed her a fat registration packet and an autographed hardback book without even making eye contact with her. She silently blessed Johnny Fontaine, a contact from the streets who had whipped her up a fake driver's license in record time. One fake ID for Randy Ward, male. Though Miranda didn't think the photo looked anything like her, it hadn't mattered. This guy had barely glanced at it. The whole thing reminded her of false IDs, barhopping, and her early college days.

She supposed this registration guy didn't really have to be that interested; after all, she'd already coughed up the eight hundred ninety-five dollars for this weekend that stretched from six in the evening on Friday until three in the afternoon on Sunday.

Almost a grand to learn how to get laid. Pathetic.

Glancing around, Miranda was surprised to see that the men who were signed up for this weekend seminar on swift seduction seemed like a real cross section of American males. Some were young, some old, some fat, some thin, some bald, several with long hair. But most looked rather clean-cut, like regular businessmen. For some reason this depressed her.

"Your partner," Mr. Uninterested said, handing her a

small envelope. "His name. And he's got yours. You'll meet tonight during the first hour."

"Great."

And she shouldered her duffel bag and headed toward the check-in.

Jake had checked in earlier in the day and registered for the seminar. He'd gone up to the room, tossed his registration packet and book on the chair by the desk, and slung his bag beneath that same desk without unpacking it. Then he'd stripped down to his boxer shorts, flinging his clothes on a nearby chair, and crawled beneath the covers of one of the queen-sized beds in the room.

He hadn't slept well last night. He figured he'd better try to get some sleep now so he could keep up tonight and not doze off in front of everyone. Insomnia had plagued him for some time, but he was determined to tough it out.

Just before he drifted off to sleep, he wondered if this assignment he'd given himself was such a good idea after all. No article was worth thinking too much about the fantasy that was called relationships, and why he was never going to have a decent one. . . .

"Sharing a room?" Miranda said to the desk clerk. "Do I have to?"

The slender clerk, his light blond hair slicked back off his head, nodded.

"I'm afraid so. Mr. Levine is adamant about this. My understanding of this seminar is that there's a considerable amount of homework outside the actual lecture time, and he insists each participant room with another participant so they can work on the homework together and discuss what they've learned so far. He called it"—he tapped a pencil against the countertop—"total immersion, or something like that."

"Great. Fine." This was *not* good. Miranda had thought she'd have the privacy of her own room in order to undress and have a little downtime from being a guy. Now she'd have to keep the act up constantly. But while following other stories, she'd had to turn on a dime, change plans instantly, and this story was proving to be no exception.

She could do it. It wouldn't be that hard. Thank God her pajamas were unisex and not feminine at all. And she could dress in the bathroom, just claim she was modest.

"You're in room three hundred twelve," the desk clerk said, and Miranda thanked him and took the key card.

Cautiously, feeling like she was Goldilocks entering the three bears' cottage, Miranda inserted the key card, slowly turned the doorknob, and stepped across the threshold.

The hotel room was dark, the heavy curtains drawn. And totally silent.

Taking a deep breath, she walked farther inside, then stopped just beyond the door as it gently swung shut. She placed her bag on the luggage stand.

So far so good, she thought as her eyes adjusted to the dim light.

Then she saw him.

Gorgeous.

It was the one word her brain seemed capable of forming.

Gorgeous and exhausted.

Two words. *That's good.* But her brain seemed incapable of functioning further.

She simply stared. The man fast asleep in the queen-sized bed on the far side of the room had kicked off most of his covers. Clad only in a pair of light blue boxer shorts, he afforded her an amazing view of his glorious body as he lay on his back, an arm thrown over his face, deep in sleep as that chest slowly rose and fell.

She flashed on Brad Pitt in *Thelma and Louise*, that sexy, seductive scene that had made her knees go weak when she'd first seen it. Sex. That *body*.

This guy had that kind of body, that kind of presence—in his *sleep*!

I am in so much trouble. . . .

Miranda stopped that line of thought, determined to tough this out. How much time would they actually spend in this room, except for sleeping? He'd think she was a guy. And she could handle him. She took a deep breath, gave herself a mental pep talk.

Come on, you know men.

Oh, she knew men. She was comfortable with them. With four older brothers, there was nothing a man could do to surprise her or gross her out that hadn't already been tried, times four. But even though her brothers had delighted in shocking her and had walked around in the nude a great deal of the time, she'd never, even in all the time she'd been dating, seen a male body that had affected her the way this one did.

Get your eyes back in your head. . . .

One arm was flung over his face so she couldn't see it, and a muscled leg peeked out from beneath the sheet. She could see an incredibly sexy chest, with just the perfect amount of dark hair, arrowing down toward where the bed-sheet was gathered at his waist. . . .

"Hey," said a deep masculine voice, and she realized he was awake.

Mortified, she yanked her gaze from his body up to his face and saw him. In a kind of sick, slow-motion response, almost as if she were in shock, Miranda recognized who her partner for this long weekend was.

Jake Blackhall.

The Jake Blackhall.

The one man she'd thought would never have to take

any sort of seminar on seduction. The man was simply testosterone on the hoof, one of Los Angeles's most notorious bachelors, a guy who really got around.

And she was his roommate for the entire weekend.

2

"We're roommates," *she* said, then realized how stupid that sounded. Like summer camp or something.

"Yeah," he said, swinging those long, muscled legs off the side of the bed, reaching for his jeans and pulling them on. The man was totally natural, totally unself-conscious, and seemed unaware of how good-looking he was.

It only made him that much more appealing.

He fastened his jeans, didn't bother with a shirt, and approached her. She couldn't seem to stop staring at him; the combination of dark hair and deep blue eyes was stunning on him. His hair was longish, it would brush the back of his shirt, but it suited him. And those eyes! Clear, intelligent, so penetrating—

Suddenly Miranda felt a lot less secure with her disguise.

"Jake Blackhall," he said, holding out his hand, and she liked him even more because he didn't just assume she—make that *he*—knew who he was. Even though he was famous, or more accurately, *infamous*. And in L.A., city of celebrity, that counted for something.

She panicked as she reached for that large, masculine hand, self-conscious about how she was presenting herself. And remembering what Jim had told her while she'd gone through his closet during his crash course on "being a guy."

"A firm handshake, Miranda," he'd said. "Otherwise they'll be on to you."

She latched on to his hand and gave him a crushing handshake, vigorously pumping his arm up and down.

He winced, then returned the handshake, his own pressure firm and assured, but considerably less. She pulled her hand away.

"Randy. Randy Ward."

"Good to meet you, Randy." Jake studied her as he massaged his hand, a slightly puzzled expression on his handsome face. Miranda glanced away.

"I'll take this other bed."

"Fine." Jake glanced at the digital clock on the nightstand. "We have a few hours until the whole thing starts at six. What were you planning on doing?"

"Uh—I don't know. Maybe going over the information packet. Checking the schedule and how this whole thing is set up."

"Would you mind if I tried to sleep?"

"Not at all. I can read in the bathroom if the light bothers you."

"That won't be necessary," he said quietly. "I've slept through worse."

And with that he walked back over to the bed, slid out of his jeans—she averted her eyes, then couldn't help taking a quick look—and climbed beneath the covers. His back was turned toward her, and within minutes she heard his even breathing. She couldn't be sure he was asleep, but he was certainly making an effort.

She wondered why he was so tired—

There she went, with the writer's curse. Constantly wondering about other people's lives. She had to stop. Especially when it came to this particular man.

Miranda silently counted to ten, trying to relax and clear her mind. Here she was, in a hotel room with the man who had been voted "Los Angeles's Sexiest Bachelor" on the cover of her magazine *two years in a row*! And not only that, he'd stripped down to his underwear! And they were alone in a hotel room, and would be for most of this weekend!

How had she gotten herself into this situation?

The article. The one you want to write. Keep your eye on the prize, she told herself firmly, then opened the information packet and pulled out the thick sheaf of material inside. It spilled over her bed, piles of single pages, various worksheets, and a thick, spiral-bound workbook. She reached for the first thing that caught her attention, a glossy, professional, eight-by-ten, black-and-white photograph.

Anton Levine, in all his glory.

He was dressed in a pair of black leather pants and nothing else as he stared at the camera with an arrogant sneer, his lip curled. He'd obviously worked out and created that body; no man possessed stomach muscles like those without the requisite work.

But the expression in those dark eyes as they stared defiantly into the camera left her cold. Chilled her. This guy was no Brad Pitt, and Thelma and Louise wouldn't have wanted to get near him.

He seemed to be going for some sort of Jim Morrison look, the whole bad boy rock and roll thing, with the tight leather pants and the long, curly dark hair. She wondered if the hair was all his own or extensions.

Probably fake. Come to think of it, she wondered if he'd had pectoral implants.

"The lizard king," she said softly to herself, then

glanced over as Jake rolled easily to his side and watched her.

"Did I wake you?" she said, nervous.

"Nah. I'm having trouble sleeping. What've you got there?"

She handed him the picture and fought a smile as he started to laugh.

"Oh, this is *not* a good sign," Jake said, then tossed the picture back at her. "What's the deadline on getting my money back?"

She laughed, and realized that she liked him.

He was an absolute riot to talk to. So smart. Funny. Articulate.

She wondered what he'd be like on a date. She didn't dare think about what he'd be like in bed. She already knew the answer. Devastating. And if those intense blue eyes were focused on you—well, a woman wouldn't stand a chance. She knew she wouldn't.

Thank God she was a guy—sort of. For the weekend. Here in their hotel room, man to man as it were, she just enjoyed being with him.

"So how did you decide to take this seminar?" Jake asked her. They'd ordered up sandwiches from room service and were now sprawled on their respective beds, eating.

No girly salads for her, just manly man stuff—sandwich, fries, extra ketchup, and a piece of pie. Hell, she'd even ordered a beer, as had Jake.

"Well, I haven't had a whole lot of luck with relationships." She hesitated, then belched. This guy stuff was a lot of fun—all she had to do was remember her brothers at their very worst.

"What's the problem?" Jake said.

Miranda had the feeling that she'd just been taken under this man's generous wing. He probably considered her to be nothing in the way of a threat or competition. Of course, there was always the possibility that he was just a nice guy.

"I'm not sure. I've had two relationships, and they just never . . . caught fire, if you know what I mean."

"I do."

"And you—" The look he gave her caused the words to die in her throat. As if he wasn't used to anyone throwing his own questions right back at him. Probably no one dared, especially women.

But she was a man. Sort of. She could behave differently. Challenge him.

Miranda forged on, determined. After all, they were going to be in close quarters for the next forty-eight hours. They had to get along.

And she genuinely wanted to know what he was doing at this seminar. There it was again, that writer's mind, that endless, boundless curiosity. Because if there was one man in the City of Angels who didn't need to know how to seduce a woman swiftly, it was Jake Blackhall.

What *was* he doing here?

Miranda cleared her throat. "Mr. Blackhall, we can't pretend—"

"Jake. The name's Jake."

"Okay. Jake." She chose her words carefully, also making sure she consciously pitched her voice lower. She had to sound masculine. "We can't pretend—or let me say that *I* can't pretend—that I don't know a great deal about your past. It was all over the place, in the news, in the tabloids—I mean, I couldn't go to the market without seeing your face as I checked out."

He sighed, then ran a hand through his thick, dark hair, and she felt sorry for him. It had to have been a horrible experience.

"Not that I believed any of it," Miranda quickly added.

"Thank you," he said quietly. Those two words were so heartfelt that a part of her heart ached for this man, what he had to have gone through. A divorce was bad enough, but being devoured by the press at such a vulnerable time would have been agony.

"So," Miranda continued, "I really admire the fact that you'd come out to a weekend seminar like this one. I mean, it's tantamount to admitting that you want to get back into the whole relationship thing again."

"Yeah," he said, then hesitated. She sensed there was more, and waited.

He didn't say anything.

"Hmmm," she said. "I wish I'd known when I confided in you, trusted in you, that the gesture wasn't going to be reciprocated." *Wait, that sounded too feminine. Get to the point, the way a guy does. Think practical!* "And how are we going to do the homework assignments if we aren't open and honest with each other?" She was getting the hang of this man thing, saying what she felt and not worrying about how the other person took it. Just being a little bolder than she usually was, and she was bold by nature.

She wouldn't have survived four brothers if she hadn't been. They'd toughened her up.

"All right," he said. "Of course I'm interested in relationships. I just don't have a whole lot of faith in the fact that I'll ever choose to be in one again."

She mulled this over. Considering what she knew about this man's past, she could see his point. His ex-wife had been out for blood.

"I can understand that, with what you've been through."

He leaned back on the bed. "Now you sound like my sister."

His sister? This wasn't good. *Too feminine, you're coming off way too feminine.* She had to mix it up, make herself more masculine. Or make her feminine manner more understandable. Swiftly she thought of a few other pointers Jim had given her.

"If you come off too feminine by accident," he'd said, "say you have sisters. Men who have sisters get the whole women thing a lot better than men who don't."

Great idea. Thanks, Jim.

"Sisters," she said. "Now *that* I understand! I have—four of them." Silently she asked Mike, Mark, Mitchell, and Marty to forgive her for suddenly changing their gender.

"Jesus, you were really outnumbered. Any brothers?"

"No."

"Hmmm. Where are you in the birth order?"

"I'm the youngest. How about you?"

"One sister. A twin. I was born first, so I consider her my little sister."

"You must be very close." This side of Jake Blackhall fascinated her.

"We are." He grinned. "She wasn't that happy about my taking this seminar."

"I'll bet. Neither were my sisters."

And they laughed, two men together, acting out against their sisters, defying the feminine.

And bonded.

As Jake pulled their hotel room door shut behind him and they headed down to the first evening of the seminar, he studied his new roommate, Randy Ward.

Poor guy. Clearly overwhelmed by all that feminine energy. Four sisters and no brothers! No wonder the guy seemed slightly—feminine.

His build certainly didn't help. The guy was slender, almost delicate. Jake would bet money that Randy had probably been sickly as a child. Overprotected. And the only boy, a baby brother born into a family of four sisters? The baby boy they'd all been waiting for? He'd probably been spoiled and doted on. Coddled.

That dark red hair and clear pale skin reminded Jake of an Irish altar boy. He'd even spotted a few freckles on those high cheekbones. He seemed younger than his thirties, but with that build and those freckles, Randy had probably always looked younger than he really was.

And he obviously hadn't had success with women, otherwise why would he be here? Jake had almost considered telling him to go downstairs and get his money back, as this seminar was not the way to a woman's heart. But he'd learned long ago not to interfere with other people's plans.

He'd keep an eye out for him, make sure he didn't get in any trouble. And if after tonight Randy decided that this weekend wasn't for him, Jake would help him get a full refund. Jake kind of liked the idea of butting heads with Anton Levine, aka Jim Morrison the Lizard King.

Jake decided he wouldn't look for trouble. Randy seemed like a nice enough guy. And Jake was sure the two of them could get along throughout the next forty-eight hours. He'd get the information he needed for his article, and poor Randy here would—hopefully—get enough information so that his next relationship wouldn't be as miserable. Perhaps it would even catch fire, if that was what he really wanted and needed.

Hell, maybe there was hope for one of them.

The lecture hall was packed, with easily six or seven hundred men milling around and settling themselves in the luxurious stadium seating, then adjusting the built-in desks that swung up and opened in front of each seat.

Jake led the way, Miranda following his broad back. He cut a swath through the masculine crowd, and Miranda realized with a little thrill that other men were deferring to him. He was clearly, as an old sociobiology professor had taught her, the big monkey in this group.

Thank God she was a man this weekend, or she might do something really stupid like let him know how attracted she was to him.

She'd never dated a man like him, so self-assured and—smart. *Together.* Despite the hard times he'd endured after his messy divorce, she sensed this was a man who had rebuilt his life and would make it no matter what circumstances life threw in his way.

She admired that.

If she were totally honest with herself, it turned her on. Big-time.

"Here?" Jake said, indicating two center seats in a row about one third back from the immense stage.

"Great." She dumped all her stuff in the seat next to the one she was going to sit in, then sat down and began to wrestle with the built-in desk.

"Here. It's easier if you do it this way." Jake quickly and efficiently slid the desk up and over, positioning it directly in front of her.

"Thanks." She reached for her material and began to organize it on the small desk area in front of her. All around her, men were talking and laughing. Clearly many of the attendees had already gotten to know each other.

Jake sat down next to her, and his broad shoulder brushed against her slender one. Miranda felt a flush of heat work its way up her throat, and desperately thought cool thoughts, trying to turn down the temperature of her traitorous body. It didn't seem to want to cooperate with her male disguise, as the feelings she was feeling were all female.

Mountain lakes, waterfalls, ice cream—

It wasn't working. She'd just pictured herself sharing an ice-cream cone with Jake. *Start over—mountain lakes, waterfalls—*

"You okay? You look a little flushed."

"I'm fine, Jake. It's just—is it warm in here?" She bit her lip before she added, *or is it me?*, not wanting to speak in a feminine manner. If she were older, she'd swear she was having a hot flash.

Damn it, she'd ended her sentence with a question. Men made statements, they didn't ask questions. At least that's what Jim had told her.

"It's too warm in here," she said. *There.*

"It is kind of warm. Too many bodies crammed in one area."

The lights began to dim, and the sound of talking died down along with the rustling of papers as everyone's attention was directed toward the brightly lit stage.

"If there's a fog machine, I'm outta here," Jake muttered, and Miranda had to bite her lip to keep from laughing. Her thoughts exactly.

And then the Lizard King made his appearance.

He walked to the center of the stage and into the spotlight, and Miranda was relieved to see he'd ditched the leather pants for an expensive Italian suit. She had an eye for fashion and could swear it was Armani.

Well, the guy could afford it. She'd estimated about six to seven hundred people here, so the math was simple if you averaged it out. Six hundred fifty people times eight hundred ninety-five, no make it nine hundred, dollars came out to—

She reached for her pocket calculator and did the math, then swallowed.

Wow. A very impressive sum. Enough so this guy could afford a closetful of suits.

Then before she could think about anything else, the program began.

"Women," Anton said. "The source of all our *problems*, right?"

Several men in the audience laughed. Miranda was glad Jake didn't. He'd taken out his pen and was already making notes on his legal pad.

About what? she thought. Anton hadn't really said anything.

"They're perceived as having all the *power*," Anton went on, taking the remote microphone out of its stand and beginning to pace the stage like a restless panther in a cage at the zoo. Now he was getting into the whole rock and roll thing. Almost like performance art.

"*All* the *power!*" he said, and a guy behind them yelled, "*Yeah!*"

"But do they really?" he said.

Miranda wriggled slightly in her seat. She had a feeling she was in for a long evening, and wished she'd brought some chocolate. Or a soda. Something so she could pretend she was watching a movie.

"It's *said*," Anton continued, "that at the beginning of any date, the *woman* has all the *power* because she already *knows* whether the two of you will end up in *bed!*"

Murmurs rippled across the vast crowd.

Jake wrote.

Miranda stared at the Lizard King. She felt the beginnings of a headache.

"It's *also* said," Anton continued in that same powerful, authoritative tone, "that she makes up her *mind* if she's going to have *sex* with you within the *first thirty seconds* of *meeting* you!"

More murmuring.

"So what you've all come for this weekend is the secret to turning her *no* into a *yes!*"

Scattered applause. Miranda frowned.

"Let's get to work," Anton said. "Take out your Swiftest Seduction Workbook and turn to page three."

Miranda sighed, reaching for her notebook.

It was going to be a long night.

"*So,*" *Anton said* almost four hours later, "before you return tomorrow morning at *eight*, I want *each* of you to *push* yourselves out of your self-imposed *comfort* zones and say *hello* to at least *five new people* before you arrive tomorrow."

Miranda, feeling tired and a bit silly, turned to Jake.

"Hello."

His lips twitched as he fought to repress a smile. "I think he meant new people, Randy. You've already met me."

"I don't care. One down, four to go."

"I think he also meant women."

"Good point. I'll concede it." How often had she heard her brother Marty use those exact words? Having brothers certainly gave her a leg up on this whole man thing.

She gathered all her material and contemplated throwing Anton's picture away. Maybe burning it in some sort of protective ritual. Then she almost gagged as she saw several men heading toward the stage, photos in hand. She realized they were going to ask for autographs.

"Gag me," she muttered. *Oops.* "I mean, how gross!"

Jake followed her gaze. "I couldn't agree more." He glanced down at her. "I'm about ready to turn in. How about you?"

Her imagination went into overdrive, but she forced the words out of her mouth to be natural and neutral.

Neutered, if she were perfectly honest.

"Sounds good."

Within half an hour, they were back in their hotel room. Jake, informing her he doubted he'd be asleep before three or four in the morning, ordered up a pot of coffee.

"My ideal woman," Miranda said as she studied the detailed workbook form they had to fill out before tomorrow's workshop. "I've never really thought of my ideal woman." *Understatement of the year.*

Jake was staring at his worksheet, pen in hand. "You don't have a type?"

"Nope." She hesitated. "Do you?"

"Yeah. Vengeful barracudas." Then he sighed. "No, I— that was stupid. We were just two people whose marriage didn't work out."

Miranda thought for a moment, then said, "But she didn't have to go after you the way she did. She must have been pretty angry."

"She was."

She focused her attention on the form. "Height. Weight. I don't really care."

"Just put NA for nonapplicable."

"Good idea." She began to fill out the form, writing NA in most of the blanks. *Ain't that the truth. . . .*

"It's not as if we're going to get a grade," Jake said, his voice filled with repressed laughter.

"God, wouldn't that be awful, to have to admit you flunked The Swiftest Seduction."

He started to laugh and she found that she liked the sound of it, that deep, masculine laugh. Staring down at her worksheet, she wrote in, *Has to have a great sense of humor. And hopefully get mine.*

Their coffee arrived, and Miranda resisted the urge to pour for both of them. Instead she waited until Jake had poured himself a cup, then helped herself. She'd defer to him, as he was the bigger monkey.

Well, okay, the only real male monkey.

She was almost done with the arbitrary list of attributes for her ideal—what, mate? no, her ideal sexual conquest— when Jake got up off the bed, rummaged in his duffel bag, and brought out a pair of pajama bottoms.

He headed toward their bathroom and her mouth went dry.

Before she had a chance to compose herself, he walked back out of the bathroom, clad only in a pair of blue cotton pajama bottoms, barefoot, with that magnificent chest in full view.

He sprawled out on his bed, on his stomach, as he studied the sheet. "Let me see yours," he said.

Before she considered the repercussions, she handed it over, then her heart began to speed up as she realized she hadn't made her handwriting all that masculine.

Great.

Would he guess what was going on?

"I think I'm going to change as well," she said, reaching for her pajamas and heading for the bathroom.

• • •

Inside, she shed her clothing with lightning speed and stared at her reflection in the large mirror. Clad only in a pair of red silk bikini panties and the winding strip of cotton cloth she'd wound around her breasts to flatten them down, Miranda took a deep breath and wondered if she should come clean with Jake.

He might know, if he glanced up and really studied her in her pajamas. As baggy as they were, would he be able to make out the outlines of her feminine figure? Though she was tall, Mother Nature had blessed her with full breasts. But she didn't like the idea of sleeping all bound up—she wouldn't be able to breathe.

Damn.

Swiftly and silently, she unwound the cloth, then stuffed it in between the clothing she'd taken off. She slipped on the pajamas and studied herself in the mirror.

She looked more like a girl than ever.

Well, she'd just have to bluff it out. And if he guessed and demanded to know what the hell was going on, she'd come clean. She was doing an article for her magazine, and that was that. The way Jake had reacted to the seminar, she doubted he'd care one way or the other if she got the scoop on Anton Levine.

With her clothes in her arms and her heart in her mouth, Miranda unlocked the bathroom door and stepped outside.

"You're not all that fussy—" Jake said as he studied Randy's list, then stopped as he looked up and saw his roommate in his pajamas.

Jesus. The poor guy looked even *less* masculine, if that were possible. As much as he'd disliked the first evening of the seminar, maybe there was something there for Randy. Though the minute Jake had that thought, he rejected it. *I mean, look at his list of attributes for the woman he wanted to sleep with—most of them were NA, or "non-applicable." Except for that sense of humor.*

But what about all that talk about catching fire?

Jake frowned. Something wasn't right here.

"You okay?" Randy asked him.

At that exact instant, Jake made up his mind. Poor Randy, poor little guy. Surrounded by four sisters and his mother, he hadn't had a chance. His father was probably one of those guys who was never home. Randy had probably been a short, runty little boy who liked to play with dolls. And he'd most likely been the kid on the playground that everyone had picked on, the one who'd been beaten up by the class bully.

Maybe they'd even made him cry.

Jake made up his mind. No matter what Randy looked like, he'd treat him like a man. Perhaps that was the reason Randy was here, in a misguided attempt to reclaim his manhood. He wouldn't stand in his way.

"Yeah, I'm fine. I was just thinking as I was studying your list, and—well, it's pretty damn sparse. I don't think it's exactly what Anton wants."

"Do you think a man should have a list in his head? Don't you think that limits the possibilities? And basically objectifies a woman?"

Feminine or not, this Randy really knew how to carry on a conversation. *All those sisters of his, no doubt.*

"I just don't like the idea of a list, period," Jake said. "It strikes me as kind of juvenile."

"Exactly."

"But why don't you fill in a few details so that Anton won't bother you."

"Good point." Randy reached over and took the list, then lay back down on the bed and studied it.

Jake looked at Randy out of the corner of his eye, then smiled. He seemed so young, even at thirty-three. And that haircut! Irish altar boy, all the way.

Grinning, he got back to work on his own list.

• • •

Miranda studied her worksheet.

Hair. She thought for a moment, then wrote in, *Dark.*

Eyes. She tapped her pen against the sheet, then wrote, *Dark blue. And intense.*

Height: As tall as I am, if not taller. Let Anton think what he wanted about that answer.

Education: College degree. I like ambition in a partner. And smarts. A great mind, good conversationalist.

Figure: Muscled, athletic, graceful movements, a great walk.

Voice. She almost wrote in, *Deep and masculine*, then thought for a moment and wrote, *Distinctive. A great bedroom voice. Memorable.*

As she glanced at the other questions, she smiled, realizing what she was doing.

She was making a list of Jake Blackhall's best qualities.

Within half an hour, Miranda gathered all her homework together, piled it on top of one end of the large dresser, then went into the bathroom, brushed her teeth, came back out, and climbed into bed.

"I can turn off the light," Jake offered.

"No need to," Miranda said. "I can sleep through just about anything."

"Great. I shouldn't be much longer."

He had trouble sleeping, and envied Randy's ability to just drop off. As Jake listened to his roommate's slow, even breathing, he wondered at a fate that would pair him up for the weekend with such a strange little guy.

He turned his head as he heard his roommate's voice. Randy muttered something, then moved onto his stomach and buried his head in one of the pillows.

Even though he was asleep, he was having a rough

night. Jake frowned into the darkness. That he could understand.

Then Randy flopped over on to his back and muttered, "Oh, Jim . . ."

Oh, *Jim*?

He hadn't even thought about that possibility. Well . . .

Jake lay quietly in the darkness of the hotel room. Things were getting more complicated by the minute. And they still had a day and a half of The Swiftest Seduction to get through.

He had the strangest feeling that he was going to get one hell of an article out of this weekend.

3

Later that same night, Jake was still wide awake.

He was used to it. It amazed him how little really good sleep he was able to get, yet still function. He couldn't seem to relax, let go, and fall asleep. He paced the halls of his house late at night; he paced out by the pool, restless. But here at the hotel he could only lie in bed and breathe deeply, trying to fall asleep.

He hadn't told Jen how bad it really was. He hadn't wanted to worry her.

A noise from the bed across from him caught his attention, and he watched as Randy got up in the dark and walked into the bathroom. The door closed softly, and a bar of light came on from beneath the door. Then water ran from the sink, and Jake had to smile.

The guy was really modest. He'd never met anyone quite like Randy Ward.

The water stopped, the light went off, the door opened, and his roommate for the weekend came back out and climbed back into bed, then whispered, "Jake? Are you awake?"

"Yeah."

"Still can't sleep?"

"Nah."

A short hesitation, then, "Anything you want to talk about?"

Those sisters had trained him well.

"Nothing I can think of. But I wouldn't mind talking for a while."

"How are you feeling about the seminar?"

"I was wondering how Anton Levine got to this point." He laughed. "I doubt if he has any sisters. Or if he does, they're probably pretty pissed at him."

Randy laughed.

Jake warmed to his subject. This really helped, talking about the foundation of his article. "But what happened? Why would a man start this kind of a business? I don't think it's just about money."

"But it's a considerable amount of money. What, six hundred guys times nine hundred bucks? You do the math."

"Yeah, okay. But why this particular type of seminar? Why women? Why is he so frightened of them?"

"And why," said Randy, "are six hundred men in Los Angeles eager to sign up for this weekend?"

Great question. He'd have to include that in his article. Randy really had a fine mind. He could keep up.

"What is it you do?" Jake asked him. "Your job."

"I'm a—a freelance editor. It keeps me busy, and you wouldn't believe the number of writers who need a good once-over."

He laughed. "Oh, yes, I would."

"I forgot. You're a writer. Do you self-edit?"

"Most of the time. Once in a while, I send a piece to my sister. She's my toughest critic."

"I know what you mean. I have a friend, Jim, who helps me when I can't get an article just right."

That explained the mysterious Jim. Who knew if they were involved or not? A person could talk about anyone in their sleep.

"There's something here," Jake said, talking to both himself and Randy. "Something about this man that's just beneath the surface that explains everything. I just have to find out what it is."

He's writing an article about this weekend, Miranda realized. And it would be a good one. No, make that *great*. Because Jake Blackhall excelled in exposés; it was the type of writing that had put him on the map. This article would be no exception.

She wondered if any particular magazine had already bought the article. The one he finally sold it to would be on a national level, like *Vanity Fair* or *Harper's*. Not some local read like *Street Talk*.

He was completely out of her league.

Though one of her dreams was to break into the national magazine market with a really great article, it didn't depress her that Jake was already there. Miranda knew her own article would come from an entirely different angle. After all, how many women had the opportunity to see Anton Levine for who he really was?

She found that she loved talking with Jake. And she imagined how much fun it would be to discuss work with him whenever she wanted to—

Stop. Don't go there. This is a man who doesn't believe in relationships, who thinks a great relationship isn't out there for him, that it's just a fantasy—

Well, *her* fantasy was that someday she'd be one of the individuals in just such a relationship. With a wonderful man, a man who made her life so much better and more challenging than it could ever be alone.

"They want relationships," she said into the darkness. "All of them. They may disguise it in terms of getting laid, but underneath it all, every single man in that audience knows that something crucial is missing in his life."

Randy was one perceptive man.

And Jake realized that he'd inadvertently just found one of the angles of his piece.

"Can I quote you on that?" he said.

"Sure."

"Do you believe it?"

"Yeah, I do." She took a deep breath. "It's why I'm here."

Jake thought of Jim, then decided to keep that piece of information to himself.

"You have trouble with close relationships?"

Randy took another deep breath, then said, "Yeah. I do." And Jake felt that it had taken a lot for him to actually say the words out loud, to admit them to himself.

He owed Randy nothing less than total honesty back.

"I do, too."

Randy hesitated, then said, "I can't see how you would. I mean, don't take this the wrong way, but you seem to have everything going for you. Looks, height, status, money, intelligence—and *you* have trouble? If *you* do, what kind of hope do the rest of us have?"

"A bad relationship with a bad ending can mess with your mind," Jake said. "How did your two relationships end?"

"I ended both of them."

"Because—no fire?"

"Yeah."

"And you want that."

"I do. It has to be there. My mother told me once that marriage is hard enough at times, all the ups and downs you go through in life. But if you don't have that spark, there's even less to hold two people together during the difficult times."

"Smart woman. How long have your parents been married?"

"Coming up on forty-five years."

"That's an achievement."

"You bet," Randy said. "It just seems like it's so much harder today."

"I know what you mean."

They were both silent for a moment, lying in the darkness, then Randy said, "You know what I really want? I want to come home from work and walk into a house and know that there's a—there's someone there for me. Someone waiting for me. Someone who's always in my corner, who's in the trenches with me, who's in it for the long haul. Who's thrilled to see me, and I'm thrilled to see them."

"And fire," Jake said softly.

"Yeah. And fire."

He considered that. "I've always wanted that, too."

"And you thought you had it with your marriage?"

"I really did."

"I'm sorry it didn't work out."

Jake stared into the shadowy darkness. There was something about Randy, some quality to his personality, that made it easy for Jake to open up to him. Extraordinary, as he was a man who usually kept so much inside. "I was, too."

"I've never been divorced, but it must be a lot harder than a breakup."

"Yeah." He took a deep breath. "I had no idea she had so much anger inside of her."

"It probably didn't have a whole lot to do with you. I talked to a psychologist once, and he said that we kind of play out things from our families in our marriages. For all you know, she wasn't fighting you, but her father."

Jake thought about that. Randy was one perceptive guy.

"I think you may be right. She came from money. Her father had always given her anything she wanted, but—"

"None of his time. No real attention."

"Yeah. I knew something was wrong within a few months. She never really believed that I loved her. She had to hear it six, seven times a day. There was something really eating at her all the time."

"Jake, no man could have made that marriage work."

He felt something shift within him, felt the tight emotion he'd been holding inside his body ease. Who would have thought that he'd be having a conversation that would affect his life with a man he'd met mere hours ago?

"You're right."

They were quiet for a time, yet he knew Randy wasn't asleep.

"You know what I want?" Jake finally said.

"What?"

"The way you want that partner who's in your corner, in the trenches with you? I've always wanted—" He stopped.

Randy didn't say anything, merely listened.

"It's kind of a fantasy of mine—"

Absolute silence from the other bed.

"You know that feeling, when you know you really love a woman and want to be with her for the rest of your life?"

"I've never really felt it."

"Okay. Just imagine it. But—ah, it's such a guy thing. Such a fantasy. I've always just wanted to be able to lay the world at her feet. Give her everything. Give her all of me."

Silence. Then Randy said quietly, "That's beautiful, Jake."

He thought he'd feel stupid, admitting this to a man who was practically a stranger to him, and would be again after this weekend was over. But, in that very human way in which confidences were easiest given to strangers, Jake felt relief.

He'd finally admitted it to himself. How much he

wanted a relationship, and how his defense, his attitude
that he was never going to be in one again, was just that. A
defense.

"So we're both here, searching," Randy said. "Multi-
ply that by six hundred, and you've got this weekend.
The only thing is, I don't think Anton is going to help any
man in that audience get any further than a few nights in
bed."

"Yeah. Would you mind if I turned on the desk light?"

"Not at all."

She watched from her bed as Jake set up his laptop and
began to write. She liked watching him as he worked, and
she did until her lids were too heavy and she had to close
them. Sliding her hands up beneath her cheek, she slowly,
reluctantly, drifted into sleep.

And dreamed of him.

He wrote until about four in the morning, then saved his
work to disk and turned off the laptop.

And finally felt sleepy.

Glancing at the clock, Jake realized he could get in a
few good hours of sleep before they had to get up and go
downstairs for their first full day of the seminar.

As he slid between the sheets of his bed, he glanced
over at Randy. He looked like an angel, his face relaxed in
sleep, that delicate facial structure totally vulnerable. Jake
studied him for a moment and found himself hoping that
Randy would find that partner in the trenches, that person
who would be thrilled to see him walk in the door at the
end of the day. He was a nice guy, and he deserved a little
happiness.

As he watched him, Randy stretched, then murmured,
"Jake—"

This guy definitely talked in his sleep. Jake decided not

to get all paranoid. His roommate's sexual orientation was really none of his business. And Randy probably mentioned his name because they'd been talking. The brain was amazing the way it processed information. He'd had some pretty crazy dreams himself.

Not worrying about it too much, Jake lay down, closed his eyes, and finally managed to fall asleep.

They had breakfast in the hotel's large, sunny coffee shop. Miranda caught sight of Bertie Hunt wolfing down an enormous stack of pancakes. She swiftly turned her back and made sure she and Jake were seated out of Bertie's line of sight.

That was all she needed, for Bertie to blow her cover before she got to the real meat of the seminar.

After they finished breakfast, she stopped off at the hotel's gift shop and bought two chocolate bars, a packet of chocolate sandwich cookies, a can of guava juice, and a copy of both the *Wall Street Journal* and *People*.

Nothing like being prepared.

Having paid almost nine hundred dollars for the privilege of sitting in this seminar and listening to Anton Levine, Miranda had never thought she'd be bored to death.

She should have bought amphetamines.

"Redheads," a heavyset man said, standing at one of the microphones that had been set up in the aisle.

"So you like *redheads*," Anton parroted back.

Yes. We all know this. Can we please move *this* along! Miranda doodled on her pad, sketching the man at the mike.

"Yeah. Always have."

"And the woman you're *dating* is—"

"A brunette."

"You see," Anton said, pacing the stage, addressing the

crowd. "This man is being *dishonest* to his *own true self*. He's *denying* who he *is* by *settling* for a woman who *doesn't* fit his ideal!" He wheeled sharply, pivoting on his heel, then dramatically pointed an accusing finger at the man. "I'll bet she falls short of *so* many other requirements on your *list!*"

"Yeah," the man said sheepishly. "She does."

"So do you *see* how the relationship *isn't* working? You should *go* out to a bar, *find* the woman on your list, and then *get to work seducing her*!"

The crowd broke into spontaneous applause. Miranda couldn't join in. She noticed that Jake wasn't clapping either.

And she'd finally figured out why Anton talked in that strange way, emphasizing particular words, almost punching them out.

It was to keep his audience awake.

Was it too much to ask that, having shelled out almost a grand, she be entertained?

Thank God that today they'd decided to sit far in the back of the auditorium. In the back row.

Bored? she wrote on her pad, then slid it over so Jake could see it.

Brain dead, he wrote back, and she almost laughed out loud. Then she nearly swallowed her tongue as she saw Bertie stride up toward the mike. He adjusted his pants over his enormous belly, then looked up at Anton.

"All right," Anton said. "Review your list of requirements, please."

Bertie's list was so predictable. Enormous breasts. Long blond hair. Blue eyes, a submissive demeanor, and she couldn't have children from a previous relationship. Or cats. Especially cats. *Maybe* a dog, but only if it was well trained.

In the course of reviewing his list, Miranda learned a lot more about her co-worker than she'd ever wanted to, including that he had a desire for a relationship that "flirted with bondage and dominance."

"I think that what I really want," Bertie said, "is a bad girl. Someone really naughty. You know, a nasty little girl I can tie up."

"Yeah!" yelled some jerk in front.

Mother of God, Miranda thought. This was swiftly disintegrating into group therapy for Bertie, and Anton showed no signs of getting things back under control. How was she ever going to face her co-worker on Monday? What would he do when he realized she'd attended the seminar? She wondered what Jim would think when she told him about this.

Then Bertie dropped his little bomb.

"But this is what I can't understand," Bertie whined into the mike. "I have this ideal woman in my mind, a picture of her, but there's this woman at work—"

"A *blonde*?" Anton interrupted sharply.

"No, she has short red hair. Her name is Miranda—"

Anton smiled down at Bertie. "And do you think she's a *nasty* little girl? Is that why you're *attracted* to her?"

Miranda dropped her pen. Jake glanced over at her. She couldn't reach it, so he bent down and picked it up, handed it to her.

"Thanks," she whispered. She couldn't take her eyes off Bertie. She felt as if she'd been punched in the gut. *Bertie* wanted her for his nasty little playmate?

The universe was playing an incredible practical joke on her. It was her punishment for attending this seminar under false pretenses.

"I don't know. I just keep thinking about Miranda," Bertie continued, his tone petulant.

"No *names*, please," Anton said smoothly. "That gives them more of an *identity*, and we *don't* want that. You just want to see them as *the other*."

"Okay. This woman—I walk by her desk at work, and

all I can think about is—having sex with her. Tying her up."

The chocolate bar Miranda had just split with Jake threatened to come right back up. She swallowed, feeling faint. Oh, God, this was worse than she'd expected. Being tied up by a man like Bertie was her own idea of a personal hell.

"Have you *asked* her *out*?" Anton demanded. "For a *drink* after *work*?"

"No," Bertie said. "I'm scared of her. I just—whenever I can, I try to get close to her. You know, stand close to her. Talk to her. But—I get scared. She's kind of a—a ball buster. You know, the hard type, balls of steel, a real career woman."

"I hear you!" yelled another man.

Miranda's eyes widened. Bertie, scared of her? That made her feel a bit more safe. And she'd take balls of steel over being tied up by Bertie any day.

Unconsciously she moved toward Jake.

Jake noticed when Randy moved closer.

The poor guy. This talk of bondage was making him nervous.

He felt sorry for this woman Miranda. Having someone like Bertie hovering around her at work couldn't be all that pleasant.

"Let's read," he suggested, finally giving up on the seminar and reaching for the *Wall Street Journal*.

"Good idea," said Randy.

Jake studied his face. Poor guy—he actually looked almost sick.

She read the movie reviews in *People* while Jake concentrated on the stock market. Anton droned on, taking several other men through their lists. Miranda opened the sand-wich cookies and offered them to Jake.

When she cracked open the guava juice, he whispered, "We should sneak out to the bar. I need a drink."

She smothered a laugh and offered him the can. He took a swig, then handed it back to her. Their fingers touched and she felt that slight spark. Well, not so slight.

That fire.

Damn it. She'd found someone she could catch fire with, and he saw her as his little brother.

How mixed up could life get?

The spark caught Jake by surprise.

For one insane moment, he wondered if he'd com-pletely suppressed his real sexual orientation. How could he be—there was no other word for it—*attracted* to a man like Randy?

It was worse than that hot little spark when their fin-gers had touched. While his roommate had showered this morning, he'd still been sleeping, in the middle of a dream. An extremely erotic dream. He'd been making love to a woman, completely absorbed with giving her pleasure, but when he'd finally looked down at her face, he'd seen—

Randy.

Those delicate, high cheekbones. Hell, those freckles. Those hazel eyes had been almost drugged with pleasure. It had been a very vivid, sexual dream—only Randy had been a *woman.*

Freud would have a field day.

And to top it all off—it had aroused him.

Sick. He was a sick bastard. But you couldn't pay him enough to get up in front of this crowd, stand at a mike, and spill his guts. Though he had to wonder how Anton would handle it.

The only conclusion Jake could come to was that he

wished he could talk to a woman the way he'd talked to Randy last night. They hadn't spent much time with small talk—they'd gotten right to the deep stuff. And he found that he had a longing, a need to connect that deeply, but with a woman. Not with Randy, his strangely effeminate roommate.

He hadn't been overly concerned—until that damn spark. What the hell was going on? Jake glanced over at his roommate and saw the faint flush of a blush on those cheekbones.

Shit. He couldn't ignore all the signs. First Randy talked about a Jim in his sleep, then said his name. Now he was blushing when their fingers touched.

Jake knew he'd have to nip this in the bud. They'd do their homework tonight, but they wouldn't talk. He'd feign sleep. As much as he'd enjoyed his conversation with Randy last night, he couldn't risk—anything. Giving Randy any kind of encouragement. It would be dishonest to both of them.

And tomorrow they'd both return to their regular lives. This whole seminar would be an unpleasant memory.

Something had happened. Over lunch, Miranda felt Jake pulling away from her.

She had a feeling it had something to do with the spark. The way their fingers had touched when she'd shared her guava juice with him. Maybe he'd felt it, too. Maybe he was scared that he had feelings for—Randy.

Bertie walked by their table, surrounded by admiring men. Miranda glanced down at her soup, trying to avoid being spotted by her co-worker. If he saw her, the jig was up, big-time.

"Man," said a guy with a military crew cut, "I admired your guts, standing up there and really admitting what you want!"

"You are the *man!*" said another seminar participant.

"Thanks!" Bertie said, and Miranda realized he was basking in the attention. All of a sudden she felt sorry for Bertie. She wondered what he'd ever wanted out of life, because she was a hundred percent sure he hadn't gotten it.

"Randy?" Jake said. "Are you okay?"

"No." She put her soupspoon down. "I'm beginning to think that this whole seminar wasn't such a good idea."

"I know what you mean."

"No, I don't think you do." She hesitated, knowing that he deserved the truth. "Do you have any idea what it's like to—live a lie?"

Oh, no. The poor guy was going to come out of the closet. He was going to tell him—

How did he get himself into these situations?

"Toward the end of my marriage," Jake said carefully, "I lived a lie. I tried to convince myself that I was happy. But I wasn't."

"So you do know."

"I think," Jake said, setting down his fork, "that all of us live lies once in a while. It's a part of life, until we figure out what it is we really want. Maybe you're just being too hard on yourself, Randy."

"No, I don't think I am. I haven't been entirely honest with you, Jake."

He didn't want to hear this. Not now. Not here.

"Could we not talk about this right now, Randy?" He hated himself for the words the moment he saw the vulnerable, disappointed expression on his roommate's face. "I need to go up to the room and get a few things. Could you wait here? I'll be right back."

"Yeah. Sure."

Miranda watched as Jake wove his way through the coffee shop and out the door. And she wondered what she'd hoped to accomplish by telling him the truth about who she was and what she was up to.

They still had one more night in their room. If he found out she was a woman, would he boot her out?

No. He was a writer. He understood the need to get a story, to write something with a unique point of view, to understand something that intrigued or infuriated you.

Miranda sighed and picked up her soupspoon. Okay. They'd get through tonight, but on Sunday morning, over breakfast, she was telling him the truth.

Jake let himself into the hotel room. He did have to get a few things, but it had really been an excuse to get away from Randy—

As he strode swiftly past the luggage stand, he accidentally tipped over Randy's duffel bag, sending some of the contents spilling out on the carpet. He knelt down to pick them up and stilled when his fingers came into contact with a pair of emerald green silk bikini panties.

Women's panties.

His tired brain fought to make sense of it.

This Randy was a complicated man. Not only was he on the brink of publicly admitting his true sexual orientation, he seemed to have a fetish when it came to women's underwear.

It was none of his business. He didn't want to know. Stuffing the contents of the duffel back into place, Jake slung it back up on the luggage stand and headed toward his laptop.

Miranda loaded up for the afternoon. *Entertainment Weekly*, *Vanity Fair*, and just in case the first two choices seemed too feminine, she grabbed a copy of *Men's Journal*. She could give it to Jim when she went to work on Monday.

After checking out with a few more candy bars and two bottles of soda on top of the magazines, she felt ready for anything.

She and Jake found seats in the far back and settled in for the afternoon.

"And so," *Anton* shouted from the stage, pacing like a manic tiger, "with *all* that you've learned today, you're *ready* for your *final exam!"*

"This should be good," Jake muttered. He was in the middle of an article in *Entertainment Weekly*, while Miranda was trying to finish *Men's Journal.* Candy wrappers littered the floor in front of them, as well as two empty plastic soda bottles.

"Oh, I can't wait," she said. Somewhere in the middle of the afternoon, she and Jake had gotten back on track. A shared sense of humor helped a lot. That, and the fact that he'd put on a killer pair of reading glasses. How could one man look so sexy?

"You will *go out* tonight and have *dinner* with your *roommate,"* Anton shouted. "And after *that,* you will *go* to one of the *bars* along the *beach* and, supporting and encouraging each other, you will each *pick up a woman!* And after using *every* technique I've taught you *today,* you will take it *as—far—as—you—can!"*

The audience roared. Miranda blinked. Pick up a *woman?*

She glanced at Jake and blurted out, "I don't think I can do this." Then, realizing what she'd just admitted, she covered her mouth in horror.

"Randy," Jake said quietly, "I'm not going to tell on you if you don't do the assignment." He hesitated. "And I know. About Jim."

She felt the color drain out of her face as she stared at Jake. In the background, Anton was still yelling, exhorting the men to "take it *all the way! Pass* this final *exam!"*

The audience reaction was deafening. A true crowd mentality.

"You do?" she said weakly, still facing him. "How? What gave me away?"

"You talked about him in your sleep." Jake hesitated. "Do you love him?"

Comprehension dawned.

He thought she was gay.

4

"Love him?" she said. "Jim? No, I don't."

"Okay," Jake said, studying her. "Listen, Randy, I might have overstepped a boundary here, and if I did—"

"No," she said swiftly. "You didn't."

"Maybe I assumed something I shouldn't have, and if I did, I'm sorry."

"No, it's okay. But I need to explain something to you."

"Are you all *ready*?" Anton yelled from the stage, pumping up the crowd.

"Yes!" roared the collective audience.

"Which one of you is going to become *Mister Speedy*!" Anton yelled back, but Miranda barely heard him. She had to get Jake to understand.

But not here, not when there was a chance that someone might overhear what she had to say. It was bad enough that she had to tell Jake she'd lied to him, let alone admit she'd duped an entire auditorium full of men.

She didn't want that kind of attention directed at her.

And she certainly didn't want Bertie to know she'd witnessed his entire confession. Work would be absolutely unbearable if he found that out.

"Can we—can we just go out to dinner?" she said, feeling miserable.

He gave her a long, measured look. "Sure."

They walked to a tiny little Italian place just off Ocean Avenue. And though the food was excellent, Miranda found she didn't have much of an appetite. She knew Jake noticed the way she merely pushed her food around her plate.

"I didn't mean to upset you," he said. "That wasn't my intent."

"I know." Things were going terribly wrong. She'd have to tell him the truth tonight. What was the worst that could happen? He'd ask her to leave, she'd go back to her apartment in Culver City and return the following day to finish the seminar. He'd already told her he wouldn't turn her in for not completing tonight's assignment.

Still, there was a part of her that was scared to tell him. Jake Blackhall was a notoriously private man, and they'd really talked the night before. About private, intimate things. And she wondered if he would've talked to her the same way if he'd known she was a woman.

Probably not.

She could see a distinct potential for him to be really pissed off at her. Especially when she told him she was going to write an article about the whole weekend. It would be tantamount to stealing his thunder.

How had everything gotten so complicated?

"Jake," she said as their waiter cleared their plates away, "I don't really want any dessert. Do you think we could leave?"

"Sure."

They were walking down Ocean Avenue when they

passed a noisy bar, and as Miranda glanced in, she recognized several of their classmates there, trying out their Swiftest Seduction techniques. She slowed as one man in particular, the one who liked redheads, caught her attention.

Jake came to a stop beside her.

"Want to go in?" he said after a moment. "Just to see how they're doing. If this stuff actually works."

She was curious. Actually, she wanted to see if any of the stuff Anton had taught them today *would* work in the real world. It would add a lot to her article, how this seminar played out in real life. Readers would want to know.

And it would delay the inevitable, going back to their room and confessing all.

"Okay."

He found them a table in a far corner of the immense bar. As it was a Saturday night in Santa Monica, the place was packed with both men and women on the prowl. The music was loud, the lights low—and the drinks surprisingly good.

Mr. Redhead seemed happy; the auburn-haired waitress that he'd started flirting with was paying plenty of attention to him. But then again, maybe she just wanted a hefty tip. Miranda scanned the area. Thank God, Bertie was nowhere in sight.

She'd watched as Jake had gently flirted with the hostess, then several of the waitresses, and finally a female bartender. Actually, he'd only been responding to what they'd started with him. The man was a walking magnet for the opposite sex.

"You don't seem to be having any trouble with women," she observed. "You could probably go home with any woman here."

He gave her a look.

"I'm serious," Miranda said. Then she realized that these women meant next to nothing to Jake. Though it was clear he enjoyed the sexy, flirtatious interaction—and what man wouldn't?—he really did want that one special woman he could feel close to, and give everything to. What had he said last night?

You know that feeling, when you know you really love a woman and want to be with her for the rest of your life? I've always just wanted to be able to lay the world at her feet. Give her everything. Give her all of me.

That was Jake's fantasy.

And Miranda found herself jealous of this woman who would get all of Jake. All she would get was his pity and compassion, because he thought she—rather, *he*—was a total loser in life who couldn't even seem to make up his mind about his sexual orientation. Who was a total coward when it came to relationships.

This was too hard. Too painful. She had to tell him the truth.

"Jake," she said, touching his arm. "I have to tell you the truth." She took a deep, steadying breath. "I'm not who you think I am."

He leaned forward, attentive. The look in his dark blue eyes was kind, and she just couldn't stand being the recipient of his pity.

Get it over with.

"Inside," she said, pointing to her chest. "Inside, underneath all this, I'm really a *woman*."

His expression incredulous, he sat back in his chair.

There. Well. She'd finally done it. The truth was out; there was no going back.

He seemed at a total loss for words. Then he leaned forward and said, "You mean you're—you're—transgender?"

If it hadn't been such an emotionally loaded conversation for her, Miranda would've laughed. He thought she was a man who felt he really should've been born a woman! Like on the *Jerry Springer Show*, "Women Trapped in Men's Bodies! What Should They Do?"

"No, I mean I'm really a *woman*!"

"I heard you the first time. Have you—Jesus, have you had the surgery done yet?"

Tears of frustration sprang into her eyes. This was *not* going well. And the last thing she wanted to do was break down and cry in front of this guy. Then he'd really think she was a total loser.

"Give me a minute," Miranda said, her voice choked with emotion, then she got up and started across the large bar, heading for the rest rooms. She needed a moment of privacy; she wanted to lock herself into a stall until she got herself under control. Then she'd come back and, if she had to, unbutton her shirt and—

What? Show him her bound-up breasts?

A sob escaped her as she strode across the floor, then came to a stop in front of the two doors to each rest room.

Which one do I use?

She was dressed like a man, had a man's haircut, shoes, shirt, suit. If she went into the ladies room, she might start an incident. Yet she didn't want to go into the mens room—

Swallowing down her feelings, blinking back frustrated tears, Miranda turned and stared at Jake. No time like the present. She'd ask him if they could leave, they'd go back to the hotel room, and if she had to change in the bathroom and walk out in her underwear to get her point across, well then, that's exactly what she'd do.

And if *that* didn't work, she'd call one of her brothers and ask him to identify her as a woman over the phone. Marty, her youngest brother. They were closest, and he would understand that she'd gotten herself into another mess in her quest for a story.

And keep it quiet.

Transgender!

She ran her fingers through her hair in frustration, then started back toward their table. That was the exact moment she bumped into the sexy blonde.

And all hell broke loose.

•   •   •

Jake sat at the table, pondering the new twist his relationship with his roommate had taken. Forget the seminar, he should do an article on Randy. The kid was a lot more tortured than he'd thought. Talk about a messed up sense of who he was.

Or maybe not. Maybe he wasn't screwed up at all, just wanted to be who he truly was and honestly connect with another person. In the end, wasn't that what they were all trying to do, in the seminar or not?

He realized he had another piece of his article, and took the small pad and pen he always carried with him out of his pocket.

Miranda careened into a busty blonde in a cling-wrap-tight pink minidress and white boots—a Pamela Anderson lookalike—and almost knocked her over.

"I'm *so* sorry," she said, grabbing the blonde's arms and steadying both of them. "My fault, I wasn't looking where I was going."

"Aren't you a sweetie pie!" the busty blonde cooed. "Imagine that, a man who actually apologizes!"

Several of the women standing around her laughed. Miranda smiled and started to back away.

"Not so fast, sweetie," said the blonde. "I should thank you."

And before Miranda realized what was going on, the blonde grabbed her shirtfront, pulled her close, and began to kiss her.

The sudden burst of laughter from the crowd caused Jake to look up just in time to see a blonde woman with an amazing little body in a tight pink dress kissing Randy.

Really kissing him.

What the hell—

Did Randy think he had something to prove? Was this his idea of doing their final assignment?

And why did Jake have the distinct feeling that everything was spiraling out of control?

She was a great kisser, Miranda realized dizzily as she pulled away and looked at the woman, at her glistening, bubble gum pink lips. Her lip gloss had tasted sweet, like candy.

This was easily qualifying as one of the strangest nights of her life. Okay, make that *the* strangest.

"Thanks," the blonde whispered. "For being nice."

"Okay." Miranda took a deep breath. She wondered if this qualified as their homework assignment. *Sure, why not.* "Gotta go."

"Not so fast," said a deep male voice, and she turned to see a man who looked like a mountain, glaring at both of them. "Lizzie, what the hell was this man doing to you?"

"Nothing, Steve," whispered the blonde, and Miranda knew in that split second that she was afraid of him—and with good reason. If he'd been a dog, he would've been a fighting pit bull.

"Oh yeah? Don't you bullshit me, I saw the way he was kissing you!"

"Listen," Miranda began.

"No, you listen to me," Steve said, and, grabbing her shirt, he hoisted her up into the air and started outside.

Jake couldn't believe what he was seeing. The guy had picked Randy up as if he were a doll. Jake started up out of his chair and began to push his way through the mass of bodies crowded around the bar, but it was slow going. People were partying, and not in the mood to move.

"Fight!" someone yelled. *"Fight!"*

"Move!" yelled Jake.

Randy wouldn't stand a chance.

Jake continued to struggle toward the exit, hoping he'd be able to stop what was about to go down.

"Listen," said Miranda, who had shot to her feet the moment Steve had dropped her in the alley, "can't we talk about this like reasonable—"

Steve charged her. She darted out of the way, then raised her hands in front of her face, palms out. Her heart was hammering so hard in her chest she was afraid she was going to be sick.

"Hey, come on, please don't hit me, I don't want a fight—"

She dodged him again, but knew he was closing in for the kill.

He could see Randy through the glass windows, out in the alley behind the bar, dodging and feinting like a little lightweight boxer trapped in the ring with a heavyweight champ. And as Jake pushed his way out the door, not even caring who he bumped into in the process, his brain registered something—awful.

Randy fought like a girl.

Then— *Oh shit, he* is *a girl!*

Randy's a woman. A real woman.

That was what he'd—no, *she'd* been trying to tell him.

How could he have been so dense? Because he hadn't been looking at what was right under his nose. Now it all made sense, the way she'd talked, the excessive modesty, even the silk underwear he'd found in her suitcase.

Randy Ward was a woman. A woman who was about to get the shit beat out of her by the Incredible Hulk.

Jake raced toward the two of them just as the man punched Randy in the stomach. She doubled over in agony and fell to her knees.

• • •

She fell against some trash cans, knocking them over, spilling something smelly all over the good suit Jim had loaned her. She couldn't feel anything but the intense, overwhelming pain in her stomach. Tears burst out of her eyes and ran down her face, and all she could hope was that this guy wouldn't pick her up and hit her again—

Then, mercifully, she passed out.

"What the hell is wrong with you, hitting a woman?" Jake turned on the huge man, confronting him. Jake knew he was out of control; he was almost shaking with his anger. Several other men had gathered outside the bar and were watching. This fight was really getting interesting, now that the two opponents were more evenly matched.

"What do you mean, a woman?" the Neanderthal demanded as he rounded on him. "He messed with my woman, and I taught him a lesson! You want one?"

"No," said Jake, turning and starting to walk away toward Randy. Then he changed his mind, turned back, and decked the guy.

"Randy. Randy, come on, stand up."

She was fighting to regain consciousness, then she felt a pair of hands, very gentle hands, beneath her armpits, hauling her to her feet. A sudden wave of nausea swept over her, and she threw up on her shoes.

"I don't feel so good," she whispered, and this time didn't even try to lower her voice. Then she started to cry.

"Ah, *shit*," said a recognizable voice, and she felt herself being swept up into a pair of strong and capable arms.

And of course, to make matters even worse, the paparazzi had been tipped off and flashbulbs exploded in a frenzy of light as he carried Randy out of the bar and down the street.

He didn't even care what kind of headlines they'd put to the photo. He only knew he had to get Randy to a hospital. A punch like that, to a woman's stomach—

Jake didn't even want to think about it.

He walked right out into the traffic on Ocean Avenue and held things up until he managed to hail a taxi, then tersely told the driver to head for the nearest hospital.

The doctor in the emergency room hadn't even blinked as Miranda had started to unwind the length of cotton fabric from around her breasts after taking off her suit. This was L.A., after all. She was sure he'd seen much stranger things.

"Quite a hit you took," he said quietly, a little later. "You'll be black and blue for a while, but the X ray showed no internal damage. You were lucky. You could've broken a few ribs."

She nodded her head.

"I'll go ahead and send your husband in," he said, leaving the curtained cubicle before she could open her mouth to say, "Oh, but he's not my—"

And then Jake was standing there, staring at her. And she was dressed in one of those disgusting little blue-and-white-patterned hospital gowns, open in back and totally without style.

They studied each other for a long moment, and she sensed he knew the truth.

"You know, it probably would've been better if he'd just killed me."

Jake's lips twitched as he walked closer. "Is your name really Randy?"

She couldn't look at him; she was so ashamed of the way she'd deceived him. So she concentrated on her right hand as it pleated a piece of the hospital gown. "Miranda," she said softly. "Miranda Ward."

"Miranda Ward?" he said, and she glanced up at him. "The jig's up."

When they got back to their hotel room, she said, "Could I take a shower before we talk? I smell like garbage and—vomit."

"Sure," he said.

She locked the bathroom door and stared at herself in the mirror. She'd scraped one side of her face on the cement as she'd fallen, and the doctor had given her some ointment for it. Her hazel eyes looked huge and dark in her pale face, and her freckles stood out starkly.

She'd looked better.

Sighing, she started the shower, took off her clothes, adjusted the temperature, and stepped in.

He stayed close by the bathroom door, in case she needed his help.

And halfway through the shower, he heard her start to cry.

It tore at him, and he gently tried the doorknob, only to find it locked. He sat down by the door and listened, picturing her sitting curled up in the tub in a fetal position as the water sluiced down over her. She'd been in shock, and now she was coming out of it. And he'd bet money it was the first and only time she'd ever been struck in her entire life.

That kind of violence could be terrifying to experience.

He waited patiently until he heard her turn off the water and step outside, reach for a towel. Only then did he get up and walk silently across the hotel room to his bed and sit down.

• • •

She came out dressed in her blue cotton pajamas, incredibly tired. Her very short, dark auburn hair stood up in little spikes all over her head.

She'd never felt less attractive.

Jake was sitting on his bed. He'd taken off his suit jacket and rolled back his shirtsleeves. He'd also kicked off his shoes. She sat down on her bed, facing him.

He'd drawn the curtains, and the only light in the room came from the bathroom's open door. She didn't make a move to turn on the bedside lamp. Somehow she knew it would be easier to talk to this man in the almost-dark. Like last night.

She cleared her tight throat, then said, "I'm really sorry I messed up your weekend."

"You didn't."

"And the photographers—I'm sorry about them, too."

"Screw them. It doesn't matter."

She clutched the mattress with her hands, one on either side of her. "I guess I'm just sorry about everything."

"What were you doing, Miranda?" he asked, and she felt like crying at the gentleness in his voice.

"I was working on—a story. About this whole Swiftest Seduction thing. I researched Anton Levine and brought the idea to my editor, and he wouldn't let me do it because Anton won't let women in. You know, we're 'the other.' So he assigned it to Bertie Hunt."

Comprehension dawned. "Bertie, the guy who wants to tie up—Miranda. Oh, no."

"Oh, yes. That's me. I learned far more about my co-worker this weekend than I ever wanted to know."

"I guess." He frowned. "You're a writer? Where do you work?"

"I work for a magazine called *Street Talk*—"

"I've read it. It's a good magazine. I think I even read one of your columns. Did you do that piece on animal rights about three months ago?"

"Yeah, that was me."

"It was really good."

"Thanks." She chanced a glance at him. "Are you mad at me?"

"No. I'm relieved."

"Relieved?"

"Yeah. I thought I was going a little crazy this morning."

"In what way?"

"I had this dream. And in it—you were in the shower while I was dreaming, by the way—but in this dream, I was making love to a woman. And when I looked at her face, it was you."

"Randy?" she said, the word coming out in a soft squeak.

"Yeah. So you can see how I was kind of concerned."

She nodded her head. "So you were . . . attracted to me when I was a man? I mean, pretending to be one?"

"Yep." He just continued to look at her, and she had to look away. Her heart had started to speed up, and a blush was working its way up her neck.

"You're blushing," he said softly.

"Good eye."

"Care to tell me what you're feeling?"

"I'm feeling kind of beat up."

"Anything I can do for you?"

"Don't—don't do anything for just a minute, okay? I have to get my bearings."

"Okay."

The silence overwhelmed her. Sitting in this semidark hotel room, with this particular man, knowing he'd had an erotic dream about her—it was all too much. She didn't dare tell him the thoughts she'd had about him.

"Do you even like me?" she finally said.

"I think you know that I like you a lot," he said. "I've enjoyed our weekend together."

"Hmmm." She considered this, then bit her lip as he got up from his bed and sat down next to her.

"Don't," she said, her voice coming out in a nervous rush as he took one of her hands in his.

"Don't?" he said softly. "I thought you wanted—fire."

She swallowed, realizing how effortlessly it would happen with this man. She couldn't seem to think straight with him this close.

"It would be taking advantage of me, after the trauma we both went through tonight—"

"I feel just fine. You?"

"Jake." She turned her head away from him. He let go of her hand.

"Tell me to stop, Miranda, and I will."

She couldn't seem to find the words.

"But you have to tell me."

She couldn't do it. Almost as if something beyond her rational will was guiding her actions, she slowly turned her head toward him. Looked at him. That face. Those eyes.

"Go slow?" she said, and hated the way her voice trembled.

"As slow as you want."

He was leaning toward her when she said, "This doesn't have anything to do with that homework assignment, does it?"

"Absolutely not." His hand cupped the side of her face and she leaned into his touch.

"I look like shit," she said feebly, searching for excuses. "I can't do this, looking like this."

"You look great," he whispered.

"In pajamas, with short hair. Oh no, not this way—"

"Oh yes, just this way," he said, seconds before he kissed her.

And then she was lost. He continued to kiss her as he eased her back on the queen-sized bed, and Miranda just gave it up, gave up all resistance to what was going to happen. What had to happen. It was so strange, she never would've met Jake in any other situation; they traveled in totally different social circles. But this weekend, she'd gotten to know him and discovered she really liked him.

Could love him, given time. Maybe loved him a little right now.

But really lusted after him at the moment.

He stood, then unbuttoned his shirt and shrugged out of it, and she remembered that first moment she'd seen him, almost naked in his boxer shorts. The way she'd stared at his chest. Well, she was looking at that chest now, and watching as he removed his belt and tossed it on the other bed.

She was thankful he didn't undress any further, just came back down on the bed and took her into his arms.

He kissed her again and she found that she liked the way he kissed her. Liked it so much that she didn't even realize he'd unbuttoned her pajama top and pushed it aside until he broke the kiss and said, "How did you hide these?"

She started to laugh, realizing he was referring to her breasts.

"I tied them down."

"Did it hurt?" he said, gently cupping one breast and rubbing his thumb over nipple. She arched her back slightly in reaction.

"It was—a little uncomfortable, but not bad."

"Let me know if I hurt you," he whispered, and she knew he was referring to the area where she'd been punched. "Tell me."

"I will," she whispered back, then slid her hand up into his hair and gently pulled. "Kiss me," she whispered.

"Whatever you want," he said, a breath before their lips met.

She'd asked him to go slow, but now she was urging him to speed things up. The minute he'd touched her breasts she'd been ready for him, amazed at the speed with which he could get her going.

"This is slow?" he said as she urged him up over her.

"Don't talk," she said, and he laughed. Then he braced his weight on his forearms so she didn't have to have any pressure on her sore stomach.

"I could get on top of you," she offered.

"Don't talk," he said, and she started to laugh, then the laugh turned into a moan as he parted her thighs and slid inside her, hard and hot and strong.

"Oh," she said, stretching out the one word into a moan.

"I hope that's good," he whispered as he started to move.

"Oh, yeah, oh, oh—" She grasped his shoulders tightly, totally overwhelmed.

"That's it," he said. "Yeah, just like that—"

It didn't take either of them long. She came apart in his arms and he followed right after, rolling off her as soon as he finished. But his arms came back around her immediately, and one hand slid down to rest on her stomach.

"Okay?" he whispered, and she knew he wanted to know if he'd hurt her.

"Great," she whispered against his ear. "Much better than a punch in the stomach."

He started to laugh. "I should hope so."

Then, exhausted, they both fell asleep.

Jake woke up, Miranda tucked tightly against his side. He glanced at the bedside clock and read the glowing digital numbers.

Four in the morning. The time he usually went to bed.

He'd actually slept. Not only slept, but slept well, that deep, dreamless, restful sleep that he hadn't been able to find for the longest time.

It felt wonderful.

He glanced down, realizing that his slight movement had awakened Miranda. She was looking up at him, and he recognized uncertainty in those clear, hazel eyes.

"Hey," he said. He reached out and ran a gentle finger over one of those high cheekbones, the one that wasn't bruised. "How are you feeling?"

"Good."

"How good?" He was amazed to find that he wanted to make love to her again, but he didn't want her to think he was a brute.

"Really good."

He reached out and ran his hand over her short, spiky hair. "You did this for a story?"

"Yep."

"What did it look like before?"

"Short, but not this short."

He considered this. "You have beautiful cheekbones. When I first saw you, I thought you looked like an Irish altar boy."

"My dad would be pleased to hear that. He's Irish." Her smile reached her eyes as she looked up at him. "When I first saw you, I thought you were beautiful."

"Huh."

"I did. You were asleep on that bed, in nothing but your boxers."

He remembered. He'd been trying to make up for one of his usual sleepless nights. And in she'd walked, a woman disguised as a man, and it hadn't even fazed her.

"You're a cool little customer, you know that?" He kissed her, then felt her gentle touch on the side of his face. Her fingers threaded their way up into his hair, held him close. By the time they broke the kiss, he was absolutely sure what they both wanted.

"This time," he whispered, "you can be on top."

5

Miranda came awake with a start early Sunday morning.
She eased herself up on her elbow, wiggled out from under
Jake's arm, and glanced over his sleeping body at the
softly glowing face of the hotel's digital clock.

Seven ten in the morning. They were due in the auditorium for the final part of the seminar at nine.

She studied Jake for a long moment, the pure exhaustion that had been on his face finally relaxed. He was
sleeping well, and she was glad of that. But she'd decided,
before she'd fallen asleep last night after the second time
they'd made love, that there was no way this relationship
could work. The last time she'd kissed him, just before
they'd fallen asleep, she'd known it had to be for the last
time.

And that had just about broken her heart.

They were too different. At different times in their lives.
They were too far apart on too many levels. He was Pacific
Palisades, she was Culver City. He wrote for national

publications, she could barely get assignments from a local magazine.

In time, he'd tire of her, even though their attraction to each other was immense. And she wasn't sure she could take how irresistible he was to the opposite sex. How would she possibly hold her own?

They'd come together because of circumstance, and so she'd decided their affair had to end the same weekend it had begun. Practically the same day. So Miranda had resolved to take this particular decision out of his hands, make it easy for him.

Getting silently out of bed, careful not to wake him, she wrote a quick note on the hotel stationery, dressed, then packed her bag and slipped quietly out the door.

He woke up totally rested, glanced at the clock, and swore when he realized it was almost two in the afternoon.

And the seminar had started at nine. Why hadn't Miranda nudged him awake?

He glanced around the quiet hotel room.

Because she wasn't there.

He got out of bed in record time, searching the room until he found the note she'd left.

Darling Jake,

Don't try to change my mind. It can't work, no matter what you say or think. Thanks for saving my butt the other night and for not being too mad even though you had every reason to be. And whatever was said in this room will go to my grave, no secrets revealed. I wouldn't do that to you.

I know your article will be wonderful, and I'll never forget the time we spent together. But I'd rather that it stayed a happy memory than the

*breakup I'm sure we'd face down the road. We're too
different, don't you think?*

Have a happy life—Love, Randy Miranda

"Have a happy *life*?" he muttered to himself as he threw
the note down and reached for a worn pair of jeans, then
pulled a sweatshirt over his head. "What is she, de-
ranged?" He talked to himself as he quickly laced up his
running shoes. "Too different? What the hell's *that* supposed to mean! We were too *different* when she was a guy,
but now—*damn* it, Miranda!" Grabbing his seminar materials and his key card, his hair uncombed, his eyes feeling
gritty, he let himself out of the hotel room—and noticed
the DO NOT DISTURB sign hung on the door. That, and late
checkout, had allowed him to sleep in.

He was going to kill her. Jake slammed the door and
headed for the seminar.

And for Miranda.

She was in the front row, planning her strategy, when she
saw him walk in. And she found she couldn't quite take her
eyes off him.

He looked awful, his hair uncombed, his expression . . .
pissed, there was no other word for it. The jeans and sweatshirt looked like he'd slept in them, but he had a tightly
wired energy that told her he was angry she'd left him
without letting him know. Or even given him a choice. And
she realized that she really wasn't that good at the whole
relationship thing.

It had been kind of a juvenile move, leaving, but she'd
left the way she had because Miranda wasn't sure she
could've left if he'd asked her to stay.

"Ah!" said Anton, calling attention to Jake's late entrance. "Jake *Blackhall*, one of the most *notorious* bachelors in this *city*! I'm assuming you got *lucky*, since you're

coming in so *late*! I hope she was *worth* it and didn't require too much *effort*."

The look Jake shot him said it all. Something along the lines of *shut the fuck up.* Anton's smile wavered slightly, then he turned his attention back to his audience.

"Well, we're *just* about *done*. We have *time* for *one* more *story*. Does *anyone else* have anything about last *night* that they'd like to *share*?"

Miranda glanced at her watch. Time to get it over with. Time to launch her attack and then skip out.

She raised her hand high in the air.

"*I'd* like to say something," she called out.

What the hell was she up to? Jake had headed for the back of the auditorium, thinking Miranda would be sitting where they'd sat together yesterday. But instead she was dressed in a conservative dark suit and sitting right up front and center.

He went ahead and sat down. He'd catch her afterward; she wasn't going to get away from him a second time.

And now she wanted to share? Jake had a feeling that this couldn't be a good sign.

Anton stared down at Miranda from the stage. "Yes—Randy, is it?"

Miranda stood up. She unbuttoned her suit jacket and threw it down, revealing her upper half, a very feminine and curvy upper half, dressed in a clingy black halter top. As it was practically backless, it exposed a gorgeous female back. He knew that back; he'd spent some time admiring it last night.

Jake sat forward in his chair.

"Nope. *Miranda*. And buddy, do I have a few bones to pick with *you*!"

"Oh, my God!" shrieked Bertie, several rows away. He actually got up and ran out of the auditorium, his belly jiggling frantically. Miranda watched him go, then turned toward Anton.

"That's right. Be afraid. Be very afraid, 'cause *I'm* your worst nightmare!"

Anton stared at Bertie's large departing backside, then turned his attention back to Miranda. "Who the *hell* are you?"

"A woman. You know, the *other*? The one Bertie mentioned who has balls of steel? And I have something to say to you and to every single man in this auditorium—well, maybe excluding one."

Jake grinned and sat back in his seat. He had a feeling he was going to enjoy this.

"You're doing a disservice to every single person on this planet by running these seminars! It's not like men and women don't have enough problems without your filling everyone's heads with this crap!"

Several men in the audience started to protest, but a few started to clap.

Miranda didn't even pause for breath, and Jake breathed, "Good for you." What a woman.

"Almost a grand to teach a man how to get laid? Hell, I could tell a guy the big secret in two minutes and I won't even charge for my time!"

"*You* have to *leave*," Anton began.

"Oh, I will," Miranda said.

"What's the secret?" a man called out.

"Stop thinking about women as 'the other' and start thinking about them as people, just like you. People with hopes and dreams and fears, and also people with a sex drive that *rocks*!" She punched her fist into the air, and several men actually howled.

She took a breath and didn't even let Anton protest. "*Everybody's* scared of relationships, every man or woman on this planet from the moment we reach puberty and figure out that we're different. And we put up all these walls when it doesn't have to be that way—"

The auditorium's doors were opening, and cameramen and women from the local news stations started to move in with newscasters in tow.

"Oh, my *God*!" screamed Anton. "I *cannot* allow this!"

"Where's the woman who took the seminar?" one newscaster called.

"Right here!" Miranda shouted. "Right this way!"

Anton looked to the right, then the left, then the Lizard King covered his face with his hands and simply ran off the stage.

Jake waited until she was done with all her interviews before he approached her.

"Nice work," he said. "You'll probably get a movie deal out of it."

"That's not why I did it," she said.

"I know. But you should be prepared for the offers." He lowered his voice. "Why did you leave?"

She started to walk out of the auditorium, and he fell into step beside her.

"The answer to that should be obvious."

"We're too different."

"Yeah. I said so in the note."

"And if I don't think so?" he said.

"We're still in lust. That's what's going on."

"It is, huh?"

"Yeah."

"And what if I don't think so?"

She stopped walking and looked up at him. "Don't make this harder than it has to be, Jake."

He could tell she was close to breaking, after revealing her true identity and giving out countless interviews to the press. And he didn't want to bring her back into the relationship this way, when she wasn't at her best. So he pulled her into his arms and held her close. When he spoke, his lips brushed her ear.

"You and me. We're not done, not by a long shot. I'll see you soon."

And then he turned and walked away.

Later that day she went to Jim's condo and returned all the clothing she'd borrowed from him. And told him most of the story. The parts that weren't X-rated.

Jim just stared at her.

"You did *what*?" he finally managed to croak out.

"You'll see it on the six o'clock news tonight," she told him. "All of it."

"Ron's going to kill you!"

"Ron has nothing to do with this. I used my own money to take that stupid seminar, so he has no say in this."

"Wow. You're really on a roll."

"Well, yeah. Oh, by the way, I hurled on your black shoes."

"I didn't like them that much anyway."

"And I got garbage all over one of your suits."

"What the hell kind of seminar was this?"

"Okay, let me start from the beginning . . ."

Jake sat out by his pool that night and thought of ways to win Miranda back.

When his cell phone rang, he picked up immediately. It had to be Jen.

"Hey, how did it go?"

He simply told her the entire story. From beginning to end.

"And she walked out on you?"

"Hold on, Jen, she has her reasons." He told her what Miranda had written in the note, and then the way she'd revealed all at the end of the seminar.

"The woman in the black halter? I saw her on the news tonight!"

Jake closed his eyes. Great. She'd made the national news. That certainly spelled the death knell for Anton Levine and his workshops.

"She was terrific! I wish I'd been there to see it!" Jen started to laugh. "Jake, I think you've got your hands full with this woman!"

"Oh, don't enjoy yourself too much," he said dryly.

Once Jen had stopped laughing, she said, "So, how are you going to win her back?"

"I was hoping you could help me with that."

"Okay, start at the beginning again and don't leave anything out. I mean, leave out the parts I shouldn't hear, but other than that, tell me everything! There has to be a way to reach this woman . . ."

She went back to work on Monday to curious stares and whispers.

Well, first there was the haircut. No matter how she styled it, it would be a few months before she looked anything like her old self and didn't resemble a twelve-year-old Amish kid. Or that Irish altar boy.

Then the newscast. Though several of her co-workers had come up to her cubicle to congratulate her, others had stopped talking as soon as she'd approached their huddle by the water cooler, and Miranda could tell that jealousy was already rearing its ugly little head.

Too bad. She'd already decided not to do the article.

Needless to say, Ron, her boss, wasn't too pleased with her decision.

"I don't understand," he said, when he called her into his office. "You were so hot on this article Thursday night, and so angry that Bertie was going to the seminar."

She couldn't possibly tell her boss about Jake.

"I changed my mind," she said simply.

"Better offer?" he said. "We all saw you on the news last night."

"No offers. I just—changed my mind." She didn't want to relive the weekend and remember what she'd had with Jake.

"All right. I'm disappointed, but I have to respect your judgment."

She was walking out of his office when Ron said, "Miranda?"

"Yeah?"

"Good work. I hear Anton Levine has left the country."

"What do you know," she said. And smiled.

She'd finished her lunch and was trying to drum up some enthusiasm for another article when Jim came to her cubicle and whispered, "Jake Blackhall just stepped off the elevator and is asking for you."

"Jake?" As she stood, she smoothed down her skirt and patted what was left of her hair.

Looking over her cubicle wall, she could see Jake striding toward her, a huge bouquet of flowers in his arms, a riot of color.

Her eyes widened.

Every single staff worker stopped what they were doing, stood up, and watched his progress as he walked steadily toward her cubicle. No doubt about it, he—*they*—were the complete center of attention. There wasn't one person in the office who didn't know who Jake Blackhall was. After all, he'd graced their cover two separate times.

"Jake," she said quietly when he reached her.

"Miranda," he replied, then glanced around. "Do we have to do this out in the open?"

"You can have my office," one of her co-workers eagerly offered, never taking her eyes off Jake.

"That would be good," Jake said. Those blue eyes of his were like lasers as he studied Miranda.

"Thanks, Carrie," Miranda said, and started toward the

private corner office, conscious of his gaze on her every step of the way.

Once inside, she walked to the far side of the office, behind the desk, behind the chair. Jake stayed by the door, flowers in hand.

There was a short, sharp knock on the door. Jake turned and opened it.

Carrie, holding a vase.

"I thought—" she began, looking up at Jake.

"Thank you." Jake took the water-filled vase and shut the door. Then locked it. He glanced at her as he set the vase down on the desk, along with the huge bouquet of flowers.

"Miranda, why are you all the way over there? You aren't scared of me, are you?"

She moistened her lips. "No, just . . . overwhelmed."

He wouldn't stop looking at her. "Yeah. Me, too."

He glanced out the office's huge glass window. A crowd had gathered. With determination, he walked over to the blinds and snapped them shut.

They were alone.

Neither spoke for one of the longest minutes Miranda could remember.

"Are you pregnant?" he finally said. "I mean, could you be?"

Her cheeks flamed as she remembered how eagerly both of them had made love. Twice. With no thought of protection.

Idiots. They were idiots.

"No. I'm pretty sure I'm not. Is that why you're here?"

He kept looking at her. "No." He seemed to consider what to say next, then said, "Did you turn in the article?"

"No. I'm not going to write it."

"Why not?"

"The—the fun went out of it. You?"

"I'm not—I'm not done with it yet. I don't know if I ever will be."

She narrowed her eyes at him. "Oh, come on! Don't tell me you're not turning it in either."

"I'm not sure. Actually, the editor at *Vanity Fair* called and asked me if you'd consider doing the article with me, sort of one man's and one woman's opinion of the entire thing. A dialogue."

She simply stared at him. How ironic that one of the dreams of her life should be handed to her on a silver platter. But it would entail working with Jake—

She couldn't do it.

"No," she said softly. "I can't."

He sighed. "I kind of thought you'd say that. So you leave me with no other alternative."

He stuck his hand in his pocket and pulled out what looked like a baseball. On closer inspection, she realized that it was a ball. A small globe of the earth.

Smiling, he knelt down and gently tossed it so that it landed right at her feet.

She stared at him, remembering a conversation they'd had in the dark just a few days ago.

"You know that feeling, when you know you really love a woman and want to be with her for the rest of your life?"

"I've never really felt it."

"Okay, Randy, just imagine it. But—ah, it's such a guy thing. Such a fantasy. I've always just wanted to be able to lay the world at her feet. Give her everything. Give her all of me."

"That's beautiful, Jake . . ."

Her eyes filled as she looked down at that tiny little globe.

"I've always just wanted to be able to lay the world at her feet."

Oh, Jake . . .

She glanced up at him, tears streaming down her cheeks, and saw the stark uncertainty in his eyes. Yet her throat was so tight, she couldn't answer him.

"You know that guy?" he said softly.

"What guy?" she whispered, her throat tight.

"The one who's there when you walk in the door, waiting for you to come home. In your corner, always. In that trench with you, Miranda. In it for the long haul. The one who's thrilled to see you?"

"Oh. That guy."

"Yeah. Well, I want a chance to be that guy."

He was blasting through every single defense she had. She didn't know how to stop him, and wasn't even sure she wanted to.

She bent down and picked up the tiny globe, then set it on the desk between them, next to the vase and flowers.

"Please, Miranda. Just a chance."

"We're too different," she said.

"Not in the ways that matter."

"I'm—you'll get tired of me."

He laughed at that. "Not in this lifetime." He held out his hand. "Come here. Just for a minute."

She knew that if she took that hand she was lost. But suddenly being lost didn't seem so bad. Stepping from behind the desk, she walked slowly over to him, put her hand into his, let him pull her into his arms.

He kissed her, then held her gently, stroking her short hair.

"You're the most stubborn woman," he whispered.

She sighed. "Yeah. I am. But only when I'm scared."

"So, we're okay?" he said.

"Yeah. I can't fight this anymore."

"Give in," he whispered. "It's a lot more fun."

She leaned into him and surrendered.

"I'm assuming you want to write for the rest of your life."

She looked up at him. "But of course."

"Kids?"

She loved the tender expression in his dark blue eyes. "With you? Sure."

"Maybe a dog?"

"Two. And a big, fat cat."

"Do you have a real attachment to working here, or would you rather freelance?"

"Oh, what do you think?" Freelancing had been her dream for as long as she could remember.

"I think we should blow this joint." He swung her up into his arms, then dipped her toward the desk so she could grab her flowers and the tiny globe. When they opened the door and started out of the private office, several people suddenly scattered.

"Purse?" he said.

"In my desk."

He set her down long enough so she could unlock the bottom drawer of her desk, get out her purse, and kiss Jim good-bye. He was grinning, so happy for her.

"You take good care of her," he said to Jake, shaking his hand.

"Oh, I plan to." And with that, he swept her up into his arms, flowers and all, and started down the aisle. Heads peeked over cubicles as they headed toward the bank of elevators.

"You know, this is the first time I've ever seen you in a skirt. You have first-class legs, Miranda."

She laughed.

The elevator door slid open, and people stared at them, puzzled. Who carried a woman around in broad daylight?

Jake stepped inside the crowded elevator and the door slid shut. No one moved or talked as they descended more than a dozen floors, then he lowered his head and his lips brushed her ear.

"If this is a fantasy, don't wake me up." Then he kissed her.

She couldn't have agreed with him more.

The Awakening

Christine Feehan

1

The warm wind gently carried the message through the lush vegetation of the rain forest, traveled high into the dense canopy that shrouded the jungle in mystery. Wild honeybees built combs just beneath the crown, out of reach of most of the animals. If they heard the wind whispering, they ignored the tales and went about their business. Birds of every kind, parrots clothed in a riot of color, helmeted hornbills and falcons, picked up the gossip and conveyed it swiftly on bright wings, shrieking with delight throughout the forest. Noisy troops of long-tailed macaques, gibbons, and leaf-eating monkeys heard and leapt from branch to branch joyfully, shouting with anticipation. The orangutans moved cautiously through the trees in search of ripe fruit, edible leaves, and flowers, maintaining dignity in all the fuss. Before long, the news was everywhere. There were few secrets in the community and everyone had been waiting with concern.

He heard the news long before her scent reached him.

Brandt Talbot shrank into the heavy vegetation, his chest tight and his body taut with sudden anticipation. She was here at long last. In his domain. Within his grasp. It had been a long hunt to find her, nearly impossible, yet he had managed it. He had deliberately lured her to his lair and she had come. He was so close, he had to use iron self-control to keep from moving too quickly. He couldn't spook her, couldn't tip his hand, allow her to realize for one moment that the net was closing around her. It was essential to close every avenue, drive her to the center of his domain, and cut off each escape route.

His strategy had been planned for years. He had had time to plan while he searched the world for her, while he reviewed every document in his hunt for his prey. When he was certain he had the right woman, the *one* woman, he put his plan into action using his lawyer to draw her into the rain forest, into his territory.

He moved swiftly through the thick fauna, silently but quickly, effortlessly leaping over fallen trees as he made his way toward the outer edges of the jungle. A rhinoceros grunted nearby. Deer scrambled in fear as they caught his scent. Smaller animals scurried out of his way and birds fell quiet at his approach. The monkeys retreated to the higher reaches of the canopy but they, too, remained hushed, not daring to raise his ire as he passed beneath them.

This was his kingdom and he seldom flaunted his power, but every species was aware interference would not be tolerated. Without his constant vigilance and his continual care, their world would soon disappear. He watched over and protected them and asked little in return. Now he demanded complete cooperation. Death would come silently and swiftly to any who dared defy him.

Everything was different the moment Maggie Odessa set foot into the jungle. *She* was different. She felt it. Where the heat on the coast had been oppressive, *stifling,* within the forest that same heat seemed to envelop her in a strange perfumed world. With each step that took her into the deeper interior, she became more aware. More alert. As if awakening from a dream world. Her hearing was much more acute. She could hear separate insects, identify the trilling sounds of birds, the cries of monkeys. She heard the wind rustling in the branches overhead and smaller animals scurrying among the leaves. It was strange, yet exhilarating.

When Maggie had first learned of her inheritance, she had thought to sell it off without seeing it, out of respect for her adoptive mother. Jayne Odessa had been adamant that Maggie never enter the rain forest. Jayne had been frightened by the very idea of it, repeatedly begging Maggie to promise that she would never put herself at risk. Maggie loved her adoptive mother and didn't want to go against her wishes, but after Jayne's death, a lawyer had contacted Maggie to inform her that she was the daughter of a wealthy couple, naturalists who had died violently when she was a child, and that she had inherited their estate deep in the rain forests of Borneo. The temptation was too much to resist. Despite the promises Maggie had made to her adoptive mother, she had journeyed halfway around the world to look for her past.

Maggie had flown into the small airport and rendezvoused with the three men sent by the lawyer to meet her. From there they'd traveled in a four-wheel-drive utility vehicle for an hour before they left the main highway and took a series of unpaved roads leading into deeper forest. It seemed as if they had bumped over every rut and pit in the dirt road. Eventually they had parked the vehicle to proceed on foot, a prospect Maggie hadn't been happy about. The humidity was high and she knotted her khaki shirt around her backpack as they trekked into deeper forest.

The men seemed enormously strong and well prepared. They were well built, quiet when they walked, intensely alert. She had been nervous at first, but once they were walking along the trail in deeper jungle, everything seemed to change; she felt as if she were coming home.

As she followed her guides, winding deeper into the darkened interior, she became aware of the mechanics of her own body. Of her muscles, the way they moved sleekly, easily, her strides almost rhythmic. She didn't stumble, she didn't make unnecessary noise. Her feet seemed to find their own placement over the uneven ground.

Maggie became aware of her own femininity. Small beads of moisture ran in the valley between her breasts, sleek with sweat, her shirt plastered to her skin. Her long, thick hair, her one call to glory, was heavy and hot against her neck and down her back. She lifted the heavy mass, the simple act suddenly sensual, lifting her breasts beneath the thin cotton tee, her nipples rasping gently on the material. Maggie twisted her hair with the expertise of practice, fastening the thick rope to her head with a jeweled stick.

Strange that the heat and primitive jungle should suddenly make her conscious of her body. The way she moved, her hips gently swaying, almost an invitation, as if she knew someone was watching, someone she wanted to entice. In her entire life, she had never been a flirt or a tease, yet now the temptation was overwhelming. It was as if she had come to life, here in this dark, overgrown place with vines and leaves and every kind of plant imaginable.

Shorter trees vied for sunlight with the tall trees. They were draped with liana vines and creeping plants of various shades of green. Wild orchids hung above her head and rhododendrons climbed as high as some of the trees. Flowering plants grew on the trees, stretching for the sunlight that managed to make its way through the heavier canopy. Brightly colored lorikeets and other birds were in constant motion. The raspy call of insects was a noisy hum that filled the forest. The air was sweet with perfumed flowers that teased her senses. It was an exotic, erotic setting where she knew she belonged.

Maggie tilted her head back with a small sigh, rubbing at the sweat on her throat with the palm of her hand. Her lower body felt heavy and restless with each step she took. Needy. Wanting. Her breasts were swollen and achy. Her hands trembled. A strange elation swept through her. Life pulsed in her veins. An awakening.

It was then she became aware of the men. Watching her. Hot eyes on the movements of her body. The curve of her hips, the thrust of her breasts straining against the fabric of her T-shirt. The rise and fall of her breath as she walked along the narrow path. Ordinarily, knowing that she was being watched would have embarrassed her, yet she felt wanton, almost an exhibitionist.

Maggie examined her feelings, and was shocked. She was aroused. Totally aroused. She had always thought she was a bit on the asexual side. She never noticed men the way her friends did, never really was attracted to them. They certainly didn't find her attractive, yet now she not only was aware of her own sexuality but was reveling in the fact that she was turning men on. She frowned, puzzling over the unfamiliar feelings. It didn't feel right to her. She wasn't attracted to the men, even as aroused as her body was. It wasn't the men. It was something deep within her she couldn't comprehend.

She moved along the path, feeling eyes caressing her body, feeling the weight of stares, hearing the heavier breathing of the men as she went deeper into the darkened interior of the forest. The jungle seemed to close behind them, vines and bushes spreading across the trail. The wind gusted, heavy enough to drop leaves and small twigs onto the forest floor. Flower petals, vines, and even a few smaller branches settled onto the ground so that it looked as if it hadn't been disturbed in eons.

Her eyes were seeing details differently, much more sharply, catching movement she shouldn't have been able to notice. It was exhilarating. Even her sense of smell seemed enhanced. She was trying to avoid walking over a beautiful white lacy plant that seemed to be everywhere. It gave off a pungent odor. "What is this on the ground?" she ventured to ask.

"A type of fungi," one of the men answered gruffly. He had introduced himself merely as Conner. "Insects love it. They end up spreading its spores everywhere." He cleared his throat, glanced at the other men, then back at her. "What do you do in the big city, miss?"

Maggie was startled that he asked her a question. None of the men had encouraged much conversation. "I'm a veterinarian for exotic animals. I specialize in felines."

Maggie had always been drawn to the wilds, studying and researching everything she could find on rain forests, animals, and plants. She had worked hard to become a veterinarian of exotic animals, hoping to practice in the wilderness, but Jayne had been so unwavering, resolute in her determination to keep Maggie close, she had eventually settled for working for the zoo. This had been her big chance to go to the place she had always longed to see.

Maggie had dreams of the rain forest. She had never played with dolls like other little girls, but with plastic animals, lions and leopards and tigers. All the big cats. She had an affinity for them; she knew when they were in pain or upset or depressed. Felines responded to her and she had quickly acquired a reputation for her ability to heal and work with exotic cats.

The men exchanged a brief look she couldn't hope to interpret. For some reason their reaction made her uneasy, but she persisted in attempting to converse now that he'd given her an opening. "I read that there are rhinoceros and elephants in this forest. Is that true?"

The man who called himself Joshua nodded abruptly, reached back, and took her backpack out of her hand as if the weight of it was forcing them to slow down. She didn't protest because he didn't so much as break stride. They were moving fast now.

"You're certain of where you're going? There's really a small village where there are people around? I don't want to be left all alone with no one to help me if I get bitten by a snake or something." Was that her voice? Throaty? Husky? It didn't sound like her.

"Yes, miss, there's a town and supplies." Conner's tone was guarded.

A ripple of unease went through her. She struggled to tame her voice, make it once more her own. "Surely there's another way to get there without going on foot? How do they bring in supplies?"

"Mules. And no, to reach your home and the village, you must walk."

"Is it always this dark in the forest?" Maggie persisted. What landmarks were they navigating by? There were so many trees. Ironwood and sandalwood. Ebony and teak. So many different kinds. There had been numerous fruit trees such as coconut palms and mango and banana and orange along the outer perimeters. She recognized the various types of trees, but couldn't tell what the men were using to identify the actual trail. How could they tell where they were going or how to get back? She was intrigued and a bit awed by their ability.

"The sunlight has little chance to penetrate the thick branches and leaves above," came the answer. No one slowed the pace, no one even glanced at her.

Maggie could tell they didn't want to converse. It wasn't exactly as if they were being rude to her, but she could tell when she addressed them directly that they were uneasy. Maggie shrugged carelessly. She didn't need conversation. She had always been comfortable with her own company, and there were so many intriguing things in the forest. She caught a glimpse of a snake nearly as thick as a man's arm. There was a tiny spot of spectacular color that turned out to be a frog of some sort on a tree. And so many lizards she lost count. It should have been immensely difficult to spot such creatures. They blended with the foliage, yet somehow she could see them. Almost as if the jungle was changing her in some way, improving her sight, her ability to hear and smell.

Sudden silence took hold of the forest. Insects ceased their endless hum. Birds abruptly stopped their continuous calls. Even the monkeys ceased all chatter. The stillness disturbed her, sent a chill cascading down her spine. A single warning was shrieked high in the canopy, an alert of danger, and Maggie knew instantly that it was danger to her. The hair on the back of her neck raised and she nervously turned her head from side to side as she walked, her eyes restlessly probing the thick foliage.

Her apprehension must have communicated itself to the guards. They tightened up the distance between them, one dropping back behind her, urging her to move more quickly through the forest.

Maggie's heart accelerated, her mouth went dry. She could feel her body begin to tremble. Something moved in the deep foliage, large, heavily muscled, a shadow in the shadows. Something paced along beside them. She couldn't really see it, yet she did, the impression of a large predator, an animal stalking her silently. She felt the weight of an intent, focused stare, the unblinking eyes of something savage. Something fixated on her. Something wild.

"Are we safe?" She asked the question softly, moving closer to her guides.

"Of course we're safe, miss," the third man replied, a tall blond with dark, brooding eyes. His gaze slid over her. "Nothing would attack so large a party."

The group wasn't that large. Four people tramping on a nonexistent path toward an uncertain destination. She didn't feel all that safe. She had forgotten what the third man's name was. It suddenly bothered her. Really bothered her. What if something did attack them and the man tried to protect her and she didn't even know who he was?

Maggie glanced back. The trail had disappeared completely behind them. She lifted her chin, another shiver finding its way through her body. Something watched and waited to attack. Were they walking into an ambush? She didn't know any of the men. She was trusting a lawyer she knew very little about. She'd investigated him, of course, to ensure he was legitimate, but that didn't mean she hadn't been deceived. Women disappeared every day.

"Miss Odessa?" It was the tall blond. "Don't look so frightened. Nothing is going to happen to you."

She managed a small smile. His reassurance didn't take away her fear of the unknown, but she was grateful he had noticed and had tried. "Thank you. The forest went so quiet all of a sudden, and it feels so . . . " *Dangerous.* The word was in her mind but she didn't want to speak it aloud, to give it life. Instead she matched her stride to the blond's. "Please call me Maggie. I've never been very formal. What's your name?"

He hesitated, glanced toward the left into the heavy foliage. "It's Donovan, Miss . . . er . . . Maggie. Drake Donovan."

"Have you been to the village often?"

"I have a home there," he admitted. "We all have homes there."

Relief swept through her. She felt some of the tension leave her body. "That's reassuring. I was beginning to think I had inherited a small hut in the middle of the forest or maybe at the top of one of the trees." Her laughter was low. Husky. Almost seductive.

Maggie blinked in shock. There it was again. She *never* sounded like that, yet twice now her voice had become an invitation. She didn't want Drake Donovan to think she was coming on to him. What in the world had gotten into her? Something was happening to her, something she didn't like at all. She knew it was wrong, everything about it felt wrong, yet her body was raging at her with an urgent, primitive need.

From several yards away, Brandt feasted his eyes on her through the thick foliage. She was everything and more than he had expected. She wasn't tall, but he hadn't expected her to be. Her body was curvy, with lush breasts and hips, a small waist, strong legs. Her hair was thick and luxurious, a wealth of red-gold silk. Her brows were reddish, her eyes as green as the leaves on the trees. Her mouth was a sinful temptation.

It was oppressively hot and she was sweating, a dark vee down the front of her shirt molding to her high, firm breasts. There was a damp line down her back, drawing attention to the sweep of her spine, the curve of her hips. Her jeans rode low on her hips, exposing an enticing expanse of skin and revealing a belly button that he found exceedingly sexy. He longed to capture her right there, drag her away from the other men, and claim what belonged to him. He had taken far too long in finding her and the Han Vol Dan was nearly upon her. He could tell. The others could tell. They tried not to look at what didn't belong to them, but she was so naturally sensuous, so alluring and compelling, the men were reacting with the same ragged hunger as he felt. Brandt felt bad for them. They were doing him a favor, despite the danger to all of them from the overpowering emotions. He had been tracking poachers when she had arrived, and the men had gone to meet her in his stead, to bring her to him.

The rain began, great sheets of it, working to penetrate the heavier foliage above them, sending the humidity up another notch. The downpour bathed the forest in iridescent colors as the water blended with light to make prisms so that rainbows washed across the vine-draped trees. The woman, *his mate,* Maggie Odessa, turned her face up in delight. There was no grumbling, no squeals of shock. She raised her hands over her head in silent tribute, allowing the water to cascade over her face. She was rain-wet. The drops ran down her face, her lashes. All Brandt could think of was that he needed to lap every drop from her face. To taste her petal-soft skin with the life-giving water running over it. He was suddenly thirsty, his throat parched. His body felt heavy and painful, and a strange roaring started in his head.

Maggie's white T-shirt instantly soaked through in the sudden deluge, rendering the material nearly transparent. Her breasts were outlined, full, intriguing, a swell of lush, creamy flesh, her nipples darker and twin hard buds of invitation. The richness of her exposed body drew his gaze like a magnet. Beckoned him. Mesmerized him. His mouth went dry, and his heart hammered out an urgent tattoo.

Drake glanced back at Maggie, his gaze lingering for a hot, tension-filled moment on the sway of her breasts.

A warning rumbled deep in Brandt's throat. The growl was low, but in the silence of the forest, it carried easily. He coughed, the peculiar, grunting cough of his kind. A threat. A command. Drake went ramrod stiff, jerked his head around, peered uneasily into the bushes.

Maggie's gaze followed Drake's to the thick vegetation. There was no mistaking the sound of a large jungle cat.

Drake tossed her the backpack. "Put on something, anything, to cover yourself." His voice was clipped, almost hostile.

Her eyes widened in amazement. "Didn't you hear that?" She held the pack in front of her, shielding her breasts from their view, shocked that the men seemed more concerned with her body than with the danger approaching them. "You had to have heard that. A leopard, and close, we should get out of here."

"Yes. That is a leopard, Miss Odessa. And running doesn't do a bit of good if they've decided to make a meal of you." Keeping his back to her, Drake shoved his hand through his wet hair. "Just put on something else and we'll be fine."

"Leopards like naked women?" Maggie quipped as she

hastily pulled on her khaki overshirt. If she didn't make light of the situation, she might panic.

"Absolutely. First choice every time—you might want to remember that," Drake said, his voice tinged with humor. "Are you decent?"

Maggie buttoned the khaki shirt right over the soaking wet tee. The air was thick, the scent from so many flowers almost cloying in the oppressive humidity. Her socks were wet, her feet becoming uncomfortable. "Yes, I'm decent. Are we even close yet?" She didn't want to complain but she suddenly felt irritable and annoyed with everything and everyone.

Drake didn't turn around to check. "It's a bit farther. Do you need to rest?"

She was very aware of her escorts watching the heavy foliage warily. Her breath caught in her throat. She could have sworn she saw the tip of a black tail twitching in the bushes a few yards from where she stood, but when she blinked, there were only the darker shadows and endless ferns. As hard as she tried, she could see nothing in the deeper forest, but the impression of danger remained acute.

"I'd rather keep going," she admitted. She felt very out of sorts. One moment she wanted to entice the men to her, the next she wanted to snarl and rake at them, hiss and spit at them to go away from her.

"Let's continue then." Drake signaled and they were once more on the move. The three men were carrying guns slung carelessly across their backs. Each of them had a knife strapped to his waist. None of them had touched the weapons, not even when the large cat had made its presence nearby known.

The pace the men set was grueling. She was tired, wet, sticky, and far too hot, and most of all, her feet hurt. Her hiking boots were good ones, but not as broken in as she would have liked. She knew there were blisters forming on her heels. She was growing hungrier by the moment, but

Maggie wasn't about to complain. She sensed the men weren't pushing her to be cruel or to test her endurance, but for some other reason that had to do with safety. She complied as best she could, hurrying along the trail in the sweltering heat, wondering why the jungle felt so close and where the trail had disappeared.

2

The house was surprisingly large, a great three-story structure set back in the middle of a thick stand of trees with a
wide verandah that circled the entire building. Balconies
on the second and third stories were intricately carved—a
skilled artisan had etched the most beautiful jungle cats
into the wood. It was nearly impossible to see through the
branches intertwined around the house. Each balcony had
at least one branch touching or nearly touching the rail to
form a bridge into the network of trees, a highway high
above the ground. Vines curled around the trees and hung
in long, thick ropes.

Maggie studied the way the house appeared to be a part
of the jungle. The wood was natural, blending into the
trunks of the trees. An abundance of orchids and rhododendrons cascaded with at least thirty other species of
plants and flowers from the trees and walls of the house.

The rain fell steadily, drenching the plants and trees.
The rain was warm yet Maggie found herself shivering.

She turned up her face to watch the individual drops fall to earth, threads of silver gleaming in the sky.

"Maggie, night comes fast in the forest. Wild animals prowl around. Let's get you settled in the house," Drake advised.

Dry clothes would be more than welcome. Or, the thought came unbidden, no clothes at all. Briefly she closed her eyes against that stranger inside of her, a part of her that the jungle was slowly awakening. She was uncomfortable with that side of herself, a sensual, uninhibited woman who wanted to be the object of a man's desire. She wanted to tempt. To entice. To seduce. But not these men. She didn't know whom she was looking for, she only knew her body had come to savage life and was making intimate demands she had no way of coping with.

Maggie took a deep, calming breath and forced herself to look around her, to concentrate on other things beside the edgy need crawling through her body.

"Maggie?" Drake prompted again.

"You're certain this was my parents' home?" she inquired, staring in awe at the craftsmanship. The way the house blended into the trees, vines, and flowers made it virtually impossible to spot unless she was staring directly at it or knew exactly where to look for it. It had been cleverly designed to appear a part of the jungle itself.

"It's been in your family for generations," Drake said.

In the waning light it was difficult to see, but it appeared as if there were several flat areas running the length of the roof, almost like paths. The room was steeply pitched and with jutting dormers and matching minibalconies. "Is there an attic?" The house was already three stories. It seemed incredible that it could have a full-length attic but the large windows indicated otherwise. "And what are those flat spots on the roof?"

Drake hesitated, then shrugged casually as he unlocked the front door. "The roof is flat in spaces to accommodate easy travel if it has to be used as an escape route. There's a basement with a tunnel, too. And yes, there's an attic."

Maggie stood at the threshold, watching Drake's face closely. "Why would I need an escape route? Who or what would I be escaping from?"

"You don't have to worry. We'll all watch out for you. The house was designed well over a hundred years ago and is meticulously maintained. Over the years its been modernized but all the original features designed for escape were kept."

She blinked rapidly, her hand going protectively to her throat. He was lying to her. It was in the sound of his voice. Her new, acute hearing picked up the strain, a sudden tension in him. His gaze slid away from hers for just a moment, touched on the forest long enough for her to have certain knowledge of his deceit. Uneasiness washed over her, through her.

Maggie took a tentative step inside, feeling as if she were being lured by the unique beauty and eccentricity of the house. By the secrecy of her past. She had such little knowledge of her parents. They were shrouded in mystery, and the idea of learning about them was far too great a temptation to resist. She remembered very little, vague impressions only. Angry shouting, the flash of torches, arms holding her tightly. The sound of a heart beating frantically. The feel of fur against her skin. Sometimes the memories seemed the thing of nightmares; other times she remembered eyes looking down at her with such love, such pride, that her heart wanted to burst.

Standing in the middle of the front room, she looked uncertainly at Drake as Conner and Joshua paced through every room in the house, ensuring there were no stray animals hiding. "Are you certain the village is close?" Before she had wanted to be alone, to rest and recover from the long journey. She was truly exhausted, having traveled for hours and definitely suffering jet lag, yet now she was afraid to be left alone in the large house.

"Just through those trees," he assured her. "The house has indoor plumbing and we set up a small power plant on the river. Most of the time we have electricity, but once in a while it goes off. If that happens, don't panic; there are emergency candles and flashlights in the cupboards. The house has been stocked, so you should have everything you need."

She looked around at the well-kept house. There was no dust, no mold. In spite of the humidity, everything appeared highly polished. "Is someone living here?"

Drake shrugged. "Brandt Talbot has been the caretaker for years. If you need anything, you can ask him where to find it. He's had the run of the house, but he's going to be staying in the village. I'm certain he'll help you with anything."

Something in the way he said the caretaker's name got her immediate attention. She glanced up at him as a frisson of fear chased through her body. *Brandt Talbot.* Who was the man that Drake had said his name so softly? Drake had sounded wary and his eyes had shifted restlessly to the heavy foliage outside the house.

The other men left her luggage in the front room, lifted a brief hand, and hurried away. Drake followed them at a much slower pace. He paused at the door, looking back at her. "You keep the bars on the doors and windows, and don't go walking around at night outside the house," he cautioned. "The animals around here are wild." His sudden smile removed all traces of grimness from his face, leaving him looking friendly. "Everyone has been looking forward to meeting you. You'll get to know us all quickly enough."

Maggie stood uncertainly on the shadowed porch of her parents' ancestral home and watched him go with a sinking heart. It was everything yet nothing like she had expected, a place of mystery and shadows that awoke something primitive and wild and very sensual deep within her.

Leaves rustled high in the trees above her head, and she glanced up. Something moved, something large but very silent. She continued to stare into the thick foliage, straining to make out a shape, a shadow. Anything that might make the leaves flutter in the night air against the wind. Was it a large snake? A python perhaps—they grew to enormous sizes.

She felt a dark premonition of danger, of something dangerous hunting her. Stalking her. Watching her intently with a fixed, focused stare. Defensively she put a hand to her throat as if warding off the strangling bite of a leopard. Maggie took a cautious step backward, toward the safety of the house, her gaze never leaving the tree above her head.

The wind plucked at the trees, stirred and shifted the leaves. Her heart slammed hard against her chest as she found herself falling into the hypnotic gaze of a large animal. She had always been fascinated with large cats, but every encounter had been in a controlled environment. This leopard, a rare black panther, was free, wild, and on the hunt. The stare was terrifying, unnerving. Power and intelligence shone in those unblinking golden eyes. Maggie couldn't look away, caught in the gripping intensity of the focused stare. She knew from her vast experience with exotic cats that the leopard was one of the most cunning and intelligent predators in the forest.

A single sound escaped her, a soft moan of alarm. Her tongue darted out, traced her suddenly dry lips. Maggie knew better than to run—she didn't want to trigger an attack. She took another step backward, felt for the door. All the while her gaze was locked with the panther's. The cat never looked away from her, a hunter beyond measure, a fast, efficient killer that was concentrated on prey. *She* was the prey. She recognized danger when she saw it.

He could hear her heartbeat, the fast acceleration that signaled intense fear. Her face was pale, her eyes wide as she stared deep into his. When her small tongue touched her lush bottom lip, he nearly fell out of the tree. He could almost read her thoughts. She believed he was hunting her, stalking her. She believed he was hungry. And he was. He wanted, *needed* to devour her. Just not in the way she thought.

She backed inside the house, slammed the door shut solidly. He heard the bar slide into place. Brandt remained very still, his heart hammering out his joy. She was his now. It was only a matter of time. The intensity of his need for her shocked him. The instinctual drive for a mate went far beyond anything he had ever experienced.

The night was falling. His time. It belonged to him, to his kind. He listened to the whispers as his world stirred to life. He heard the softest calls, knew every creature, every insect. Knew who belonged and who did not. There was a natural rhythm to life and he was in the midst of a change. Disturbing, disquieting, but he was determined to exert his discipline and handle it as he did all things, with iron control.

He shifted, roped muscles rippling beneath the thick fur as he padded in silence along the heavy branch, intent on following her progress as she moved from room to room. He couldn't take his eyes from her, drinking in the sight of her, torturing his body, his senses, with her. She moved him as nothing ever had. She stole his breath and aroused his body to such a fever pitch of excitement he found himself enthralled.

Nothing stood between them but his honor. His code. Nothing. No time or distance. He had resolved that issue with his cunning intelligence. He lifted his head and forced his body to take in air, to read the night, to know he was in control in the midst of the upheaval. His body was different. Heavy with need, throbbing, aching. Every sense was alive. Every cell needed. Hungered. His head roared and ached, an uncomfortable state for one of power and discipline.

Maggie leaned against the door for a long time. She had been crazy to come here to this far-off place with danger at every turn. Her heart was racing and her blood rushed madly through her body. Yet a small smile touched her mouth in spite of the adrenaline pumping through her. She couldn't remember feeling so alive before. She wasn't even certain she had been afraid, she was so excited. It was as if she had been walking through life asleep to all the possibilities. Now, here, in the primitive jungle, every sense was enhanced and on fire.

She stepped away from the door, looked up at the ceiling with its fans and wide beams. This house suited her with its wide-open spaces and interesting carvings. She began to walk through it, confident that there were no animals in her home. It was exhilarating to feel as if she had closed out all danger and left it on the other side of the door. She picked up her packs and began an inspection of the downstairs. The rooms were large and each had the same high ceiling and sparse furniture, all made with a hard, dark wood. Curiously, in two of the bedrooms she discovered claw marks, as if some very large cat had marked the wall up near the ceiling. Maggie stared at the marks, puzzled by how they had been put there.

In the large kitchen she found a note on the small refrigerator penned in a masculine scrawl explaining how the lights worked and where to find everything she might need for the first night in her family home. There was a bowl of fresh fruit left for her and she gratefully ate a juicy mango, her parched throat savoring the sweetness. She touched the large, looping letters of the note in a silent thanks with a caressing fingertip, strangely drawn to the handwriting. She turned the note over and over, brought it to her nose, inhaling the scent. She could actually smell him. Brandt Talbot, the man who had written the note, had lived in the house.

He was everywhere. His scent. He seemed to envelop her with his presence. Once she was aware of him, she realized his touch was everywhere. He *lived* in the house. The polished wood and gleaming tiles had to have been his doing. The artwork, which appealed to her, had to be his.

The stairs were wide and curved in a sweeping circle up to the next level. Incredible photos of every wild creature imaginable hung on the walls going up the stairs. The photographs were rare treasures. The photographer had captured the very essence of wildlife, unusual action shots and beautiful pictures of plants, close-ups that depicted the dewy petals. She leaned closer, already knowing who had taken the photographs. In the corner of each picture was a four-line poem. Reading the words made her feel as if she had accidentally connected intimately with the poet. Each poem had been written in a looping masculine scrawl. The sentiments were thoughtful, beautiful, romantic even. It couldn't have been written by anyone else. Brandt Talbot had the soul of a poet. He was an unusual man and she was already intrigued.

She inhaled again as she climbed the stairs, drawing the scent of him deep into her lungs. He seemed to belong. Here in the house. Deep inside of her where she breathed. The mysterious Brandt Talbot with his incredible photography skills and his love of wood and wildlife and beautiful words. He seemed familiar, a man who shared her favorite things.

Weariness was making her droop. Maggie became aware of how uncomfortable her skin was, wet and sticky, as she made her way up to the second story. She found a bedroom at the end of the hallway that was to her liking. The bed was made up invitingly, the fans were already circulating air, and there was a spacious private bath off the room.

She put her packs on the dresser, silently claiming the room as her own. Above the bed, up in the corner, she saw the claw marks etched deeply into the wood and she shivered. Her gaze remained there as she tossed the khaki shirt aside and peeled off the wet T-shirt. It was a relief to have the soaked material away from her tender skin.

Maggie stood in the center of the room wearing only her low-riding jeans, and she sighed with relief. Wet clothes clinging to her skin called up a strange sensation, almost as if something lying dormant beneath her skin stirred for a moment, tried to break through her pores, then subsided, leaving her itchy and tender and very irritable. She stretched her sore muscles, lifted her hands to take down her hair, shaking it loose so she could wash the heavy mass in the shower.

Her boots came off next, then her socks. It was heaven to be barefoot, her soles cool on the floorboards. Much more comfortable, she took the time to look around the large room. The second-story bedroom was spacious with wide beams and little furniture. The bed was huge with four intricately carved posters rising halfway to the ceiling. Several fans whirled above her head, providing a welcome breeze in the room. Her gaze touched once more on the strange claw marks, slid away, then returned as if drawn by some unseen force.

She crossed the room to stare up at them, finally climbed up on the bed and stretched to touch them with her fingertips. She traced each mark. The wood was shredded; the claws had dug in deep. Was it from a long-ago pet kept in the house? Something wild that had marked its territory?

The moment the unbidden thought came to her, she shivered, the marks taking on life, burning her fingertips so that she pulled her hand quickly away from the wall. Surprised, she glanced at her seared fingers but found them without a blemish. Maggie put her fingers in her mouth, soothing the sensitive nerve endings with her tongue.

She wandered across the room to the windows. The panes in the room seemed overlarge, big enough to climb through should she need to do so. Each room had similar size windows with the inevitable balcony around them. A grid of bars shielded each window, making her very aware she was in a wild setting.

Maggie stood at the window, staring out into the night. Into the rain and the forest. She could see the leaves waving and dancing in the trees as the wind increased in strength. Bone tired, she began to slowly peel away her jeans, wet from the tropical rain and sticking to her. She wanted a shower and then to lie down and sleep as long as possible. She didn't want to think about how wild her surroundings were, how she seemed so different here in this exotic setting. She didn't want to be aware of her body, every nerve ending heightened by the sultry air and danger surrounding her. She stood naked, staring out the window into the darkness, unable to look away.

The glass reflected back her image as a mirror might. The strange heaviness was on her again, a burning that pooled low and wicked in her body, throbbing and demanding relief. It was even stronger than the last time, as if a wave of sexual hunger gripped her, settled in her, demanded satisfaction. Maggie leaned closer to peer into the glass, inspecting her body. Her skin was unmarred, smooth and inviting.

Separated only by a thin pane of glass, Brandt's breath stilled in his body. She was so enticing with her innocent eyes and sultry mouth. Her body was made to be touched, to be enjoyed. Made for him. His heart thundered out a savage beat and his body shuddered with anticipation.

He could almost feel the texture of her skin, soft and inviting. He knew the way their bodies would come together in frantic heat, in a firestorm of passion and hunger. When she moved, her body was a seductive invitation, her full breasts drawing his heated gaze. There was a thin sheen of sweat on her skin so that she glistened like the petals of a flower after a rain. He locked his muscles to keep from leaping through the window and lapping at every inch of exposed skin. He wanted to suckle her lush breasts, feel her fiery heat surround him. He wanted to be buried deep inside of her. He had so many plans, each more erotic than the last, and looking at her, he vowed to have her in every way possible. Drawn by the sight of her body unveiled to him, he pressed closer, his eyes gleaming gold in the dark.

Strangely, Maggie felt eyes on her, watching her. The impression was so strong she stepped even closer to the window. She doubted if any human would be out standing on the balcony in the deluge, especially with a panther near. Yet the feeling persisted that her lover had arrived and he waited for her. Wanted her. Was desperate for her. The feeling was strong, overwhelming, as if she could feel his savage hunger beating at her in her mind. His eyes were caressing every inch of her body.

Her hands moved up her narrow rib cage on the path she wanted him to take. She cupped the weight of her breasts in her hands, an offering, a blatant temptation. She needed to feel him touching her, his thumbs teasing her nipples into hard peaks. Maggie's skin was hot and flushed, her body aching for release. When she moved, it was a sensual flow of muscles and curves, her hands following the lines of her body, drawing attention to the fiery triangle of curls at the junction of her legs.

Her thighs felt smooth, her hips rounded. She ached for her lover to find her, to come to her, to touch her skin and find every secret place on her body. Her long hair fell around her like a silken cloak, strands sliding over her breasts and back as she moved, caressing her breasts and buttocks. The sensation caused her body to clench tightly in reaction, her blood to thicken and her breath to grow labored.

Maggie placed her hands on the glass pane. She wanted. She hungered. For whom she didn't know, but the feeling was strong in her. And it wasn't sweet or pleasant. The erotic images dancing in her head were rough and consuming, not of a gentle, considerate lover, but one taking her in a wild frenzy of lust, of elemental, savage desire.

The pictures in her head bewildered her and she turned away from the window. Maggie padded barefoot to the shower, hoping to wash away the strange ideas in her head. The strange sensations in her body. She wasn't at all prepared for the way the tropical forest affected her, and she just wanted it to go away.

The water was cool on her skin. Maggie closed her eyes and savored the feel of it, the way it seemed to absorb into her tissues and pores. She was exhausted, wanting only to sleep, yet the fever in her blood was strong. A force of nature. She leaned against the wall of the shower and allowed the water to cascade over her breasts, massaging the terrible ache. If she belonged in this wild, primitive setting, did it mean the reaction of her body would never go away? Maggie patted her body dry, leaving some of the cooling water to dry beneath the fans.

She lay on the bed in the dark, listening to the rain. Outside her window the wind blew, and unfamiliar sounds of the jungle penetrated the walls of the house. She lay still with her heart beating in tune to the rain. She could feel the sheet beneath her skin. She found herself rubbing her body along the material, wanting to feel every inch of her skin touching it. She rolled seductively, stretched, came up on her hands and knees to push her bottom up in the air. All the while she throbbed and burned and nothing she did gave her relief.

Brandt watched as she was caught in the throes of the sexual heat of their race. She was the most sensuous creature he had ever seen. His body was on fire, painful, as she moved against the sheets. He watched her fingers move over skin that belonged to him. Touch places that were made for him. A snarl escaped, a low moan of hunger. The lust, the need was so strong he no longer cared about honor, about the future. He would have her tonight. Now. There would be no waiting.

And then she buried her face in the pillow and wept as if her heart were breaking. The sound stopped him cold.

He stared at her, seeing her easily in the dark, and felt her fears, her loneliness. Felt her confusion and humiliation for things she couldn't hope to control or understand. He hadn't thought what changing her life so drastically would do to her, only what it would do for him. He crouched on the balcony and listened while she cried herself to sleep. Unexpectedly, his heart nearly shattered.

Maggie dreamt of a man's soothing voice. Of comforting arms. Of fur sliding sensuously next to her skin. Over her skin. Of padding through the darkened forest on four legs, not two. Of behaving outrageously, seductively, rolling and crouching to entice a male to her. She dreamt of torches flashing and the sound of gunshots. She dreamt of a man with a scent that filled her with longing.

She woke in late afternoon, her body sprawled naked, tangled in the sheet, with the memories of strange, disjointed dreams etched clearly in her mind. She became aware of sensation first, then sound. The raucous calls of birds. The hum of insects. The chattering of monkeys. The rain.

It was already humid and the fans were whirling to provide a semblance of relief from the sultry air. She turned her head toward the window and was surprised to find mosquito netting surrounding her bed. She reached out idly, not quite all the way awake, and pulled the netting to one side. She found herself blinking up at the most compelling, mesmerizing eyes she'd ever seen. Molten gold. Liquid. Hypnotic.

Her heart jumped and then began to pound out a rhythm of joy. Her small teeth bit into her lower lip. "What are you doing here?" Her voice came in a rush. He was the most physically intimidating man she had ever seen. She lay paralyzed, unable to move. She could only stare at him helplessly, shock mixing with a strange excitement.

Brandt pushed the netting into the corner, his gaze sliding possessively over her body. The sheet was tangled around her, revealing more than it hid. Her silken hair spilled around the pillow, a spun reddish-gold that matched the thatched curls peeking at him from the shadow between her legs. He swallowed the sudden dryness in his mouth. "I wanted to make certain you were all right. It occurred to me it wasn't safe leaving you alone in an unfamiliar house in the middle of a rain forest, so I stayed to protect you. I'm Brandt Talbot." One rounded breast was tantalizing him, drawing his heated gaze no matter how much he tried to impose discipline on himself.

Maggie felt the brush of flames from the burning intensity of his eyes as he looked at her body. With a small gasp of alarm, she sat up, dragging the sheet over her. "Good heavens, I don't have any clothes on!"

His perfectly sculpted mouth curved gently into a small smile. "I noticed."

"Well, don't notice." Holding the sheet up to her neck with one hand, she imperiously pointed toward the door with the other. He was the most alluring man she had ever seen. His hair was long and thick, jet-black, shiny enough to make her want to run her hands through it. Given the way she had been feeling the night before, she wasn't altogether certain it was safe for him to be in her bedroom. Especially when she was naked. "I'll get dressed and meet you downstairs in the kitchen."

His smile widened into a melting grin. "I brought you

up food." He pulled a silver tray from atop the dresser and placed it on the bed. "I don't mind your state of . . . er . . . undress. It livens up the place."

She blushed, color creeping up her neck. There was fruit on the tray, a glass of cold juice, a mug of hot tea, and a colorful orchid. The flower was fresh. Exquisite. What kind of man would think to bring her something so beautiful on her first awakening in the rain forest? She stared from the tray to his masculine good looks. The man was all muscle, rippling biceps and wide shoulders. His eyes were mesmerizing, a burning intensity Maggie was lost in the moment their gazes met. She had never seen eyes like his before on a man. His eyes belonged on a creature of the jungle, a hunter, focused and intent on prey. Yet he had thought to bring her a flower on a silver tray of food.

Maggie looked hastily away from his eyes before she was lost forever in their mysterious depths. Lost forever in the contrast between predator and poet.

"I don't think this place needs livening up," she murmured, trying not to gape at him. There was no way she was going to try to eat fruit stark naked in bed with him staring at her with his sinful eyes. He was robbing her of speech. Of breath. Of good sense. Her entire body came alive with him in the room. It wasn't safe. That was all there was to it. "Really, you just wait downstairs and I'll be right down."

His gaze moved over her. Hot. Possessive. She held her breath. His look alone could send her body into meltdown.

His white teeth flashed briefly, leaving her with the impression of a predator as his smile faded. "I'll be waiting, Maggie," he said quietly as he left the room. His voice was low, compelling. A tone that seemed to seep through her pores to heat her blood. He had a voice, a body, eyes, and a mouth that were too sensually sinful, and she was afraid of succumbing to his blatant sex appeal in her present state. Fortunately, he had sounded a bit too aggressive. Too arrogant. There was something proprietary in his tone that set her teeth on edge. It was almost as if he had rubbed her fur the wrong way.

Maggie laughed aloud at the analogy. She was in the forest a day, but already she was embracing the wildlife. She tossed back the sheet and hurried to the bathroom. Brandt Talbot had the keys to every door in her house. The bar on the front door hadn't even slowed him down. She should be grateful to the man for being so concerned about her. *He had slept in the house with her.*

Had he come to her room in the middle of the night? Had he crept into her dreams with his amazing voice? She tried to reach for the elusive memories but all she could really think about was the way she had been on fire, the way she had needed to be touched, to be stroked. Had he seen her like that? The idea made her burn inside and out.

She stared at herself in the mirror, wanting to see if she looked as different as she felt. For the first time she noticed how incredibly large her green eyes were. Her pupils were tiny pinpricks in the light of day, protecting her eyes from the bright glare of daylight, although there was little sun. She stared, wondering at the illumination of her vivid green eyes as she spread toothpaste onto her brush. Her heart stopped, slamming hard in her chest, as she exposed her small white teeth. Sharpened canines gleamed at her, a wicked addition to her delicate looks.

Maggie covered her mouth, frightened, of the strange illusion. It had to be an illusion. Very slowly she took her hand away and stared at her exposed teeth. They were perfectly straight. Perfectly normal. She was losing her mind. Maybe Jayne had been right and she didn't belong in such a primitive setting. She had loved the thought of it for so long, maybe she was just too susceptible. On the other hand, it was the only time in her life she would be able to learn about her parents. She had never been a timid woman, or a nervous one. She had no fear of traveling on her own. She was well versed in martial arts and had confidence in herself in a tight situation, although here, in the wild forest, she felt so different, so unlike Maggie Odessa. Yet it wasn't in her to run.

She dressed with care, as lightly as possible. The humidity was oppressive. Her hair was twisted into a neat French braid and pinned to the top of her head like a crown. It left her neck bare. She found her lace bra and matching panties, scraps of material she hoped wouldn't rub against her skin in the heavy cloying air. She was not making the same mistake twice, being caught without her bra in the middle of a tropical rainstorm.

She had very little time to research her parents' history. She was determined to make every moment count. As she ran down the stairs, she prepared a mental list of questions for Brandt Talbot.

Brandt stood up as she entered the kitchen, and every single word in her head melted away. Scattered. Dissipated so that she just stood in the doorway staring at him. He made her weak. Actually weak when she looked at him. Maggie feared if she tried to speak she might stammer. His effect was overpowering.

He smiled at her, and a thousand butterfly wings brushed at the pit of her stomach. As he came toward her, he moved in absolute silence, not even his clothing daring to rustle. He took her breath away. Maggie had never been so susceptible to anyone before and it was exceedingly uncomfortable.

She forced an answering smile. "Thank you for spending the night in the house with me. I really wouldn't have been so foolish as to try to take a walk around the grounds but it's nice to know someone was worried." Self-consciously she seated herself in the high-backed chair he held out for her. "I suppose you have the keys to the house?"

"Yes, of course. I reside here most of the time. The forest has a way of reclaiming what belongs to it very quickly. The creeper vines wind beneath the eaves if I don't stay alert." He sat facing her at the end of the table.

Maggie watched his strong fingers find a mango wedge

and bring it to his mouth. Strong teeth bit down. Her entire body clenched in response. She forced herself to look away from him. "Can you tell me anything about my parents? I was adopted at the age of three and really don't remember anything at all."

Brandt watched her expressive face, the conflicting emotions chasing across it. Maggie was fighting her attraction to him, determined to ignore it. She was much more potent up close. The chemistry between them sizzled and arced so that the very air around them was electric. "All of us in the forest know of your parents, Maggie," he said softly, watching her closely. The mango tasted sweet, the juice trickling down his throat like the finest wine, but it couldn't take her place. She would taste sweeter, more intoxicating.

"Tell me then." She took a cautious sip of the juice and was instantly entranced. It was a nectar she couldn't identify, but her mouth absorbed her first sip as if parched for the taste. Embers smoldering in the pit of her stomach leapt to life, spread like a living flame through her bloodstream. The hand holding the glass trembled.

Brandt leaned closer, his fingertips brushing back a tendril of hair as it escaped from her upswept crown. His touch lingered, sent flames dancing over her skin to match the building conflagration inside of her. "The taste is unique, isn't it?" His lean, strong fingers closed over hers, brought the glass to her lips. "Drink, Maggie, drink all of it." His voice was husky, seductive, a tantalizing invitation to a feast of pleasure.

She wanted to resist. There was something in him that frightened her even as he attracted her. A power, the possessive way he touched her. Maggie was certain she was placing herself in his control, but the scent of the nectar enveloped her, tempted her. One strong hand was at her nape, his fingers curling around her neck, making her all too aware of his strength. He tilted the glass and the golden liquid slid down her throat. Fire blossomed in her, pooled low, and burned out of control.

Panicked, Maggie jerked her head back, her green gaze meeting his. He was so much closer than she had thought, the heat of his body seeping into her. She couldn't look away, hypnotized as he brought the glass to his own mouth. His lips settled intimately over the exact spot where her lips had touched. He tilted the contents down his throat, all the while holding her gaze with his own.

Her lungs burned for air. She watched his throat work, watched as he caught a drop of amber liquid on his fingertip and deliberately carried it to her mouth. Before she could stop herself, her tongue darted out, swirled along his finger, absorbing the taste of him along with the nectar. For one moment her mouth was tight around his finger, sucking on his flesh, her tongue dancing and teasing provocatively. Maggie could feel her body dampening, burning with sudden hunger. Her hips moved restlessly and she ached for relief.

Brandt inhaled sharply, caught the enticing scent of her invitation. It nearly drove him crazy. He was half-mad for her already. The sensation of her mouth, hot and moist, tight around his finger, made him as hard as a rock. It was an easy enough step for his body to know what it would feel like to have his mate give the same attention to his heavy erection. His hand tightened possessively around her neck, he bent his head closer.

Maggie abruptly pulled away, nearly tumbling out of the chair as she hastily backed away from him. "I'm sorry, I'm sorry." Tears burned in her throat, glittered in her eyes. "I don't know what's wrong with me. Please go." She had never, at any time in her life, *ever* acted in such a manner. And Brandt Talbot was a complete stranger. No matter how much his scent and looks attracted her, no matter how *right* he felt, he was a stranger.

"Maggie, you don't understand." Brandt stood also, stalking her across the expanse of the kitchen. His body was compact, muscular, and he reminded her of a great jungle cat, ropes of rippling muscles, power and coordination.

She retreated until the counter brought her up short. "I don't want to understand. I want you to go. Something's wrong with me." There was a fever in her blood, her mind was in chaos. Images of writhing on the floor with Talbot were etched in her brain. She could hardly think clearly. Her body betrayed her, her breasts aching and tender. In her deepest, most feminine core she burned for him. "Just go. Please just go." She honestly didn't know which of them was in more danger.

He put a hand on either side of her body, trapping her between his hard frame and the counter. "I know what's wrong with you, Maggie. Let me help you."

Her fingers actually curled into a claw. She raised her arm, going for his eyes even as her brain screamed a protest. Brandt was fast, whipping his head to one side, shackling her wrist tightly. Maggie closed her eyes, terrified of reprisal. Although his grip was like a vise, he wasn't hurting her.

"Maggie, what is happening to you is very natural. This is your home, where you belong. Can't you feel it?"

She shook her head, dragged in a lungful of air to regain a semblance of control. She wanted to go home, far from the influence of the jungle, of the heat. "I don't know what's happening, but if this is the way this place affects me, I don't want to be here."

He was suffocating, reason gone, the world spinning madly. Brandt battled his savage nature, the fierce primitive need and hunger as elemental as time. She was frightened, unaware of her legacy. He needed to remember that at all times. Maggie couldn't get away from him, it was too late for her. He had to court her, persuade her gently, coax her into accepting her inevitable fate. The urgent demands of his body could not be allowed to destroy the fragile thread between them.

"Maggie." He used his voice shamelessly, a blend of temptation and heat. "The forest is calling to you, that's all it is. Nothing else. You haven't done anything wrong. You haven't offended me. I don't want you to be afraid of me. Are you? Have I frightened you in some way?"

She was more afraid of herself than she was of him. She shook her head, unwilling to speak, the masculine scent of him nearly overwhelming.

"You want to know about your parents, don't you, and all the work they did with endangered species? They were legends in their own way with the progress they made." Brandt felt the tension began to slowly dissolve in her body. "Let me tell you about your parents, because, believe me, they were two very extraordinary people. Did you know that they protected the animals here? That without them, poachers would have succeeded in killing off the sun bear? That's only one of their triumphs. They made it their life's work to protect rare endangered animals. Your mother was much like you, with a smile that could light up a room. Your father was a strong man, a leader. He lived here, in this house, and he took over his father's job of protecting the rain forest. Each year it has gotten more difficult. Poachers are bold and they have tremendous firepower."

As he felt the apprehension drain from her, Brandt slowly released her, turned away from the danger the close proximity of her body presented. Her breasts were heaving with every breath she drew in, dragging his gaze to the firm, tempting mounds he longed to touch. He had feasted his gaze on her body, knew the swelling curves were a creamy invitation to sheer soft satin. Her heat fired his blood, and the scent of her aroused him to a painful need, his jeans stretched taut, his body in rebellion against the dictates of his brain.

Maggie's hand trembled as she gripped the counter to support her rubbery legs. She wanted to hear every word he had to say with regard to her parents. "What do you mean, without my parents poachers would have succeeded in killing off the sun bear?" She made every effort to sound normal. She knew he had to think she was psychotic, one moment trying to seduce him, the next clawing at him.

"With deforestation, plantations, and poachers encroaching every day, the sun bear, like many other animals, are in a tremendous decline and have been for a number of years. Your parents recognized the immediacy of concern."

"Why are poachers after the sun bear?" She was genuinely interested. Maggie had worked hard to learn about endangered wildlife, drawn to the cause from the first time she had seen a large cat.

"Several reasons. It is the smallest of all bears and is marketed as a pet. The largest it gets is about a hundred forty pounds, very small for a bear. And the bear is beautiful with a crescent-shaped yellow or white mark across its chest. It's really the only true bear living in our rain forest, and we don't want to lose it."

"My parents were game wardens? Is that what you do?" Somehow the idea of Brandt being a game warden was even more appealing. She persisted in seeing him as a hunter, yet in truth he was a protector of the creatures in the forest and a poet at heart.

He nodded. "All of us in the village have dedicated our lives to the preservation of the forest and the trees, plants, and animals dwelling in it. Your parents had two particular animals they fought to preserve, and eventually it killed them."

Her heart beat into the silence. "What killed them?"

"Poachers, of course. Your parents were too successful at what they did. Parts of the sun bear are worth a fortune." Brandt sat at the table and picked up his mug of tea, wanting to set her at ease.

"Parts?" Her eyebrows shot up. She frowned at him, rubbing at her arms. She was itching again. That strange, uncomfortable feeling of something moving beneath her skin was back. "Poachers sell off parts of the bear? Is that what you're telling me?"

"Unfortunately, yes. The gallbladder is especially popular for medicine. And in some places the conversion of forest habitat to plantations of oil palm have put an even larger price on their heads. Because the bears don't have their natural foods, they feed on the heart of the oil palm and destroy the trees. Naturally the plantation owners pay money to have the bears hunted and destroyed." Brandt watched her closely, following the movement of her hands as her palms rubbed back and forth along her arms.

"That's horrible."

"Leopards are disappearing as well." His voice was fierce now. "We cannot allow the leopards to become extinct. Already the numbers are dwindling at an alarming rate. Once these species are lost to us, we cannot recover them. We owe it to them, to ourselves, and to our children to preserve these animals."

Maggie nodded. "I've certainly done research in the area of saving habitats and I know the necessity, Brandt, but if it killed my parents all those years ago, I would think the danger would be even greater now."

"Danger doesn't matter. We accept that as part of our lives. We are the keepers of the forest. It's our duty and it has always been our privilege. Your parents understood that, and their parents before them." His golden eyes moved over her, a brooding perusal. "There are only a few of us, Maggie, carrying on what your parents worked so hard for. It's your legacy." Noting her distress, he stood up slowly so as not to startle her. "What's wrong?"

"My skin itches." She bit her lower lip. "Do you think I could have picked up some kind of parasite? It's strange, like something's moving inside of me, running under my skin." She was watching his face closely and saw the fleeting, cunning expression in his eyes. He knew. He was looking at her innocently, but he knew much more than he was letting on. She tilted her chin at him in challenge.

"You know what it is, don't you, Brandt? You know what's happening to me." She moved around the counter, putting it between them, the only way she felt safe.

"Are you afraid of me, Maggie?" he asked quietly.

His tone chilled her to the bone. It was the second time he had asked her that. The silence in the house beat between them. Outside the walls, the forest was humming with life. "Should I be?"

"No," he denied quickly, his molten gaze burning intensely, searing her. Branding her. "Never be afraid of me. I'm sworn to protect you. Above all others, above the forest and the animals in the forest. Never be afraid of me, Maggie."

"Why? Why are you sworn to protect me, Brandt?" His very intensity frightened her. No matter how hard he tried to look civilized, she saw the hunter in him. She saw the predator. He could camouflage his savage nature for brief periods of time, but not from her, not when they were alone together. She felt edgy and irritated. Why would she know him? Why would she see through him? The ground seemed to be shifting out from under her feet.

4

The silence stretched between them until Maggie wanted to scream. She could feel the turmoil raging deep within her, almost as if something wild were struggling for control. She was aware of so many things. The spacious room, the total isolation. The fact that few people knew where she was. Maggie was alone in the rain forest with a man whose sheer power overwhelmed her.

Brandt took a single step toward her. She reacted without thought, without plan, springing in a swift leap to the tabletop across the room. She landed in a crouch on all fours. Lightly. Silently. Her lips were drawn back in a snarl. The pins holding her hair scattered to the floor, spilling her heavy braid down her back. It took a few moments for reality to sink in, for Maggie to realize what she had done.

A soft moan of despair escaped as she surveyed the distance from the counter to the table where she was crouched. It was impossible to have jumped the area in a single leap. It wasn't humanly possible.

"Maggie." He said her name. That was all. His voice was soothing. Gentle. Tender even. He knew what was happening to her—she could see the knowledge in the molten gold of his eyes.

"Get out now." She bit the words out at him, shaking with fear, with terror. She jumped from the table and raced out of the room, up the stairs to the bedroom. She was leaving, as quickly as possible. There had to have been something in the nectar, something to bring about the change in her. Whatever it was, she was going back to safety. Away from the jungle and far, far away from Brandt Talbot.

Maggie dragged her backpack out from the under the bed and began to stuff her things into it. Her hands were shaking so badly she dropped her clothes on the floor before she could get them into the pack. When she raised her eyes, he was standing there. Looming over her. His thighs were like oak trees, strong columns of power.

He reached out and took the pack from her hands, casually tossed it aside. "How do you think you can find your way without a guide, Maggie?" He touched her face with his fingertips, trailed a caress down her collarbone, then lower to the neckline of her shirt. It felt like a stroke of heat, of flame.

"People know where I am," she told him, her green gaze locked in combat with his golden one. "The lawyer . . ."

He shook his head. "Is one of us; he works for me. The moment you set foot in the forest, letters—brilliant forgeries I might add—were sent to your work to give notice, and to your apartment. Your things were packed up, some stored and others shipped. No one expects your return; they believe you are staying in your new estate after all."

"I'm a prisoner here? Why? What could you possibly want with me?" Maggie struggled for control. She needed to be calm, to breathe air and think. Brandt Talbot was enormously strong and he had the advantage of knowing the forest. She was as good as his captive. Yet even knowing that information, she couldn't deny the chemistry arcing between them, sizzling and alive and potent beyond imagination.

He was close to her. So close she could smell him, feel the heat of his body right through her clothes. So close her breasts were only a scant inch or two from his chest. His fingers wrapped around her throat, his thumb tipping her head back. "This is your home, Maggie. You belong here. You were born here in this forest. And you belong to me." His hand slipped from her throat, slid over her tank top to cup the fullness of her breast. His thumb caressed her nipple through the cotton and the lace.

The breath slammed out of her lungs. Flames shot through her body, from her breast to her deepest core. The strange roaring was back in her head. Need was on her. Not some gentle emotion, not a pleasant feeling, but a raging tidal wave of hunger, of craving. She wanted his hand to tighten, to knead and massage. His mouth to close over her aching flesh, to devour her.

Both hands flat on his chest, she shoved him away as hard as she could. "You drugged me. The nectar. You put something in the drink to make me like this."

As hard as she shoved him, his body barely rocked in response. "Listen to me, Maggie. I haven't lied to you. I won't lie to you. You're close to the change, that's what's wrong. It took me so long to find you, and you're ready for me. Your body needs mine. Let me help you." He still cupped the weight of her breast in his palm. Intimately. Possessively. His hand slid lower, over her rib cage, over her slender, tucked-in waist, to rest on the curve of her hip.

"What the hell does that mean?" Her green eyes glared at him. He couldn't help but notice the way she was breathing, starved for air. Frightened. Resolute. Courageous. Maggie was determined to fight him even in such distress, yet she didn't jerk away from his touch and she didn't become hysterical. His admiration for her grew.

He used his voice, a soothing caress, to tame her fears. "Let me tell you about your family. Who they were. What they were." His fingers stroked her hip tenderly because he needed to touch her; he couldn't stop himself. "We can go for a walk if you'd like. If you would feel more at ease. I'd like to show you the beauty of the forest." *Your home.* The unspoken words were between them.

Brandt's touch was so intimate, so possessive, so completely right, Maggie stilled beneath his drifting hand. Absorbed his touch. Craved more. He seemed so familiar, and yet tiny tongues of flames licked at her skin wherever he stroked. She wanted to protest, to fight him; at the same time she wanted desperately to fasten her mouth to the perfection of his. Sheer sexual chemistry. That was all. That was everything.

Maggie nodded. The house was too stifling. And he was too compelling. She wanted him more than she had ever wanted anything in her life, and yet she knew nothing about him. She would have thought him crazy if she didn't have the proof of his words in her own body. The strange sensations, the wild, savage need to have him buried deep inside of her.

This was her one chance to get out of the house, away from his influence. If she could get to the village, perhaps the others would help her leave.

Brandt shook his head, his white teeth flashing with a small, enigmatic smile. "I'm not crazy, Maggie. Really. Let me tell you the story before you decide."

"I'm listening," she agreed as she pulled on her boots. She didn't look at him again. It was the safest thing to do. She would need every ounce of courage. She would need her wits about her. One look at Brandt Talbot and good sense scattered away instantly. She wasn't making that mistake again. "Are your parents alive, Brandt?" She wondered what his mother would have to say about his behavior.

"My father is alive," he answered softly. "My mother died a few months after your parents. Poachers killed her, too."

Maggie shivered at his grim tone. He tried to hide it from her, but she heard it all the same, tuned as she was to his every nuance. She led the way out of the house, watching as he carefully locked the door behind them. "Are you expecting visitors?" she asked with a raised eyebrow.

"It pays to be careful, Maggie. That's the first rule you learn here. You must never forget we're in a war. They want us dead, and if they find our homes, they'll be waiting for us. This area has been protected for hundreds of years, but each year the forest shrinks. There will come a day when we will have to leave here and go somewhere safer." He sounded sad. "Our people have guarded here nearly as long as the trees have existed. It will be a terrible loss for all of us and for the forest."

She heard the regret, the genuine sorrow in his voice. "I'm sorry, Brandt. I know what you're saying is true. We can only hope awareness of the importance of the rain forests and the various species here on earth is growing."

He walked very close to her, protectively, his larger body occasionally brushing against hers. His proximity was exciting. He made her feel feminine, sexy, even seductive, all things she had never considered herself to be. She glanced sideways at him, not wanting him to steal her soul away along with her good sense. It was the way they moved together, as if they had known each other always. The silence stretched and lengthened. A companionable silence when she should have been nervous and afraid.

The forest was extraordinarily beautiful. Flowers of every color rained down from the twisting vines and trees. The world hummed around them, a vibrant, mystical paradise. The perfumed scents of so many flowers filling the air were intoxicating. There was movement everywhere around them as birds soared overhead and monkeys flung themselves from branch to branch. The world seemed in constant motion, yet as still as the lizards and brightly colored frogs clinging to the trunks of the trees.

Maggie felt a strange peace stealing into her body. *As if she knew this place. Was familiar with it. As if it were home.* The thoughts were unbidden but crept into her mind all the same. The wild forest should have frightened her, but the setting was as natural to her as breathing.

"Why aren't the insects bothering me?" She suddenly realized that she heard continual buzzing around her but not even a mosquito had settled on her skin.

"The scent of the nectar repels them. We use it in the houses also. It makes life much more bearable here. We mix it in the village and use it daily. It works best if ingested." He answered matter-of-factly. "There are many properties here in the forest that can be used for medicine and repellants and other worthwhile things."

"Tell me more about my parents." She was enjoying walking with him too much. Maggie didn't want to take the chance that she might succumb to the attraction between them. She couldn't see herself having a hot flaming affair with a jungle lover and walking away unscathed. She was too drawn to Brandt. Too wrapped up in his allure.

He swept a hand through his dark silky hair. "I'd like to tell you a story first. It's well-known here in the forest. Every villager knows it and it ties into your parents."

She glanced at him quickly but he was looking at the path, choosing a way opposite of the direction Drake had pointed out as being toward the village. Whatever Brandt Talbot was up to, he had the upper hand. Maggie didn't care. She was determined to glean as much information from him as she could. "Please do."

He did glance at her then. She felt the power of his burning gaze, but she kept her face averted and looked as innocent as possible. Brandt shrugged his wide shoulders carelessly. "The village was younger then, with its homes closer together and in a clearing. No one thought they would be in such danger. The village had been large but time and circumstances had dwindled it down to a few pairs. The youngest were already in their thirties. They wanted a child. Everyone in the village wanted it for them. They were a deserving couple, working hard to preserve the forest, braving the poachers, destroying traps, freeing captured animals, striving tirelessly to keep the creatures under their protection safe. And finally the miracle happened." He smiled as if remembering a wonderful moment.

"The couple was going to have a baby."

He nodded, the faint smile lingering, reaching his golden eyes so that he took her breath away. "They had a beautiful daughter and they were very happy. The people were excited. Most of the pairs were older and had few children, so they were eager for the ritual of promise."

Maggie pushed her hair out of her face. Strands were escaping the braid as leaves and twigs caught it and pulled as she passed by. "What is the ritual of promise?"

"These people were not merely human, Maggie, but something much more, a separate species. They were not wholly animal nor wholly man, but something of a mixture. These people were of nature itself, using a normal human form but able to become large leopards, prowling the forest to keep order. They had dominion over other creatures, and with that came inevitable responsibility."

She had to sneak another look at his face. He was telling her a story, but he was implying the story was much more than that. She couldn't believe such a tale—she wouldn't believe it, no matter how charismatic Brandt was.

"Half-human, half-leopard, like the leopard men in the legends?" She tried very hard to keep the skepticism out of her voice. She had spent plenty of time reading and researching on the various tribal beliefs on half-human deities. She had always been somewhat obsessed with the subject.

"Those of this species are able to change shape at will. Not at first; when they're young, they are regular children. The change comes later. It is known as the Han Vol Dan. The way of the change. They are not half anything but all their own species. They live and work as humans but shift when necessary. They are the guardians of the jungles, of the rain forests. A people as rare as the treasures in their keeping."

Brandt's fingers tangled with hers as they moved together in perfect step. Perfect rhythm. There was no stumbling over the uneven ground. No rustling of leaves or snapping of twigs. They moved as a single unit, with natural stealth and complete ease. Unexpectedly he stopped, stepped directly in front of her so that she nearly ran into him.

Maggie had no choice but to tilt her head back and look up at him. Look into his golden eyes. At once she was lost, falling under his spell, her breath leaving her lungs in a rush. Rays of sunlight filtered through the heavy foliage, casting delicate radiance through the shadows, illuminating the brilliance of colors. Birds flitted from tree branch to vine, a flutter of wings overhead. She was aware of life pulsing around them, of the ebb and flow of nature singing, of the sounds of wildlife and water. Until she looked into his eyes.

Her world narrowed to Brandt. To the mysterious secrets swirling in the depths of his eyes. To the burning hunger and need she read there. He looked at her as if she were the only woman in the world. His molten gaze moved over her face slowly, drinking her in. He brought her hand up between them, so that her palm skimmed over the muscles of his chest. Her fingers brushed his chin sending butterfly wings brushing at the pit of her stomach as she felt his mouth moving against the back of her hand. His eyes continued to hold her captive. Maggie was mesmerized, a hunted rabbit caught in the intensity of his stare. He turned her hand over, opened her fingers, and, still holding her gaze, bent his head to scrape his teeth gently in the center of her palm. His tongue swirled, a hot, moist flame, and his sculpted lips completed the brand, pressing, firm yet velvet soft over the pulsing heat.

"I know you don't understand any of this yet, Maggie, and I thank you for your courage." His voice wrapped her in intimacy. "I just want you to know I have the advantage of knowing about you, about your life. I know about the time you fell off your bike and had to go to the hospital for stitches. I know about you caring for your mother while she was so ill, coming back from college to stay by her side for two months, nursing her yourself."

Maggie stared at him with wide, shocked eyes, tried to pull her hand away from his. He merely tugged her closer. "Don't be afraid of who you are. I'm not. Of course I investigated; I couldn't afford to be wrong. I know you've always loved the forest and the animals in it. So you see, I do know you. I know what kind of woman you are."

Brandt turned away from her, walking once more, taking her with him, unable to look into her frightened eyes. He kept her hand firmly in his. He had fallen for that tenderhearted young woman he had read so much about. Like a drowning man, he had clung to every scrap of information he could ferret out about her. His emotions were already involved, and each moment spent in her company or simply observing her drew the net tighter around his heart. She didn't know him other than as a man who tricked her, brought her to foreign soil, and attempted to seduce her into accepting him. He detested the fear and uncertainty in her eyes.

Maggie bit down on her lower lip, a sharp bite to give her courage to spar with him. "Why do you do that, Brandt? Deliberately keep me off balance? I know you brought me here, I just haven't figured out your real motive. I don't have enough money to make it worth your while. I'm not beautiful or famous. Why don't you just tell me the truth?"

"I have been telling you the truth. You aren't listening to the truth." There was no impatience in his voice. He kept walking, veering slightly along a faint path.

Maggie could hear the continual roar of a large body of water. She glanced back in the direction they had come and saw only forest, no path, no house. She was well and truly lost, dependent on Brandt to return her home safely. Her fingers were tangled with his. She told herself she didn't want to bother with a struggle in the heat and the humidity, but the truth was, she liked the feel of him strong and protective beside her.

"I'm listening," she said, because she could feel the heat wave starting in the pit of her stomach, spreading like a wildfire through her blood. "Tell me about the change." Something was happening deep inside of her. Something she didn't understand or want. She tightened her fingers around his, holding on to the only security she had while her body went up in flames. She didn't look at him, but stared into the trees ahead of them, trying to ignore the sensations assaulting her.

"Let me finish the story, Maggie. The ritual of promise is a wedding of sorts. Two lost hearts bound together as one. The story goes that cats have nine lives. The male is reborn remembering what came before. He must find his mate. No other will do. He must recognize her and lay his claim before the onset of the Han Vol Dan. Before the change overtakes her. The ritual of promise occurs when the two live in close proximity and the male recognizes the reborn female. Or, if the soul is new, when the male recognizes his mate at an early age."

"How can he do that?"

His eyes moved over her again. Moody. Brooding. Dark with some hidden mystery. "The aura of the woman or child calls to him, melds with his. The elders can see the two colors merge. The little girl was recognized and promised in the ritual. But the poachers had their revenge. They had been tracking the couple, trying to find their home, wanting to be rid of them. A very clever trap was set."

Maggie could feel the acceleration of her heart. Of his heart. She could hear them both pounding, remembering, reliving the terror. Her mouth went dry and she shook her head. "Don't tell me any more. I don't want to hear."

"Because you know. You were there when they came with their guns and their torches. When your father woke your mother and bundled you up and put you in her arms. When he kissed you for the last time and turned to fight the mob, to hold them back to give your mother a chance to save you. You remember his change, the way his fur felt against your skin. And you remember your mother's sobs as she wept and ran with you through the forest away from the village that was already being burned."

He turned up her hand, brought her knuckles to the warmth of his mouth. "I remember it vividly, every detail, Maggie, because my mother died that night, too—oh, not right away; she lingered for months before her physical body gave up." He couldn't feign his sadness. It was as real as her own. She saw it in his eyes, and his poet's heart wept.

She did remember the frightening, nightmare images— a leopard leaping, snarling, a mass of teeth and claws cutting a path while they ran with dizzying speed. She remembered her mother flinching as a shot reverberated. Her mother ran several yards, staggered, recovered valiantly, and continued. Maggie pressed a hand to her mouth. Memories? Were they real? Could her mother have run through the forest in the dead of night, away from all she had known? Away from her husband and people? Run with a terrible wound draining the life from her?

She dragged in her breath. "And she took me to Jayne. Jayne Odessa."

"A very wealthy woman who had never had children and had always wanted them. Who was your mother's friend and shared her concerns for the rain forest and endangered species. Who knew nothing about what your mother was, only that she loved her and would do anything to keep you safe. She witnessed your mother's death and she took you back to the United States and legally adopted you."

5

Maggie stood absolutely motionless. It was insanity to believe anything Brandt Talbot said, yet she knew it was true. She did have memories of that night. And Jayne Odessa had spoken often of a friend she loved very much who had died violently, tragically. A woman named Lily Hanover. The two women had worked tirelessly to preserve the rain forest and all the endangered species within it. Saving the environment had been the cause that had brought Jayne and Lily together. But Jayne had never told Maggie that Lily was her mother.

Brandt caught her chin. "Don't feel sad, Maggie. Your parents loved you very much and they loved each other. Few people ever have that in their lifetime."

"You knew them?" Her green gaze locked with his, daring him to lie to her.

"I was a boy, but I remember them, the way they always touched each other and smiled at each other. They were

truly wonderful people who always practiced what they
believed no matter what the danger."

Maggie glanced up into the trees, caught sight of the
several frogs sitting openly on the leaves. Their eyes were
huge, enabling the amphibians to hunt at night. Higher up,
clinging to the branches of a tree, was a small tarsier with
its round shiny eyes staring down at her. He looked like a
fuzzy, huggable alien creature. Her mother and father had
seen these little creatures just as she was seeing them, perhaps had stood under the same tree.

"Thank you for telling me about my parents, Brandt. I
understand better why Jayne was afraid for me to come
here to the forest. I used to talk about it all the time and she
would get upset, even cry. I longed to come to the rain forest here and in South America and in Africa. When I became a veterinarian, it was with the idea that I would be
working in the wild to preserve rare species."

"Jayne Odessa witnessed the poachers murdering Lily.
She had no idea of Lily's heritage, that she was a shape-
shifter." Brandt took a breath, let it out, all the time watching her expression carefully for signs that she was
rejecting the things he was revealing to her. "It must have
been so frightening for Jayne to know that poachers would
murder someone just because they tried to protect the animals. And then you had to grow up just like Lily, wanting
to save exotic animals."

He stroked her hair, the lightest of caresses, but the
touch sent heat spiraling through her body. She ached for
him but did her best to ignore it. Though he appealed to her
on so many levels, she was leery of the sheer force of the
attraction between them. "I may have inherited the tenden-
cies from my birth mother but Jayne certainly influenced
me, too. She surrounded herself with books and information on habitats and endangered species, supported the
causes monetarily, and volunteered for all sorts of things.
Of course some of her passion rubbed off on me."

"Do you believe the other things I told you, Maggie?"

Brandt framed her face with his hands, bent his dark head toward hers as if he couldn't bear the inches separating them. "Do you believe another species could exist? A species of shape-shifters? Do you believe you're one of us?"

He was so close, so tempting, his golden eyes glittering with intensity. "I don't know," she answered carefully. "I guess it wouldn't be all that difficult to prove." There was a challenge in her voice.

"And have you run screaming from me?"

"I may run screaming from you anyway," she pointed out with a small, self-mocking grin. She was watching his face, saw his sudden resolve, and her heart began beating overtime in her chest.

In the canopy overhead a monkey screamed; the flutter of wings told of birds taking flight. Brandt swung his head around quickly, alertly, his eyes suddenly flat and hard. "James! What are you doing here?"

Maggie looked in the direction Brandt was staring just as the wind shifted. She caught a vaguely familiar scent. She had smelled that presence a couple of times now, in the forest as she journeyed on her way to her parents' home and then outside the house, near the verandah. She could barely make out the man hidden in the shadows.

"Just curious, Brandt." The voice floated to them, almost a challenge.

Maggie instinctively moved closer to Brandt, feeling that odd "fur ruffled the wrong way" sensation she didn't like. Brandt seemed to recognize her discomfort and circled her waist with his arm, drawing her beneath the protection of his shoulder. Before he could introduce the other man, James had melted into the bush.

Maggie held her breath, waiting, but she didn't know for what.

Brandt left her side, tracking the other man into the foliage. When he returned he took her hand, drew her to him. "He's gone. Don't look so afraid."

"Who is he?" Maggie asked.

"One of our people." Brandt sounded grim. "One I would caution you to keep a distance from. He holds a fundamental belief that the rules apply to everyone but him."

For no reason that Maggie could think of, she shivered violently. Her body held an aversion to the man who was hidden in the heavier foliage. Brandt immediately reacted, running his palms up and down her arms in a massage.

"Why do you touch me as if you have the right?" And why did she crave his touch? "You touch me as if it's perfectly natural." As if she belonged to him.

"Does it bother you so much?" His voice dropped an octave, became a husky seduction. The pad of his thumb slid over her full lower lip in a caressing stroke.

Her stomach did a flip of delight. "It bothers me because it feels . . ." She trailed off, her eyes locked with his. It felt right. Perfect. Exactly what she wanted. His mouth was a scant few inches from hers. The temptation of his perfectly sculpted lips was more than she could resist.

Maggie honestly didn't know who moved first. She only knew there was magic in the brush of his mouth on hers. He was unexpectedly gentle, his lips moving over hers like the soft drift of the breeze. She felt his ravenous hunger, yet he touched her so tenderly, coaxing her response instead of demanding one. She pressed closer to him, circling her arms around his neck, needing the feel of his body against hers.

At once his lips firmed, hardened. He deepened the kiss, his hands sliding over the contours of her body, shaping her curves, dragging her closer. Brandt pushed the edge of her shirt up to give him access to bare skin. His palms found lace over her breasts, the thinnest skimming of materials to cover luscious treasure.

His touch sent fire racing through her blood. It shook her that she could have such a reaction, such an overwhelming need. A tremor ran through her body, and she stiffened slightly, something deep within her still fighting.

He abruptly pulled his mouth away from hers, his hands lingering on her breasts, his forehead resting on hers. There was the sheen of sweat on his skin and his breathing was ragged, his body fiercely aroused. "We can't stay here alone like this, Maggie. I don't have nearly the control I thought I did." He kissed her again. Gently. Persuasively. "Unless you want me the way I want you."

Everything feminine in her rose up to answer his call. She wanted him. Craved him. But as hot as she felt, as much as she wanted to wrap herself around him, something deep within her perversely denied them both the ultimate release.

"I can't, Brandt, I'm sorry. I don't know why. I can't." She curled her fingers in his shirt, held on to him for comfort.

His hands reluctantly left her breasts, skimmed over her rib cage, caressed her flat belly. "I understand, honey. Don't worry." He kissed her forehead, breathing deeply to pull himself back from the edge of sexual hunger. "Let's go somewhere safe."

"Is there somewhere safe?" She looked up at him, knowing her eyes were shining at him. His understanding only served to make him more attractive. Brandt Talbot was an incredibly sensitive man and she was falling deeper and deeper beneath his spell.

He bent his head to kiss the corner of her mouth, feeling he should be a candidate for sainthood or at the very least knighted. He took her hand and started off confidently in another direction. "I guess the village would be safe enough. We might find a person or two there." He scowled as he said it.

Maggie knew he was thinking about the mysterious James, hoping he wouldn't be at the village. "I would hope so. I'd like that. I've wanted to see it." She enjoyed walking beside him as he named plant species and pointed out animals and reptiles she might have missed. She became aware of how completely safe she felt with him. The forest was a dark place, mystical and even haunting, yet Brandt moved so quietly, so fluidly, with such complete assurance, she realized just how much a part of it he really was. "You took all those photographs hanging in the house, didn't you? They're very good." There was raw admiration in her voice.

He actually flushed. "You noticed those, did you? I hope you didn't read any of that nonsense. I should have taken them down but I didn't think about it."

"I liked the poetry."

He groaned. "It isn't poetry. I just was trying to find something for titles but nothing fit." His excuse sounded lame even to his own ears.

Maggie reached out and touched his hair, tangling her fingers in the silky mass for just a moment because she couldn't resist. "Are you a professional photographer?" He was so appealing in his embarrassment that she was reluctant to help him out but she couldn't stop herself.

"I freelance for *National Geographic*," Brandt admitted reluctantly. "I write articles and do consultations for various governments. Along with my job here, I try to raise world awareness about the value of the forest."

Maggie stared at him in shocked amazement. How could she not have put it all together? "You're *the* Brandt Talbot, the renowned leading expert on the rain forest? *Doctor* Brandt Talbot. I can't believe I'm talking to you. I've read everything you've ever written!" Maggie found herself falling deeper under his spell. He loved what she loved. She heard it in his voice and read it in his articles. He couldn't fake that kind of passion. "Tell me more about the species you say my parents were," she encouraged, uncertain whether she could believe him or not. Her body seemed living proof of his revelations. Something was going on inside of her, something she seemed not to have control over, yet his explanation seemed beyond the realm of reality. She tried to keep an open mind. "Are there many of them left?"

"Of us, Maggie—you're one of us—and no, there are not many of us left. Our race has dwindled. We've been hunted and killed nearly to the point of extinction. It was partly our own fault. We don't have the most noble history." There was regret in his voice.

"What happened?"

"In the early days, some tribes worshiped us as deities. Some of our people became obsessed with power. Like any species, there are those among us who choose a life of common good and service, and those who want to reign, to conquer. We have our own diseases and our own problems. We're passionate, a mixture of human and animal instincts that means good and bad from both sides." He stopped walking. "The village is just ahead of us. Maggie, even today, some of our males are obsessed with power," he cautioned her carefully.

"Leopards don't mate for life, Brandt. The females raise the cubs alone. Do the men walk away after sex?" She forced herself to ask the question without looking at him.

He caught her to him, his arms steel bands. "No, Maggie. We are not leopards, not animals, nor are we human. Our species mate for life. It's how it's done. For nine lives. All of our lives. Over and over. You're mine, I know you are, you've always belonged with me."

Relief and joy washed over her, so much so that she couldn't respond. The thought that he might want her for all their years rather than just a mating made her happy in spite of the fact that she wasn't altogether certain any of it was real. She let him hold her in silence while she looked around her, trying to see through the rain and trees. Sure enough, there were a couple of small structures woven into the trees and camouflaged by the wealth of plants growing in every conceivable manner. She shook her head. "This is the village? This is where everyone lives? All two buildings?" She was trying not to laugh. She had pictured something much different. A thriving busy hub, at least, like a native village.

"We never live in the village. We simply meet here to enjoy company or get supplies. Homes are scattered in and around the trees. We make certain there are no trails and that we're constantly vigilant, looking for signs of anyone near. The poachers destroyed the village the night your parents died, and since that time we've kept it quite small for protection."

"That makes sense, but it seems a sad way to live."

"We have our own community and not all of our people reside in the rain forest. Some have chosen to live on the outskirts. We change at will, with the exception of the Han Vol Dan. The first time shifting occurs is uncomfortable and can't be controlled. It's best to have someone with you to talk you through it."

"So children don't shift shape. Only adults?"

He nodded. "And we don't know what triggers it in each individual. Some are earlier shifters than others." Brandt slipped his arms around her shoulders, needing to touch her, to have her close. He was feeling edgy and combative, knowing the other males were in close proximity. His friends, he reminded himself. Men he trusted. Men who had saved his life a dozen times, as he had saved theirs. They knew Maggie was his mate. They would be just as uncomfortable around her as he would be with them there until he had bound Maggie to him.

And then there was James. Brandt and the others had scented him in the forest, watching Maggie's arrival. Twice Brandt had smelled his spoor near the house. Brandt didn't trust James and didn't want the man anywhere near Maggie. Their species had too much animal influence, so much so that they had to fight their very natures at times. They reacted like territorial males until the bonds were fully established. It was dangerous for all of them.

Maggie felt the fine tremor running through his body. "What is it?" She slid her arm around his waist, something she might not ordinarily have done, but he seemed to need her. There was a strange kind of power in having a strong man need her so much, to have him so intent on his pursuit of her. "You're uncomfortable with our being here. I can feel it, Brandt."

He pulled her back into the shelter of the trees and turned her into his arms, brought her body tightly against his so that she could feel his every muscle imprinted on her. His scent enveloped her. Brandt leaned down to nuzzle her hair aside so he could find her shoulder with his mouth. Teeth scraped back and forth gently over her bare skin. "I want you." He whispered it softly against her ear, his warm breath teasing her senses. "I want you so badly I can't think sometimes."

Her entire body answered his whispered confession. Clenching. Pulsing with heat. With hunger. With anticipation.

His lips drifted up her throat, his teeth tugged tenderly on her chin, skimmed along her cheek to find the corner of her mouth. His tongue stroked. Lingered. Traced her lips until she opened for him. At once she was lost. His mouth was a mystery of intrigue, of masculine expertise and hot promises. His tongue swept inside, swept her away from her inhibitions. From sanity. From any clear thought.

Her arms crept up around his neck. Locked there, held him to her while she moved against him, a slow rubbing of her body against his. Arousing him further. Savoring the way his body hardened in response. All the while their mouths were welded together. His hands moved over her, shaped her breasts, memorized the curve of her hips, slid possessively over her buttocks. Kneaded. Massaged. Stroked.

His mouth became hotter and silkier, his tongue danced, dueled with hers. He trailed kisses over her chin, her throat, leaving tiny flames behind. His mouth settled over her breasts, suckling right through the thin cotton of her shirt.

Maggie cried out, cradled his head, arcing into him

while her body nearly drowned in a tidal wave of desire. Nothing had prepared her for the heat, for the hunger.

"Let's go away from here," he whispered, "right now, Maggie. Come with me away from here. I need you so much right now."

She nodded, needing him, needing him to stop the terrible ache, to fill the emptiness. "I've never done this before, Brandt," Maggie admitted, wanting him to go slow, to let her catch up to his obvious experience.

His entire body went rigid. His golden eyes blazed at her with a mixture of consternation and hunger. "Are you untouched, Maggie?" There was shock in his voice.

She stiffened immediately, drew away from him. "Not anymore." Her chin went up with a hint of defiance. "I'd have to say you changed that."

He had inadvertently hurt her. Brandt shackled her wrist, brought her resisting body back to him. "I'm sorry, Maggie, I didn't mean it that way."

"I know exactly what you meant. You wish I were experienced. I'm so dreadfully sorry, but I'm not. I've never found a man I loved that much or was so attracted to that I wanted to have a physical relationship." She was furious. *Furious.* She was not about to defend her morals to Brandt Talbot. She turned away from him, away from his pathetic little village.

Brandt knew Maggie wanted to be angry with him. He was certain she was telling herself she was angry with him, but her eyes were shiny and if tears spilled over he would have to kiss every drop from her face. Deliberately he dragged her hand to his chest and held it against him, ignoring her halfhearted struggles.

"How could you think I would want another man to put his hands on you? To touch you?" His arms circled her body, held her to him while he nuzzled the top of her head with his chin. "The last thing I would ever want would be for you to believe, even for a moment, that you cared for another man enough to want him to make love to you." He kissed her temple. "I was only concerned for you. You should have told me immediately. What you're feeling, I'm also feeling. I could have lost control. I must take great care with you." He held her to him, waited for the tension to drain out of her. He was beginning to know her. She might flash at him, but she got over things quickly.

Maggie tilted her head back to look up at him. Instantly she knew she'd made a mistake. His eyes were dark, liquid, melting her, tugging at her heartstrings. She shook her head, knowing it was too late. The hurt, the anger was slipping away while her insides turned to mush. She took a deep breath, let it out slowly, and forced her hungry stare away from his hypnotic eyes.

"Take me to the village. I want to see what it's like." She needed a space from him, breathing room. She needed a semblance of normalcy and a reprieve from the continual sexual assault on her senses.

He rubbed the bridge of his nose, looking thoughtful. "All right, we'll go, but just remember I'm as on edge as a male leopard when a female is . . ."

She whipped her head around, glared at him, provoked beyond endurance. "Don't you dare say I'm in heat. I am *not* in heat!" She flushed a bright scarlet, stepped away from the temptation of his masculine body. "What a thought!" Though she'd been thinking it herself. She had all the signs of a feline in heat, but Brandt saying the words aloud was humiliating. Suddenly her eyes widened and her hand went to her throat. "Wait a minute. Are you implying I can conceive? Is that it? I'm ovulating and I want to have sex because I can conceive?"

She backed hastily away from him as if he might contaminate her. When he started to follow her she pointed an accusing finger at him. "You stay right over there, away from me. *Far* away from me."

He was grinning at her and Maggie found herself staring at his mouth, fascinated. Intrigued. Her mouth curved in an answering smile in spite of her intentions to be serious. "It isn't funny. Stay over there where I know I'm perfectly safe and explain this to me. Do . . ." What in the world did they call themselves? "Do leopard-people only have sex when the female ovulates?"

Brandt burst out laughing. "You're looking disappointed, Maggie, which I'm thankful for. No, we are a highly sexual race and lovemaking is frequent. But, yes, when our mate nears the time of ovulation, the need becomes much more intense. Sex can be rough. That's why I was concerned with your being a virgin, not because it displeased me." His gaze was hot as it moved over her. Possessive. "We'll get around it."

"We won't need to get around it! You aren't coming near me! I'm not getting pregnant. I'm not! So you can just stop looking at me like that. Unless you have a box full of protection, you can forget it." She felt wild, upset, needy. Raging hormones out of control. She felt sorry for every female cat she had ever come into contact with. "Weren't you even going to tell me?"

"Eventually. I'm taking things slow, letting you get used to the idea of what you are. It carries a certain responsibility with it." He shrugged his wide shoulders, and she nearly groaned at the way his muscles rippled enticingly.

"I'll say." She glared at him when she wanted to fling herself at him and beg him to rip her clothes off. The village was the only safe place. They needed people, not privacy, not an exotic rain forest with its flowers and trees and steamy assault on the senses. "Get away from me, Brandt. I'm feeling extremely catlike toward you just about now, and raking my claws down your face seems a good idea." Raking her claws down his body would be better. Over his back. Clinging to him. The image the words evoked sent her body pulsing with need.

He saw it in her expression, inhaled her beckoning scent. Male satisfaction gleamed in his eyes.

Maggie rubbed her hands up and down her thighs. "For heaven's sake, do we have litters? Cubs? Inquiring minds want to know." She couldn't stand still, she couldn't think clearly. Another wave of need was rushing through her body like a fireball.

Brandt's gaze narrowed, focused on her completely. He simply reached out and caught her hand. "Neither one of us is in any shape to go visiting, Maggie. You're going to have to trust me to know what to do."

Night was falling fast as it often did in the rain forest. She felt tired and muggy and her clothes felt uncomfortable against her skin. She could tell she was getting edgy, wanting to rake at Brandt. The best thing was to be alone, somewhere quiet and soothing.

6

Maggie woke unbearably hot, a soft cry of protest on her lips. She heard the echo of the haunting sound as she lay in the dark room with her heart beating too fast and her mind racing. The room was pitch black, yet her vision was remarkably good. Instead of reassuring her, the fact left her curling her fingers in the sheets. Her body had awakened her with urgent need, burning for relief so that she couldn't control her restless shifting.

It was only then that she thought to inhale. At once she went still, her stomach flipping and hot liquid heat surging through her body in instant invitation. She smelled fruit and the musky scent of a male. *Her* male. Brandt. She would know that masculine scent anywhere, a blend of outdoor and spice. She knew immediately he was as aroused as she was.

Maggie moistened her lips. "What are you doing here?"

"Looking at you." The words were soft, seductive.

Truthful. His voice came from the chair positioned in the deepest corner opposite from her. "Watching over you."

She smiled in the dark. "Do I need watching over?" The thought of his eyes on her, intense and burning, was a powerful aphrodisiac. She moved along the sheets, trying to get comfortable when every nerve ending was alive and sizzling with awareness.

"You were moaning in your sleep. The sound tore me up." Brandt was sprawled out in the chair, his long legs stretched in front of him, his eyes devouring her. He had positioned the chair at the best advantage to watch her. She was so beautiful, so real, lying on his bed, all lush curves and gleaming skin. He ached to hold her. To lap his tongue along her throat and in the deep valley between her breasts, to swirl it in that intriguing little belly button he had such difficulty tearing his gaze from.

She belonged in the house. Here with him. The sight and sound of her, the *scent* of her completed him. He had to clear his throat of the unexpected lump clogging it so he could speak. "There's fruit on the tray there if you're thirsty or hungry. It was hot so I brought ice in the small insulated bucket."

Maggie sat up, pushed at the hair tumbling around her face. "You're always taking care of me, Brandt. Thank you, it was very thoughtful of you." She was thirsty and hot, her throat parched.

Brandt watched as she reached a slender, bare arm through the mosquito netting and lifted a piece of mango to her lips. She tilted her head slightly, exposing the long column of her throat, smooth and vulnerable, to him. Her lips parted slightly, and he caught a glimpse of her small teeth, her tongue, before she took the fruit into her mouth. His entire body clenched when she sucked the juice from her fingers. Her tongue darted out to catch the last drop of juice on her lower lip. His hand dropped to his thick, hard arousal pulsing with hunger and urgent demand. A single sound escaped him.

Maggie's head went up. "Do you want to share with me?"

Her voice sent jackhammers tripping in his head. He thought he would burst from his skin. "Look at me, Maggie," he commanded gruffly.

"You're in the shadows. I can't see you."

"Yes, you can. Use your eyesight. Look at me and tell me if you want me sharing with you." There was a moody, edgy feel to his voice, one that sent a shiver of awareness down her spine.

She pushed the mosquito netting aside and leaned forward, picking up another piece of mango as she did so. It took a moment to make him out, as still as he was in the chair. He seemed to become part of whatever his background was, a highly developed camouflage. Maggie could see him then, his powerful body draped on the chair. Entirely naked. Starkly aroused. He made no attempt to hide the pulsing staff thrusting upward from between his legs. He sat there, motionless, his brooding gaze on her, simply awaiting her decision.

Beneath the thin tank top her breasts ached tenderly. A trickle of hot liquid dampened the sheets. He stole her breath. Just looking at him, so hungry for her, robbed her of air. Deliberately she licked at the fruit, knowing his eyes were on her. She sucked the piece into her mouth, followed it with her fingers. Maggie took her time. There was no need to hurry; she could see his reaction as she sucked the juice from her hand. His nails dug into the arm of the chair and his body jerked.

She heard his swift intake of breath as she slowly caught the hem of her tank top and pulled it over her head to bare her breasts for him. "I definitely want you sharing with me, Brandt," she invited.

Some of the tension left his body but he remained across the room from her. Maggie's body tightened even more in anticipation. He liked looking at her—she could feel him drinking her in, devouring her with his heated gaze. Deliberately she leaned back on the bed to hook her drawstring bottoms with her thumbs. Carefully she slid the material down the curve of her hip, shimmying a little as she pushed the pajamas from her legs, discarding them beside the bed in an unwanted little heap.

Maggie reached for another piece of fruit, but he was there before her, picking up the orange pulp and bringing it to her mouth. He squeezed so the juice ran over his fingers and across his palm. Maggie took a bite, watched him pop the rest into his own mouth, and he offered her his hand. His knee wedged between her thighs, leaving her open, damp, pulsing for him.

Maggie caught his thick wrist and brought his fingers to her mouth. Her tongue slid over his skin, probing, teasing, exploring the contours of his hand while she lapped up the juice. All the time she was very aware of his body, silky hot, so close to hers.

The sensation of her tongue lapping so delicately over his fingers, tracing the crease in his palm, nearly made him explode. The tips of her breasts skimmed his arm, flashed fire along his skin. The junction between her legs, as he nudged closer, was fiery hot, damp, giving off the rich scent of her calling to him. The hammering in his head became a roar. He was thick and hard, but her tongue was increasing his measurements beyond anything he'd ever experienced. He couldn't imagine what would happen if her hot mouth pulled as strongly at another portion of his anatomy.

Brandt curled his hand around the nape of her neck and tilted her head back, fastening his mouth to hers. Heat exploded inside of her. Erupted into a hot molasses that spread through her body until she was burning up inside. His mouth fed on hers, his tongue dueling, tangling, stroking while his hands explored her satin-soft body. Maggie couldn't breathe, yet he was providing her air. She couldn't think, her mind in a chaos of pleasure, as he guided her through the whirling sensations, anchoring her to him with his commanding mouth and strong hands.

His hands cupped her breasts, his thumbs gliding over her nipples to bring them to two taut peaks. "I need a piece of mango," he whispered into her open mouth.

Brandt didn't stop kissing her, eating at her mouth while she bent to get the fruit. His mouth was hot and masculine and she was lost in his passion. He didn't take the mango from her. "Rub it on your nipples for me," he instructed, pulling back to look down at her full breasts cupped in his palms.

A small explosion went off in her deepest most feminine core, and moist heat seeped and beckoned to him at his provocative words. She could feel ripples of fire deep within her. His gaze was burning, possessive, his face hard and edgy with need. Maggie nibbled at the fruit so that juice ran down the corner of her mouth. Brandt leaned forward and caught the drops with his tongue, tracing her lower lip until she opened her mouth for him again. Her body clenched in reaction.

Watching his golden eyes grow hotter, almost liquid, she rubbed the mango over her nipples in slow, deliberate circles, then in a wider pattern over the curve of her breasts. Her breasts seemed to swell with the attention, aching for him. She held the fruit to his mouth, watched him suck it inside without breathing. Her lungs refused to cooperate. She pressed her body tightly against his knee, rubbing like a cat, seeking a measure of relief.

Brandt leaned in to kiss her again. "Thank you, honey." The three words were said against her throat. Maggie closed her eyes as his teeth skimmed her sensitive skin. His lips traced a path to her breasts. Everything stilled inside of her. Waiting. Longing. Needing. He huffed out his breath, blowing warm air over her nipples. Her body wound even tighter.

His hair spilled across her arm, over her skin, brushing tiny flames over her. And then she felt his tongue. A tiny

stroke. A light caress. She jumped. Her hips shifted restlessly. Maggie closed her eyes, savoring the pleasure as his
tongue began to lick and lap slowly at the fruit juice. It was
designed to drive her out of her mind and it did. She caught
his head in her hands to hold him to her breast, thrusting
into the hot, moist cavern.

Brandt closed his mouth around her offering, sucking
strongly. She cried out, writhing against him, her body
brushing against him, a thousand points of flames. Her
arms dragged him closer. Maggie threw back her head, jutting more fully into his assault, while wave after wave of
sensation rushed from her breasts to her belly in a fireball.

He bent her backward slowly until she was resting on
the mattress, sprawled beneath him while his mouth pulled
strongly and his hands claimed her body for his slow exploration. His strength was enormous—she felt it in the
smooth ripple of muscle beneath his flesh. Unable to resist,
Maggie traced her hands over him, each angle and plane,
the ridge of his muscles, wanting to feel his thickness in
her hands.

Brandt had other ideas. "I'm going to shatter if you do
that," he admitted, his hands moving over her rib cage, her
small waist to her belly. He loved the smooth expanse, the
way her hipbones felt beneath his fingertips. Her curls
were nearly as fiery as her core, bright and hot and waiting
for him to dip his thumb through them.

She jumped, catching at his hands. Brandt ignored the
restraint and pushed her thighs more fully open. "Let yourself go, Maggie," he said softly. "There's only the two of
us. I was made for you. To love you, to bring you pleasure." His finger stroked over her damp core, swirled inside
to find her hot and slick with need. "Am I bringing you
pleasure, Maggie?"

"You know you are." So much so she couldn't think
straight.

"Maggie, it's me you want, not just anyone," Brandt
said, his golden eyes suddenly fierce. His finger plunged

deep, so that she gasped, her hips bucking against his hand. "Say it, Maggie, say it's only me you want." He reveled in the feel of her muscles clenched around him, but he had to know it was for him. She had to give herself to him fully. Her body wasn't enough for him, it would never be enough. Maggie was his other half, a woman born to be his best friend, his companion, and a lifelong partner. Their sexual chemistry was a huge bonus, but it wasn't enough. She had to want him.

Her green eyes went wide as he pushed two fingers deep, stretching her, wanting her tight body to accept his easily. "Say it, Maggie, I need to hear you say it."

"Who did you think I wanted?" she gasped, nearly coming up off the bed. She was certain she wasn't going to live through wanting him.

"Say you'll stay with me, live with me, Maggie, learn to love me, here in the rain forest where you were born." He bent his head to her soft, taut belly, so firm and flat, his palm lying across her thatch of curls. As he lapped gently at her sexy belly button, he pushed his fingers deeper inside of her, closed his eyes as her body clamped down in response.

"I want to be here with you, Brandt. I longed to come here," she admitted. He was driving her out of her mind. "Please . . ." The word broke from her, a soft gasp of need. The waves of pleasure were so intense, Maggie had to struggle to stay grounded in reality. "What about protection, Brandt? You said I could get pregnant."

His teeth nipped her belly, his tongue swirled and caressed. "Right here, Maggie. Our child would grow here in your belly. *My* child." His teeth nipped again. "Would that be a terrible thing for us? To have a child together?"

There was seduction in his whisper, a temptation. Maggie had always craved a family and had been so lost without one. His whisper spoke of permanency, of commitment. She was so tempted with her body going up in flames. She couldn't think straight with wanting him. She didn't want him to stop but she needed time with him, to know him inside and out. There was the blaze of possession in his eyes, a ruthless stamp to his mouth and an insatiable sexual hunger in him when he looked at her, when he touched her. He was thoughtful, protective, intelligent, and had a sense of humor—but was that enough to really know him?

His fingers slid out of her and his teeth nipped a little lower, his soft laughter against her curls. "Our males stimulate the females into pregnancy, honey; you don't operate exactly like a human. I just wanted you to know, I wouldn't mind my child growing deep inside of you. I wouldn't mind your breasts full with milk." He smiled again, self-assured, no longer looking vulnerable, but intensely masculine. "I'm a cat, after all. But waiting until you know me, until you trust me, is essential. I'll be very careful, I promise." He lifted his head and looked at her, his golden eyes gleaming. "Don't move, baby, just lie still for me," he whispered, his hands parting her thighs. "The first night you were here, in my bed, I sat in that chair and dreamt of this. Of how you would taste." He lowered his head.

A scream ripped its way out of her throat. Her body bucked and convulsed. His tongue was relentless, stabbing, probing, sucking at her body, creating earthquakes and fireworks, shattering her into a million pieces. It went on and on, a storm of pure pleasure she was lost in, thrashing beneath him without inhibition, crying out for him, pleading with him to be deep inside of her where she needed him, where he belonged.

Brandt caught her hips in his hand, pulled her down the bed until her bottom was on the edge and he was tight against her. His erection was heavy and thick, the head so sensitive as he pushed into her, his body shuddered with pleasure. She was like a hot, slick fist, velvet soft but so tight he nearly lost all control. He forced himself to take his time, to fill her slowly, to push deeper and deeper into her body, wanting her to take every inch of him.

Maggie heard a keening sound, realized it was she. His body was invading her, a thick, hard fullness that brought a fiery friction of intense pleasure. She could feel her body adjusting, accommodating his size. And then he began to move and she was lost to everything but the conflagration he was building, feeding.

He moved slowly at first, watching her for signs of discomfort. When she lifted her hips to meet his, he began to lose himself in the perfect rhythm, hard and fast, plunging into her, driving deeper. The little noises escaping her throat drove him wild. "Take all of me, honey, all of me." It was a plea, a demand. She burned hotter and hotter, gripping him tightly.

He thrust hard, reveling in the way her body trembled with pleasure, the way her breasts jutted upward, her stomach rippled, her eyes glazed slightly as their bodies came together. The sight of her, the feel of her was his undoing. He wanted it to last forever, but he had wanted too long, too much, and his body had other ideas. He felt it start in his toes, rising higher and higher, his belly on fire, hips thrusting ferociously, almost brutally, his hands pinning her to him, while he erupted with jets of hot cream, filling her, triggering an intense orgasm so that her body gripped and tightened, milking his until he collapsed over her, spent and momentarily sated.

They were locked together, their hearts hammering loudly, their scents mingling, both so sensitive they were afraid to move. Brandt kissed the corner of her mouth, her chin, the tip of her breast. "Are you all right? I didn't hurt you, did I?" Reluctantly he rolled his weight off of her. His hands tangled in her hair possessively.

"You know you didn't hurt me," she assured him. She didn't think her body would ever belong to her again. "It's hot in here. Did the temperature shoot up when we weren't looking?"

He laughed softly, deep in his throat. "We had other things on our minds." He sat up, reached past her. His naked body was flexible, a miracle of movement.

"What are you doing?" Maggie asked drowsily. She rolled over onto her stomach and lifted her head to watch him. There was something very intimate about the dark night enfolding them in its cloak, yet they could see each other very clearly. She watched him lift the insulated bucket of ice to his mouth. Fascinated, she propped herself up on her elbows to watch his throat work as he swallowed the ice-cold liquid.

He was so sexy, the simple act took her breath away. Just drinking water. And how had he managed to get her to trust him the way she did? She trusted everything he said with an instinct, a knowledge, that he was telling her the truth. Or maybe she just wanted him, burned for him, and nothing else mattered.

Brandt looked at her over the bucket, his eyes so gold they glittered. A slow, wicked smile curved his mouth, revealed his teeth. Catlike. Wild. Primitive.

Maggie had no idea of the picture she presented, thoroughly loved, thoroughly sensual. The tips of her breasts swayed slightly as she moved, and the smooth rounded curves of her buttocks quivered, drawing his attention. She had a beautiful bottom. Already his body was stirring. He felt the familiar tightness.

Plucking a piece of ice from the bucket, he held it up. "I think I have a way to cool you off."

Her eyes widened. She looked at him warily. "I don't like that wicked look in your eyes."

He lifted her hair and rubbed the ice over her nape, felt her shiver. At once her nipples tightened. "Feels good, doesn't it?" He traced her spine in a slow deliberate caress, lazily watched the heat of her skin melt the small piece, leaving behind a trail of water. He bent forward to lap at her skin, catching the little beads, savoring the liquid.

Maggie let her head fall on the mattress and closed her

eyes. Her body was completely relaxed, pliant under Brandt's hands. His heart swelled, knowing she was his, that she belonged in his home, in his bed. He would wake up and find her there. He could touch her body, make love to her when and where they wanted. And he wanted.

The next piece of ice made lazy patterns in the small of her back. The water melted and pooled into the two dimples there. Brandt sipped it as if it were the finest champagne. He found a larger piece to rub along the crease of her buttocks, so that the icy drips trickled to cool the heat at her core. To mingle with his cream and soothe any soreness. He bent his head to nip her gently on her left cheek. "Are you sore?" He pressed kisses into the two dimples, his hand finding her wet entrance.

"I'm sleeping," she lied, too lazy to move, but she pushed back against his palm.

He removed it, disappointing her, but then it was back, his fingers probing deeply. Maggie nearly came up off the bed as the piece of ice met the fiery heat of her core. "You devil! What are you doing?" She could feel the ice-cold water melting, trickling deep inside her body. The sensation was intriguing.

Brandt caught her hips as she rose up on her knees and dragged her back against him, his body bending dominantly over hers as he took her from behind, plunging deep to follow the ice-cold trail through her hot, tight sheath.

"You can't possibly," Maggie objected, grinding her buttocks hard against him as flames spread through her and hunger shot up fast and strong.

"Did you know that a male leopard was once observed mating with his female over a hundred times in a two-day period? I can live with that; can you?"

At that moment, Maggie thought she could.

7

Brandt answered the knock on the door, waved Drake inside. "It's late," he greeted, knowing there was trouble. Drake would never have interrupted them unless it was an emergency. He and Maggie had had only one night and one day alone together, not nearly enough time for him to feel secure in Maggie's commitment.

"I know." Drake glanced at Maggie. "I'm sorry, Maggie, really. I wouldn't have come if we didn't need Brandt."

"Poachers?" Brandt guessed.

"We've been checking the area you were so worried about and sure enough, one of the bears is missing. We spotted another trap." Drake paced across the gleaming floor. "I know this is a bad time, Brandt, but there's too much activity. We think they'll come tonight to try for more. We have a breeding pair we can't afford to lose."

Brandt shook his head. "Maggie is too close to the Han

Vol Dan. I won't leave her alone. You know how frightening it can be, Drake."

"It could happen anytime," Drake protested, shifting his gaze away from Maggie. "You know we'll need you tonight if we're right. They'll be in force, Brandt. And they're too close to our people. If we're discovered, if one person was careless and left a trail . . . Those men read signs almost as well as we do." He glanced at Maggie uneasily. "And James's scent was all over the poachers' camp. He's nowhere to be found."

"Of course he'll go." Maggie put a hand on Brandt's forearm, rubbed her palm gently over his tense muscles. "Just go and get it over with. I'll be fine."

Brandt shook his head, his sculpted lips frowning, his golden eyes moody. "It isn't safe, Maggie."

"You have to go," Maggie said quickly sensing Brandt's hesitancy. "You can't worry about me. I'm a grown woman; I can handle things here." She said it with complete confidence. Maggie had been handling the details of her life a long while before Brandt Talbot had come into it.

"Maggie, you're very close to the change. I feel it. I need to be with you when you go through it for the first time," Brandt protested, clearly torn at having to choose between his duty and his mate. He raked a hand through his dark hair, his gaze dwelling on her serene face.

Maggie produced a self-assured smile. "Go. I'll be right here when you get back." She slipped her arms around his neck and leaned into his hard frame. "I'm not afraid, Brandt. This is important, what you do is important."

Brandt hesitated, then locked her to him, his mouth finding hers in a hard, apologetic kiss. "You're my everything, Maggie," he whispered fiercely, "you remember that. My everything. For you it's all happened too fast and you're unsure. For me, I've known for all of my life that you were my other half. You hold my heart and my soul. Don't destroy me. I'm trusting you not to destroy me."

Maggie feathered a series of teasing kisses along his

shadowed jaw. "You need to have a little more faith. Go now." She was glowing at his words and she knew it. Secretly she had been afraid of falling for his dark good looks and the highly charged chemistry between them, his poet's heart and his hunter's eyes. Afraid after hot sex and coming together with such fire, he would simply walk away like the male leopards they so closely resembled at times.

Brandt kissed her again. Hard. Possessively. Thoroughly. His molten eyes burned over her. "You be here when I get back. Don't you leave this house and go exploring or trying to save some creature you've heard bleating. I mean it, Maggie. Poachers are dangerous. I don't want you anywhere near them. And while I'm gone, don't open the door to anyone, even if you know he's one of ours."

She walked with him to the door, her fingers tangling with his. "I have no intention of allowing anything to happen to me, Brandt."

He turned to follow Drake into the night, hesitated, swore softly, and framed her face with both hands. "Maggie, be here. I can't tell you what it's been like searching the world for you, feeling so alone. Afraid for you, alone, without the knowledge of your people to protect you. Don't leave me."

Her vivid green eyes searched his golden ones. "What is it? Tell me."

He shook his head. "I have a feeling, a premonition if you want to call it that."

She went up on her toes to press a single, lingering kiss to his frown. "Then you be extra careful, Brandt. I'll be sitting safe in the house while you're off chasing poachers. Maybe *I* should be worried about *you*."

"Brandt." There was urgency in Drake's voice and this time Brandt responded, hurrying down the steps after his friend.

Maggie watched from the verandah until they were out of sight; and then she returned to the house, closing and locking the front door. Deliberately she flicked off every light so that there was no telltale glow to lead anyone to the house. Her night vision was extremely acute, much more so than ever before. She wondered at the changes taking place in her body. It seemed as if every hour she discovered something new, her senses enhanced a hundredfold.

Her body was wondrously sore from their continual lovemaking, and Maggie wanted a long soak in a hot bath. The air, as always was sultry, but the thought of hot water was more than she could resist. In the bathroom she lit a single candle to fill the room with aromatic spice. The flame produced a soft flickering luminosity that danced on the walls. The water lapped soothingly at her sore body like a thousand healing tongues. She could see a dark smudge on the side of her hip where his fingers had dug into her curves in the deep throes of his passion. Her breasts were tender and slightly burned, matching her chin, from the shadow on his jaw. Even the insides of her thighs held the evidence of his possession. Deep inside her she still felt him. Still craved him.

She fell asleep there in the hot water, dreaming of Brandt and his hard, capable body thrusting deeply into hers. Her body clenched, tightened; she thrashed, bumping her head on the tub. Maggie woke, blinked drowsily, and rubbed at her head. As she patted her skin dry with a towel, she noticed how tender she was. Her skin felt raw and inflamed. It was painful to pull on her clothes but she did, worried Brandt might need her.

Maggie paced restlessly across the tiled floor. She was feeling sick to her stomach and there was a strange roaring in her head. She clutched her head, trying to massage her temples. The throbbing was increasing so that her head pounded and ached. Her bones felt too big for the confines of her skin. It felt as if her head might burst to accommodate the expanding skull. Was this what Brandt had worried about? Had it started? Experimentally she ran her tongue along her teeth to feel if they were sharper.

Staggering a little under the weight of the pain, Maggie went to the bedroom, certain that when she lay down she would feel much better. She tried to rest, but the pressure of the mattress was too much to bear. As she sat up she felt a strange rippling of muscles across her belly, in her arms. When she looked down at her skin, something moved.

Maggie thought she screamed. Her muscles contorted, rippled, and knotted right under her horrified stare. She could see something running beneath her skin, something like a parasite, raising her skin as the thing rushed beneath the surface. Her heart rate accelerated and her mouth went dry. All at once her clothes were too tight, too constricting. The material hurt her skin. Alarmed, she tore off her jeans, flinging them away from her.

Fire raced through her belly and her legs went rubbery. She fell to the floor. "Brandt!" She screamed his name, her one hope in the midst of insanity. His name came out somewhere between a cough and a grunt. Her throat was closing on her, swelling, changing, so that her vocal cords weren't working.

The Han Vol Dan was upon her and she was alone and terrified. Her body writhed, a rush of adrenaline pumping through her system like an erupting volcano. Her skin felt raw, oversensitized. The merest touch on her body hurt. Maggie struggled to control her fear, to think while she could. She had to rid herself of her clothes before she no longer had fingers. Tears were running down her face as she stripped off her blouse and underwear. She couldn't bear to look at her contorting body. She had thought it would be a quick change, not a vicious assault on her muscles.

She crawled across the floor to the balcony door. The confines of the house were so stifling, she could hardly breathe. Maggie didn't want to look at her hand as she reached up to slide the door open but she couldn't help herself. Her hand was curved, knotted, knuckles extended.

She managed to get the door open and dragged herself onto the balcony.

A wave of fur broke through her skin as her spine seemed to bend and crackle, a thick matting of reddish hair with rosettes stretching endlessly. For a moment she was caught between human and beast, half and half. She could only wonder at the mystery of such a thing, how it could be that it had never been discovered, but then she was absorbed in the takeover of her body by the animal inside of her.

She heard the noise of it—bones cracking, muscles snapping, tendons popping—as her body was reshaping. The sounds were horrifying, but the wildness caught at her, her senses heightening. The night rushed at her, into her, a world she hadn't known existed.

There was a long silence while the wind held its breath. Then the rain fell from the sky, drops landing on the cat sprawled on the balcony, panting so heavily. Maggie lifted her head and looked around her. Without moving her head, she could detect motion in the trees in a visual field of nearly 280 degrees. The shock was enormous to her, her mind nearly numb as she attempted to comprehend what had happened. She could think, but she was trapped in a body not her own, one totally alien to her. And deep within her, something wild and ruthless was striving to blend with her.

The leopard came to its feet. Easily. Gracefully. Nothing awkward about the way the animal moved. The leopard was built for total awareness, with grace and intelligence. Deep within the animal's body, Maggie had only one goal. To get out of the rain forest. To return to civilization where nothing like this could ever happen again. It wasn't interesting or fun—it was terrifying beyond belief. Maggie Odessa would be lost in the forest, but the leopard had senses far beyond her own. Leaping from the balcony, making her way down the network of tree limbs, she ran fast, utilizing the unique radar in the cat's whiskers to help her find her way.

She had no idea how to get back into her own skin, her own form. This leopard's body could not be hers. Worst of all, the female was spreading her tantalizing chemical signals throughout the forest as she raced away from the sanctuary of the house to find the borders of the forest. The leopard was in the throes of sexual awareness, rubbing on trees, scent marking, and scratching. Maggie was horrified when she suddenly became aware that the animal and she were both in need of a male.

She ran faster, determined to remove herself from the influence of the wild rain forest with its sultry, steamy heat and from the effects of her overactive libido. She ran a long distance, loping easily over fallen logs and up steep embankments. The river didn't slow her down; she plunged in and swam, leaping to shore and shaking delicately. As she continued, she became aware of the mechanics of the leopard's body.

The faint sound of shouting, of voices carrying through the forest, nearly stopped her heart. The noise was a great distance away, but she instantly was aware of what it meant. Brandt could be in trouble. She was running like a wild thing and Brandt could be in danger somewhere. The thought was sobering. But what could she do, trapped as she was, imprisoned within an animal form? She wanted to sob with fear and frustration. Maggie forced her mind away from hysteria and tried to think logically.

She had persisted in thinking of herself as two identities. One human, one animal. But she was neither and the creature running through the forest so easily was part of her. She continued to think, to be Maggie Odessa, but now in another form, one that was unfamiliar to her, yet felt as if it fit her.

Once she identified that Maggie was still Maggie only in another shape, she felt much calmer. She slowed down, huffing out a breath, looking about her with the eyes of enhanced vision. Her vision. She'd had it all along, she just had never used the ability. She inhaled, drew in the scents of the jungle. She wasn't a leopard, nor was she quite human. She was different, yet still Maggie.

Cushioned paws allowed her to move in complete silence. She could feel the enormous power in the body she occupied. Unable to prevent herself from testing the possibilities, Maggie leapt easily onto a thick branch some six feet above her head. It was a simple, easy jump, and she landed perfectly balanced as if she'd been doing such things all her life.

Maggie crouched in the tree and thought about Brandt. He had told her the absolute truth. She wasn't two people divided; she was one who would remain Maggie Odessa. She simply could take on more than one form. A feeling of unbelievable power washed through her. What a gift. Her birth parents had given her a priceless legacy. She thought about the things Brandt had told her and she understood the need for discipline. She could control the emotions and sexual tension while she was in the shape of the leopard. Being in the form of a leopard made no difference. She didn't have to act more of the animal, she simply wasn't exercising control over the wild nature rising so strongly.

The emotions were strong, but not unfamiliar. She certainly had wanted to be with Brandt, had enticed and tempted and seduced him as much as she would allow herself. The leopard was feeling those same things magnified by its primitive nature, the nature that was so much a part of her. Maggie relaxed, allowed the tension to seep out of her body. She could reason, use her intelligence; she could think things through, not run like a frightened child. And she could exercise discipline and restraint on her wilder cravings. The power belonged to her and she could do with it what she willed.

Brandt had been afraid she would be unable to handle the transformation, had wanted to stay with her instead of going after the poachers. She was proving him correct with her childish actions. She needed to return to the house and calmly wait for him to aid her into returning to her other, human form. If he didn't come within a reasonable length of time, she would use this form with its abilities to hunt for him and help him in any way possible.

Maggie thought of Brandt's words. How he had searched the world over for her. How he had always known she was his mate. How certain he was that they belonged together. She didn't have that certainty based on years of knowing her heritage. She'd known him only a very short time, yet she *felt* it was right in her deepest soul. He had begged her to be there when he returned. She didn't want to let him down. She wasn't going to let him down. Brandt Talbot was *her* choice.

Maggie leapt from the tree to land softly on the ground. She had been more alive here, deep within the rain forest, than she had ever been in her life. She had no intention of allowing fear to take that life from her. Of taking Brandt from her. Everything she had ever worked toward in her life was right here, in this wild exotic setting.

She didn't fear it, she reveled in it. The canopy, the flowers, the abundance of fauna in no way made her claustrophobic, as she knew it often made other people. The heat didn't adversely affect her. She loved the rain forest and everything in it. And Brandt. She loved the poet in him, the unexpected surprise of his gentle side. He was the biggest reason why she wanted to stay and face what she was. Who she was. She would research the history of her species and do what she could to fit into the lifestyle.

Maggie began her journey back to the house. The leopard knew the way, padding silently, scenting the wind, her night vision excellent. She was nearing familiar ground when the loud crack of a gun split the night. A volley of shots followed. Animals shrieked, a cacophony of sound. The trees above her head became a riot of movement, wings fluttering, monkeys shrieking and leaping from tree to tree. The warning was loud and insistent in the darkness of the forest.

Maggie winced, jerked to one side, curling her lip to expose her canines as she took shelter in the thick vegetation. Her heart pounded out a rhythm of fear. At once she heard the answer of her people, a peculiar drumbeat, as old as time but effective, a kind of Morse code she should have known but had never learned. She couldn't read the message sent by her kind, but she was aware of news being passed.

Her first thought was for Brandt. She could taste the bitter edge of fear in her mouth. She didn't want to lose him, now that she had found him. Why hadn't she committed to him? Why hadn't she reassured him that she wanted to be with him? Maggie burst from the foliage and began to lope back toward the house. She would pick up the scent of Drake and Brandt from there and track them to where the poachers had set traps.

To her surprise, the leopard faltered, the front legs wobbling unsteadily. She somersaulted over a small branch, skidding along the ground. Maggie lay flat out, hearing the ominous creaking and pops that accompanied change. "Not now," she groaned, the sound emerging from the leopard's throat as a grunting cough.

It wasn't as painful, or maybe it hadn't ever been. Maybe she had been so frightened that it had seemed painful because she had expected it to hurt. She itched, her skin erupting with fur one moment, then smooth and bare the next. She found herself sitting on the ground, stark naked. Maggie leapt up quickly, afraid of insects burrowing into her skin.

With a little sigh she began to jog toward the house. She knew her way now—she had the same abilities as the leopard, she had had only to acknowledge them, accept them, and learn to use them. She had to cross her arms over the fullness of her breasts as she hurried, the jolting as uncomfortable in her chest as the ground was on her bare feet. The leopard form was designed for easy movement through the jungle, while her present form was a nuisance. Sharp leaves and bark lacerated her tender skin. She hardly noticed the discomfort as she pushed hard to get back to the house, wanting to track Brandt.

The noise stopped her cold. A high keening sound, the moan of an animal in pain. She had heard it many times, but this time she inhaled the scent of blood. Without conscious thought, Maggie turned toward the sound. She had to go to the injured animal—the sound tugged at her.

The bear was much smaller than she had expected, with smooth jet-black fur. It had a beautiful white crescent marking its chest. Its long tongue was lolling out of its mouth. She couldn't help but notice the long and pointed claws it used for ripping into the bark of trees to uncover insects and honey. The bear was whimpering in fear and pain. It swung its head toward her as she emerged from between two trees and attempted to roll to its feet, but instead thrashed dangerously. She could see the thick blood coating the bear's left side. The ground was dark with it.

Maggie lifted her hand and went completely still, keeping her distance prudently. "Be calm, little one, I'm going to help you." She needed her backpack, her medical supplies. She could tranquilize the bear and see to the wound, but she wasn't certain the animal would survive while she raced to the house. The sight of the small bear in such distress angered her. She knew they were a rarity even in the wilds.

Above her head, some fifteen feet up, she saw the branches of the tree were bent and broken to form a nest. The bear must have tried to make it to its resting place. From the nest the bear would have a good view of the forest floor. She could see the hairless soles of the sun bear's feet and the sickle-shaped claws as it lay panting, watching her with tragic eyes.

The bear suddenly reared up, tried to charge, but was prevented from reaching her by the savage wound in its side. It fell back helplessly, baring teeth at her in warning. "I'm going to help you," she promised. "Just give me a couple of minutes to get my things." How far was she from the house? A distance still, she was certain.

Maggie swung away from the unfortunate creature, knowing the best thing to do was to get her supplies as quickly as possible. The bear made a second pitiable attempt to rise, this time whining at her, a clear call for help. The sound tore at her heart. The bear was clearly afraid, straining to pull its weight into cover. She caught the scent of another large cat as she turned back toward the sound of the distressed bear. A leopard was in the vicinity, a male, and he was stalking prey.

Maggie lifted her head to test the wind, much as the agitated bear was doing. She knew immediately this animal was more than a beast, he was part of the community Brandt lived in. And he knew Brandt had staked his claim. *James.* The idea of meeting him filled her with trepidation. His very scent offended her in some strange way.

Had he come to help? Maggie hesitated, aware she was completely naked and extremely vulnerable. She hadn't been afraid of the wild animals in the forest, or the dark, or even the wounded bear, but knowing another man, whatever form he took, was stalking her, filled her with fear.

She turned to escape. If James was coming to help the sun bear, he didn't need to find her there. She could get to the house and return with supplies, fully dressed. She took two steps, and the large cat broke through the heavy foliage.

8

Maggie's breath caught in her throat. The spotted leopard was large and heavily muscled. It tore through the thick undergrowth no more than six feet from her. Blazing yellow-green eyes focused on her, the pupils dilated and fixed. She could feel danger emanating from the male, see the piercing intelligence. Instinctively she stepped back, recognizing the smoldering tension in the eyes.

The animal growled a warning, and Maggie glanced behind her to see where the bear was. Her gaze shifted only for a moment, but the cat had inched forward so that it was only a foot from her. The male stared, wrinkled his nose, curled his upper lip, and grimaced with an open mouth, a wide yawn. Maggie recognized the classic Flehmen response of the male to a female.

She tilted her chin in challenge. "You think I don't know who you are? I can smell you. Whatever you're thinking doing, you can forget it." She took a breath, hissed his name with disgust. "*James*. Change your form and help me save this bear." She was almost more furious than she was afraid. Maggie realized he had followed her deliberately. Brandt had attempted to warn her earlier that James wasn't "right." His scent bothered her, as if she detected a depravity within him. "I know you understand me. We're the protectors of the forest. Before anything else we have to help these creatures survive." She could only hope he had been indoctrinated since his birth and would respond.

James pushed forward, displaying his savage teeth, his eyes staring at her with a certain cunning viciousness. His head pushed hard against her legs, nearly knocking her to the ground, clearly a signal to go where he wanted. His tongue deliberately licked across her bare thighs, a slow, painful threat. The raspy papillae on the big cat's tongue could draw blood if he chose.

Maggie shuddered visibly, his touch making her feel ill. The idea of going anywhere with him was terrifying.

The bear lay on its side on the ground, panting. The wind stilled. The rain began its slow, steady drizzle all over again. Maggie and the leopard stared at each other in the darkness, the heavy green canopy and thick layers of mists and clouds overhead blocking out the moonlight. There was complete silence, the hush of expectancy. Maggie's heart beat out a rhythm of fear.

Without warning a black panther exploded out of the foliage, moving with the force of a freight train, slamming into the spotted leopard so hard he knocked the cat off his feet. The night erupted into violence. Monkeys shrieked loudly, scrambling from branch to branch overhead. Birds took flight despite the darkness. The spotted leopard rolled, leaping to his feet to avoid the panther's teeth going for a suffocating hold on his throat.

The ears on the black panther were twisted so the backs were visible from the front, signaling aggression as he faced the wary spotted leopard. His mouth snarled, revealing the sharpened canines. Fights between male cats were often to the death, and Maggie backed away, screening her body in the leaves of the ferns, her horrified gaze fixed on the two combatants.

The panther attacked with blurring speed. Grace and flexibility combined with strong muscles to twist and turn, leap and rake, change direction in midair. The battle was brief but fierce, each cat going for a death grip on the other's throat.

The spotted leopard was knocked off his feet a second time, rolling, shifting shape as he did so, as if the blow had been so hard he no longer could hold the feline form. James ran, his back to her, naked, displaying the same muscular build she was beginning to recognize as characteristic of Brandt's people.

Maggie watched as the black panther shifted shape, almost running as he did so, easily and so quickly she could hardly believe her eyes. Brandt caught the fleeing man by his hair and brought him up short. Brandt's lip curled into a snarl of menace. She could see the cold fury on Brandt's face. "Did you think we wouldn't figure out who was helping the poachers, James? Your stench is all over the poachers' camp."

"I was investigating them," James denied, his gaze shifting away from Brandt toward Maggie. "I wouldn't betray the animals to poachers!"

Brandt's heavy fist connected solidly with James's shoulder. "Don't you look at her. You look at me if you want to live beyond this moment."

Maggie shrank at once into the deeper cover of the foliage, not because she was embarrassed at being naked—she seemed to have lost all inhibitions here in the jungle—but because the idea of James looking at her body sickened her. And because it seemed to antagonize Brandt further to see another man looking at her.

James immediately complied. That frightened Maggie, the swift compliance, as if James knew Brandt really meant he might end the other man's life. She pressed a shaking hand to her mouth. Conditions in the rain forest were extremely primitive. There were no policemen on the corners, and Brandt and his people had no allegiance to any local government. Isolated, they lived by the swift, lethal law of the jungle.

"I swear to you, Brandt, I wasn't helping the poachers. I should have shifted my shape and helped the woman with the bear but the violence, the scent of her being so ripe, and the blood kept me from thinking straight."

Brandt cuffed James so hard he rocked back on his heels. "Don't you blame Maggie for your lack of control. We always can think straight. You wanted something that didn't belong to you, James. You watched her when Drake was bringing her through the forest. They smelled you. I smelled you. Your stench is outside our home. What did you think would happen when you were finished? Were you going to kill her?"

"No!" Maggie was gratified to see the man look shocked, even horrified at the idea. "I don't know what I thought. That she'd prefer me, want me instead."

"You know you can't steal someone else's mate, James." Brandt cuffed the man a second time, an expression of disgust on his face. "Get out of here, present yourself to the council, and tell them what you did. If you don't, James, I'll consider you my enemy and I'll hunt you down." He shoved the other man away from him, his golden eyes glittering with menace. "You know me. I'll hunt you down until I find you."

James stumbled, took a few steps forward, glancing back over his shoulder. "I swear I wasn't going to harm her, Brandt. I wouldn't do that to one of our women."

Brandt watched the man go before turning his attention to Maggie. He could breathe again, think again, now that Maggie was safe. He stalked her across the small space. "You said you'd be waiting for me," he reprimanded, caging her body between his hard, masculine frame and a tree trunk. He was stark naked. There was a long, thin, angry red streak across his belly. Her eyes followed the laceration with dismay and she found herself staring at his thick erection.

"You can't possibly be aroused," she whispered. "You could have been killed." She was fascinated by him, by the thickness, the shape of him. Without thought she brushed her hand along his shoulder, touched the edge of the wound on his belly, and stroked her fingers over his heavy staff.

He caught her chin in his hand, his eyes still glittering. Still menacing. Adrenaline was pouring through his body. She felt it in the fine tremor of his body against hers. "You'll always arouse me, Maggie." He dropped a hard kiss on her upturned mouth. "I'm heading to the house for your medical supplies. I can travel faster without you. Don't you move."

She was breathing heavily, wanting him, needing him, strangely affected by the sight of such a terrible battle. "I'm sorry, Brandt. I put you in danger."

"We thrive on danger, honey. It's our way of life." His teeth teased at the pulse at the base of her throat. "I'll be back soon, I promise. Don't be afraid."

Maggie watched him disappear back into the foliage of the jungle. She wasn't afraid. Not at all. She belonged here in the jungle, belonged with Brandt Talbot. Every moment she spent here, no matter what seemed to be happening, she knew the rain forest was her home and Brandt was her mate, the man she wanted to spend her life with. She had no real idea how it had all happened, but she knew she wanted to be with him. She was willing to live with the strange differences here in the jungle. There was nothing she had left behind in civilization she wanted badly enough to give him up for.

Maggie looked at the bear lying almost quietly now, eyes staring at her without hope. "But I'm going to learn how to change shape fast like he does," she told the animal. "And I'm going to do some research into your little life, too, Mister Bear."

Maggie was crooning softly to the animal when Brandt returned. She was almost disappointed that he was fully dressed. He handed her clothes, jeans and a T-shirt, which she hastily donned while he tranquilized the bear.

Working with Brandt was easy. He seemed to know instinctively what she needed. His hands were reverent as they moved through the bear's fur, as he held the head to ensure the animal could breathe properly while she repaired the damage. "He should be caged," she said, wiping her forehead with the back of her hand, smearing dirt across it. "He might not get enough to eat or some other animal might get him, as injured as he is," she explained, moving a safe distance away from the bear where she could watch it wake up. "The injury isn't that bad. No broken bones, and he's lost some blood, but if someone was actually shooting at him, they were a poor shot."

"I think he was hit by a stray bullet. The poachers sprayed the area when they realized they were under attack." Brandt shook his head. "He'll do fine. He'll stay in his nest and I'll drop by each day to make certain he's eating. I don't want him caged."

"What happened to the poachers?"

There was a grimness about his mouth and his golden eyes were flat and dangerous looking. He shrugged his broad shoulders with casual carelessness. "I don't think they'll be bothering us again. The rain forest has a way of dealing with those who violate its trust." His gaze moved over her face, dark and brooding, a certain ruthlessness to his expression. "I left you in the house, Maggie. The rain forest also has a way of dealing with those who are careless."

Maggie hesitated, but she was too tired to argue with him. Rays of light were streaking through the canopy, signaling daylight had arrived. She sat down on the forest floor and looked up at him. "I wasn't careless, I was afraid,

Brandt, and I ran away like a coward. I'm sorry. I thought I was prepared for the way it would feel, but the change was slow and frightening and I panicked. It wasn't what I had imagined." She looked down at her hands. "I think I just ran instinctively. I thought if I left the forest, it would never happen again. I wanted to be me."

The bear grunted, its long tongue lolling out. They watched as the body twitched and the legs jerked. "You were always you, Maggie," Brandt said softly, aching for her, angry with himself for letting her down. Brandt reached out and pulled Maggie to her feet. "Come on, baby, let's go. You're tired." He drew her into the shelter of a large, lacy fern while the bear rolled over, shaking its head.

"You're angry with me." She made it a statement as she leaned up against his larger frame. He was solid. Steady. She could feel his anger seething beneath the surface, yet his hands were incredibly gentle.

"You scared the hell out of me, Maggie. There's something wrong with James. He's always been off when it comes to women. He's been caught shifting to impress the native women. They sleep with him thinking to gain his power or some such nonsense. He doesn't care about them; he uses them. He wants to control them."

"Like the men you were telling me about who wanted to be worshiped as gods."

He nodded. "He likes power over women. I really don't think he was involved with the poaching—that would be a death sentence to him—but he isn't someone I want you around. Ever. I'll never feel you're completely safe with him in the forest. I hope the council chooses to exile him."

His fingers tightened around hers as the bear clawed its way up the tree to its nest. When the bear had settled in completely, Brandt drew Maggie with him, weaving his way in and out easily through the plants and trees. It was a measure of the change in her that she knew immediately they were not headed to the house.

"I'm tired," she objected. "I just want to go home."

"You won't be too tired to see this place; you'll love it, Maggie. And you can sleep if you like once we're there. There's a small clearing right around a pool so you can lie in the sun. The forest is your home. All of it."

She glanced up at the sky. "It's sure to rain."

"Maybe," he agreed. "But trust me, you won't care."

She did trust him. She went with him willingly.

The sight robbed her of speech. She stood close beside Brandt, just staring, enthralled by nature's beauty. Water cascaded from a hundred feet above them, a white frothy foam pouring over the smoothly rounded rocks. It fell into a large natural pool, deep, the water almost crystal clear out away from the falls. It gleamed an inviting blue, the surface shimmering with a rainbow of colors. Abundant ferns created a living, lacy screen around the exotic pool. Flowers of every kind cascaded like the falls from the trees so that colors and perfumed scents filled Maggie's senses and turned the spot into a magical, mystical paradise.

Maggie was tired, her muscles aching from the unexpected change, and the soles of her feet hurt from walking barefoot earlier. In the steamy heat of the forest, the cool water was an inviting sight. Maggie looked uncertainly at Brandt. There was still a hard edge to his mouth in spite of her explanation, so she ignored Brandt, not wanting to look any longer at his masculine body, not wanting to inhale his spicy scent. Not wanting to know that she had put that edge to his sculpted mouth. She chose a spot where the massive boulder forming the basin was flat and she could seat herself near the water's edge. Removing her shoes and socks, she rolled up her jeans and without hesitation plunged her feet into the water. She expected it to be icy cold, but it wasn't.

Maggie was hot and sticky, the jungle sultry and humid despite the early hour. A bead of sweat trickled along her skin, in the valley between her breasts. She glanced up at Brandt to find him watching her in silence. At once her stomach did a melting flip and her heart began to pound. Naked desire burned in his gaze. Maggie rubbed her hands on her thighs nervously. "It's going to be hot today." Her voice came out a croak.

"Yes, it is." His gaze holding hers, Brandt stripped off his shirt in one fluid motion and flung it carelessly aside.

She stared up at his chest. The slow burn in her belly began to spread, building into something wild. Without thought, Maggie stretched languidly, her arms above her head, tilting her face toward the sky, exposing the line of her throat, lifting her breasts beneath the thin tee.

"It isn't fair that you can do this to me with just a look," Maggie said. "I came back, Brandt. I came back when I didn't have to." But she did have to come back. She was afraid that if she was away from him, she might cease to exist. She would be Maggie, but walking through life, not living it.

"It's my fault you were out there alone," Brandt said. He allowed his gaze to drift over her, a slow, lazy inspection of her lush curves. "I'm not blaming you for being afraid. I blame myself for leaving you alone when I knew you were close to the change." He moved to stand beside her while she sat at the water's edge. His fingers tangled in her hair, rubbing in the silky strands. "I didn't mean to snap at you, Maggie. The Han Vol Dan is a frightening experience even for those of us who know what to expect. I'm proud of you that you went through it alone and still had the courage to come back to me." It humbled him as nothing else could have.

Brandt knew he looked stiff and grim and aloof, but fear for her was still an ugly presence in his heart, and he couldn't seem to calm the demons raging in him. He had wanted to break James's neck, and the thought of the man roaming freely, presenting a threat to Maggie, made him resent his decision to allow James to escape the jungle justice.

His hand trembled as he reached down and simply

pulled her shirt over her head and tossed it on top of his own. "We can change easily and naturally, fast and on the run if there is need. It's only another form, not a change of character." Her skin gleamed at him, as smooth as silk. She was utterly beautiful to him, as exotic as any of the creatures in his care. "I'm going to show you, Maggie."

His hands were on the waistband of his jeans and her heart pounded as she heard the rasp of the zipper. She tilted her head to get a better view as he pushed the jeans away from his body without a semblance of modesty. He was ferociously aroused, thick and hard and tempting beyond her ability to resist. She instantly forgot she was tired.

"I love looking at you." The words slipped out of their own accord. Honest. Simple. Life in the rain forest.

For the first time he seemed to relax, some of the tension seeping out of him. "It's a good thing, honey, because I'm very partial to looking at you." He stepped away from her. "I think about the leopard in my mind first, Maggie, before I actually start the change. It takes practice, but you'll be able to do it."

She was sweating. Just looking at him and hearing the sensual note in his voice was making her ache in the most wonderful places. He robbed her of air even in wide-open spaces.

Brandt reached down, locked his fingers around her wrist, and effortlessly pulled her to her feet. "Watch, Maggie." He held his arm away from her while the fur raced over his skin.

Maggie had eyes for other things. She allowed her palm to slide up his thigh, to cup his heavy sac, to linger playfully along his erection.

"I'm showing you something important here," he said, trying to sound stern.

"And I'm looking," she answered truthfully.

"You're doing more than looking." His breath caught in his lungs as her fingers danced, closed tightly around him, slid, and caressed.

She arched an eyebrow at him, her smile teasing. "Poor baby. And you were feeling all mean and bad, too. I'm soothing you. You should thank me."

"Mean and bad?" he echoed, every muscle in his body taut with need.

"Snarly. You were snarling. You know, curling your lip and exposing your teeth." She went up on her toes, pressed her breasts against his chest to nibble at his lip. "You have wonderful teeth, by the way." Her tongue slid tantalizingly over his lips. She pushed away from him when he reached for her.

Laughing, Maggie wiggled out of her jeans. Instead of turning back to him, she jumped straight into the water.

9

The water was cool, bringing instant relief to Maggie's body. It was a perfect temperature in the sultry heat of the morning. She ducked beneath the surface, wanting to feel clean, wanting the thick mass of her hair wet and cool for a change. Most of all, she wanted Brandt to play with her. The hard edge to his mouth, the glittering menace in his eyes were intimidating. She had made a monumental decision, her entire life changing in the blink of an eye, and she needed comfort. They both did.

Brandt watched Maggie's body move through the water, cutting cleanly, a flash of her smooth, inviting buttocks, a kick of her feet. Her head came up out of the water, long hair shaking off droplets of water in every direction. She looked like a water nymph, ethereal, desirable. A mermaid with blazing hair and inviting skin.

She was life itself, family—she was worth all the long hours, all the danger and tedium of his job. She was why he did it, why he wanted the environment saved, why wildlife was so important. One woman with more courage than good sense, willing to take him on instinct. Willing to forgive the trap he set for her, to look beyond it to a life with him.

Brandt sighed and slipped into the water to rinse the sweat from his skin. She had another life. One in a city, one she had lived for years before he had come along. He swam swiftly, furiously across the pool to the other side, coming up behind the waterfall and off to the side of it. He heaved his weight onto the small shelf he knew was there, fitting his hips onto the smooth rock, his legs dangling down. Water lapped at his thighs and groin, soothing waves when his mind was roaring a protest.

"Maggie." He waited until she stood up in the shallows, the water lovingly ringing her hips, droplets running off her breasts and down her beautiful belly to her navel. "This isn't right. What I've done isn't right. It's been all about me, what I need, what I want, not about you and what you want or need."

Her green gaze slid over him speculatively, heightening his awareness. Maggie had a sensual, sultry quality that left him hard and hungry and so edgy he sometimes wanted to leap upon her and devour her on the spot. She tilted her head to one side, twisted the length of her hair as she looked at him. "Is that what you think, Brandt?"

Where had she gotten such confidence, this self-assured woman who was looking at him with amusement when he was trying to be noble? She was in the middle of the rain forest, had just gone through the Han Vol Dan alone. She had committed her life to her mate, accepted her heritage, embraced it even. Where did she get such courage? Brandt could only stare at her, the beautiful, sensual picture she made standing hip deep in the clear pool.

"I think you haven't heard everything, Maggie," he said quietly. "Our people don't always choose to live here. We're a small band, very small, older couples mainly and Drake, Conner, Joshua, and James. One female, young

Shilo, not quite old enough and without a mate. No others. Most of our kind are long gone or living and working in the cities. They rarely, if ever, shift shape, and some do not have their mates."

She flung her hair back over her shoulder and slowly lowered her body beneath the surface of the water until her breasts floated, a temptation of lush, creamy flesh. She swam closer to him. "I had the impression there weren't many of you left."

He blinked, tore his fascinated gaze away from the perfection of her feminine body. "Us. Many of us left," he corrected. "The point is, you had a life somewhere else. You can still have that life."

Maggie stopped swimming, stilled there in the pool with the water cascading behind her and mist falling softly across the surface. "What are you saying?" Her voice was tight, the joy fading from her face, from her eyes.

"I'm saying, if you prefer to live in the city, we can go there. I expected you to give up your life for me and that was wrong. I love the rain forest and everything in it. But I watched what you did for the bear. You worked so fast, with no hesitation. You're so skilled, Maggie. You have no idea, you take it for granted, but you were amazing."

The tension drained from her body and she swam through deeper water to him, nudging his thighs open so she could hook her arms over his legs to stay afloat. Her hair fanned out around her head like silk on the surface of the water. She rested her chin up high on his thigh, deliberately close to the junction of his legs so that her hair teased at the insides of his legs. So that her mouth was tantalizingly close. So that when she breathed, he held his breath.

"So much the better for my work here," she answered, and nuzzled his leg. Her teeth teased his skin while her gaze grew hot watching the effect on his body. He thickened, hardened, reaching for her with male ardor. "I love it here, Brandt. And I trained with the idea of working in the wilds." Her tongue collected drops of water from the crease of his legs. She smiled when he shivered, when his hands came down to fist in her hair. Her tongue went on a little foray, exploring, teasing, testing her power over him.

"I mean it, Maggie. I'll try living in the city if you want me to. I want you to be happy." His entire body seemed to be suspended. Waiting. Every nerve ending was alive. Screaming. Centered in one place.

Her arms slid to his waist, her body wedging closer as she shifted slightly. "I'm happy right here, Brandt. Incredibly happy."

Her mouth closed around him as tight as a fist. Hot. Moist. Sucking hard, her tongue doing some kind of dance to drive him mad. His head fell back and his world narrowed. Time stood still while the mist came down and the prisms of color floated in the air behind his eyes, in his blood. His fists tightened, bunching in her hair, and he held her to him. A growl of pleasure escaped from the back of his throat. Leaves wavered in the breeze. The waterfall thundered into the pool.

Life gave gifts sometimes. He had been given one to treasure. Brandt tugged on her, not wanting to lose control, wanting to be inside of her, sharing the same skin. "Come here, baby." He reached for her, hooking beneath her arms and pulling her straight up out of the water with his enormous strength.

Maggie was shocked by how casually he revealed his hidden strength. He lifted her as if she weighed no more than a feather. She stood with a foot on either side of his hips while he pressed his hand to her, his fingers testing her desire.

"I want you," she assured him, her hands on his head to steady herself. He was making certain her body would accept his comfortably. She should have known he would. That was Brandt, seeing to her needs. Her wants. He thought himself so selfish, when he had given her life. Maggie allowed his hands to invade her body, her mind, to drug her bloodstream and fill her full of sheer pleasure.

She pulsed with it, rocked with it, pushing against his hand, her body drenched in liquid heat.

As she began to settle onto his lap, taking him into her body, inch by slow inch so that he filled her, stretched her, completed her, she leaned close to find his mouth with hers. No one could kiss like Brandt. No one could melt her the way he did. She was lost in the heat of his mouth, in the strength of his body, in the way he built the fire between them.

The rain started, a fine drizzle to add to the mist of the waterfall. Maggie began to ride, rocking her hips, sliding him in and out of her sheath like a sword, clenching her muscles, holding him tightly in her fiery center. His hands were at her breasts, his mouth devouring hers, then her throat. He bent her backward, his marauding mouth latching on to her breast, his hand urging her to ride harder, faster. The friction was all-consuming, robbing her of breath, of sanity.

The rain tried to find their rhythm, coming down faster and harder, but they became frenzied, wild, bucking together in a firestorm of passion. Drops fell on sensitized skin, creating the illusion of tongues sliding over their heated bodies. The passion grew, an inferno out of control. The release was shattering, a fire consuming them, an explosion of senses.

They clung to one another for the longest time, simply holding each other. Maggie's head on Brandt's shoulder. His hands stroked caresses down her hair, her back.

"I want you to be certain, Maggie, that I'm what you want. That this is the life you would choose no matter what."

She pulled back to search his expression. Her fingertips traced the lines etched into his face. "I want to be with you here, right here, Brandt," she assured him, kissing his strong jaw. "I'm choosing to be here with you."

He pressed his mouth to hers, his heart still beating too fast, too hard. Something was wrong. It shouldn't have been, but he was uneasy with her decision. Uneasy with the fact that she accepted him when she didn't know what he really was. Who he really was. Maggie saw the man she wanted to see, the poet, the man who brought her flowers. She didn't see the beast raging against the poachers, protecting what should be held intact for the world.

She managed to get unsteadily to her feet, her body throbbing and pulsing with aftershocks, singing with joy. He stood up, too, close to her, so that his body touched hers. Their fingers clung. Maggie leaned into him. "You still have that look. What can I do to make you more certain?"

Brandt swallowed hard. There was nothing she could do. Nothing she could say. He kissed her. Hard. Possessively. He put everything he felt for her into that kiss. Told her everything he couldn't say in words. Poured his heart and soul into the kiss.

The wind shifted and Brandt abruptly lifted his head, scenting the air. At once his expression changed, his lip lifting in a silent snarl. He shoved Maggie away from him so that she stumbled backward and fell into the pool, the water closing over her head. He was already in motion, turning toward the thick bank of ferns, his form shimmering with fur as a leopard exploded out of the foliage and hit him at full speed. It was like getting hit with a battering ram, jarring his insides, bones and muscle and tissue. Losing his footing was not an option—the spotted leopard already had the advantage—so Brandt took the impact, absorbed it in his muscles and sinew, allowed it to rock him, but he leapt in the air, whirling to fight, raking claws laterally as he did so.

The spotted leopard's momentum prevented him from avoiding the claw, and Brandt scored across the eyes and down the slavering muzzle. The cry was half-human, half-beast as James turned and drove in again.

Brandt understood this time he had no choice. James was determined to get rid of Brandt for good. It was kill or be killed, a very real way of life in the rain forest. He spared a thought for Maggie, how she would react, and then he was lost in the fierce battle.

Maggie kicked to the surface, her heart pounding. She dragged herself from the pool. The sounds were terrifying, the noise so loud the forest would carry it throughout the interior. The black panther and the spotted leopard were raking and biting, ramming each other to force the other into submission. She looked around for a weapon, anything she could use to help Brandt. James had caught him off guard, had torn a gaping wound in his side. He was at a disadvantage.

The change started in her mind first. He had told her that. With tears running down her face, she tried to block out the sight and smell of blood, the sight of two powerful males in real combat. She knew the leopard inside and out. She *was* the leopard. Her fur was reddish with beautiful rosettes, her tail long and tipped red. She heard the noises, the cracks and pops, felt the stretching of her skin and bones.

Maggie lay on the rock, astonished that she had managed to do such a thing. She stretched, snarled to show her canines. The wildness of the battle was already in her, thickening her blood and pumping adrenaline through her. A warning growl escaped her throat as instincts took over. She trusted that part of her, accepted it. Reveled in it. The threat was to her mate. To her family. To everything she cared about.

She leapt on the back of the spotted leopard, sinking her teeth deep into his neck, raking with claws. He shook her off easily, but the distraction was all Brandt needed to gain the advantage. He was on the other cat before it could recover, taking the throat, twisting until the leopard was on his side, the hold impossible to break.

Maggie was already inspecting Brandt's injuries, padding around him on her soft cushioned paws. When he let go, backing away, the spotted leopard didn't rise.

Brandt could hear the others coming fast, coming to his aid. It was too late for any of them. He'd had no choice but to make the kill, but it sickened him that he had to do such a thing to one of his own kind. He looked at Maggie bleakly, his head down, his heart filled with sorrow. His sides were heaving as his lungs worked to recover.

Her tongue soothed a rip on his shoulder, lapped at another along his side. She nudged him to his feet, already aware of the others on their way. She was clearly stating her position. His people could deal with the aftermath of jungle justice. Brandt was to go with this mate, allow her to take care of his injuries. Her tongue was busy, and her smaller body continually urged his toward the forest, away from the sight and smells of his savage way of life. Urged him toward their home.

Maggie had clearly chosen her destiny and Brandt finally accepted she knew what she was doing. His heart overflowing, he went with her, basking in her love and care.